# ARCHITECTS OF
# MEMORY

# KAREN OSBORNE

# ARCHITECTS OF MEMORY

**TOR**

A TOM DOHERTY ASSOCIATES BOOK

NEW YORK

ARCHITECTS OF MEMORY

Copyright © 2020 by Karen Osborne

A Tor Book
Published by Tom Doherty Associates
120 Broadway
New York, NY 10271

www.tor-forge.com

Tor® is a registered trademark of Macmillan Publishing Group, LLC.

The Library of Congress Cataloging-in-Publication Data
is available upon request.

ISBN 978-1-250-21547-5 (trade paperback)
ISBN 978-1-250-21546-8 (ebook)

Our books may be purchased in bulk for promotional, educational, or business use. Please contact your local bookseller or the Macmillan Corporate and Premium Sales Department at 1-800-221-7945, extension 5442, or by email at MacmillanSpecialMarkets@macmillan.com.

First Edition: August 2020

Printed in the United States of America

0  9  8  7  6  5  4  3  2  1

*To Glenn*
*my together*

# ARCHITECTS OF
# MEMORY

Ashlan Jackson slammed her retrieval pod into an abrupt standstill. She stared into the rictus grin of the dead warship's open belly, not breathing, as a piece of live Vai ordnance passed within an inch of her pod's forward camera, twinkling in the light of the Tribulation star.

Predictably, the commlink flared to life.

"Ash. Holy crap." She expected her captain Kate Keller's familiar, wry tones, not Leonard Downey's worried pitch and gravel. The presence of the engineer on the other side of the comm did nothing to make her feel calmer. Keller would understand her mistake, but Len might investigate. Ask questions. *Damn.* "What the hell are you doing to my pod down there?"

Ash gulped down stale, end-of-shift air and keyed the button to respond. "The pod's fine. I'm fine, too. Thanks for asking." She winced as she lied. "I just miscalculated the approach vector to *London*. Had a near miss with something live. I think it was Vai, but I'm not getting a good read on it from here."

"It's not like you to miscalculate."

Ash sighed. "Forgot my coffee this morning."

"Coffee's important. Nat says . . ." Len's voice crackled through the comm. "Nat says it looks like a zapper and that she can defuse it. It's on the Christmas list, so if you can snag it, we'll all get a nice bonus."

Ash felt a headache flare to life as she switched the view on her camera. The alien bomb peeled away from her pod, blinking merrily. "I like my head right where it is, Len, not five hundred klicks away and on fire."

"You'll be fine. Zappers aren't molecular. They're kinetic. You won't evaporate. They'll only blow you up if they hit a plasteel hull."

"My pod has a plasteel hull."

Len paused. "You'll be fine. Snag it with the net and Natalie will meet you in the cargo bay, do her thing, and we'll all be that much closer to citizenship."

Ash cut the audio and looked back out toward the black beyond. The zapper blinked, twisted, and twirled in the starlight. She thought of the Christmas list—the long, dangerous schedule of explosive extras Aurora Company set as bounties for its salvage teams—and, not for the first time, wished her indenture was up, so she could be somewhere warm, with pretty women, real alcoholic beverages, and something other than standard Company decking underneath her feet.

Maybe just one *particular* pretty woman.

"Fine," Ash said, erasing the thought of Keller from her mind. "One alien death trap, coming right up."

Ash keyed in a new vector, doing the math in her head as the targeting computer brought up a red, blinking path for her to follow. The zapper was heading on a trajectory that would take it out of the former battlefield and into the freeze without hitting anything too valuable. Letting it go would be easy, but all of them needed the extra credit. The zapper's easy velocity made it a perfect target, and her pod was just fast enough to catch up.

Unfortunately she didn't feel the same way about her instincts. *A five-year-old could have seen that damn thing coming,* she thought, swallowing panic.

Ash grasped the sensors, and the metal rigging around the pod shook to life. She fired the engines long enough to bring the pod alongside the bomb, then released her net. The zapper pressed gently into the quiet squeeze of the collapsing fibronet, losing all forward momentum and hanging, a coruscating emerald marble in the sky.

"The master at work." Len sounded pleased. "Natalie, you're on and looking good."

"You're not so bad yourself," Natalie said.

The team's salvage ordnance engineer, Natalie Chan, was in her late twenties, a three-year Aurora anti-Vai combat vet with the scars and attitude to match. When Ash first heard Natalie's comm voice, she'd guessed her age to be around fifteen, a teenager playing with gaming tablets rather than someone who could defuse entire minefields before breakfast, a virtual hero of the line.

Ash forced out a chuckle. "Stop flirting, you two. I'm about to drop a present down the chimney."

"Too much chatter." Keller had returned to the comm from wherever she'd been, and with her, a ragged sense of decorum.

Ash stared into the open maw of the salvage bay. Her ship, *Twenty-Five*, looked like all the others of its line, stocky and serviceable with a safety rating of 97 percent and a drab name to match. *Twenty-Five*'s square, commonplace hull was built to slot into any number of Auroran maintenance ports on any number of Company-run space stations. The ship's dark matte paint and hard curves were meant to conceal rather than impress. Most of *Twenty-Five* was cargo space and storage bays; the crew lived on the cramped middle deck, stuffed between the medbay and engineering storage. The ship's full integrated antigrav was a reward for their stellar work on last quarter's Company goals. Compared to the mine on Bittersweet, it was paradise.

It had been Ashlan's home for well over a year.

She felt better these days. More confident. *The zapper was an isolated incident, that's all*, she told herself. *It isn't a symptom. I'm still too close to my exposure date for symptoms. Nobody's going to notice. I can still finish my indenture and make it to citizenship.*

She could see Natalie's guide-light and adjusted her trajectory in millidegrees, pushing the pod and its precious contents back toward the ship. When Ash was close enough, Natalie rushed forward in an EV suit. Her smart brown eyes gleamed through the faceplate. Natalie detached the net using a pair of long pliers. For a moment, Ashlan thought she was looking at a small child in a large and dangerous Halloween costume.

"Oh, what Christmas morning fun," Natalie said.

On the bridge, Keller sighed. *"Please* concentrate."

Ash made sure Natalie cleared the cargo safety line before engaging a new trajectory back toward *London*'s R&D ring, taking a hard right at some railgun debris. She liked flying in vacuum. She was good at it. *Natural talent,* Keller had said. The comms went silent as the dead cruiser leered at her once again in the ancient silence of the living stars.

She aimed her pod at *London*'s science level and spiked the burners, taking the trip slow and steady to calm her zapper-fried nerves. The starship's open belly swallowed the stars around the fore camera, and she dropped down a corridor-turned-access shaft.

Last week's work had been quiet and gruesome. The Vai coup de grâce had surprised *London*'s research cadre as they'd gathered in their lab-level conference room to look over some sort of mid-battle development. There they remained, floating silent and shocked, until the salvage team arrived to take them home.

That had been Ash's least favorite part of this job—finding, identifying, and cataloging the bodies, their nails and eyelashes crusted with frost, their eyes wide with sudden, eternal surprise, their white coats filled with the gruesome evidence of explosive decompression. It reminded her entirely too much of the last days of her time in the mines on Bittersweet, after the Vai attack, after she'd been dragged out of the wreckage by Keller and her new Auroran family. Her friends on Bittersweet had been loaded like this, coffin by coffin, onto *Twenty-Five*. Onto an Auroran salvage ship, because Wellspring Celestial Holdings had been too decimated to show.

She'd towed the scientists' bodies back, one by one, cradled careful and sure in the pod's pincers. Keller ran their DNA, identified them, and said their names, while the rest of the crew stayed quiet in respect for the dead. Some of them had been allies from another Company, carrying Manx-Koltar jackets, bags, and guns. Those were placed in separate pods in the *Twenty-Five* cargo bay, to be returned to their families the next time the crew made a supply run to one of the outlying stations.

Now that the R&D bodies were packed away, she could relax. They'd open the bridge-adjacent decks later, go through the entire rigamarole again. Today was all about lasers and lifting, machinery and discovery, Natalie's quips and Len's jokes. Today was coffee and chatting in the morning with the others, lunch bathing in the Tribulation sun, card games after dinner. She felt a hopeful little hitch in her chest as she imagined Keller smiling at her behind the ragged curtain of her light brown hair, warmth in her eyes, and she wondered, maybe she'd want to talk after dinner, maybe she'd—

*No. She doesn't want to see me. Not that way.*

The comm lit up, rescuing Ash from feeling sorry for herself.

"So. We know the scientists were having a meeting," Len said. "Check for doughnuts. They might have real coffee. Oh, and see if you can snag me some of those new haptic interfaces, too. I'm sick of having to type everything manually."

"You're terrible." Ash moved the pod alongside the crash-locked door next to the conference room. "Have some respect."

"Frozen doughnuts are the best kind."

"Shut up, both of you," Keller said. "Space plus bullshit equals death."

Ash flicked on the pod's lasers, waiting for them to warm up. A crash-locked door might stop a human infiltrator in standard gravity on a functioning starship, but it wasn't going to stop a salvage worker in a Company pod who could literally lift away a wall and cast it into the void. She waited for Keller to give her the go order but heard nothing.

"Captain? Should I engage?"

Len's voice had gone quiet. "Captain's still here, but she's a little distracted. Corporate just called. Go ahead and open the room, but hold up for further instruction before you go in."

*Great. Exactly what I need on a bad day. Corporate watching my every move.* Ash swore under her breath, aimed her laser cutter and fired, separating what had once been a ceiling from what had once been a wall. The work reminded her of the little that had been good about her Wellspring Celestial mining indenture: the pride she took in her exacting cuts, the meditative repetition of clearing a vein. Instead of extracting celestium from the rocky skin of a crappy planetoid, though, she was extracting secrets from the dead. It paid better and, plus, mining had never been this exciting. There was so much to be discovered from a ship's final moments, and *London* told its stories in spades.

The laser cutter finished its work, and Ash engaged the pod's pincers, pushing them forward to snag the wall. She fired the backburners to nudge the pod into position, lifting and setting the wall aside as if it were a plastic building block. She directed the lights into the room beyond, starting the standard scans for heat and radiation signatures.

"Indenture Ashlan," Keller interjected, using her careful corporate voice. "Mr. Solano is watching on the ansible from the *Rio de Janeiro*. When we fixed the Tribulation system ansible array three weeks ago, corporate received a data dump that'd been waiting in the buffer ever since the battle. There's a lot of data missing, but he thinks you're close to something very interesting."

"Is that all I have to go on?"

Keller cleared her throat. "Mr. Solano believes that whatever we're looking for was the object or phenomenon that caused the Vai to retreat behind the White Line."

"Is it ours or theirs?"

"Unknown. It's in a quarantine locker, and all we know is it's going to be unlike anything we've seen before," Keller responded in that no-nonsense, corporate-is-watching tone of hers. "That's all the scientists were able to dispatch in the data dump."

"They didn't take any readings?"

"No. Whatever it was, it came up from the planet on an unscheduled shuttle. The scientists had just enough time to snag it, dump it in quarantine, and gather the science crew before—"

"Bam. Vai attack."

"And Vai retreat," Keller said.

"All right. I'm heading in."

Ash focused her pod's lights into the closet she'd uncovered—an Aurora standard quarantine room with long, octagonal lockers set into the walls and just enough space for someone to walk through with a transport dolly. As she'd hoped, most of the lockers were still operating, sealed from the rest of the ship with their own power sources whirling away. Three showed the slow, blinking red light indicating that there was something inside.

"Three live ones," she reported, uploading the registration information to the ship.

There was no immediate answer from *Twenty-Five*.

Ash tapped her fingers, restless in the silence. She imagined Keller conversing with the CEO, imagined her crooked smile and her graceful collarbones and her—*Damn it,* she thought. *She said no, and no means no, so you're not helping yourself by thinking about her that way.*

"Two are biological research samples," Keller finally said. "What about the third?"

Ash fought off a skittering, nervous energy. The third locker blinked at her, the registration blank as the gray walls of the room itself. She queried the system with the Company's salvage hack number; the box operating system reported back that the interior weighed 9.85 pounds and that it contained nothing at all.

"Mr. Solano would like you to open the box," Keller answered after a few seconds.

"I'd feel safer with more scans."

"He wants you to open the box," said Keller, her voice still careful. "But I'm Aurora out here. I want Dr. Sharma to have a look as well. Hang tight."

Ash stopped slouching as soon as she heard the doctor's enthusiastic voice in the background.

"I don't see any indication that what's inside is dangerous," Sharma said. "But it's a quarantine box. An isolette. Storing dangerous things is the whole point."

"So, I could be pressing a suicide button," Ash said.

Keller coughed. She wasn't talking to Ash. "Look, I don't want to put my people at risk if we don't know what's in there, sir. Yes, I know she's an indenture."

Ash waited another tense fifteen seconds.

"Mr. Solano would like you to go ahead, Ash," said Keller, her voice tight and commanding.

Ash wondered why the captain would make the mistake of using her personal nickname in front of the Company CEO instead of her hated title of *indenture*. Was Keller *that* nervous? "Acknowledged," she said. "Opening the box now."

Ash slid her right hand back into the sensor glove that controlled the pod's human-interaction arm. Her hand shook. Her eyes swam. She felt her stomach bottom out in sudden fear; she was out on a job, driving expensive Company equipment, and *symptoms* were the last thing she needed. *I can't be sick right now,* she thought. *I can't have symptoms now. Not while the CEO is watching.* The robot arm rattled. Hoping beyond hope that Keller and her high-placed friend on the ansible hadn't noticed, Ash slowed, taking a long, quiet breath.

She pushed the robot arm's controls with a light touch of her index finger and connected it to the locker's basic interface. The front panel slid open to reveal a main chamber filled with a sick, slanted violet-green light. It was fierce and starbright, choking and painful; she raised her hand in front of her eyes until they adjusted. She wondered what it would be like to see it in person, without a pod or an isolette dampening the transmissions between them. She wondered if it would be a good idea.

*Probably not.*

She tried to turn on the polarizing filter on the cameras, but the pod was unresponsive. Buttons and toggles shuddered and crackled. Noise built from a faraway point—a great, crashing rush—and she felt it wrap around her chest and crawl into her ears, smothering her in one wide, frightening moment. She struggled to breathe. Tried to blink away the blinding light. Tried to yell for help, but she couldn't hear her own voice. She was buried in memories of dirt pouring down her throat.

The pod's exterior cameras crashed, one by one. Its main systems failed in a cascade that had Ash out of her harness and elbow-deep in the innards of the maintenance panel in seconds. Her nose ran; when she wiped it, blood stained her fingertips. The temperature around her plummeted twenty degrees in the second before the pod went dark as a tunnel on Bittersweet. She saw her breath in the second before the light faded for good.

Ash tried to stay calm, panic licking at the old memories of the mines, of the long dark days and darker nights. She reminded herself that since she was still breathing, structural integrity hadn't been compromised, and eight hours of oxygen was more than enough to survive.

*Twenty-Five* was right around the corner.

Keller would never leave her.

She'd trained for this.

Ash pushed back in her chair and peered at the quarantine locker, allowing her eyes to adjust. She could see the outline of a spherical inferno that burned like a supernova and roiled like an ocean. She extended her fingers, squinted, tried to block out enough of the light to really see what was out there. She heard whispers, somewhere high above her, coalescing in spatters of sibilants and breathy vowels, and she looked away, trying to see who was talking—

*Glory,* she heard.

*Christopher's* voice.

She pushed forward in the chair, her stomach twisting, too dizzy to stand, attempting to hit the robot arm with the last dregs of the pod's power. There was no reason for her to be hallucinating her dead fiancé's voice, not unless she was truly, wholly screwed. The pod was quiet as the expanse outside, as the shocked seconds after the mine shaft collapse, before the screaming.

*This is it,* she thought. *I'm going to die.*

The robot arm moved. The quarantine locker closed.

The pod rebooted.

Ash thought the blessed, bright blue Company logo would be imprinted on her grateful retinas for the rest of her life.

She sucked down freezing, canned air and stabbed the comms hard enough to hurt her fingers. "*Twenty-Five,* this is Ash, come in, *Twenty-Five.*"

"I'm seeing her. She's alive, she looks okay. Christ, Ash, you gave us a scare." It was Natalie, sounding frantic and relieved at the same time. Ash opened her mouth to speak, but her throat felt numb from the cold. She checked the porthole and jumped in surprise; *Twenty-Five*'s second pod was floating right next to hers, hanging over the quarantine room like it had been there the entire time. She could see the black-haired, pixie-dangerous ordnance engineer working at her console, her face drawn and pale.

Her own cockpit looked like the aftermath of a tornado. Subsystems had been toggled that shouldn't have been, as if she had pressed a bunch of buttons at once. She had bruises running up and down her arms. Ash busied herself with turning off the charge on the mining laser, the backup atmo scrubbers, and the exterior secondary arm that snapped at nothing. *Did I turn them on? Is this another symptom?*

"Natalie? How did you launch so fast? It's been what, two minutes?"

Natalie, looking worried, peered out the aft porthole. "What?" she said. Her words came over the comms a half second after she spoke; for a moment, Ash felt she was the star of a badly dubbed movie.

"It's been twenty-six minutes," Natalie said. "We thought we lost you."

# 2

Natalie towed Ash back to *Twenty-Five* in relative silence. The solar backup charger kicked in halfway through the debris field, and Ash was able to slot the pod back into its housing on the outer hull under her own power. She felt the pod shudder into somnolence and sighed as the airlock cycled and the door opened: she was safe.

At least one thing had gone well today.

Len waited just beyond, the corners of his mouth creased in relief and worry. He gave Ash a sturdy hug with one brown, muscled arm. "This is not *Alien Attack Squad*," he said, his voice clogged with rare emotion. "Cliff-hangers are for vids, Ash."

"I'm sorry." She leaned into the warmth of the hug. "Don't worry. I made it out."

He didn't laugh. "You look like hell."

"I'm *fine*."

"Well, you won't be in ten minutes. Doc's on her way down, and the captain's blazing mad."

Ash gave him a playful push away. "I can handle Kate Keller."

He rolled his eyes. "I'm sure you can. But, Ash, about the doctor—"

"Sharma's not going to even touch me this time."

His eyes darted, half nervous, over to Natalie's pod; the younger woman was still inside, running postflight tests. His voice dropped, went half husky. "The last twenty minutes were a shitshow for all of us. I just . . . want you to take this seriously, okay?"

Ash snorted in response. "Leonard Downey, chief executive of snark, is asking me to take something seriously?" She laughed. "You remember when I got that concussion from hitting debris near the *Mumbai*? I took *that* seriously. The Company bill set my citizenship date back three whole months. Len, I'm walking, I'm talking, I'm fine. There's no reason to be worried."

"And what'll that savings do for you if you're dead?"

She tensed. Thought of the light in the pod, of the dizziness, of the darkness. Of the things she couldn't tell him. "It's not that easy. You *know* it's not that easy."

Len sighed, rubbing the back of his head. "No," he agreed. "It's not." He paused. "I'm going to take a look at your pod, and hopefully, we'll get some answers."

"Thanks, Len," she said. "Don't worry, I won't let anyone know you care."

"You're the best." He laughed, tossed some diagnostic tools into the pod, gave Ash another quick hug, and climbed in. The door to Natalie's airlock slid open, and the younger woman jumped out, her short hair spiked and lawless from where it had been crushed in her helmet. Dr. Sharma ducked out of the ship's spine, wearing a blue sweater and an unusually fascinated look on her face, a lancet and vial cupped in her manicured left hand.

"Indenture, we'll need—"

Ash's breath froze and she backed up. *I can't let her do a blood test. She'll find out.* "You know I can't afford the needles, Dr. Sharma."

Sharma shook her head. "You're going to have to get over it. I'll bill it as mission-critical, so it won't go against your indenture. We're all lucky this isn't an autopsy."

Ash ran her hand through her hair. "Look. I feel fine. I just need a glass of water. I need to wash my face. Give me five minutes."

Sharma cracked a sour little smile, stepping forward. She grabbed a penlight from her pocket and turned it on, shining it straight in Ash's eyes without warning. Ash winced and turned her chin to one side, the bright light exacerbating her stabbing headache.

"*Ow*, doctor, for the love of God—"

The doctor pursed her lips in thought. "You said you were breathing the entire time?"

"I suppose I had to be."

The doctor turned off the penlight. "Because you have petechiae on your face, on your neck, broken capillaries in your eyes—you've been punched, or spaced, or strangled. That's strange. And not expected."

"I feel fine. Why do you care so much anyway? I'm just an indenture."

"You're not *just* an indenture, Ashlan. Not to me, at least." Sharma sighed. "But right now, I suppose I'm simply concerned that you don't fall on your face on the way up to the bridge. Luckily for you, we have a captain who believes your health is secondary to listening to the whims of our chief executive." She gave Ash a once-over and pointed toward the bridge, the tools still dangling in her hand. "I'll be waiting in the medbay when you're done."

Ash released a pent-up breath of relief and turned toward the entrance to *Twenty-Five*'s central spine. "I'll be down as soon as I can. Promise."

"Please do. You've been through a trauma you don't even remember," Sharma said. "That's not a good sign."

"I don't mind not remembering trauma," Ash said, grabbing the ladder with one hand and swinging up onto the bottom rung.

Ash heard the soft, put-upon sigh of the doctor as she pulled herself up to the bridge, and the relief felt featherlight once out of direct sight. She'd led Sharma to think her fear of medicine was understandable, that it stemmed from the brusque, prodding mannerisms of the Wellspring doctors back at the Bittersweet mines, men and women who viewed the Company's human workforce less as people to be healed and more like machines to be patched up. It was a convenient mask for Ash's very real fear: that Sharma would discover her illness, an illness that would disqualify her from citizenship anywhere but in a gutter back on Earth. Lately, she'd thought the doctor had become a little suspicious, less likely to humor her, less likely to bill a procedure as mission-critical, to force her into it, to make her pay for her own downfall.

That was bad enough. A new blood test would ruin everything.

Auroran citizenship was a better deal by far than Wellspring's version, which came after decades, if at all—but Ash knew she still trod dangerous ground. Aurora Company prided itself on cross-vertical investments, pairing agricultural colonies with hubworld industry for a stable revenue stream. Wellspring Celestial's main strategy relied on mining celestium and water ice, and for a while, it had been sound; they had a near monopoly on the celestium-rich hubworlds and moons, and a steady stream of poverty-stricken uncitizens like Ash's family, willing to sell themselves into indenture for the opportunity to get cit tags. Refined celestium ore was 65 percent of the fuel mix that powered the grav-drive, and 25 percent of the tough plasteel hulls that made escaping gravity wells possible. It had made Wellspring's executive class rich as hell—at least until the Vai arrived to smash their business model and their desperate underclass.

Ash hadn't even known things could be different until Keller and the others yanked her screaming from the Bittersweet wreckage.

She pulled herself up to the bridge, feeling tired. Like everywhere else on *Twenty-Five,* the command space was tiny, every single open space used for floor-to-ceiling interfaces, storage, toggles, and consoles. It was full of noise, lights, beeping things, and constant activity. After the quiet of the pod, the thousand small distractions of a smooth and stable *Twenty-Five* sounded positively beatific.

Ash was surprised to see vehicular control occupied by Keller's XO, the red-haired and taciturn Alison Ramsay, who normally spent her time on the night shift. Ash started to apologize, but Ramsay grinned and brought her index finger to her lips, indicating the ansible monitor. Keller's back was to Ash, talking with a somewhat familiar brown-haired man wearing an executive's torc around his neck. It took a few seconds for his face to register.

*Shit.* Ash colored, shoved down a mouthful of panic and dropped into the salvage control chair.

Ramsay kept her eyes on the ship's power levels, tapping with little purpose, her real attention clearly on hearing the conversation Keller was having with the Company CEO. Joseph Solano was known for his hands-on management style and propensity to show up at important work sites, but even he rarely enjoyed this long of a chat with any of his captains. Ash ducked, staying out of the visual range of anyone involved.

"My head of R&D is desperate to begin. Is the quarantine box onboard yet?"

Keller straightened her shoulders. "I don't think that's a prudent decision—not after what it did to my indenture. I'd need your express authorization."

Solano loomed. The man was the skinny side of plump and wore his hair in curls, with a well-kept black beard and the white, stretched tattoo of a birthright citizen curling around his ear. He sat at a desk in front of an illuminated Company logo like a newscast plutocrat and wrung his hands while speaking. "You have it. I obviously don't want you to do anything that would put an investment like *Twenty-Five* at risk. But we've been trying to put together the events of the Battle of Tribulation for over a year, and this is the closest we've ever been to a real answer."

"We know what happened at Tribulation, sir," said Keller. "*London* led the battle. The Manx-Koltar cruiser took the right flank, and *Mumbai* the rear. They won, sir."

"But *how* did they win? The Vai slaughtered *London* in fifteen minutes, Captain Keller. They could have pushed on past Tribulation, into Aurora's shipping lanes and straight on to Europa with just a few gunboats to stop them. But they didn't. They stopped fighting. They retreated behind the White Line. We shouldn't have won, Captain, and the secret to that victory is right under our noses. I don't need to tell you we need to obtain this device before the competition does. Once they find out that *Rio* is moving toward Tribulation, we'll have a lot of unwanted company. It would be prudent to get started before our arrival."

Keller took a quiet breath. "What about the intercorporate treaties?"

"Those haven't been enforceable for months. Other companies should be classified as hostile for the duration of your deployment here. This mission is our future, Captain Keller, and we need to secure it right now. Aurora is prepared to offer whatever support you need to properly secure the device before our arrival," Solano said.

Ash's hand curled, her breath catching. Solano had basically just dared Keller to ask for overtime. Hope kindled in her chest. *Come on, Kate,* she thought. *Push.*

Keller looked over her shoulder, acknowledging Ash's arrival with a quick tilt of her chin. "Actually, we could do more than get started. We have Dr. Sharma on staff, and she worked in R&D for over ten years."

"Hm," Solano said. He paused and looked off-screen. "All right. If you can give us a basic dossier on the item by the time *Rio* arrives to take over, you get a bonus."

Keller paused, then licked her lips. "I was actually thinking hazard scale pay, sir. For everyone."

The CEO laughed. "I knew you'd ask. Fine, I'll authorize hazard scale. You're the best, Keller. Don't make me regret it."

"Of course, sir," Keller said.

Solano's voice softened. Out of the corner of her eyes, Ash could see Ramsay stab at her keyboard, biting the bottom of her lip. "This is not just salvaging equipment and bringing our soldiers home, Kate. This is history. Ensuring the future of humanity. We have to be ready if—*when*—the Vai attack again."

"We'll do it, sir," Keller said.

"Fantastic. Do us proud. *Rio de Janeiro* out."

The screen went dark, and Keller turned to look over her shoulder. "Thoughts?"

"He's not wrong," Ash volunteered. "This could be a breakthrough. And we all could use the extra credit."

Keller twisted around in her chair, pointing at Ash with one ill-manicured hand, her unwashed dishwater hair loose around her peaked, angry face. She rose, stalking across the bridge in two steps. "You. I thought I lost you. Twenty minutes. No life support. You should have died. You broke my cardinal rule. I'm not happy."

Ash managed a weak smile. "The cardinal rule: Don't scare you?" she ventured.

"Got it in one. Come here, damn it."

Keller clasped her hand in Ash's and dragged her out of her seat into a moment's tight hug. Keller smelled like anger and the engine room, and her nails dug into Ash's back, her warm skin pressing against Ash's neck for a few more seconds than was necessary. Ash let go first, and Keller looked relieved. She cleared her throat.

Ash looked over at Ramsay, who was making a show of peering at her monitors, giving them the formal illusion of privacy. "She woke you?"

"Yes, and since you didn't die," Ramsay said with an amused twist to her voice, standing and brushing off her coveralls, "I'm going back to bed."

"Just an hour, Alison, then I'm going to need you on the bridge," Keller said, taking Ramsay's place at vehicular control, bringing up footage of Len with his head stuffed in a panel, still downloading readings from Ash's pod. The red-haired woman muttered a few words about needing more coffee, inclined her head, and dropped into the access tube, yawning. When Ramsay's steps could no longer be heard, Keller turned her chin, so her eyes focused on Ash.

"All right, she's gone. What the hell happened out there?" Keller asked.

Ash's memory flashed in bright light, a searing headache, sheer, choking panic, then the calm of realizing it was all over. Christopher's voice. "I opened the locker to see what was inside. Whatever it was, it knocked out every circuit I had."

Keller frowned. "Before that. When you were having a seizure."

"I didn't have a seizure."

"Your hand was shaking."

"Hands shake."

Keller sighed and stood, straightening the hair hanging in strands over Ash's forehead. "Do not bullshit me out here, Ash. You know my mantra."

"Space plus bullshit equals death," Ash recited.

Keller nodded. "Your illness is getting worse."

Ash bit her bottom lip. "No."

"Yes, it is."

"Damn it, Ms. Keller. I'm not even forty."

"Stop using my citizen's name when we're alone. I'm Kate to you. And I care about you, and I'm sorry about—"

Anger flared bright in Ash's chest, and the words came as fast as a cascade failure. She couldn't stop them. She didn't want to stop them. "*Sorry?* You know what's *actual* bullshit? This. Stringing me along, making me fall in love with you when I was still hurting over Christopher, then telling me we can't be together—" She hauled in a breath. "And then shit like this, making me *hope,* getting us hazard scale pay, when I know where it's actually going to end up. Making me look at you, saying you *care* about me, every single day, while you know how *I* feel—"

Keller's fingers grabbed her upper arm. Ash tried to yank herself away, but they tightened, the lights of the bridge catching in the stones of Keller's citizens' rings. Her grip almost hurt.

"I didn't *make* you do anything. I wouldn't. I would never. But you know what would happen if anyone discovered we'd been together," Keller said. "You know they'd reassign you, probably to a shit detail like the one you had at the Wellspring mine, and when your new doctor found out—it would be *over* for you. Never say I don't care. If I *didn't care,* if I still didn't want this to work, I would have had a *very* different conversation with Solano. You need to be patient. I'm working on it."

An ugly displeasure kindled in Ash's belly. "You arranged for my indenture to be served aboard *Twenty-Five,* and you can arrange for it to be served elsewhere just as easy, huh?"

Keller looked hurt. "That's not what I mean. You're really talented. I would have wanted you here, regardless."

"Regardless. You're giving me one hell of a mixed message, Kate," Ash said. "And I'm sick of it."

The captain's eyes hardened. "You want mixed messages, look

at yourself. You say that you're part of this crew, but you don't tell me that you're *hallucinating*. You could get us all killed."

"That's not supposed to happen!" The words tore free. "I can't be patient. I've only been infected for a *year*. Hallucinations, voices, seizures, it's all stage four endgame shit. Not *tomorrow*. Eight years from now. Maybe nine. But you still talk like we've got *time*."

"Don't we?" Keller said.

"No."

Keller closed her eyes and let go of Ash's arm, and she slouched forward. "We still can't make any rash moves."

"Why not? I would. For you."

"It's different when you run the show." The other woman swallowed before continuing. "I can't be your girl out here. I have to be your captain first. That's why. I'm responsible for your life, and for Len's, and Natalie's, and Sharma's. Not just yours. I need to be honest with you, and you need to be honest with me for their sake. And we need to continue to work on getting you citizenship, and—"

"You want honesty, Kate? I'm *dying*," Ash spat.

A chime from the reporting system sliced through the tension between them. Keller's attention was stolen immediately, and Ash felt a swell of momentary grateful heat in her cheeks. She leaned forward to look over the captain's shoulder; Keller had received a data dump from Len, full of numbers and graphs Ash didn't quite understand.

When Keller was done reading, she grabbed Ash's hand.

"This could be something," she said. "Let's get through these next few days. *Rio* will be here before we know it. Let's see what the hazard pay nets us. We'll make it work. Please, Ash."

Ash thought about Keller's skin on hers, the other woman's hair running through her hands, her quarters in the dark. She felt light-headed, angry and assuaged, dizzy and as certain as she'd ever be about anything. "All right."

Keller squeezed once more, then put the report on the ansible monitor so Ash could see it as well. "So. The thing in the locker. Do you think it's Vai?"

"Sure felt like it," Ash said softly. *Quiet suffocation. Death. Voices.*

She heard a clattering at the access tube. Sharma pulled herself out, breathless and full of blue-sweater bluster like she'd just won the lottery. "Oh, it's Vai. For sure. But that's not the interesting part."

Keller sat back down. "I'm listening."

Sharma brought up her medbay interface on the main ansible monitor, then ducked into the same report Len had just filed. "Look at those usage numbers. The Vai weaponry we've seen—zappers, screamers, even greenhouse bombs—even at Grenadier, they rarely registered over a six-point-two on the Miles scale, right? This one's a fourteen-point-five. Isn't that exciting?"

Ash's hand started to shake, and she shoved it in her pocket. *Not in front of the doctor.* "I think the word I'd use is *terrifying*. That could take out dozens of ships. A *planet*."

"Could it have killed Tribulation?" said Keller.

Sharma's eyes widened. "It certainly could have. But that's still not the interesting part. Number one, from the compositional analysis taken by the indenture's pod before it failed, we know it's not a kinetic, but it's not a molecular style with which we're familiar. It's doing two things we don't expect Vai moleculars to do. Number one, it functions when there aren't any Vai around. Number two, it let Indenture Ashlan live."

Keller whistled.

The doctor's face was formal and excited all at once, and she waved her hands in the air like a child at a birthday party. "That's nothing compared to number three. What if the fourteen-point-five isn't power output, but power input?"

It took Ash a few moments to catch on, but Keller's eyes

widened immediately, and she stood, crossing the bridge until she was nose-to-screen with the data. "A battery. An engine?"

"A zero-point battery. This could change everything," Sharma said. "I mean, it's been posed by some people at HQ for a while that the Vai use zero-point energy, but it's always only been a theory. And if this is real, the fact that it drained the pod battery and disrupted Ash's memory is . . . worrying. It could be messy. That doesn't mean it's out of the question. General quarters or not, all the scientists on *London* would have wanted to see it. And power loss explains why we never received most of the battle data."

Sharma went silent. Keller stayed where she was, staring at the numbers, swaying like a squirrel charmed by a cobra. Ash's mind was a sudden deluge of implications, rolling over each other faster than she could open her mouth to say them, but one of them was in front of all the others.

"An end to scarcity," she said.

She might as well have dropped a bomb in a quiet forest.

Sharma pointed to her. "We *hope,*" she said. "We don't even know what the Vai look like, let alone have any idea how Vai energy exchange works. Human spaceships are easy to describe: refined celestium fuel powers the grav-drive, the grav-drive powers virtually everything else. But for all we know, Vai ships are powered by magic. We figure out how this works, and everything changes for Aurora. This could be the difference between survival and suicide if they come back, the thing that keeps Aurora as a market leader until the end of time. We *must* figure out how it works. We must get this to some proper engineers. *Immediately*. We can't wait for *Rio*. We need to call a colleague of mine on *Medellin*, then get back to Europa Station straightaway."

Ash's heart thudded. "And give up top-tier hazard pay?"

"This is bigger than any of us, indenture."

"Oh, I know," said Ash. She pushed off the wall, taking two

steps toward Sharma. "You're a birthright, so let me remind you of why Len, Natalie, and I are even *here*."

Sharma narrowed her eyes. "You can't be a citizen if you're dead."

Len popped up from the access hatch, followed by Natalie; she'd combed her hair and changed her uniform. "I heard that," he said, "but Ashlan's right. We're doing this ourselves."

Keller sighed. "Guys."

"We need to wait for the professionals, indenture," said Sharma, shooting a glance at Len.

Len flexed his arm. "You're looking at them, doc."

"Guys," said Keller, louder this time. She rubbed her temple, as if fighting off a headache. "I appreciate your thoughts on safety, Reva, but I can't ignore the fact that this mission could be life-changing for our indentures, and if they're willing to try, I think we should listen to them. How do we run tests on this thing without turning *Twenty-Five* into Tribulation?"

Sharma crossed her arms. "We call *Medellin*. We push hard for Europa Station."

Keller sighed, then leaned forward in her chair. "What about going to the planet?"

There was silence on the bridge. Natalie shuffled her feet. "Aren't we, ah, not supposed to land there?" Natalie asked.

Sharma tapped her chin in thought. When she spoke, it was with a hint of dark, professional anger. "It isn't as safe as a proper, locked Company lab with proper, trained Company scientists. But you can't suck power out of dead plasteel. The worst that would happen is that you'd have to wait around for the solar rechargers to work."

Keller rubbed her eyes. When she looked up, her gaze rested on Ash for a few seconds longer than she probably should have. "Okay, planet it is. Ash, you have the most experience with this thing, so you get to run this show down on the planet. Get it set up. I'll get back on the ansible with corporate to tell them what we're doing."

Ash closed her eyes for a moment. The weapon's painful light was still there, a seared, violent memory. She felt weight like a band around her throat. Someone was whispering behind her eyelids, someone that sounded like dead Christopher, and she opened her eyes to stop it. Keller had her arms crossed, and she tapped her thumb against her opposite elbow, a rapid and erratic tattoo.

"Mr. Solano did say we're the best," Ash replied.

"Damn straight we are," whispered Natalie. "Come on, Ash, let's go get this thing."

Ash followed her, grinning at Keller before she swung a leg over the lip of the hatch and dropped into the ship's spine. The captain had a faraway look on her face and a short, amused smile on her lips. Ash let herself think of a planet and a lake and a cabin, Keller in a sweater with her head on Ash's shoulder, and the thought kept her so warm she put aside her worries about the quiet, prickling lights and her shaking body.

Citizenship was just around the corner.

# 3

Natalie and Ash left *Twenty-Five* in the ship's two retrieval pods, taking a graceful arc back toward *London* and the quarantine locker. Natalie spent the time humming wartime pop songs under her breath.

"Hey, do you know this one by the Smashboys? The one that samples the machine roar they recorded on Cana? *Vvvvvvaaaaaaiiiiii*—"

Ash snorted. "You sound like you just ate a cat. And, no. I grew up on the Wellspring dole. There was a lot we didn't get. Mostly we got WellCel vids, some Manx-Koltar movies."

"What about *Alien Attack Squad*?"

"Never even heard of it until I met Len."

Natalie made a small noise of disbelief. "But you lived on a colony."

Ash shook her head. "Bittersweet wasn't a real colony. Not like Tribulation. It was a mine. We were all indentures. There were strict rules."

Natalie smirked at her through her porthole and gunned the pod forward. "There are rules everywhere you go."

"Not like Wellspring's. I just didn't know any better. I thought they were fair." Ash took a breath. Christopher had called their indenture *slavery* once he'd learned enough about the word, but how could it have been slavery if they'd both agreed to it? Signed a contract, even?

"What do you mean?"

"Wellspring's indenture period is supposed to be a decade,

except for the fact that they own your ass once you sign up, and if you've got family, they own them, too. It's not like you have any other option, though. My parents were Wellspring. Debtors so far in they were never going to get out. So were all my friends. We were uncitizens, so we all ate off the dole and accrued debt. I was only able to settle my own debt with those bastards and enter indenture with Aurora because my fiancé put me down for his death benefit and Aurora thought I could be a decent pilot."

When Natalie spoke, it was with quiet embarrassment. "I didn't know you had a fiancé."

"That's because I don't like to talk about it." Ash checked her altimeter.

Natalie hummed a few bars of the *Alien Attack Squad* theme, trying to return the conversation to the easy back-and-forth of before. Ash bit her lip, trying to force down the unmoored feeling she always had when someone mentioned Christopher, and focused on flying.

They cleared a particularly thorny patch of spinning debris, revealing the hulk of dead *London* beyond. During the battle, Vai weaponry took to *London* like a machete to a water balloon, making the ship the graveyard's largest and most valuable corpse. Three of its six levels were laid open, their contents spilled in an ever-whirling, sun-glistening spiral.

"Sounds like Wellspring was a bit like the military," Natalie said.

Ash switched her trajectory toward the science deck and sent the new numbers to Natalie's pod. The second pod matched the change in less than a second. "Not quite. You've only got a year left, right? That's because you had a savings account. You could put credit toward your contract. You were learning useful skills. On Bittersweet, everything you owned came from the Company store, and you had to pay it out of your indenture. The prices were so high that you'd spend your entire paycheck on food and soap, let alone buying yourself out."

"But the death benefit was enough?"

When Christopher came up, she generally shifted the topic to something else—anything else. "He'd been promoted, I think," she said. "Those last few months are a little fuzzy. He'd been going off to the exec wing for his new job, at least. Hey, we're going to want to focus up here; this part's full of spinning debris, and you need to keep your mind on the target if you want to keep yourself and your cargo out of the mix."

"You're begging off?" Natalie said.

"Not begging off." *I just can't trust my hands right now and I don't want you to know.* "I just want to see you work, Miss Minefield."

"Flatterer. I work in an EVA suit, not a pod."

"Just another skill to learn on your way to citizenship."

Natalie groaned and pushed the pod forward, taking the lead. The quarantine locker with the Vai device was waiting, stripped of all power, in the exact place Ash had left it. She moved her pod alongside Natalie's, and slid both hands into the pincer controls, just in case. Natalie's breathing was heavy and deliberate in her ear. Ash switched to her fore cameras and watched the other woman carefully push her pincers toward the quarantine case.

"Slower."

Natalie laughed. "C'mon, live a little."

Ash winced and watched the pod's pincers, molasses-slow, slip around and under the quarantine locker. She heard the satisfying click through the comm and let loose a breath she didn't know she was holding. Natalie's pod turned back toward its stocky, square mother ship.

"Ready to go," Natalie said.

"Setting return course."

The two pods fired their burners, taking them out of *London's* debris field and back toward *Twenty-Five*.

After depositing the locker just inside the cargo airlock, Ash stowed her pod in its station for the second time that day and headed for the ship's spine, dropping down to the habitat ring and applying her thumbprint to her storage closet. It was quiet; everyone else would be in the cargo bay, loading the shuttle.

Her closet wasn't any larger than Sharma's storage, and it was ignored as a rule, the blankets rumpled, and yesterday's shirt cast on the floor. She was still trying to get used to the Auroran spacers' obsession with being scrupulously clean and her own surprise at having her own space. Other than two pictures on the vanity, she'd brought little else to her new life with Aurora. Natalie liked to tease Ash about her Spartan surroundings; the younger woman's own walls were covered, top to bottom, with photographs of people in Alliance uniforms and campfires under dark skies, groups and gatherings of people her age, on beaches and on leave, holding bottles of scotch and smiling with wide, white teeth.

Natalie's room made Ash feel sad and alone.

Ash went straight to the drawer, picking out her cold-weather coat and gloves, her expedition socks and her lined exploration pants, then, as usual, stopped to touch each of the two photographs with reverent fingers. There was the picture of her parents as she liked to remember them, at the billiards hall on Wellspring Station, standing side by side against bright blue lights, smiling after a win. Next to it hung the picture of Christopher in his miner's uniform, his dirty platinum hair long and drawn over his left shoulder, holding a steaming cup of coffee.

Ash had forgotten when the picture was taken. Christopher's shoulders drooped, and his eyes seemed sunken and tired, so it must have been some time into the contract. His smile was still gorgeous and crooked. He hadn't yet started to show signs of the celestium madness that would come to claim anyone who got off Bittersweet alive.

"Miss you, baby," she whispered, like she always did, then went above. *Miss you, and I'll always be sorry.*

When she walked into the cargo bay, Len was loading the last boxes of scientific equipment in the back of the landing shuttle, and Natalie was locking up boltguns for travel. Sharma tiptoed, looking into the airlock with determined eyes. "There it is," she said. "What a beauty. Can't you bring it in?"

"It's a quarantine locker, Dr. Sharma," Ash said. "I like my life."

Sharma narrowed her eyes. She adjusted her scarf, sliding on tight leather gloves. "I'm sorry. I just want to get to work. Have you ever seen a Vai molecular up close? It's the closest you're ever going to get to synesthesia. First time I saw one, I threw up. Then I nearly died."

Ash stared.

Keller grinned, sweeping in from above. "Are you *scared*, Dr. Sharma?"

"No," said Sharma, deadpan. "I'm dismayed that we're not burning for Europa right now. *You* should be scared."

"All right, Ash is in charge," responded Keller. "We've loaded enough provisions for three days. If you all do your jobs, we're going to accrue a lot of credit. Are you ready?"

The others cheered. Ash looked down at her hand. It was steady enough. She turned it over and took a breath. Thought of Christopher, and what he would say. Thought of her citizenship account. Their dreams. *I can handle this. I'm so close.*

"Let's go," she pronounced.

She thought she heard someone laughing, but when she looked around, she didn't see anyone smiling.

Ash shivered.

"I love you guys," Keller said, looking relieved. "Now get out there and get us a bonus."

# 4

As the shuttle approached the planet, Ash tightened her hands around her safety harness and tried to swallow the starving, tight nausea threatening to derail her afternoon. She wanted to place the blame for how she felt directly on Len's shoulders—as the only one on the planetside team with atmospheric flight certification, he was cackling at the tiller, acting like he'd gotten into Keller's special whiskey stash—but Ash couldn't forget the bright hallucination from earlier in the afternoon or the miscalculation that had nearly gotten her killed. She felt guilt as keen as the acid in her throat and looked out the window to distract herself.

Tribulation yawned underneath her, a sick, striated marble clothed in cloudy green seas, golden deserts, and burgundy-blue forests. With the atmospinners settled into a hush as dead as the colony itself, the planet's original flora and fauna were crawling back from the brink of annihilation. As the shuttle tumbled toward the ground, she could see the central city and the hub-and-spoke clearings leading out to the agricultural settlements where indentures like her had once lived and dreamed and tended the land: a ragged stain left over from the Vai smallpox, a human oasis losing the fight against an encroaching wine-red tide.

"Hang on," said Len. "We're entering the atmosphere now. Heat shield deployed."

Natalie squirmed in her seat while Sharma read a packet of flimsies like she was back in her office. Ash kept her gaze focused on the ground tumbling up to meet her, the hold of gravity clawing around the shuttle, grabbing violent and sure at her soft body and the protective metal keeping them all from the flames and the fall. A massive roar filled her ears as the shuttle slipped into the planet's ionosphere, and she clutched the harness tight enough to cause her knuckles to go white.

Ash was an asteroid brat, daughter of the dole, descended from celestium miners and ice cutters. Going downwell just felt wrong. The closest she'd ever gotten to living on a planet was in the mine on Bittersweet—not that Wellspring had even tried to terraform that choking dust ball, not that she'd ever been outside in the interminable years she'd been indentured there. When Keller and Sharma showed her pictures of how Auroran indentures lived, they'd been pictures of Tribulation before the war, pictures of smiling homesteaders earning their way to their own land, to agency over their own bodies, to their own dreams, their own money, their own children—

—and in only *seven years guaranteed.*

*Seven years guaranteed* had made the decision about abandoning Wellspring a lot easier than she'd thought it would be.

It still wasn't enough.

The shuttle bounced to the side, and Ash's belly shuddered into the back of her throat. This time, she was pretty sure it wasn't her fault.

"Len, stop fucking up," howled Natalie.

"I'm just making it fun." Len smirked at her, righted the shuttle, ramped up the anti-grav, and started looking for a place to land.

The war-torn version of this colony looked nothing like the photographs Ash had seen. Trashed and overgrown, the asphalt roads lay infiltrated by fibrous local grasses like broken crackers, and unprocessed food wrappers rolled in a gentle eastern wind from the recycling center. The doors of prefab houses sat open like cracked eggshells. The whole city felt like it had taken a very long breath and never let it go.

Len found a municipal shuttleport near the center of the city that looked mostly clear of rubble and set the shuttle down on a clear civilian pad with a jarring clank. By the time Ash had loosened her restraints, the others were already outside, squinting against the too-bright afternoon sun. Natalie opened one of the gun lockers, loading the boltgun with a quick, practiced *snick*. The air was flush with fetid rot and sweet sulfur, and when Ash filled her lungs she still felt slightly dizzy.

"Where do you want to go, Dr. Sharma? Will right here do?" Ash asked.

The doctor raised her hand to shade her forehead and wrinkled her nose. "If you don't mind, I would actually prefer to head to the center plaza. The admin center is defensible and will have adequate afternoon light, which we'll need in case this is a zero-point charger and we lose power to our equipment. We don't want to screw up the shuttle."

Natalie rubbed her hands together. "I like being able to get home."

"How far?" said Len, loading the dolly.

"Half mile."

Ash considered. "We can do that," she said.

Len finished loading the boxes on the dolly, and pushed off, leading the way through the southwestern axis of the city. Ash walked in silence, flanked on either side by silent plasteel prefab homes with half-cracked doors, the black shadows inside promising grisly discoveries. Nobody knew why the captain of the *London* hadn't been able to inform colonial administration of the Vai advance. As the Battle for Tribulation wailed above the planet, many of the colonists had still been going about their normal evening schedules, and Ash imagined families slouched dead at their dinner tables, the meals still moldering where they sat.

*Or maybe not,* she reminded herself. The Vai used molecular weapons here, the kind that screamed through the streets on

the wings of devils, tearing apart women and children and soldiers and farmers and scattering their ashes to the sulfur wind. It
seemed unholy to leave the colony to rot like this, but triage was
triage. Survivors first.

There were no survivors here.

Ash's eyes were caught by a group of black ashen outlines on
the wall—she thought it was street art at first, but then recognized bodies bent in fear: the chins tilted toward the sky, the
arms folded over their heads, the delicate, defiant turn of one
woman standing over a child.

"Is that them?" she whispered.

Natalie set her jaw, her face dark, then continued walking toward the plaza. "Yeah. That would have been the work of a C-6
Hornet."

"I didn't expect—"

"You expected bodies? Rubble? That's not how the Vai do things."

Ash stared. She could almost imagine the dusty outlines moving, their fingers trembling—*Or maybe that's the celestium sickness talking,* she thought. "I know. But . . . this whole city is in a
lot better condition than I thought."

"They didn't use kinetics here, like armor-breachers or hullcrackers, not like Gethsemane," Natalie said, an edge of respect
in her voice. "Can you imagine what would happen if we could
just figure out how it was done? You could take a ship, a colony,
in seconds, without spending a lot of time scrubbing bloodstains
and brain matter off the walls you're set on occupying. Or burying
bodies."

Ash shuddered. "Just slide right in and take your place."

"No wonder people want to figure out how they work," Len
added.

"Yeah," Natalie said. "Would make the crappy part of war
much easier."

Sharma cleared her throat. "Can we not speculate on things that make me sick?"

The rest of the trek was short and silent. The main administration building occupied the entire block on the north side of a plaza paved with bricks sticking up from the ground like jagged, bloodstained teeth being eaten alive by tough red blades of native grass. *Just a hundred years and there will be no city here at all*, Ash thought. *Archaeologists are going to need isolation suits and chainsaws.*

The lobby was the only place in the city that hadn't been built from prefab blocks. The space was open and airy and aesthetically pleasing, with a wide reception desk made of dark local wood and a mural depicting happy farming families of all colors and origins. The glass doors yawned open, smashed. Glass crunched and crackled under Ash's boots in the uncanny quiet.

Sharma pointed at the open center of the floor. "That space looks fine," she said.

Ash turned to search the room as they unpacked, and her eyes were caught by a flash of color: a stuffed unicorn toy with a golden horn and a rainbow tail, sitting half wrapped next to a plain white coffee mug, a roll of tape, and a scattering of flimsies. She walked over and picked it up, flicking on the power button. The animatronics kicked into gear, and the toy neighed, kicking its fabric hooves in the air.

"Huh. Battery's still working," Ash said. "Birthday present?"

"Birthday present?" the toy repeated.

Sharma looked up. "Cute. My granddaughter would like that." Ash waved it in the air. "Want it?"

"Want it?" said the unicorn.

"That seems gauche," Sharma said, after a considering moment.

Len stopped unpacking and walked over, yanking the unicorn out of Ash's hand and shoving it through his belt. "We're a salvage crew, and that's a character from *Alien Attack Squad*, so I'm salvaging it for my room. I have no problem with gauche."

"No problem with gauche," said the unicorn.

"Oooh, Len," Natalie said. "You have someone who will actually listen to you now."

He snorted in response and got back to unpacking boxes.

Ash shook her head, then turned her attention back to the coffee cup and the flimsies on the desk. The liquid inside had long since evaporated, leaving a brown film. The flimsies were strewn on the desk, chair, and floor, as if someone dropped them in surprise while rising from their chair.

Ash peered over the desk to see a dark shadow. It took her a moment to register it as a body: the body that had dropped the flimsies, the body that had been in the middle of wrapping a child's present, lying blackened and rotten on the floor behind the desk, curled into a ball, clutching its head with hands made of thin, white bone.

Her lunch rocketed back up her throat.

The others snapped up to Ash's side in a second. Natalie's hand rubbed Ash's back as she spat recalcitrant chunks of protein bar onto the floor, then sucked the vomit out of her teeth, retching again, her vision pinpointed with black scrollwork. She'd seen dead bodies before, she'd seen *Christopher's* dead body, but she'd never seen anything like this, couldn't imagine this dark terror was what he looked like, now, buried in the Bittersweet sand.

Sharma padded around the body, crouching, examining the dead man with a curious light in her eyes. "Poor man. This isn't consistent with death by blue screamer, or anything else we've seen so far. I can't even tell you how long he's been dead because of the slight difference in atmospheric composition since the atmospinners on the colony stopped working," she said after a quiet moment. "Definitely over eight months. Could be a year."

Len heaved a sigh and stepped back. "After the attack. Free-lancers. I'll pack up, then."

"Pack up, then," said the unicorn.

"No." Sharma straightened, her voice calm and sure. "We're losing the afternoon light. We don't have time to relocate."

"We're going to do it right here? With this guy staring at us?" Len said, aghast.

The doctor blinked. "It's not like there's anything we can *do* about it. He died a long time ago."

"We can *bury* him."

Ash's stomach unclenched, and she spat on the ground one more time, listening to the engineer and the doctor bicker. She liked Len better—everyone liked Len better—but in this case she'd have to agree with Sharma. Bringing the isolette back to a more controlled situation on Europa would rob her of a bonus that could save her life. "I think it's probably best that we do what we came to do and then get the hell off this planet," she said.

"Shit," said Len.

"Shit," said the unicorn.

Natalie patted her gun. "I'm going to clear the perimeter," she said. "I'm worried about that body."

"Ain't nobody here," Len said, crossing his arms.

"Len," Ash warned, pointing at the body. "Space plus bullshit. And *that* is bullshit. So is going out there alone, Natalie."

"I'll be fine," she said.

"Yeah. Of course. Everybody here is fucking *fine*," muttered Len.

"Everybody here is fucking *fine*," repeated the unicorn.

The toy's bright, thin voice pierced the tension. Nobody laughed, but the corner of Natalie's mouth lifted as she turned and left. Sharma let out a pent-up breath and turned back to unloading her mess of tablets and sensors. Len took off his jacket and laid it over the dead man's face and torso, then turned back to his own work: running cables from the battery he'd brought to Sharma's equipment and a local-area comm system meant to feed data back to *Twenty-Five*.

Ash walked a few steps away to calm down. She uncapped a bottle of water and washed out her mouth, then took a few deep, calm breaths until the black dots peppering her vision slowed and stopped.

Living on *Twenty-Five* felt like a permanent holiday visit with relatives Ash had to tolerate but didn't necessarily like. They knew entirely too much about each other: their annoying habits, their tics, their most boring stories. She knew too much about Len's gambling debts, had heard Natalie's story about the Bailey skirmish eighteen times, and, thanks to Keller, knew how to catch a trout in a Neversink lake with a rope and her teeth. She probably knew more about her crewmates than their own families did.

*But maybe not,* Ash thought, taking a swig. She'd told a lot of stories of growing up a Wellspring uncitizen, but had avoided her mining indenture and Christopher's death until recently. Ramsay's deflections about her family were absolute. And, of course, there was the desperate, important, terrible thing Ash had never said to any of them but Keller, in the dark of her quarters: the madness that was the biggest secret of them all.

And then there was Sharma. Ash knew very little about the Auroran scientist. Busy like a perpetual motion machine and full of relentless formality, Sharma regularly mentioned a son and a granddaughter living on Mars but had never taken a family call. She was a birthright citizen—her parents were top-ten earners, and she'd been born with full rights. Her dossier said that she'd spent a lot of her career doing medical research for Aurora HQ. For a person like her, moving to a salvage vessel staffed by indentures was like ditching a sky-top penthouse for an uncitizen dorm.

When Ash was finally feeling well enough to breathe in without wanting to vomit, she looked up. Sharma was checking the seals on the quarantine equipment, the isolette humming quietly in the center of a clear second quarantine box. Len was screwing in the housing on a robot arm.

"Both quarantine levels are sealed and we're ready to proceed on your mark, Indenture Ashlan," said Sharma. "This is your last chance to go outside."

"It's safe, isn't it?" said Len. "I thought you said this was going to be safe."

Sharma's mouth quirked in a sly half smile, and she indicated the unicorn. "Quite safe. This is a K-1 isolette, tested on some of the most sensitive bits of the Christmas list that we've got. If I'm right, we're about to change everything. Isn't that worth watching?"

Ash's stomach twisted again, and she flipped open her talkie. "She's going to open it, Natalie. Stay out there in case we need a rescue?"

Sharma sighed.

"Acknowledged." Natalie's voice was tinny and tight. "I'll be outside."

"Just get back here in time for dinner." Ash flipped off the device, stuffing it in her pocket.

Len wrung his hands. "All right," he said, jumping up and moving to a secondary console. The lights inside the isolette brightened his worried face. "Let's get this party started."

Sharma took hold of the robot arm and used it to punch the button on the quarantine locker.

The lobby filled with light and sound, and the temperature dropped. Fast.

Inside her pod, the light had been overwhelming, ancient, roiling; it had crawled behind her eyes and kept her from seeing much else. Behind Sharma's K-1 isolette, she could see the device free and clear. It was spherical, containing the same sparkling, roiling interior of any Vai weapon in a housing that was far more ornate than any of the zappers they'd retrieved from the area around *London*. She had no reference for it but the old pictures she'd seen of ancient ironwork fences, the scrollwork on Earth's dead cathedrals, the eyes of gargoyles and the scent of incense. She saw teardrops, human hands in filigree, the curve of inhuman eyes, the quiet of the graveyard. A cold wind spun in from somewhere; Ash felt like the heat was being leached out of her bones, and she shivered like she'd never be warm again.

Len shook his head, keeping his eyes on the tablet like he wasn't even affected by the deathless alien beauty ducking in and out of Ash's head. "I've never seen anything like this. This is *beyond* me. I didn't think it was even possible. It's drawing power from the tablet batteries through some sort of advanced heat sink. *Draining* it. I can't tell how."

"Cover it up. I feel terrible," Ash whispered. She struggled to speak. Her words seemed locked away, sewn in the seams of heavy, suffocating velvet curtains.

Len blinked. "I'm hearing some really weird shit, Dr. Sharma."

Sharma's hands moved over her tablets with quick, practiced motions. Her words slurred. "No. Stay focused. Is it speaking to you, Ashlan?"

Ash watched her fear slip out of her fingers in black ribbons, coalesce and knot together in front of her chest in a slithering, sable Gordian knot. Far away, she heard the whispering of familiar voices: Kate's, her mother's, Christopher's, all in wordless vowels and sibilants, or some strange language she did not know. Her tongue felt heavy and coated with vomit.

"Yes," Ash said.

Sharma kept working. "Good. Fantastic. Ask for a connection."

Out of nowhere, the voices started to resolve into Christopher's. *Trying to connect. Trying to connect. Trying to connect. Connection failed. No routing to node.*

"It, um," Ash said. "It doesn't. It can't connect. You ask it. What the hell?"

"Glory," said the unicorn, still stuck in Len's belt.

"*Finally,*" Sharma said, her eyes lit with a strange intensity Ash had never seen before. She started to cry, her body shaking as if she was fighting a deep and dark power clutching her heart. Sharma reached for the button that kept the K-1 isolette in place; the curtains fell, and there was no longer anything between Ash and the weapon.

That was when things started falling apart.

# 5

Being eye to eye with the weapon was one of the most fascinating and terrifying experiences of Ash's life.

She felt dizzy, as if she were perched at the top of a mountain of bewildering height, as if she were looking down at a roaring sandstorm, watching the dirty winds batter the city over and over again, watching them abandon themselves on the encroaching forest, watching them chew on the planet's burgundy trees. Sharma's instrumentation went wild. Len's hands moved over his console as the tablets flashed and flickered. The unicorn in Len's belt loop opened its diminutive red mouth and roared in a two-toned, high-pitched alien shriek, screaming *Glory, glory, glory*—

"What do you see now?" screamed Sharma. "Can you touch it, Ashlan?"

"You're closer!" said Ash. "You do it!"

"I have to be able to hit the shutdown!"

"Fine. Okay." Ash pinched herself, and the pain helped her tumble back into her skin. The voices told her that *everything is well now that you are with me,* and the unicorn was saying it, too, opening and closing its stitched-up jaw, electricity glistening in its quiet glass eyes, speaking in chorus with the voices of the man and woman she loved: *Glory, glory, no routing to node*—

"What do you mean, 'no routing to node'?" Sharma yelled. "What else does it need?"

Ash reached out to touch the roiling light, the beating heart, the voice of the man she would have died for—

—but as she did, she noticed Len's hands had gone still. He

wasn't working; he stared straight ahead, past the tablet, past all of it toward the weapon, his eyes glassy and filled with tears. His shoulders shook. She could see his breath. She blinked a weight that felt like cotton away from her eyes. *Why is it so cold?*

"Something's wrong with Len," Ash said.

"He's fine," Sharma said. "Stay focused. We don't have much time."

The spell spun up in her head once more. Sharma was right. All three of them only had a few more seconds before they lost consciousness, like she had in the pod. (Or minutes? She had no sense of time, not here, in the screaming light of *glory*.) Somewhere in the distance, the Vai sailed in their white ships against the copper Bittersweet sky. Somewhere, she was a child. Somewhere, she was lying on the ground, watching the sky, near death, but not dying. She wanted to consume the light, bury it in her fingers, burst open with the power of the thousand *together,* get revenge for—*revenge for what? for whom?* Somewhere, time was slowing down, and Ash breathed air like water, a great wide nothing pouring down her throat, her mouth full of stone and death and everything was cold, oh so cold—

"I'm shutting this down," Ash said.

"No," the doctor yelled, but Ash pushed past Sharma, yanked the robot arm and pressed the quarantine button. The lid came down, jamming the panel closed.

The blackening world cleared.

Len blinked and lifted his arms, staring at them, as if he was a child and he'd never seen them before. Sharma stumbled back into life, throwing herself at the robot arm. "No!" she hollered.

Freed of the dark molasses holding her back, Ash moved quickly, catching Sharma's arm with her own and dragging her away, the doctor kicking and screaming like a preschooler or an addict denied a fix. Finally, the doctor's anger resolved into choking sobs, and the tension leached out of her shoulders. Ash wrapped her arms around the doctor's body, holding her close until she was quiet.

When they'd begun, the golden light of midafternoon had reigned; now, a darkening sun bathed the whole plaza in a chablis glow. She had lost time again. Twenty-six minutes? More? She knew how that kind of thing felt, now, knew the quiet song of the device, whatever it was, the way it slipped deep inside her chest and made everything cold and slow and terrible. A change had been made in some dark part of her heart, and she couldn't put her finger on it.

"What the hell was that, doctor?" she whispered.

Sharma's eyes closed. Her voice sounded raw and shredded. "I'm sorry," she whispered, lifting her chin, attempting to recover a modicum of gentility. "I don't know what came over me."

"We're going to talk about it when we get back to *Twenty-Five*."

"I told you we should have gone to Europa."

Ash looked up. "Maybe. Len. Call the captain, then call Natalie."

Len blinked, moving slowly, as if he were being given information he didn't understand. He turned to the tablets in front of him and frowned. He jabbed the tablet once, twice, three times, and that's when Ash realized that the tablet he was using was dead. She released Sharma, then ducked to check the battery below. Dead, too.

"How?" Ash said. "Len, check the satphone. What about the rest of the tech?"

Sharma's eyes widened, as if she was finally considering the implications of dropping the quarantine. She picked up her talkie, thumbing on the power, but nothing happened. Ash grabbed her own, ripping open the back of the comm to find a breached, dead battery, then yanked open a gun locker to find a dead boltgun.

The only way this gun would hurt anyone was if she used it as a club or a battering ram.

"What's the range on this thing?" Ash asked. "I thought you said a half mile was safe. Could it have drained the shuttle?"

Sharma's jaw wavered. "I thought it was fine."

"What about Natalie's talkie?" asked Sharma.

"What about her *boltgun*," Ash responded. "If she was close enough to the building, she might be unarmed, and she might not even know it."

"Go find her," Sharma said. "Leonard and I will pack up and meet you on the shuttle."

Len tilted his head. "What shuttle?"

"The shuttle you flew here. I'll be back in an hour, tops," Ash said. "I'll meet you on the road."

"Here," Sharma said, reaching into her medkit, taking out a scalpel. "It's nothing, but you should be armed. Just in case."

Ash slid the scalpel into her boot, then took off through the shattered glass doors. She picked up speed as she ran down the broken southwestern road. Whatever footprints the younger woman might have left behind had been covered over by blood-colored local dust blown in by the afternoon winds and a light rain. On the slow, lazy westerly wind, there swept in the barest hint of fire. The screaming smell of burning celestium. She turned to see where it was coming from. In the distance, she saw a quiet column of smoke rising from where the shuttle was parked.

*Shit.*

Ash took off down the main drag. She slowed as she came closer, sticking near to the prefab walls around the shuttlepad, staying in the shadows of the skinny, fibrous trees. Closer, now, she could hear two bass voices—male voices, new ones. Holding her breath, she ducked behind a vine-choked bush and peered through the leaves.

The men were freelancers, dressed in plain black. They were armed with bullet guns—*damn,* guns for planet use, guns that would actually work—and were siphoning celestium fuel out of the shuttle. Her pod had only rebooted that morning because of the celestium running in its veins. It wouldn't matter if the shuttle's solar charger worked if the shuttle didn't have any fuel.

Ash felt ill and angry and very small.

"Boss said they'd do the test in orbit," said the first man. Bearded and tight-muscled, he checked the generator. "I don't like it when the plan changes."

The other man, a clean-shaven brawler with a hangdog smirk, continued to pump fuel out of the tank. "It's a bunch of nancy Aurorans, man, and we've got the only soldier. This is not going to be a problem."

The bearded man narrowed his eyes. "I'm sick of them asking us to improvise."

"What do you think you signed up for?"

"When are they due back?"

The clean-shaven one indicated the ground with a tilt of his head. "Ask her."

*Her. The only soldier. Natalie.*

Narrowing her eyes, Ash ducked behind another bush. Natalie was shoved in the shadows, her hands tied around her back with thin rope. She hollered through a gag—muffled profanities that were meant to tell them she most certainly would not answer— and Ash felt pride alongside a clear moment of panic.

The edges of her vision clouded, and her right hand began to shake. Her vision went gray, and then popped again, a wild chiaroscuro, into stunning color. *The sickness.* She couldn't avoid it. Not when it had nearly killed her this morning. Not now, when the others needed her most. It felt like Bittersweet, like the cave-in, like the dirt filling her mouth and the mineral shards Sharma removed from her lungs. It felt like crawling in the dirt, through rocks, her ribs broken, just to find blood and darkness. It tasted like defeat.

*No,* she thought. *Not now. Not when Natalie needs me.*

She slipped the scalpel out of her boot, then stood, tossing it at Natalie.

"Hey!" she hollered.

The competitors whirled and reached for their guns. The scalpel hit the dirt a foot away from Natalie, and she threw herself back, grabbing it with one hand. That's all Ash needed to see; she stumbled, then turned, barreling away back toward town. The clean-shaven man pulled the trigger on his rifle, and the bullets whizzed by her shoulders, her ears, and she had sulfur burning in her throat and air and her feet hitting the pavement—

—until pain erupted in her shoulder, more pain than she'd ever felt in her life.

Shock pushed her off her footing and she crashed into a wall, feeling warm, sticky blood on her back. She scrambled forward, adrenaline and fear pushing her to her feet, making it four more steps before she tripped over a plant growing in the middle of the road and fell, her face cracking against the street, the stones forcing blood into her throat and rattling her brain. She managed to turn over just to see the bearded man raising his rifle, pointing it at her face. She thought she heard an explosion, thought she felt the ground shake, but maybe that was just her heart, the remnants of the alien weapon clawing at her mind—

"You must be the mission commander," the bearded man asked, far too calm for how heavy he was breathing.

She wanted to scream in pain. "You must be an asshole," she spat.

"Just a guy doing his job, like you." He raised his gun. "Tell me where the weapon is."

Ash spat out blood and a broken tooth. She fell back, looking away to the pink-soaked afternoon sky, and tried to think of Christopher. Keller's face came up instead, unbidden.

"Up my ass," she whispered.

The man walked forward and cocked his gun. "Where's the weapon?"

Ash tested another tooth with her tongue, and tasted blood. The pain grayed out the sky, the buildings, everything but her body and the man and the gun in his hand.

"I wouldn't get involved with Vai shit if I were you," she said. "As you can see, it ends up bad for everyone."

The man raised his gun. "Last chance."

"Bite me," she said, sucking down her last breath.

A shattering noise came from behind the mercenary—another bullet gun firing, an all-too-human crack against an alien soundscape. The man's forehead erupted in a fountain of blood. He died instantly, collapsing like a mine shaft under fire.

Ash, not breathing, looked up.

Natalie stood before her, legs wide, covered in blood, holding the bearded man's bullet gun. Shaking, she dropped it and knelt before Ash, reaching for her. Ash's hands found purchase in Natalie's, and she crawled toward her shipmate, sobbing.

"It's okay," Natalie said, grabbing Ash's forehead, pressing her hand against it, drawing her close. "It's your first time seeing something like that. I know it's not your job. It's my job. You shouldn't have had to do that."

Ash took a shuddering breath. "The other guy?"

"No longer a problem." Natalie leaned closer, peering at Ash's wound. "Okay. Ash, I need you to get it together. The bullet looks like it'll be fairly easy to remove, but we need to get you back to Dr. Sharma."

"I—I know—" Ash wiped her nose on the back of her hand.

"I'll stabilize you until we can get there."

Natalie drew out a needle from her pack, and Ash felt the

agony of a shot for the pain and the sweet, rushing numbness that followed, then Natalie bound the wound with a battlefield sealant. "At least—" Ash sucked in a deep breath. She smelled fire, worse now than before. The stink of electronics burning: plasteel, wood, metal. "At least Aurora's going to pay for this."

"Hah," Natalie said.

"We need to talk about the freelancers."

"Competitors," Natalie said. "He knew who I was."

"Think they're here to take the weapon from us?"

Natalie swore, then slid her arm underneath Ash's as an answer. They limped down the road, smelling the stench of scorched metal as they came closer to the plaza.

The admin complex was on fire. Natalie stood in front of the cracked glass doors, blocking her body from the heat with her hand. The equipment they'd used to test the Vai weapon was a twisted, melted wreck inside, and the quarantine locker was gone. Ash watched in horror as Natalie threw herself into the fire, grabbing still-smoking pieces of metal and throwing them aside.

"They're not here," Natalie said.

Ash scanned the burning room. No bodies but the man draped in Len's uniform coat. No doctor's sweater, no engineer's overalls, no shock of glossy black hair. Fighting the heat, her eye was caught by a sparkling scrap of rainbow mane, tossed in the corner away from the fire.

She dove for it, picked it up, turned it over and over. The eyes were dead, the animatronic leg broken and held together by scorched pink fabric. The underside had been torn open and the stuffing hung out—white, puffy, cloudy blood and guts. This was a quick, surgical strike with the sharp edge of some tool, not the ragged, careless treatment of a bomb. She saw the outline of a dark mass there, dug in, and was rewarded with the touch of hard plastic. She narrowed her eyes and yanked the stuffing aside with two thumbs, noting a hard memory card straight from an Aurora console sisterboard. It was a move straight out of an episode of *Alien Attack Squad.*

*Len, you magnificent asshole,* she thought.

"They're not here. Probably taken. Got to go," Natalie said. She jumped a burning girder to walk over to Ash, grabbing her by her good arm and tugging her out of the building, back to the relative chill of the alien afternoon. They ran to the center of the plaza, coughing, gulping clean, warm air. Searching the sky, Natalie sighed and straightened.

"We're right in the middle of a Company war," she said. "All the people that died, after how we held the line against the very devil—and we're going back to *profiteering* with *human blood.*"

Ash shook, wiping sweat out of her eyes. "We've got to find Len and the doctor."

Natalie looked down at the unicorn. "Of all the things you could have dragged out of there, you chose that?"

Ash fished out the chip, showed it to Natalie, then shoved it in her pants pocket. Paused. Shoved the unicorn down the front of her jacket. "He saw the other Company coming."

Natalie whistled. "That's Len, all right. Why are you—"

"He wanted the stupid thing," Ash said. "I'm not going to leave it here. You can give it back to him."

"Why would I—" Natalie blinked, and shook her head. "You know, let's just get out of here."

They ran from the burning building and the silent plaza, barreling back down the boulevard. Arriving at the shuttle, Ash tried not to look too closely at the clean-shaven man, who lay dead in a puddle of blood under the shuttle's right nacelle, his jaw yawning, his neck snapped at an inhuman angle, and his eyes stuck in permanent surprise. Natalie and Ash dragged the whole lot of it—the first-aid boxes, ready-to-eat meals, and extra jackets that the mercenaries had tossed out—back on the shuttle. They raided the man's pockets for his wallet and his multi-tool. Then they jumped in the back of the shuttle and hit the door seal.

Natalie pushed Ash toward the pilot's seat and then stuck her in the shoulder with another painkiller in one quick, fluid motion. Ash sat down and felt a rush of dizziness tilting the planet to one side. She poked at the interface and it responded—they had just enough fuel, and power, to break atmo.

"I can't fly if you give me more of that," she said.

"Yeah, you can." Natalie flopped into the copilot's seat, jamming the seatbelts into place and reaching up to flick the right toggles and press the right buttons. "And you only have to be awake for another, what, fifteen minutes? Then we'll be out of atmo and back on *Twenty-Five*, and in a proper medbay. We did worse in the war."

Ash took a breath. *I'm not a soldier. I'm sick.* "I can't fly."

"So, I need to give you more adrenaline." Natalie rooted around in her bag.

"No, it's not that." Ash paused. "It's—" *I can't tell her. I can't tell her why I'm sick.* "It just hurts like hell."

Natalie leaned over Ash's lap. Her hand hung over the start-up. "Not for the next hour, it doesn't. Then you get medical attention. Then you live. Right now, you fly." She thumbed the toggle. The shuttle shuddered to life. Ash saw the tiniest flicker of keen emotion in Natalie's eyes before her soldier's training trampled on it.

Ash looked back at the familiar preflight readings and took a breath. She grabbed the checklist. Her hand shook. Somewhere, her hindbrain was screaming in animal fear.

She pushed all of that away. She was Auroran. She could do this.

She ignited the launch sequence.

# 6

"Coffee, Captain?"

Keller jolted awake, her nose full of the caustic, familiar scent of *Twenty-Five*'s store of sour instant coffee, her cheeks hot with the scandal of being caught dozing on the job. Ramsay hovered between Keller and the data feed she'd been pretending to watch, mouth pulled into a smirk, holding a steaming mug two inches from Keller's face.

"Just resting my eyes for a moment," Keller said.

She took a deep, stabilizing breath and straightened her spine, pushing herself into a more professional position before reaching out to take the mug from her executive officer. She felt every inch of the mid-mission exhaustion that had dogged her steps over the last week, but that didn't mean she could just let the crew see that she was tired.

Even if Ramsay was a citizen.

"What am I going to do, tell Mr. Solano?" Ramsay let out a chilly little laugh, then slung herself back into her own chair, bringing up her work for the afternoon. She had placed her own mug of coffee close to the pitch and yaw controls, so close it worried at Keller like a nail scratching at the back of her neck. She took a long sip of coffee, then turned back to the main monitor, pretending to understand the numbers and graphs streaming back.

Ramsay followed her gaze. "Is this the data from the surface?"

"You missed the most interesting gobbledygook about a half hour ago. Should have sent them all down with the body cameras."

Keller waved her hand at the raw data streaming in from Sharma's experiments—complex numbers in baffling combinations, filling up the main viewscreen in an impatient, hypnotic fashion.

Ramsay narrowed her eyes at the data. "I see what you mean," she said. "No wonder you were asleep."

Keller laughed. "That's the terrible curse of the captaincy, Ms. Ramsay," she said, looking back over her shoulder at the other woman. "You'll never see anything fascinating ever again. You'll just sit on the bridge, waiting for things to go to hell while everyone else gets to do all the cool shit."

Ramsay snorted. "Speak for yourself. I'm heading straight on to middle management. On a cruiser. With a proper water shower."

"Big dreams, huh," Keller said.

"No use in thinking small."

Keller knew she should keep her mouth shut about her subordinate's snap judgments, but if Ramsay's ambitions got her a new assignment sooner than later, Keller wasn't going to be upset. Ramsay disparaged *Twenty-Five* entirely too often for Keller's taste. "I don't consider *Twenty-Five* to be small."

Ramsay took a sip of her coffee. "It's so small it doesn't even have a proper name, Ms. Keller."

"I like it fine." Keller fought a twinge of anger.

Keller thought of the years she'd put into her career—her indenture as a teenager on bustling *Medellin*, then the lonely solo work on the tug, then doing Ramsay's job on *Fifteen*, and back to a kind middle on *Twenty-Five*. She'd never seen *Twenty-Five* as small and never viewed the salvage corps as a stepping-stone, like Ramsay obviously did. Keller reminded herself, as she often found she must, that Ramsay's many talents didn't include having excellent people skills.

*She'll be middle management for sure,* Keller thought, hiding her smirk behind her coffee cup.

Ramsay looked back at her work, starting her typical beginning-of-shift tasks. Keller brought up Ramsay's logs from the previous day, and her monitor blinked with the comfortable familiarity of *Twenty-Five* returning green status lights across the board. Keller held the mug in both hands while rechecking Ramsay's work, appreciating the warmth against the slight chill of the bridge, listening to the familiar, comforting hum of the engine.

"What are you going to do with your share of the hazard pay, if not try for a bigger ship? Go exec?" asked Ramsay.

Keller had a quick, cockeyed flash of herself wearing an executive's heels, an ill-fitting diamond-cut jacket sitting on her angular shoulders, a white tattoo clutching at her neck like Solano's, and she laughed out loud.

"No. No way. Not in a million years."

"Why not? You'd be a good executive."

Keller's cheeks colored, and she heard Ash laugh somewhere in the back of her mind. She waved her hand at the ship, the stars, the darkness beyond. "Because I like it out here. This is where I always wanted to be."

"You could at least get away from the indentures."

"Hah," Keller said. "It's nice to be around people that have dreams."

Ramsay's thin shoulders shrugged. "Well. I've got plans that include not getting caught up in their drama."

Coffee caught in Keller's throat. She coughed. *How much of the story had Ramsay guessed?* "What drama?"

"Just the typical indenture drama. Ashlan in particular," Ramsay said.

Keller tried to treat Ash like everyone else on the crew, but she knew as well as the rest of them that secrets were in short supply on a ship too small to have a name, even if they did manage to keep the honorifics and niceties in place most of the time. She'd been an indenture. She'd come up from the uncitizens' dole herself. She knew what it took to pay off debt. Her friendship with Ash had been different from the first moment they talked in the *Twenty-Five* sickbay during the Bittersweet rescue effort. She'd tried not to love her. God, she'd tried.

*Trying* was bullshit.

No. She loved Ash because Ash *tried,* too. Because Ash had lost everything, yet kept hoping, kept her heart open. Because Ash was facing the fight of her life and she still picked up the sword every day, and tried, and tried, and tried. Ash was worth a hundred ladder-climbing Ramsays.

"You okay?" Ramsay was staring.

Keller cleared her throat. "You know what? The worst thing in the world is a party full of citizens. They don't want anything. They don't need anything. They don't care about anything. If that's the life you want, then go straight ahead. Walk off the dock when we get back to Europa and don't look back. But you'll never understand how free you feel on a ship like a tug. Mine was barely a boat. I didn't even have my own quarters. It was just me and one hell of a grav-drive. It was incredible. Best experience of my life."

"Was tug work how you got into salvage?"

"At the beginning of the war, we ended up hauling a bunch of the smaller wrecks to the Europa yards, but we couldn't work fast enough because of the Vai advance, so they told us to start breaking them down on the way. There was one run on the tug where I cracked a cooling brace. Had to fix it without a mechanic. I thought I was going to die."

"And you were good at it."

"Yeah. But it helps that I have a good crew now, too."

"That is such a line."

Keller laughed, then turned back to watch the graphs scroll by. Ramsay was quiet for a minute or two, then tilted her head and sat back in her chair.

"You never told me what you wanted to do with the money."

Keller groaned internally. "I didn't, no."

"That's not quite fair. I told you mine."

"I'm your captain. I don't have to be fair." Keller dropped the smirk and turned back to the readings coming in from the planet, feeling the bare beginnings of a headache. Satisfied by the numbers rolling by in quick succession, she brought up the ansible dialogue and sent out a ping to the new hub *Twenty-Five* had installed to replace the one damaged in the war. If she kept working, maybe Ramsay would forget about her questions.

The bridge flooded with the white light of the ansible dialogue. The sudden change caused Keller's vision to swim, and she raised her hand to her head. She'd been right about the headache: tiny, angry fingers clawed at the edges of her mind. A migraine. *Damn* it. She tried to blink away the way the bridge began to sway back and forth for a moment and dismiss the telltale black halo at the center of her vision. No dice.

*I don't need this right now.*

"Are you going to drink up?" Ramsay asked, pointing at Keller's coffee.

"What, do you want it?"

"Maybe."

"Trust me. I need this."

The migraine was a sudden one, coming on steady and savage, and her mind wandered to the medbay and Sharma's accessible store of easy painkillers. She couldn't tell Ramsay that she planned to dump this year's profits into Ash's citizenship account, but she still felt like she needed to toss the other woman an olive branch.

"You asked what I wanted," Keller said, adding a soft edge to her voice. "I want haptics installed on this bucket, even though I know the salvage line's last on the list. I'd like some better coffee."

"That's the dream, right?"

*I'd like to be with Ash.* She'd been the one to encourage it, those first few months in *Twenty-Five*'s tight space, with a tilt of a chin or a gaze that lasted a few seconds longer than it should have. Keller knew she should have stopped, but her heart campaigned in a way her mind did not, and she found she couldn't push Ash away as much as she knew she needed to. There were the nights talking quietly in the mess together, the connection, the unstated knowledge between them that something terrible and wonderful was developing. She knew she should have informed Sharma when Ash confided in her that she suspected she had celestium sickness.

But that would have meant she'd never see Ashlan again.

"If you want me to be realistic," Keller said, drinking the last dregs of the bitter coffee, "I haven't had any time off since before the war. I think I'll go visit my parents. They've both got cit tags, now. Stay awhile. They took a rebuilding contract instead of relocation, so they'll have a nice guest room finished by the time we get back to the hubworlds. I'll go hiking or something. Try to get some normalcy back."

"Sounds nice, I guess," said Ramsay. "Are you going to bring Ashlan?"

The last of the coffee caught in Keller's throat; she leaned forward, coughing, pounding her chest with her right hand. A few seconds later, she dragged a clear breath back into her lungs and swung on Ramsay, narrowing her eyes. "You're skating on thin ice, Ms. Ramsay."

Ramsay's cheeks colored; she focused on her keyboard, dropping her hands to her lap. A quiet darkness crossed her face. "Just between you and me," she said, her voice slow and careful, "because the others aren't going to say it . . ."

Heat flared in Keller's cheeks; her left hand trembled. "You're not going to say it, either. Leave it alone."

"Ms. Keller—"

"*Captain*," she stressed, rising. Damn it; any inroads she'd made with Ramsay this afternoon had just been smashed. Her head was akimbo, full of cymbals and marching bands; the pressure rushed at her temples with a hammering urgency. "Take the watch. My head's a mess. I need some painkiller."

"Let me go get it for you," Ramsay said, pushing herself out of the chair with a sigh. "I'll get you a refill on your coffee, too."

"Thanks," Keller said, handing her empty mug over her shoulder. Ramsay ducked down the access hatch and disappeared into the body of the ship.

Keller swore to herself and turned back to the ansible diagnostics, trying to concentrate but finding her mind sliding off the data and onto the memories of the day they'd recovered *Mumbai*'s computer core and Ash earned her first bonus. Ash hadn't known what a bonus was. She'd kept on opening and closing her credit account with wide eyes, almost like she didn't believe the years that were suddenly stored there, the possibilities it introduced. Keller opened one of her bottles of scotch to celebrate, told her that she'd help Ash earn her citizenship and the cure for celestium sickness, and after the others went to sleep, Ash had kissed her.

Keller kissed back.

She'd done more than kiss back.

She had feelings. She had strong feelings. She had memories of Ash dozing, soft and quiet in her bedsheets, lit by the beam of Keller's watch and the enormity of her guilt.

Keller didn't want to be a stand-in for Ash's dead fiancé. She couldn't be the captain and believe one of her crew to be inherently more valuable than another. She didn't want to be responsible for patching up another broken partner, or to feel the guilt if she had to choose Ash over someone else. She didn't want to take advantage of someone who was fighting a serious illness. She wanted to have realized all these things before she'd slept with her.

Had pushing her away been the right thing to do? *I'm* Twenty-Five. *I'm not my own person out here.*

She ached for Ash's smile, her easy support, the knowledge that she'd follow Keller wherever they went. She was still taking advantage of that. She relied on it. She was an asshole.

She had to stop.

She resolved to fix the problem when Ash came back onboard.

*After I fix this damn headache.* Keller rubbed her temple, making a stab at distracting herself by running diagnostics on the ansible, but the headache was a loud brass band playing in a small metal box; the entire bridge was turning on its axis, slipping aft like it was a thousand miles away. She'd never had a migraine that came on this bad or this fast.

*I'm having a stroke—something's wrong.* She thumbed the all-ship comm on her interface, trying to stand and failing miserably.

"Ms. Ramsay," she croaked out, "get back up here. Need help."

"On my way," she heard.

The entire ship shuddered once and cycled the environmentals, as if *Twenty-Five* had just docked with a station. *But we're alone out here. We've been alone out here for weeks.* Keller's hand struggled for purchase, and she fell back into her chair, her limbs heavy. She felt a rising, terrible panic clawing its way from her gut, but even that couldn't fight the encroaching darkness. The bridge quieted around her as she fell into unconsciousness.

Her last memory for a long time was the burnt scent of sour coffee.

# 7

In the old days, breaking atmo would have taken five million dollars, fuel tanks the size of houses, and a lake's worth of liquid hydrogen. Standing within a mile of liftoff would shake a human to death, unless you happened to be the lucky bastard strapped to the top of the rocket. Humanity was stuck to its own planet, victim of the spin and strain of gravity, of the never-ending tug-of-war between profit and science, between rampant capitalism and the need for human advancement.

The development of the grav-drive placed the exploration of space in the hands of corporations: first, ExR, then Laikasoft and Jin Industries, then Aurora and others, and they began to do the things the warring, starving governments, stuck in the ancient ways, could not do: to marry science and profit, to push outward, to explore, to colonize, to lift tiny ships like *Twenty-Five*'s shuttle up and away from the ground.

Ash had never been so grateful for Auroran science, for auto-assist liftoff, for the software that told her how far to angle the nose of the shuttle, how much fuel to feed the reactor, how fast to go. *Len would laugh at me for using auto-assist,* she thought. *I'm going to find him, so he gets a chance to laugh at me.*

As the chilly planetside afternoon gave way in a last spasm to the ever-black, ever-blank darkness of space, Ash felt herself afflicted with a vicious, drunken clarity, and when the shuttle clicked control back to the pilot's seat, she took a deep breath and swung the shuttle around. She was back in vacuum. It felt right. They were close to home. This day would get better, fast.

Natalie leaned on the buttons for the short-range comm once it came online. "*Twenty-Five*, this is Natalie on the shuttle. *Twenty-Five*, please come in."

Ash swung the shuttle around and punched the fuel expenditure, increasing the shuttle's speed toward the battlefield. From this distance, it was all sparkling lights in the sky, stars that were not stars, graves torn open where there shouldn't be graves. She bit her lip, feeling pain flickering under the muggy edges of the medicine.

Ramsay answered the comm in just three seconds, bright and cheery, as if nothing had gone wrong.

"Hey, Nat," she said. "How did it go?"

Natalie sat up in her chair, the relief in her voice clear. "Ms. Ramsay. We're coming in hot. We were attacked on the planet's surface by unknown assailants. They took the Vai weapon, shot Ash, killed or kidnapped Dr. Sharma and Len. You need to extend the sensor net and call *Rio*. Now."

"Shit. You're serious?"

"And you need to prep the medbay for trauma."

Ramsay sounded wary. "Will do. Got ID on the attackers?"

Ash tried to focus on the dizzying space in front of them, swinging the shuttle back toward *Twenty-Five*'s homing beacon. She blinked away black scrollwork at the corners of her eyes. "Definitely competitors," she said. "But that's all we've got."

"Shit," Ramsay said. "Okay, you guys are in an unsafe situation now and you're about to enter the debris field. That's no way to fly. Concentrate on getting home. I'll call corporate and Keller will get the medbay ready. See you guys soon. Ramsay out."

Ash squinted out the front window, pushing the shuttle hard, watching *London* and *Twenty-Five* in their spinning, parasitical dance. The Auroran ships grew larger and larger by the moment. In zero-gee, strapped to the chair, Ash could almost imagine the shuttle was the settled, parked point, and the ship, the debris, her home in the sky, all of that was in motion. The familiar sight of the warship corpses took an edge off her shock, and relief crowded her mind. In a few minutes, she'd be back home, back on the ship, back with Keller. *Rio* would come. There would be soldiers and scientists and forensic artists. They'd find Sharma and Len. They'd figure out what the hell was going on.

*You'll have to disclose your illness,* a voice whispered in the back of her head.

Ash pushed the accelerator.

*No.* Keller would help her. There had to be a way. Keller wouldn't allow the Company to push her out, not when Sharma and Len were still out there. Keller would come for her, wouldn't she? She'd promised—

Ash blinked away bright, sudden tears. There was something different about the way *Twenty-Five* reflected against the Tribulation sun. She had made this approach dozens of times; something was wrong. She squinted.

"Natalie, I'm seeing things," she said.

A new ship glinted in the sunlight next to *Twenty-Five,* where there should have only been quiet, black space.

"You're okay, Ash, I see it, too." Natalie's voice was all warning and no reassurance. She leaned forward and toggled the forward cameras, magnifying the view on the right-hand screen.

*Twenty-Five* was not alone. Settled nearby, connected by a gray umbilical, was a ship twice its size: a spindle-bound, spinning vessel the color of an exhausted, rainy sky—the shade of bare plasteel, nose painted in thin ribbons of orange and green. The design was a common Armour shape that had been sold to a dozen companies at the beginning of the war, but the blue-fire exhaust spitting out the back was the signature of a newer, post-Vai grav-drive, a reactor that ran as silent as it was expensive. The ship was armed, too, with railguns and a fat spinal boltlance pointed straight at them.

Ash pressed the button to call *Twenty-Five,* and pulled back, allowing the shuttle to decelerate. She didn't wait for Ramsay to identify herself before speaking. "Who are the visitors?"

The XO's voice was cheery. "Yes, they're here to help."

Natalie muttered something under her breath and shook her head.

"They're not Auroran," Ash said.

"I noticed your velocity has decreased," Ramsay said. "That's not good. You'll burn fuel you can't afford to burn. We'll have to come out to get you."

*What the fuck is this?* Natalie mouthed.

"Captain Keller can talk us in." Ash's hand hovered over the short-range toggle.

"She's in the medbay right now," Ramsay said. "Bit of an accident."

Ash looked at Natalie; the younger woman shook her head, her eyes wide. Ash adjusted the camera view to get a better, sidelong look at the unfamiliar ship. "Then it'll be no problem for you to transfer us down there, so we can talk with her directly."

Ramsay was quiet about a second too long for Ash's taste. "She's not available."

Natalie shook her head again.

"I think you should explain what's going on, Ms. Ramsay," Ash said, keeping her voice as measured as possible, even though she wanted to stand up, reach through the short-range, and throttle the XO with her bare hands.

She was answered by another quiet few seconds on the line. "Aurora Intersystems is no longer in control of *Twenty-Five,*" Ramsay said. Her voice was almost apologetic. "It's for the best, really."

Natalie mouthed the word *bullshit.*

"You were just like us." Ash shook with anger. "You were *one* of us. How long have you been planning to screw us over?"

Her attention was grabbed by a familiar flashing light in front of her. Ramsay was attempting to slave the shuttle's controls to the bridge. Ash turned on the fail-safe, her jaw aching. The implications of Ramsay's betrayal were fire-bright in her head. Had Ramsay's people been after the weapon this whole time? *No,* she thought. Alison had to be improvising, because nobody even knew about the weapon until Len had fixed the ansible and obtained the data dump. Three weeks was enough to call a ship waiting in a neighboring system, and there were plenty of radar shadows near Tribulation to hide behind.

"It doesn't matter," Ramsay said. "And if you knew what we knew . . . well, let's just say that you would be working with us. You'd be up here opening a vein."

"So, tell us what we don't know," said Ash.

The console lit up again; someone was trying to backdoor the fail-safe. Natalie swore and opened a code interface to counter it while Ramsay's calm voice continued over the shuttle speakers.

"Do you even know who Reva Sharma is? What she did in the war? Why she never fit in at poker night? Why she even wanted to be on *Twenty-Five* with you bunch of losers?"

"I always thought it was your winning personality," said Ash.

"You didn't even look her up. Of course you didn't. That's why you're here in the first place. You don't do things like that."

Ash's stomach was a black hole. Grief clawed at her throat. Natalie's hand seized at her chest strap, knuckles white.

"Where's the captain?"

"The captain is fine, as long as you do as we say," Ramsay said. "Come on aboard. I'll explain everything."

"This is about the weapon we found on *London,* isn't it? You took Sharma because she can understand it?" said Ash.

Ramsay laughed. "And we understand the market."

"The *market,*" Ash said.

"That's how the world works, girls."

The *market*. She remembered her Bittersweet orientation, Wellspring supervisors talking about the *market,* the sheer number of things she'd believed to be true, the way they all shattered in the Vai attack. She thought about the coruscating light she saw on the planet, the desperate cold, the way Len's eyes had gone entirely blank. She shivered. She found herself opening her mouth to respond, but Natalie leaned over and hit the mute button before she could.

"You're thinking about it," she said, accusatory.

"I'm not."

She snorted. "Yes, you are. We're not going over there."

"We don't have a choice. The captain and Dr. Sharma are over there. *Len* is over there. And whatever that weapon is—"

"We'll figure it out," Natalie said. "We can only help them if we can reach Aurora."

Ash narrowed her eyes and unmuted the conversation. "—but in the end, Ash, you get to decide for yourself if you're expendable or not. Because my doctors have just told me that you've passed on your little condition to Captain Keller."

Natalie narrowed her eyes.

"You knew?" Ash said.

Ramsay snorted. "I knew. The whole ship knew. If you don't come in, we'll take what we need from Captain Keller."

"Lemme talk it over with Natalie."

"Twenty seconds," Ramsay said.

Natalie muted the feed again. "*What* condition?"

Ash looked down at her interface and called up a map of the surrounding area. Her hand shook like a rotten environmental connector; she couldn't tell if it was fear, or the disease, or both. *I couldn't have passed it to Kate,* she thought. *That's not how celestium madness works. She's just bullshitting me. Nat doesn't need to know.* "I'll tell you if we get out of this. And anyway, it doesn't matter. Suggestions?"

"Um, maybe." Natalie pointed at the battlefield map. "Last week, when we did the air compression testing on *London*'s bridge-side decks, we found there might still be atmo. Can we get there?"

"I think we have enough fuel. Trust me?"

"Always," Natalie said.

Ash turned her face back to *Twenty-Five* and the enemy ship, shining in the sun. She unmuted the feed.

"We're coming," she said. "Make sure there's an airlock clear for us."

Ash thought of the photo of Christopher that still hung near her bunk—the sole thing in her possession that she cared to lose. She'd never see it again. She thought of trying to remember his face without it. She wondered if it would become indistinct, lost to the sickness like her parents, just another foggy fever dream to watch as she queued for the dole on Europa Station. She thought of Keller, her eyes smiling and inscrutable behind her bangs. They were going to leave her. They were going to leave her because it was the only way to save her. Ash only hoped that Keller would forgive her someday.

"Ash," said Natalie.

"Yeah?" she responded.

"Concentrate."

"Right," Ash breathed.

Natalie looked like hell—her black hair coated with sweat and dirt, her eyes tired, the blood on her jacket an earthlike burgundy-brown. The blood on Ash's own shoulder felt clammy, and the wound screamed despite the painkiller. Natalie said, "*Twenty-Five*'s bolt-loaded railguns fire immediately. But that looks like a charge lance on the other ship. Takes five, six seconds to load. If you can steer us away from the lance and we move fast enough, we might be able to make it to the debris field before we're shredded to pieces. Lance hits us, well . . . we won't know, we'll be dead."

"That's not a lot of time."

Natalie shook her head. "Gonna have to be."

Ramsay's voice, on the speakers. "I don't see you moving."

Ash engaged the engines, moving at a slow pace toward *Twenty-Five*. She called up the maps of *London* she and Len had made on their first trip around the dead behemoth, tagging the places where the Vai weapons had not breached and atmosphere might still exist. Len had marked a possible atmo area in the secondary supply area on delta deck, close to open standard airlocks that had once contained escape pods.

Ash had mapped these debris fields. She'd been in and out of them for twelve hours every day for the last few months. That was something she knew that Ramsay didn't, she thought. Ash narrowed her eyes and stared at the sparkling expanse, imagining every single piece of floating, twisted debris between the shuttle and the airlock. Until the incident with the zapper, her piloting record had been clean. If she could hold on a little while longer, she was sure she could make it through.

Ash breathed in, willing her vision to clear, willing her hands to be stable. "Okay, hang on."

"Punch it," said Natalie.

Ash kicked the throttle into its highest gear while dragging a hard right-and-up on the helm. The shuttle wheeled around and hurtled headlong into *London*'s debris field. Natalie focused her camera on the mystery ship; as promised, the weaponry spun up, orange-red plasma charges flowing into the discharge chambers of the spinal lance. Since the mystery ship's computer could calculate the same optimal path the shuttle's computer did, Ash altered the trajectory by hand, her own reflexes avoiding spinning debris, pieces of hull, broken boxes, the remains of lights and furniture and floor plating.

"They're firing!" screamed Natalie.

*One, two, three,* Ash counted, and then hauled the ship toward a higher trajectory. The slice from the spinal lance took out the aft camera and scored the plating around the engine. Natalie screamed. Ash felt her teeth rattle. She tightened her hands on the controls and pushed on, following a circuitous course through *London*'s swirling garbage. The railgun bolts scraped the hull, drawing screaming, deep cuts in the armor. One tore off a portion of the heat shield in a barrage so vehement that Ash thought that the next shot would be the one to do them in.

A second charge bolt whipped by the fore camera at a sickening velocity, filling the room with an unpleasant golden glow. It made a cracking impact on *London*'s open rings ahead, and flying debris tossed the shuttle to one side. Ash maneuvered the shuttle underneath *London*'s protective undercurve to one of the airlocks that dotted its pockmarked abdomen, and backed straight in.

Natalie had caught up by now or had made enough calculations to realize what she needed to do next, and she was already engaging the measures that blew the airlock for an emergency landing. A third lance bolt went by, missing them by a mile; as she'd hoped, the enemy ship had lost visual confirmation of their location and was moving into a new position, a drab executioner annoyed at its prey's momentary and worthless escape.

"Now or never. Less than ten seconds before they come around," Natalie said.

The airlock engaged; the shuttle shuddered. Ash didn't feel the common stomach-dropping nausea of a quick return to gravity, as *London*'s grav-engine had long been extinct. Natalie unhooked herself from her harness, grabbed a crate, and launched herself toward the back door, pushing it open to the pitch-darkness of the dead ship. Ash programmed the shuttle's next movements, unhooked herself and planted her feet against the front window, catapulting back. She grabbed Len's second-favorite tool set on the way—the only thing she could grab, the only thing that was remotely close—before the proximity alarm started hollering and clanging.

On the way out, she kicked the airlock door closed.

The airlock clicked shut, and the shuttle took off.

The corridor plunged into a screaming charcoal darkness that pressed against her retinas and crawled into her mouth and made everything silent.

She closed her eyes anyway.

"Please be far enough away, please be far enough away," Natalie whispered.

Ash listened for the sounds of the shuttle's destruction. The confirmation she craved came when debris clanged against the side of the ship in a hollow rainfall.

Natalie clawed at her arm.

"Light," Ash said.

"Oh," Natalie said. She seemed young and far away. She heard Natalie fumbling at her belt. A few seconds later, the flashlight on her army knife came on, focusing on Ash, who blinked to clear the bright light in the pitch black. It was freezing; their breath was white smoke between them.

"Oh my God, we're still alive," Natalie said.

"It's Christmas."

Neither of them laughed. The silence took over.

# 8

The air on *London*'s shuttle deck was thin but palatable, hideously cold, and tainted with metal and rot. Ash's first breath was pure instinct, the oxygen around her an intoxicant that filled her with incandescent joy.

Breathing out was another matter entirely.

Lancing pain erupted from the gunshot wound in her shoulder, and Ash screamed. Nearby, Natalie mumbled out a string of broken swear words, then grabbed at Ash's perforated field jacket.

"Off with this," she said.

"It's *freezing*."

"Don't care. The bullet needs to come out," Natalie said. "It needed to come out on the planet, but that's when I thought we could get you to the ship. Brace yourself."

"You're not a field medic," Ash said.

Natalie snorted. "I was at Cana. I can do this."

Ash answered by facing away from Natalie, hooking both palms around one of the low-grav handholds, her knuckles going white with dread. Natalie fumbled in the medkit for the med-aid machine, then slipped her cold hands underneath Ash's jacket. She tugged the jacket up and away from the gunshot wound. Ash used her chin to hold the bunched-up jacket in place, thought better of it, then stuffed its elastic edge into her mouth instead. She tasted rough fabric and angry Tribulation dust.

Her body betrayed her, bucking and kicking and shuddering

as Natalie ripped away the battlefield adhesive from Ash's broken skin. Natalie pressed the med-aid machine against Ash's wound, and Ash bit down on the jacket, stifling a howl at the pain of cold plasteel on open muscle.

Natalie guided the machine's moving parts past the broken gristle in Ash's shoulder. The pain detonated behind Ash's skin, rode her nerves until they burned, and she realized she was screaming when she stopped just long enough to fill her lungs with rot-tainted air.

"Almost done," Natalie muttered, yanking the machine away. She slapped an autobandage over the open wound. That was just as bad: the medical gunk inside yanked at bone and sinew, stitching the wound back together and lighting her nerves on fire.

"Painkiller." Ash made it a statement, not a question.

"I don't want you to overdose."

"Painkiller." The word was a shriek in her throat.

Natalie exhaled, then rustled in the medkit again. "It's your body."

Ash felt a distinct prick of the needle at her neck, then glitter-bound bliss. She luxuriated in the blank absence of pain. "Okay," she said. "Let's move."

"The autobandage needs a chance to work."

"It can work on the way to the bridge."

Natalie tossed the needle aside, then slid her hands underneath her armpits for warmth. "Let me sling your arm, at least."

"There should be a pilots' ready room on the way. We can find extra clothing there. What do you remember from the briefing about what might be working on the bridge?"

Natalie narrowed her eyes in thought. "The bridge was on the schedule for Len and I once we got through with processing the R&D section, which was a weird schedule inversion—but now, I guess we know why. The distress array was smashed during the

fight, but if there's air all the way down here, we might find functioning backup circuits on the bridge. We can reroute the cables
to power the ansible. Tell someone we're here before we starve."

Ash's jaw chattered. "Or freeze."

"Or that," Natalie said. She tied the tool set and the medkit to
her belt, then pushed off the deck ring like she'd been born in
zero gravity. Ash followed, one-armed, listing to her better side
like she was full of badly weighted ballast.

The ready room was in bad condition. Lockers gaped wide,
their contents afloat, like the room had been ransacked. Ash hovered just outside the open hatch at Natalie's instruction, feeling
dizzy and lost, while the younger woman rummaged through the
detritus, humming about survival blankets and sweaters, stuffing
half-eaten ration bars down her shirt.

"Can I help?" Ash said.

"You can help by standing there and letting the autobandage
work," muttered Natalie. "Take a break."

Ash hated breaks. Back on Bittersweet, breaks meant she
didn't get paid, didn't accrue citizenship credit, didn't move
forward. She amused herself, instead, by imagining what Keller
might say to this. *I'd expect this kind of thing from you,* maybe,
smirking from her seat on the bridge. In fact, it felt almost like
she'd heard Keller's voice aloud, like the woman she loved was
just across the room.

Which she was.

*No,* Ash thought, feeling the sudden panic down to her toes.
*Not yet.*

Keller sat smiling on one of the benches near Natalie, as if
gravity on this ghost ship was a fact, not a fever dream.

"Nat, do you see—" Ash cut herself off.

"See what?"

Ash searched desperately for another word than *Kate,* for a word that meant *hallucinations*, that meant *danger*, that meant *death*.

"Pants," she said, instead.

"I think this guy was around your size," Natalie said, throwing a sweatshirt in Ash's direction. Ash clawed it out of the air with her good hand, still staring at Keller, smiling quietly in her blue pajamas and her signature messy ponytail. "How did you get off the ship?"

*I didn't*, Keller whispered.

Natalie looked up from the locker, snatching a glinting item out of the air: a silver chain with an oval pendant tugging at the end. "You sure you aren't having problems with that painkiller?"

"I'm fine," Ash lied.

Natalie turned the necklace over, staring at it, letting it catch fire in the beam of the flashlight, then shoved it in her pocket. "If you say so."

"What about you? Are you feeling all right?" Ash said.

Natalie snorted her response to that, and before Ash could protest, she was back across the room, her work-worn hands pulling a pilot's jacket, smelling of old sweat and mold, over Ash's head. She fed Ash's cranky arm through the sleeve like she was threading a needle, made a sling from a pilot's belt to keep her arm and shoulder immobilized, then pulled on a few layers herself. In the end, the whole effect made them both look inflated in the harsh light, like punctured, lumpy balloons.

"I look stupid," Natalie muttered. "I'm going to freeze to death on a dead starship, looking stupid."

"We're a salvage crew," Ash said. "This is salvage."

Natalie rolled her eyes, picking at the lumps sitting on her breastbone, where she'd stored the ration bars to warm them against her body. "Yeah. Real professional, us. Come on. We're wasting air."

Natalie trained the torch at the rest of the corridor, checking
vectors in the thin atmosphere while Ash made a crude map with
a pencil, her memory of the floor plans for the science deck, and
the back of someone's rumpled family photograph. They pushed
off together toward the first hatch, where Keller waited in a
pitch-black corner with her brown eyes, her dark hands, and her
impossible crooked smile. Ash nearly sailed into the wall at the
sight of her.

"Don't get distracted," Natalie said.

Ash gulped down confusion. "It's the painkiller."

"I told you not to overdose," Natalie said.

*It's all right, now that you're with me,* said Keller's ghost.

"Shut up. You're not helping." The words were out of Ash's
mouth before she could stop them.

Natalie frowned, then swiped the map from Ash's hands. "No
more drugs for you. Just—give me that. How many hatches until
the spine?"

"Five, I think."

"That's unfortunate."

Ash pressed her lips together, trying to cultivate patience as
Natalie examined the map to check her work. By its nature, battlefield salvage was methodical, perfectionist, full of checks, re-
checks, and long skeins of utter boredom paired with moments
of starbright terror. Behind any door could lurk live ordnance
that would not tolerate careless disruption; beyond any hatch,
huddled survivors that would not live through a careless rescue.

Keller had recruited her for a molasses-paced, methodical
war—a war against nature, war against entropy, war against their
own technology. A salvager's weapons were rules and information, checklists and sterling technique. Coming out of the broken
hell that had been Bittersweet, Ash had craved the rules, purpose, and safety that had so characterized the prewar mine. *A
no-bullshit life,* she'd told Keller.

*That's a promise,* Keller had said.

Right now, all Ash and Natalie had was guesswork based on faulty data, and the thought of it made Ash nauseous. They were fighting a war with no weapons, no fortifications, and no reinforcements, trying to bullshit their way to victory.

The apparition hovered in the uneasy space right behind Ash's ear. *Space plus bullshit equals—*

"Death, I know, I know," she muttered.

"That's not a good joke." Natalie handed the map back to Ash. "I bet Len would have a great joke right now."

Ash anchored herself behind Natalie with the twist of one foot against a handhold. "Pass me the pressure gauge, will you?" she said. "And, honestly, don't you think he tries too hard?"

"Like he's trying to impress us?" Natalie said. "Come on, who wouldn't?" Natalie fished around in the tool belt, then handed the pressure gauge to Ash.

Ash slapped the pressure gauge on the door, watching it measure the air pressure behind the hatch. The machine hummed away for a few seconds, then displayed a bright, safe green on the indicator. She then tested the seal of the door manually, pressing her fingers against the seams. She felt no sick, starving pull characteristic of a vacuum leak, and nodded to Natalie.

"Clear. I mean jokes are a defense mechanism for some people. Len could have been working for Ramsay, too, and—"

Natalie yanked the gauge from Ash's hands, cutting her off. "No. Can't think like that."

"Can't rule it out, though."

"I always thought he liked me. In that way. You know? I don't want it to be because he was working an angle."

"I'll tell you what I think," Ash said.

"Oh, yeah?"

"On the other side," Ash said, reaching for the manual hatch release.

Natalie snorted. "You are a stone-cold bitch."

"Just a student of hope." Ash pushed the release down and out, and the door loosened and yawned outward. She heard the blessed, hollow clatter that was sound on the other side—blessed sound, real *atmosphere,* three whole compartments of it, from what she could see in the dark. She ducked away so Natalie could poke her flashlight through the hatch first.

"Pay up," the other woman crowed.

"I think he likes you, but he told me last week that he was worried you were too young. You're his sister's age."

Natalie swung her light around in the standard four-corner search pattern, checking for structural deficiencies, exit points, and possible salvage. "That's bullshit. I was old enough to go to war. And his sister's a—*Oh, gross.*"

The stink hit Ash in a gagging, fetid wave as she followed Natalie into the next compartment. Ash could see three floating bodies in torn Auroran indenture uniforms, silhouetted against a dead, silver-black Company interface bank. Dried blood hovered in shriveled brown balls around their skeletal fingers. One man displayed the ragged, crackling black skin of a single, fatal bolt-gun wound on his back.

Ash choked down sour liquid, looking away. She concentrated instead on getting to the next hatch at the end of the compartment. It was open, the oval bulkhead seal framing yet more atrocities—citizens, this time, in the white coats of the science corps.

She struggled for something to say. "Rotting bodies. This is a good thing."

"You're just a fucking ray of sunshine today, aren't you." The former soldier was trying to keep it together, Ash could see, but her cheeks were pale and her hands tightened nervously on the flashlight.

"Smells pretty stale." Ash made an attempt not to breathe. "I'm going to guess that the air's probably stable all the way to the spine."

Natalie pulled herself to the ceiling, kicking her legs behind her, intent on finding a vector devoid of death. "How the hell can you tell that?"

"Old trick from Bittersweet," Ash said. "They didn't always use all of the air pumps every day, so you learned to figure out where the fresh air was coming from, and if you got up early enough you could get on the detail that didn't stink."

"Sounds pleasant. Oh, wow, look at this guy." Natalie yanked herself into the next open compartment, stopping immediately. She waved her light at one of the bodies—a man in a long, black coat, with dark, loose hair braided with red ribbons. *An uncitizen, and proud of it, to leave his hair so uncontrolled,* thought Ash. She looked for a boltshot wound, but found nothing. He hadn't died from depressurization or oxygen deprivation. It looked like he'd just stopped where he was.

"He looks . . . off," said Ash.

"Definitely not one of ours," Natalie said.

"He wasn't shot. And he didn't suffocate."

"Well, there's no time to figure it out," Natalie said, then turned her light away, kicking toward the next open hatch. "And speaking of time, I don't think eight years is that much of a difference."

Ash was grateful for the subject change as she skirted the half-skeletal remains of a white-coated scientist. "It was more about the power dynamic, I think. It's tough getting involved with shipmates."

"Yeah, well, it's tough meeting new people when you're out on an indenture—"

She stopped halfway through the sentence.

"Nat?"

"Shh." The woman's tone was short and knife-sure.

This next compartment had taken significant fire. The entire aft wall sat slagged and scored and partially melted. There were three bodies here, all citizens with birthright tattoos, but none of them had been shot. The first—younger than Ash, much younger—was still strapped to an interface, his eyes open in shock. Ash noticed a hull breach against the exterior bulkhead, treated with a piece of decking and sealant, and two birthrights spinning nearby, close to the hatch, their rotting eyes and open mouths pointed somewhere far beyond the compartment itself, off at some heaven or hell, forever clouded. Official Aurora Company flimsies floated around them like confetti.

Over the tableau, Ash heard a faint, familiar hissing sound.

*That's not a good sound,* Keller said. She was behind Ash, now, whispering in her ear, her cheek close enough to touch.

"Bridge crew. They get shot, too?"

"No. Looks like they got *scared* to death, just like the guy in the coat," whispered Natalie. "That noise. Is it the breach?"

Ash listened, then shook her head. "They used sealant, which means they fixed it before they were killed. I'll check the hatch." Natalie tossed her the pressure gauge, looking instead to the score marks on the walls. Ash applied the machine to the hatch and waited; this time, it clicked and whined and calculated, and the more time it took, the more nervous Ash felt.

"Hullcracking laser," Natalie said, tracing the arc of the weapon with her left hand. She frowned. "But not Vai. The Vai are surgical. This is messy, inexcusably so. Look at the edges of that piece of hull—how they've been melted back. The Vai would have thrown a corer at it, yanked out a whole bunch of hull with a razor-sharp straightedge. A *human* weapon was used here."

"Were they fighting back?"

"If so, where are their guns?" Natalie's eyebrows raised.

"Why are all these people even here?" Ash asked. "These aren't battle stations. This is what, a ground survey compartment?"

Natalie made a face, then yanked a nearby flimsy out of the air. She read it quickly and grabbed another. "It's all Tribulation-related. Funny, right, and wasteful of Company resources, when we were told the ship wasn't even on course to the planet." She picked a third from the air. "Look at all of this. Import-export logs, a recent census, maps of the colony, all on data flimsies, like they were worried about not having access to a server."

"Well, you know corporate. So much 'just in case.' Redundancy plans for redundancy plans," said Ash.

*The Business Continuity Assurance Strategy,* Keller chirped from behind her, causing Ash to startle. She sounded like a training holo. *Aurora builds to win!*

The pressure gauge finally clicked over—this time, to a nauseous yellow. Natalie stuffed the flimsies in her shirt. "That looks good enough. We can figure it out when someone shows up. Gimme that. I'll go first."

Ash handed her the gauge. "If we had the option, I'd recommend going back for rebreathers."

"Well," Natalie said, hauling in a deep breath of the stinking air. "We'll just have to be quick, then. I'll go ahead, open the hatch to the bridge, and you be ready to launch when it opens, okay?"

"Got it."

Ash grabbed the hatch release lever and pushed again. The pressure differential caused the hatch to pop open, and she and Natalie tumbled out into *London*'s central spine. There was oxygen here, but not much, and Ash dug her useless fingers into her left side to keep herself from panicking or hyperventilating.

The spine stretched from fore to aft, and was filled with an acrid, electrical stench and the aftereffects of smoke. On *Twenty-Five,* the hub was little more than a dumbwaiter and a rickety ladder, but *London* had a cargo elevator, a walkway, and room for crew going both ways in gravity or free fall.

The utilitarian gray walls were marred by charcoal scoring and pockmarks from kinetic gunfire. Ash shuddered at the thought of using bullets on a ship, bullets that could punch through hulls, not energy bolts built for space travel—and at the crusted blood splattered against a wall.

"Vai?" managed Ash. She felt dizzy.

Natalie shook her head. "Human."

"Mutiny?"

"Or boarding," Natalie said. "Fucking *go*."

"Going," said Ash. She gasped again, pointed toward the bridge, and pushed off the ledge again. She collided with the bridge hatch and applied the gauge, not even waiting for Natalie to follow until she pushed it open. Ash sailed through, missing the bridge railing by a foot and hitting what used to be the weapons station with a disgraceful and slightly painful thump.

If the grav-drive had been functional, their seeming ascent would have been a descent; *London*'s bridge was shoved into the bowels of the vessel where nukes and hullcrackers would have a harder time reaching.

Natalie shut the hatch, and the two of them collapsed, breathing heavily. Ash let the oxygen fill her body, and for the first time since they left the ready room, she felt the prickling, acid pain of the arctic cold.

"Oh, hell," Natalie said, rubbing her head.

"You all right?"

"Yeah," she whispered. "But they weren't."

*London*'s expansive bridge, made for ten operators instead of two, made *Twenty-Five*'s look like a high-tech janitor's closet. The interfaces were haptic, not the direct-input, finger-to-keyboard old reliables on the ships belonging to the salvage corps. Headsets and handsets floated on black tethers in front of each station, tied to darkened holographic interfaces. Ash had heard of this kind of thing being installed in a few Auroran ships just before the war, new, game-changing tech developed in the haze of victory. Len would have drooled over all of it, except for the fact that the fight belowdecks had come here, too. The walls were scored with bloodstains and black char, and ripped holes in the upholstery of the chairs testified to kinetic gunfire.

In the center of it all was the captain's chair, and it had an occupant.

It had once been a man—the captain, perhaps—dead, decayed, still strapped to his chair, small bits of shredded, desiccated flesh floating in the thin atmosphere like tiny funeral flags, his jaw wide, blank sockets looking up at a matching blank sky. Dried brown blood painted his blue Auroran executive's suit and the ground around him.

"Something's wrong," whispered Natalie.

*That*, Keller whispered, *is the understatement of the year.*

# 9

Keller felt the headache before anything else—scratching, reactor-bright pain, tightening around her eyes like grapes in a juicer.

The room slammed into existence around her, fuzzy and slanted, and she became aware of cold metal against her arms and the angry chimes of familiar machines. The medbay. She was alone in the medbay. Sharma's white coat was draped over her empty chair, while an abandoned, unlabeled syringe lay on a table near the sharps container, red blood gathered at the tip.

She knew as soon as she took a deep, ragged breath that the ship's $CO_2$ scrubbers were broken. The air she tasted was dizzy-thin and tinged with metal. Her chest felt tight, like someone had stuffed her lungs with too much cotton. Her head continued to wail.

Keller swung her legs over the side of the examination table. Her injuries didn't matter. If the $CO_2$ scrubbers were down, she needed to be in the engine room five minutes ago.

Starting for the hatch, she stumbled and caught herself. The gravity didn't feel right. *The spin rate's off,* she thought, confirming it by pressing the pads of her fingers against the deck. The comforting oscillation that usually supported her every step instead resembled a flurry of terrified butterfly wings, which was never a good sign. She counted spin cycles, taking the ship's pulse: seventy-five a minute, when she was supposed to feel fifty-two.

A frantic calm settled on her shoulders, and Keller straightened, crossed the bay, and palmed the door.

The door stayed closed.

She palmed the door again. *Locked,* it said.

*Weird.* She jabbed the comm by the side of the door. "Ms. Ramsay. What's going on?"

The comm was dead for a few agonizing seconds. "Good, you're awake."

"What's going on with the ship?"

Keller heard clattering in the background, and a grinding cacophony that could only mean that Ramsay was already working in the engine room. The sound lanced pain through her hangover-bright brain, and she winced.

"There's a leak in the fuel injection system," Ramsay said. "How fast can you get down here? I could use an extra pair of hands."

"You locked the door."

"What? It shouldn't be lock—Shit!" Keller heard a squeal of metal on metal. "I'm so sorry. I'm elbow-deep in the fix, so can you just hang on for a little while?"

"Do you need me to talk you through it?"

"No, I'll be fine," Ramsay said.

Keller took another breath. Her lungs filled; the oxygen followed, sluggish and hot and wrong. She felt like a runner at the top of a mountain. "What about the scrubbers?"

"The . . . $CO_2$ scrubbers?"

Keller rolled her eyes. "I'm hoping this isn't a cascade failure issue. Can you check?"

"I'll check." Ramsay sighed. "I called Dr. Sharma, and she said she was worried about a concussion. Why don't you get some rest, and I'll come get you in five or ten?"

"As soon as you can," Keller said.

"Ramsay out."

The room went silent. Keller snorted to herself. Typical Ramsay, to advise her to *rest* during a possible cascade failure on her very own ship. *She doesn't know me at all, does she?*

Keller walked back to Sharma's console. Just because she hadn't logged enough profit for haptics yet didn't mean *Twenty-Five* still used the same old purpose-slaved terminals of the past. Any onboard terminal could become her personal bridge computer when fed the right codes. She called up the captain's interface, intent on starting the diagnostics that would point her to the next system to fail, the next task to do. Entering her command codes was easy muscle memory, and she was already moving to access the core dialogue when the interface blared a polite, helpful alarm and told her that her command codes were invalid.

*What the hell?*

The lack of oxygen dragged her throat. She tried again.

*Invalid.*

She breathed deep and slow to steady herself. If the computer wasn't recognizing her command codes, the cascade failure was already worse than she thought—and Ramsay, dealing with an engine leak, probably had no idea.

*Well, there's always the back way,* she thought, and entered Aurora's standard salvage codes instead. She was rewarded with the familiar back-end access to the system status monitors. She grabbed a stylus and a half-filled flimsy from Sharma's desk, ready to scribble a list of tasks in the margins.

Except there was nothing wrong.

No blood-red warning indicators.

No yellow watch alarms.

One single red light flashed next to the celestium-injection system in the engine room. The report read as *under maintenance,* not *nonfunctional.*

Keller scrolled down the list. Everything read as functioning within proper operational parameters—the ship's base code, memory storage, environmental systems. Even the five main $CO_2$ scrubbers seemed to be functioning at full capacity, despite what her starving lungs were telling her.

Keller took another long, unsatisfying breath. Something was broken. Something was very broken. She couldn't wait for Ramsay. She was going to have to do a full visual inspection herself.

*Which means I need to get that door open,* she thought.

She checked her pockets for her multi-tool, but found them empty. Figuring that it must have fallen out on the bridge when she'd fainted, she raided Sharma's desk drawers like a human tornado instead, disturbing the neat, sensible little piles of flimsy notes and medical doodads and making a mental note to apologize to the doctor when the crisis was over.

Pushing aside a framed picture—an angelic smiling child wrapped in a colorful *Alien Attack Squad* blanket, captioned with a neatly handwritten "My Granddaughter" at the bottom— she uncovered the multi-tool she'd given Sharma at Bittersweet. The doctor had left it behind, as Keller had guessed she might. Sharma preferred her own tools, and rarely needed to cut cable or solder breaches.

Keller headed for the hatch. On Auroran starships, locks didn't exist to promote privacy or personal security—their exclusive function was to keep hull breaches and fires from sucking the breath out of a broken vessel. She flipped out the captain's skeleton key, sliding the end into the lock mechanism, feeling for the slip point. She turned her wrist, yanking the tool back and to the left, and the door shuddered open.

"Thanks, baby," Keller said, patting the bulkhead and stepping into the hallway.

She was rewarded with a rustling of harsh fabric and a punch in the face from someone who wasn't supposed to be there.

Keller heard a sickening crunch and staggered back against

the doorjamb. Pain sheared from her nose to the back of her head, and blood splattered on her jacket. The man—it was a man—went for the boltgun at his waist. Keller struck at his wrist and he dropped it. She and the man locked eyes as it skittered down the corridor.

"Don't," she said.

The man ducked to retrieve the weapon, and this time it was Keller's turn to punch him in the face. He keeled back, toward the other wall, his hands snapping at her jacket, yanking her off-balance. She fell, and her ribs hit blank metal, the breath cast, quick and violent, from her body.

"Boss, 's Flynn." He yanked at his commlink, trying to call out.

*No,* she thought, *not on my ship.* She threw herself at the gun at the same time he did. She was a centimeter faster, and the man knew it. He swore. Her fingers connected and slipped around the trigger. He clawed at her jacket, her neck, her wrist. She broke free, bringing the gun around with its bright, silver whine.

"Don't," she said, pain shooting down her side. "Please."

He hovered, white-fisted. "Give me the gun, or I'll take it from your dead body," he said.

"I warned you. Stop," Keller repeated. Her heart thudded in her chest.

"Auroran *bitch*—"

He moved. Keller fired. The bolt of energy hit the man in the soft part of the stomach just below the sternum. He hollered in pain, but kept coming. Panic had control of Keller's fingers, now—she wanted him to stop, she just wanted him to stop—and she fired off another bolt. And another, and another, until he stopped.

The light slipped from the man's eyes. He toppled forward against Keller's torso, a sudden sack of useless meat, his blood wet and warm where it soaked her shirt.

She pushed the man's body away and scrambled to her feet,

unsteady and shaking and hyperventilating, her head going faint
with lack of oxygen. She stumbled back against the open hatch.
His blood clung to her shirt, cooling against her skin.

A stranger. She'd killed a *stranger.* On her ship.

Not a stranger. *A guard.*

*He was guarding the door.*

Keller closed her eyes. Her world spun. Her fingers felt numb
against the hilt of the stranger's boltgun. Her breath came in
quick, desperate gulps. Ramsay was still in the engine room. She
needed to know what had happened, needed to know that they'd
been infiltrated, that she was in danger, too, that the mission was
compromised—

*Why don't you get some rest,* Ramsay's voice echoed.

Ramsay wasn't fighting the celestium leak.

She was causing it.

She just hadn't expected Keller to wake up as early as she had.

The entire situation made a sudden, sickening sense. The only
real cascade failure on *Twenty-Five* was in Keller's own inabil-
ity to see Ramsay's lies. She had sent the others to the planet,
leaving her naked throat exposed to an enemy she should have
seen coming from the moment Mr. Solano had talked about the
weapon.

She'd gotten soft.

How else had she missed it? Ramsay's background was just
like Keller's—indentured parents, an entrance into her own indenture at eighteen, regular promotions, near perfect health, cit
tags on schedule. Goals met. Hard work. Grit. Consistent results.
And it would have been difficult to be disloyal on a ship like
*Twenty-Five,* with everyone living on top of one another. It was
difficult enough to keep from farting in front of one's coworkers,
let alone communicate with outside entities.

But Ramsay had taken the night shifts. She'd been alone on
the bridge for hours when—

—when Keller had been talking with Ash in the mess hall.
Distracted.

*Soft.*

Keller felt hot and cold at the same time, dizzy and sober. She
wiped blood from her bottom lip and pushed herself off the wall,
dredging up her instructions on what to do next.

She was the captain of this ship. She was Aurora in this for-
saken place, a citizen with the right to use her own last name, not
just Indenture Kate from Neversink Mechcenter 10. It was her
job to have a solution for every problem, to yank survival out of
the jaws of certain death, to bring everyone home. She'd trained
for decompression, life support failure, grav-drive unsync, and
illness in the crew. And she'd trained for this, too. They'd taught
her about corporate espionage, about what a captain was required
to do when a member of the crew chose to work against Aurora.

She thought of her crew. Sharma, with a war record as immaculate as her peacetime work. Len and Natalie, the rising stars on
their final pre-citizenship tour. Ash.

Of course, Ash.

She hoped they were bored out of their skulls waiting for the
tests to finish, waiting for her to get back in contact, maybe won-
dering why she hadn't checked in.

*I'm sorry I can't come get you yet, guys. There's something
else I have to do first.*

With her cit tags and the captain's rank came a second, quieter
oath, made privately to Mr. Solano. An oath that meant, above
everything, even her own life, even above the lives of her crew,
that she had to protect Company secrets.

Keller slung the boltgun into her waistband, then twisted
her fingers into the scratchy fabric of the dead man's jacket. She
hauled him back into the medbay, propping him up against the
wall, checking his pockets. He had no Company identification or
cit tags, but his comm had a biometric interface, so she applied

the man's thumb to the access port and scrolled through his text messages. They seemed to be in code, referencing orders from the past four hours, when the team had left for the surface.

*Good,* she thought. *They're not working too far ahead.*

She shoved the comm unit into her pocket, then checked the boltgun with clammy, shaking hands. It was some other Company's model, with the proprietary information filed off. It was low on charge, which might be another sign the competition hadn't had a lot of time to prepare for their assault. Either way, she could get a few more uses out of it. *And I only need one bolt to put Ramsay down, anyway,* she thought.

Changing out of her bloody jacket into one of Sharma's folded blue scrub shirts, she shoved the man's orange armband in her pocket and then grabbed gauze from the doctor's drawer, holding it to her nose and tilting her head up and back until she stopped bleeding, the metal tang of it clotted and hot at the back of her throat.

She wouldn't go soft again.

At the back of the medbay was a hatch built into the wall, leading to the duct network: maintenance tunnels that allowed the crew to reach the auxiliary parts of systems that needed updating, tweaking, or fixing. *Twenty-Five* was every inch her ship, her baby; she knew every bolt, every tunnel, every turn by heart. She knelt and unfastened the hatch, crawling in and dragging the door closed by wedging her toes against the inside latch. The sound of the closing hatch echoed down the tunnel, and Keller was left with the quiet thrumming of *Twenty-Five*'s ailing engine and the sour sadness of her own anxious thoughts.

She pulled herself along the tunnel, feeling fatigued and out of breath. She felt the ship shudder in the pads of her fingers and the angry ache of the engine spindown in her bones. The $CO_2$ spinners didn't register as broken, because they weren't. There simply weren't enough of them for the number of people onboard.

She remembered the extra scrubbers they'd had to install when they left Bittersweet with that cargo bay full of survivors, the way they hummed and clanked and kept her awake the entire ride home.

She wondered just how many strangers were rooting around in the guts of her baby right now, sucking down *Twenty-Five*'s precious oxygen. It was a sign they didn't care what happened to the ship. That they didn't have any plans to use it.

Keller wondered if they were looting her crew's hard-earned bonuses, stealing the weapons they'd discovered, the data they'd logged, making off with her future and her dreams and her last chance at a life with Ash.

It didn't matter.

She would make them pay for every last inch of it.

# 10

The captain, at least, had died where he'd served, in the black chair at the center of the bridge. If he'd been a citizen—and of course he had, all captains were citizens—Ash couldn't tell in death. His uniform was half flayed, and the jaw had long since gone slack and rotted to bone. His empty eye sockets stared, blank and rotten, at the ceiling.

"Where is everyone?" said Natalie.

"Evacuated, or went to fight."

Natalie shook her head. "Bridge like this, battle like that—every single seat should have a body in it. You need a bridge crew to fight."

"Some of the people below looked like they might have been bridge crew."

"But they shouldn't have left. This bridge should be full of bodies," Natalie repeated. "Captains fighting the battle alone? That's just for vids."

Ash leaned in to examine the captain's body. A wrongness caught her about the dead man's chest, the great, ripped-out cavity of it. She grabbed a pair of pliers from the tool set and, with a grimace, pulled back the captain's ragged clothing.

"His heart's missing," Ash said.

Natalie leaned in. "That's . . . new."

Ash replaced the shredded uniform flap so she wouldn't have to see the blackened hole, the cracked, punched-out ribs, the desiccated mess that had once been a human life. Whatever happened to this man, she thought, it hadn't been decompression that did it. Natalie lifted her hand to her mouth and bit down on her index finger, hard enough to whiten her skin.

"What kind of biological does this?" Ash asked.

"A knife does," Natalie said. "Metal. Hands, later."

"Murdered? By a human?"

"That's what I'd guess."

"Are you sure it's not Vai?" asked Ash.

"They're into evaporation, not evisceration." Natalie paused. "Or cracking open rib cages."

Ash's vision went blurry and sideways as painkiller-borne exhaustion hit the side of her head like a rock hammer. She heard Keller laughing, somewhere, and she straightened, rubbing her temples to drive the sound of it away.

"We're losing time. We can figure out this poor bastard later. Ansible now."

"One second." Natalie reached into the duffel bag and took out the silver necklace she'd found in the pilots' ready room. "Let's leave him this."

"What is it?"

"I dunno. It seems like a nice thing to do, though."

Natalie passed her the medal. It looked religious, but she couldn't place the saint it depicted in her own half-forgotten tradition. The saint was a woman, her arms spread wide, surrounded by a dented halo made of tarnished gold filigree. She stood on the Earth itself, holding arrows in one hand and an olive branch in the other. The bottom was lettered in italics: *Sacrament Society.*

Old Christian? A saint cult? *Mary Our Executive? The Arbiter of Hearts? Saint Clare?* Her memory blank, she slid the medal into the captain's front pocket. "Rest well, buddy," she whispered, and pushed back off toward the ansible.

Natalie was already working through the salvage protocol; step one, ensuring her own safety by tying herself and the duffel she was trailing to a nearby hook. Ash took step two, securing the environment; she spent some time looking for air leaks and sealed the bridge hatch. They then started checking to see what equipment was already working—step three.

The recitation of the salvage rules calmed Ash as she ducked under the comm console, opening the access port. There were salvage lights here to direct her work: they flickered silent and sure, drawing power from their own long-lasting battery supply like their world hadn't ended, blinking out their stories in a language any Aurora salvager would know. She felt a stab of grateful fealty.

"We're going to have to run some power over here," Ash said. "The draw is going to be pretty significant. We'll freeze."

Natalie's head was buried in a navigation console. "So, we're trapped in the fatal sort of way?"

"It depends on how fast *Rio* can get here. They should be able to trace the power draws. We might get hungry."

"I've been hungry before," Natalie said.

"Not like this."

"You'd be surprised."

Ash flashed back to Bittersweet, the nights when they didn't meet quota, the stale pieces of bread she and Christopher hid in their pockets and shared after dark. She decided not to argue. "Can we run cables from the nav computers? This hulk isn't going anywhere."

Natalie waved a wrench in Ash's direction. "You're not allowed to carry any of it. I'm not redoing that autobandage twice in one day. You can cut, but not haul."

"Fine."

Natalie worked efficiently, like she always did; Ash worked slower than she wanted, hampered by her dizzy vision, the tug of the half-finished autobandage, and the distant, wordless whispering that seemed to come from beyond the closed bridge hatch.

The voices sang songs of mutiny, cackled out orders in stubbed, sibilant Vai, sounded a little like Keller and Christopher. Ash did her best to ignore it all. *These aren't symptoms. You can't have symptoms right now. You can't leave Natalie. Not until you're back home. With Kate.*

*Beats trying to fix an ansible with prayers and school glue.*

Natalie pried off the decking near the nav console with Len's battered multi-tool, then hung over it, tracing the flow of the cable with her eyes, noting already marked cut points.

Harvesting cable without damaging it was one of the main skills of any decent Company salvage operator. Aurora's pearlescent, responsive lines were candy for competitors, years ahead of what most other companies strung through their ships. Removing them was difficult work. Natalie refused to allow Ash to lift any of the cables, and Ash ended up watching as the younger woman detached them, one by one, from their trusses, wound them over her shoulder, and dragged eight yards of cable across the bridge to the ansible interface herself.

Natalie took a break while Ash connected the cables to the ansible power supply. It was comforting work, reasonable work she could understand in a widening gyre where her reason was rapidly losing its grip on reality. It reminded her of the repetitive nature of mining, the comforting presence of Christopher at her side, the dull expectation of the expected—all the things she was trying to recapture when Keller inspired her to indenture with Aurora after Wellspring fell apart.

*Kate.*

The apparition was back. The thought of Keller tumbled Ash back out of her head onto the bridge, and she wavered, gritted her teeth, and tied off another cable, kicking it across to Natalie at the ansible. Keller had been quiet for a while, quiet and gracious in her absence, but now she was on the left side of Ash's vision, standing sentry just outside of her comfort zone.

"Damn it." Ash fumbled at a third cable, and it fell from her hands. Natalie watched, her lips pursed, as Ash clutched at her leg, futile in her efforts to hide her shaking hand. *Shit.*

"You look like crap," Natalie said. "Take a break."

Ash shook her head. "No, I'm fine. This is more important."

"You sound like Len right now."

"I'm goddamned *fine*."

"And the role of Leonard Downey will be played tonight by Ash Jackson," Natalie pronounced. "Go have some food and a swig of water, and I'll finish it up."

Ash let go of the cables and pushed off toward the duffel bag. "Fine."

Natalie started soldering the cable connections while Ash ripped open a ration bar. She chewed slowly, enjoying every starchy, sawdust bite. Keller's ghost slipped onto the chair next to Ash, her arms folded, her face beatific. The whispering increased. Ash tried to ignore the ghost, stuffing the last of the bar into her mouth and squeezing her eyes shut. Maybe if she concentrated on a more engrossing topic, like work, the ghost would go away.

"Break's over," Ash said.

"It's been three minutes," Natalie protested.

"You've almost got it working, anyway." Ash looked over Natalie's shoulder. Natalie slapped the power button, and the monitor started flickering in and out; the ansible was trying to connect to the local network.

"We've done it," Ash crowed, flexing her fingers on her good hand. She pulled herself around and dropped into the chair, moving her fingers over the unfamiliar interface, trying to find a keyboard.

"Haptics, remember?" Natalie snatched a headset out of the air above her, dragging it down onto Ash's forehead.

Ash clawed at it. "Wait. Wait a second." *I'm going to mess up. You're going to see that I'm sick.* "You do it. I'm on painkillers."

"It's not like this is heavy machinery." Natalie snorted. She began the process of fitting the electrodes to Ash's head. She brushed hair back from the nape of Ash's neck, fitting pinching diodes on her spine, sliding the lenses over her eyes.

"It's a fucking *starship.*"

"I need my hands free to make adjustments," Natalie said.

"I'm drugged up."

Natalie frowned. "You just said you were *fine.*"

"And drugged up," Ash said. "What if I can't, I don't know, *think* fast enough?"

"It's just new technology. That's all it is." Natalie switched on the interface.

Ash was subject to a shocking rush of information all at once— colors, data, lines, letters, shapes, all of it flickering and hovering on the monitor just inches away. She blinked, and the display shifted, resolved, reacting to the signals her brain was sending. She blinked again and tried to think only of using the ansible. Three or four garbled windows swept off to the side in a hurry, minimized by her need for the ansible. Sounds rattled in her ear—the rushing of an ocean, the barking of a small dog, distant ship engines, the understated chuckling of Christopher winning a poker game.

Natalie leaned in over her shoulder. "That is cool."

"The audio could use some help," Ash said, breathless. She spread-eagled her hands on her knees to take them out of play. The display blasted orange, blue, pink, yellow. She opened her mouth to ask the computer to display in standard colors alone, and only got as far as the first sibilant when the monitor flickered and settled into calming shades of white and blue. A millisecond later, the computer had called up a message window and was asking for a destination point.

"This is wild," Ash said.

"My friend Amrit told me that once you get good on the haptic, you don't even use the gloves much. You can fire off a torpedo within milliseconds of thinking up a solution—no more of this *pressing a button* or *pulling a trigger* business. Your captain doesn't even have to issue vocal orders; the bridge gets so quiet, it's basically telepathy . . ." Natalie's voice trailed off, impressed and waiting for the next step.

Ash blinked away the beginnings of a headache and resolved on the ansible node in front of her. There were two separate terminals pinging off the node they'd fixed a few weeks before. One was a familiar Aurora code; the other was masked. She tried to make a connection to *Twenty-Five*, but her old ship's ansible was dead.

"The first has to be *Rio*," Natalie said. "They're close!"

"And the other has to be Ramsay."

"Call *Rio*."

Ash shook her head. "Ramsay knows our codes. I'll bet you anything she'll be monitoring the frequencies."

Natalie frowned, and then brought her hand down, hard, on the back of Ash's chair. "Then we use code. We queue for a system update . . ."

"And they'll notice the discrepancy at HQ . . ."

"And come find us."

The ansible spun up with a clicking and a soft whispering, spitting the update request past *London*'s broken walls into the void. The system sounded a quiet chime, and a yellow light began pulsing at the bottom of the ansible.

"Did that . . . ?" Ash said.

"I think so."

"Wild."

They both fell quiet. Natalie rubbed her hands up and down her arms. "Getting pretty nippy in here. Do you think there's enough power to look at the logs? Maybe we can get a better idea of what went down right before the battle."

"Good idea." Ash reached toward the interface with silver-
capped fingers. She thought of the logs and something deep and
whining spun up at the center of the ansible array. Light exploded
from six points on the ceiling and swirled around the bridge,
painting holographic lines in blue and white in every chair: ren-
dering the curve of an arm, the line of a diamond-cut jacket, the
slightly parted lines of a crewmember breathing, the shield-like
curve of a fingernail. Within seconds, the bridge was full of blue-
lined holograms like animated drawings in a sketchbook, their
ghostly hands moving over dead consoles in a mockery of life.

The last figure rendered was the ship's captain; the hologram
displayed him head to toe, tracing lines of life over his moldering
body. His eyes blinked, again and again, in the dead bone sockets; his mouth moved where his jaw had fallen open. She couldn't
see his heart behind his rendered Auroran jacket, but she imagined it beating, imagined him breathing, imagined him living.

The dead captain's voice sounded over, guttering speakers.

"Francisco Valdes. Captain, Aurora cruiser *London*. Septem-
ber sixteenth, the year of our chief executive three-oh-two. We've
been diverted from our projected path to take care of an issue
on Tribulation Colony." The dead captain raised his blue-limned
hand to rub his right temple. "And it is, unfortunately, an issue."

"Whoa," Natalie whispered. "That's new."

**||**

For a moment, it felt almost like Ash and Natalie were no longer alone.

The blue-lined holograms spat out by the three-dimensional renderbots rolled their tight shoulders, blinked, and smiled; their faces were remarkably lifelike, their every move caught by the haptic security panopticon. Even their chests rose and fell with recorded breath. Ash tried to keep her mind on playing the log, while Natalie marveled as one sketchbook ghost rose from the navigation station and ambled toward the entrance to the spine. Natalie reached out to touch it, and her fingers passed through the light like rain through smoke. The figure ducked into the spine, disappearing legs first as if entering a deep, dark pool of water.

Natalie whistled. "They were not kidding when they were talking about upgrades on the cruisers. I didn't think this tech was even *doable*."

"Yeah," said Ash. "And we thought the text logs were bad."

Natalie made a face. "Well. Hopefully by the time this trickles down we'll be citizens and we won't have to deal with it off the job, right?"

The dead captain was rendered in the kind of incredible detail that betrayed the signs of his vague middle age: blue smile lines touching the corners of his mouth, stress creases dragging the corners of his eyes, the ill-kept beard curling at his chin. He had the lean, gangly body of someone who'd grown up in low gravity, and his mouth was turned down in the darkening, haunted stare of the broken and exhausted. Behind the animation, the corpse stayed still, jaw open, staring at nothing.

The audio crackled.

"We avoid a battle with the Vai on our way here only to find ourselves needing to start one with Manx-Koltar. Of course, for the record, Manx-Koltar is the one in violation of the noninterference treaty, here."

He coughed, dry and rattling, into a balled fist. Behind him, a group of executive types, wearing the tags and tattoos that marked them as birthright citizens who had blood and backgrounds clean enough to work a bridge like this, waved slender, silver-capped fingers in motions that looked like magical spells. The readouts behind Valdes showed them to be above the now familiar continents of Tribulation.

"There was nothing about a treaty violation in the public narrative of the battle," Natalie said. Ash heard the crackling of a ration bar wrapper in her ear, and the ordnance engineer's next words were pronounced around a mouthful of food. "What's wrong with him?"

"It was war. Poor bastard probably hadn't slept in days," Ash said.

Natalie narrowed her eyes at the corpse. "Kinda sad, really. He was hot."

*And totally my type,* said Keller's ghost, from the darkened aft corner of the bridge.

"Are you serious?" Ash asked the ghost.

"Deadly," Natalie said. "Look, they're all birthrights. Loyal as hell. You don't get that kind of composure growing up somewhere like Arimathea or Baltimore. You grow up on Europa, you learn how to survive in space from day one. You have the best teachers—"

"Shh, he's talking again."

Valdes grabbed at the sides of his chair and leaned forward.

"Twenty minutes ago, a ship bearing a Manx-Koltar IFF killed the Tribulation system ansible node and then refused to answer hails. We found them sending shuttles down to the surface, to an ag-center about twelve miles south of the main colony." He paused. Looked around. "If they don't disengage, we will have to move to protect Auroran assets."

He leaned back into the chair, his eyes going glassy. Ash could barely see the dead body behind his animated blue limbs. He rubbed his forehead. "Damn it, I don't want to have to fight other humans. Not right now." The captain looked down at his lap for a moment, seeming to decide. "*London* actual to all personnel. Prepare to—"

The holograms dropped out, plunging the bridge back to pitch darkness.

Natalie's voice lowered in rough disbelief. "We just assumed that the M-K wreckage belonged to an ally that had come to defend the planet. They were *allies*. They were on the Corporate Alliance Council. All those M-K people in the room with the scientists? The ones we IDed and put in coffins? We thought they were *helping*."

"You know what they say about assumptions," said Keller's ghost.

Ash bit her bottom lip, trying to keep her attention on Natalie. "So, an M-K ship got the drop long enough on *London* to board it—with *Mumbai* nearby? That's really weird."

"Fast-forward and see."

Ash narrowed her eyes. "The index is a bit fried from the battle . . . there's not a lot here. Here's the next bit I can access."

The ansible spun up again, and this time rendered the scene Ash had originally expected to see: a cruiser bridge at war. *London* was taking fire. The holograms shuddered in their seats, holding on to their chairs, snapping their safety belts around their shoulders. Natalie held out her arms, walking slowly in a circle around the bridge, taking it all in, running her fingertips through blue-sketched faces, resting her palms on heads and hunched backs, watching the holograms sweating through their last minutes of life.

"The second surface shuttle is escaping, sir. Our fighters can't break the railgun fire long enough to pursue," a young woman in the tactical seat said.

"And the first?" Valdes yelled.

A young tech looked over his shoulder. "Sir. Ordnance reports that the first shuttle has some sort of Vai molecular weapon in it. Claris says she's never seen readings like it. The shuttle was dead; it was going forward on momentum alone. Door was booby-trapped. We lost two indenture teams. Whatever it is, we have no record of anything like it being stored on Tribulation—"

"Sound familiar?" mumbled Natalie.

"Mm," said Ash.

Valdes sat back and tilted his chin. "Go for the weapon."

The image shuddered again as *London* took more fire. "Sir, I'm having problems keeping the power on in the lower cargo bays," another officer said, across the bridge. "Life support is failing."

"When it arrives, get it into an isolette." Valdes's head snapped, his dead eyes meeting the first man's. "We're getting the hell out of here. Tell Claris to get the scientists together. I want answers—I want to know what it is, why M-K's after it, why it was on our colony—"

"M-K is boarding." The woman who said this was no older than Natalie. She turned to Valdes, to say something more, then guttered out with the rest of the holograms, leaving the bridge death-dark and silent.

"Is there more?" said Natalie.

"One."

The bridge was empty this time. Captain Valdes sat in his

command chair, bowed and sweating, his hands tight-knuckled and tied to the arms of the chair with some sort of organic rope. His chin was set and tilted up at a second figure who stood in front of him, holding a long, serrated knife in one hand. In the other, he held a hammer.

"We . . . uh, we missed something," Natalie said. "Can you go back?"

Ash paused and peered into the file structure. "It's corrupted."

Valdes's attacker was human, wearing his hair long like any uncitizen, ribbons braided in like he was as proud of them as an executive was of his tattoo and torc, wearing a black coat that dusted the floor, with no outward sign of Company or status. Ash recognized his coat; it was the same one worn by the out-of-place body below, the stranger rotting in the same hallway as the scientists and the bridge crew. In the background, over the speakers, Ash could hear the screaming of human voices. Proximity alarms bawled. *The M-K forces? Where are the Vai?*

"Humans," Natalie whispered. "Humans did this."

"Natalie," Ash said. "That knife. Do you think he's going to—"

"Shit. I don't want to watch this."

"I think we have to."

Valdes spat toward the freelancer's feet; whether it was spit or blood or both, Ash couldn't quite tell. "Makes me happy," the captain said—he was missing teeth, now, and his face was stippled with blood. "It makes me happy that you're going to go down with the rest of us when the Vai get here. And when the salvage teams come—"

The freelancer's voice sounded hoarse and gravel-bound, as if he'd inhaled smoke in the battle without a breather. "When the salvage teams come, they won't care what they find," he said. "Don't you know what you've done, Francisco? You nearly ruined everything. *Everything.* You should have left us well enough alone."

Valdes wheezed and coughed up more blood. "You were

breaking the Alliance treaty," he said. "Some of us believe in the Alliance. In the future."

"You still think this is about property and profit and *peace*," the assailant groaned. "You are so far out of your depth you might as well be a nutrient farmer on Neptune Depot. I have my ride off this husk. You, though . . ." He paused. "You'll help humanity in another way."

Valdes's eyes darted to the knife, as if he knew what was coming. "No. Please. I'll get you whatever you want, citizenship, money. What do you want?"

"Revenge," he said.

The man in the long coat plunged the knife into Valdes's chest and twisted. The captain's eyes went wide, and he struggled; he screamed as if someone could hear him, but no figures entered the bridge, and the cry settled into a desperate, base gurgle. The murderer tore the blade toward the captain's kidney, using the rib as a guide, then cracked the ribs with a tool in his left hand. There was a squelching noise as the man slid his hand into the captain's—

"Don't get sick," Natalie said, grabbing at Ash's sweater.

Ash turned her head and buried it against the back of Natalie's warm hand. "Tell me when it's over."

"You think I'm looking?" she said, her voice shaky.

The murderer's comm rang.

Ash slit her eyes, peering through her lashes, trying to wait out the violence. Valdes's head lolled as it did now, his jaw wide, his face frozen forever in horrific surprise. The man held a human heart in one hand, fishing out a talkie from a coat pocket with his other blood-drenched hand, dripping on the floor. She looked down to see, for the first time, the rusty-brown evidence of the murder.

"This is Allen," he said.

"We're at the extraction point." The voice was a woman's, somewhat familiar, although Ash couldn't place it through the interference.

The assailant opened up a small cooler bag and placed the heart inside. "Thank God."

"Are you all right?"

"We've collected more samples since you had to leave the others behind. I'm making my way to the extraction point as we speak."

"Allen," the voice said, slower, "*Mumbai* scragged the Manx-Koltar ship. All we have are the shuttles. We can't get you in time. Any of you."

"What?" The man swayed.

"We've got Vai thirty seconds out and Aurora's taken the weapon aboard *London*."

"I can go—"

"No. It's too late. We have seconds before they slap it in a quarantine locker and take it back to Europa. I need to set off the weapon right now, to show the Vai that we can kill them. That we can *actually* kill them. We haven't killed one of them this entire war, and we need to show them, Allen. It's bigger than you, it's bigger than me."

The man was quiet for a moment, and then he looked down at his hands. "I understand."

"I'm sorry, my friend."

"No," he said, his voice dropping a register. His shoulders shuddered. "This was always the endgame."

"I'll remember you."

"No," he said, "you won't."

The bridge lit up in a sudden blinding cacophony of warning lights and sirens. The assailant—Allen—dropped into *London's* spine with the cooler and disappeared.

She heard the familiar, keening scream of the Vai engaging.

The hologram vanished, leaving the long-dead captain holding vigil over his glacial hell.

Ash ran her hand through her hair. She was sweating, despite the temperature.

Natalie gulped, then retched. "I knew M-K was full of fucking deviants, but I didn't know they were *cannibals*. Ash, this is bad."

"Is there more?" Ash shook her head and reached for the records with her hand, her mind. The computer whined and reloaded the logs from the beginning. The dead ship rattled; the air grew colder. "There has to be more. We can check the computer core for real-time data, maybe get a read on the tactical display," Ash said.

"Don't have the right tools." Natalie twisted around and found a railing; she hauled herself back down to the access ports. "It won't tell us anything more than the readings HQ had at the time, and we'd have to route power from the ansible—"

"And we're not doing that," Ash responded.

"God, no. I want to live." She looked back up to the screen where Captain Valdes sat in eternal pause, exhausted and un-bowed. The birthrights and their bright white tattoos hung for-ever at their stations, their faces set in serious ardor. "This is what they must have seen at HQ. This conversation. 'Set it off,' that woman said. Do you think she meant the weapon?"

"What do you mean?"

Natalie tapped her finger against her arm in thought. "If I were at HQ, and I knew any of this before we got the ansible working, I'd have recommended Aurora send a higher-ranked ship, a crew that had experience with more complicated salvage situations. *Two. Five.* Even *Ten*. Not us. Even with no ansible, Captain Valdes would still have logged it for the data dump. That's why we still have no support vessel. Maybe we should've listened to Reva in the first place and run to Europa."

Ash grimaced. "This was *our* corpse to pick."

"I dunno. It's weird that we're here, isn't it?" Natalie picked at the laces on her shoe. "That they sent *Twenty-Five* to one of the most important battlefields?"

"Not weird at all. I've seen this kind of shit before."

As Ash said the words, several unpleasant options occurred to her. She'd wanted stability, and the Company had given it to her. She'd wanted a path to citizenship. A place to belong. She'd been able to con herself into it for months now, and she'd thought that Aurora wouldn't demand anything more of her than her body and her mind. Not like Wellspring. Wellspring had taken her blood and her love and her very soul. She had nothing else left to give.

But Ash had seen this kind of thing before: the unwanted, the weakest, the least liked on the tunnel gang, sent into unstable tunnels, given the dangerous jobs, hazed, used as a human shield wall for Wellspring's more established workers. *Canaries*, they were called. The word had been whispered by Ash's team like a prayer, like a curse, the day the Vai attacked Bittersweet, as tiny clumps of gray earth loosened from the strutless walls, falling on their shoulders like dirt cast on a grave.

"Because we're expendable," Natalie said, before Ash could say more. "Makes you wonder if they're going to come at all."

*They're going to come,* Keller said, her voice warm and assured.

*Maybe you don't want them to come,* Christopher whispered.

Natalie poked her in the arm. "Hey."

Ash blinked. "I'm sorry. I was zoning."

"I'm starting to worry about you."

"Don't," Ash whispered. "I'm just thinking. *London* didn't know the Vai were coming because *London* was already dead and there was nobody left to sound the alarm. None of them had a chance."

Natalie kept a skeptical look on her face. "Yeah. But we do. What's next?"

Ash looked up and around. Keller's ghost sat in the navigator's chair, her arms folded. "We're burning power here, and it's getting colder by the second. We need to focus on the ansible. On life support."

Natalie looked like she wanted to make a retort—her mouth closed, opened, and closed again. She sighed. "Fair. I'll do the download. You get the blankets ready."

"Sure."

Ash unhooked her body from the haptic chair and pushed off to where they'd fastened the duffel to a sidebar, dragging out a survival blanket with her good arm. Made of heat-reflective material, it crackled as it expanded, creating a chiaroscuro effect on the dead bridge. Natalie rerouted power to the ansible, and the few lights that were on guttered and stopped. Ash held her breath through a few bare seconds of absolute darkness before Natalie's flashlight came back on.

They talked for a little while about *Twenty-Five*, about Len and Keller and poker night, about how Ramsay had fooled them all, but the conversation soon spun back to other, warmer places—Ash's childhood on Wellspring Station, Natalie's tales of running around hacker dens as a teenager. The temperature crashed in a slow, inexorable decline, like a feather drifting toward the bottom of a sunless cliff. Hypothermia slipped in even though they tried to seal the blanket, even though they shoved their hands in their sweatshirts and breathed as infrequently as possible. In the darkness, watching the ansible blink yellow, Ash lost any sense of time.

*They're coming,* Keller's ghost whispered.

Her voice was accompanied by flashes of light at the corners of her eye and involuntary trembling in her fingers and arms. Even in the cold, she felt heat, was grateful for the slips of delirium that began to slide into her mind. Natalie was hoarse, shivering; her body was pressed close to Ash's.

"I wanted to go home, you know," Natalie said, after a while. "After this deployment. I wanted to patch things up with my father. Did you ever want to go home?" She paused. "Can you?"

"I don't know if my mother's alive," Ash said. "She's still a Wellspring uncitizen, and she had to give me up to a child wellness center, and Wellspring doesn't even really exist, not anymore. And I can't even contact her, or hell, even the center, to find out until I have some sort of standing with Aurora."

"Maybe you could come home with me," Natalie said. "Get my dad out of Armour and into Aurora. Find your family."

"I . . ." Ash thought of Keller, sitting just out of reach in the darkness, ". . . would like that."

"So you wouldn't go home with Captain Keller."

Ash flushed, grateful for the darkness. "Let's change the subject."

"Oh. Len was right." Natalie elbowed her.

"What did he say?"

"That you liked her. That she liked you."

"Like we're kids?"

Natalie laughed. "I didn't want to be rude."

Ash was silent for a moment, then decided to go with a version of the truth. "There's nothing to tell. Maybe if we were different people."

"You said you had a fiancé," Natalie replied.

"Christopher."

"It's okay, you know. To get on with your life. You're not betraying him or anything."

Ash bit her bottom lip. "It's all just hard."

The ansible kept up its reassuring wail. "Where did he go, when you joined up with Aurora?"

"He died on Bittersweet. In the barrage."

"I'm sorry," Natalie whispered. "I'm exhausted. My brain isn't working right."

Ash shook her head, realizing seconds later that Natalie couldn't see it. "It's okay. The whole thing was kind of a blur. Like today."

"I should have remembered," Natalie whispered.

"Memories are weird sometimes. You know, you should have been there, when Dr. Sharma was running the experiment on the Vai device back on Tribulation, I heard Christopher talk. It was weird."

"What do you mean, you heard him talk?"

Ash inhaled more cold air, and her lungs complained. "His voice. In my head. I kept it to myself because you don't just go telling other people you're hearing voices, right? But looking back, I wasn't the only one who had a weird experience. Dr. Sharma asked me if the weapon was talking to me. Len didn't say what he heard, but he did hear something, and I'm betting it was pretty similar. We never got a chance to iron it out. Anyway, what I heard. It was what Christopher said directly after we signed up for Bittersweet, like the Vai just reached in and popped my memories out and played them back for me."

Natalie shivered. "Creepy."

"You don't think I'm crazy?"

Natalie wiped her nose with the back of her sweatshirt. "I think this thing sounds more dangerous every second that passes. And now Ramsay has it."

Ash wound her hand in the edge of the blanket, trying to get warmer. "And Kate's with Ramsay."

"If she's not dead." Ash heard a laugh, rueful and dark.

"She's not."

Natalie shivered. "You do have a thing for the captain, no matter what you say, Ash."

Ash's face flooded, even in the darkness. "I can't *have a thing*. She's the captain."

"And I can't have a thing for Len, but there you go."

Ash pushed a breath out of her shivering lungs, inhaling chill, metal-soaked air. Sharp pain throbbed and stabbed at her shoulder. She tried to put it out of her mind and failed. "Okay, fine. After we loaded up the *Mumbai* core, we, ah . . . um, let's just say that I didn't go back to my room."

Natalie was quiet. "Oh my God, are you serious? Len had money on kissing, but—"

Ash felt her face flush. "She shot me down in the end. It was too serious, too fast. She didn't want the complication to affect the crew. We had two more years out here. We were going to make a go of it afterward, if we both still felt the same way. I kind of doubted it, in the end."

"She feels the same way."

Ash coughed. It rattled in her chest. "She never told me that. Not directly, at least."

"It's so obvious. The way she watches you when you leave the room."

"Stop."

"She doesn't wait for me or Len after dinner."

Ash gritted her teeth against the pain in her shoulder, bit her bottom lip and tasted blood. She thought of Keller in the light of the bridge interface, the blue light tracing down the curve of her cheek; her body under Ash's, in the pitch-black of her cabin, quiet together, so as not to wake the others. "Maybe."

She thought of Keller, and like the devil of old, her ghost appeared, stepping out of the shadows.

Natalie moved inside the blanket, settling herself closer against the cold. "I learned in the war . . . it can be a thin line sometimes, with the right people."

"It can be a very thin line," Ash said.

"There was a guy in my platoon once," she said. "I get it."

Ash leaned in. "What happened?"

"Died at Grenadier. Saw him die."

A frisson of shock went through Ash's shoulders. "Were you there for the whole siege?"

"No, we were the reinforcements, as much as that helped," she said. "I just saw the dead mechs. The aliens inside vaporized themselves with suicide moleculars before we could get a decent peek. But some of them were injured before they pulled the trigger. Their blood is silver. Sticky. Gets into everything and won't come out."

"I'm sorry."

Natalie shivered again. "Don't be. Goddamn, it's cold in here."

"Why don't you get some rest?" Ash whispered back.

"You're going to be able to stay awake?"

"What would Len say? 'It's better than the alternative'?"

Natalie laughed. "I miss him," she said. "No situation's too bad with Len, you know? He'd be telling stories, joking about having a captive audience or whatever, trying to make us feel better."

"Yeah. He'd be good to have around right now."

The silence settled between them. "You've been a good friend, Ash," she said. "Whatever happens, I can't say we didn't do our best."

"We did our best. We're *Twenty-Five*."

She kept her eyes open against the darkness and imagined the life Keller promised, the one in the Aurora recruitment materials: a cabin by the sea, a name, salt air, whatever that smelled like. She drifted off to sleep with Natalie's warm head on her shoulder, and, before she knew she was dreaming, the ocean had turned red with blood and the seashore into a tall white bluff over a churning sea. She lost her balance, pinwheeled, and watched the cabin fall away as she plummeted, the voices swirling around her.

*I'm going to die*, she realized.

But the voices were still there, in the red, churning sea. *We'll catch you*. But she fell.

# 12

Keller breathed hard and hot as she pulled herself through the maintenance tunnels leading to *Twenty-Five*'s computer core. It was only a matter of time before the dead man in the medbay missed a check-in, and stopping to catch her breath would be suicide.

*Ramsay kept me alive, so she must need me,* she thought, as she struggled to drag air into her body. *The files, maybe. She's made my command codes invalid, and she has salvage codes, but that doesn't automatically mean she has access to the Company directories.*

Pulling herself into the crawl space behind the server room, she blinked away small black dots hovering in the corners of her eyes and swallowed a smoldering, furious anxiety. She pressed her ear against the secondary access hatch, screwed her eyes shut, and listened. She heard the soft clatter of a set of careful boots on the deck, the dull thud of fingers on the server interface, and the soft hiss of lungs breathing plain air.

One person. No suits. No respirators.

To be honest, she'd expected better efficiency from a crew commanded by difficult, exacting Ramsay. It made her lean toward a theory that Ramsay was competition, and that she'd been playing a long game, but hadn't quite expected the endgame to be laid out quite like this. Pirates would have come in suits. Pirates would have flooded both sides of the engine first, would have disconnected it and secured it for transport in less than twenty minutes, leaving the ship and crew helpless and frozen, bony carcasses spinning lost and endless in the everlasting night.

No, these were competitors, drilled on different equipment. And people drilled differently made stupid mistakes.

She was counting on those mistakes.

It wasn't a sure bet. Ramsay had been on the Auroran command track long enough to have been trained on how to properly yank an engine core. But she'd also know about the firewall lock that fell into place on the computer if the engine was removed from its housing outside of dry dock, and whatever else Ramsay was doing right now, she apparently still needed core access.

"Sir," murmured a woman on the other side of the hatch, "none of these command codes work." She paused. "Yes, I'm running the firewall protocol."

Keller slid Sharma's multi-tool out of her pocket. She unthreaded one of the bolts holding the hatch closed and peered through the hole, sliding the used bolt into her pocket to keep it from making noise.

A brown-haired woman in a black jacket and green armband hunched in front of the server interface, dropping blocks of code into the server backend.

*Jackpot*, Keller thought. *She's trying to circumvent the firewall with salvage codes. But she can't grab the whole core without a captain's authorization—*

*Wait. She doesn't need to. She's not after the entire core.* Keller's blood turned to ice. *Ramsay only showed her true colors when we found Ash's weapon. Our weapon.*

Her hand shook as she lifted the multi-tool and started to remove a second bolt. The competitor still hadn't left the room. Without her command codes, a full wipe was out of the question, but that couldn't stop a captain from going sector to sector, deleting the most important data by hand. She'd just need time. Access. To hold the room.

"Ramsay to Keller."

Her breath froze.

*Here we go.*

The sound came from all around Keller, rattling in from above and below—the ship's announcement mode, loud enough to shatter any sleeping crewmember's happy dreams. Ramsay's voice was still somewhat casual, and amiably obsequious. Keller bit her bottom lip, ignoring her, and moved bolt by bolt to unfasten the hatch.

"This isn't a big ship, Captain. I know you're in the ductwork. It's what you do. There's quite a few of us, and we're going to find you."

*Doesn't matter,* Keller thought. She slipped the last nut away from its housing with her left hand, then grabbed for the boltgun with her right.

The hatch fell to the deck with a clatter. The woman at the interface whirled in surprise, and Keller used that moment to fire once at her opponent's leg. The bolt caught the woman just above the knee, and she cried out, toppling over, trying to stop her fall with outstretched hands. Keller pushed herself out of the access tube and aimed the barrel of the gun at the woman's sternum. The competitor's eyes went wide and pain-bright.

"Stay down, stay quiet, stay alive," Keller said, catching her breath.

"They know— Fuck! They know where I am," the woman said, but she didn't move.

Keller moved to the interface and yanked out the woman's commlink, tossing it to the ground and smashing it with the heel of her boot.

The other woman's eyes went tight and flinty gray. Keller transferred the weapon from her right hand to her left, using the right to bring up the root dialogue on the core interface. Only then did she allow her hands to start shaking.

"You're Auroran. You're not going to be able to kill me," the woman said.

Keller kept the gun humming, and she cast the woman a withering glance. "You never know. I might miss and plant one in your head by accident."

The competitor stared back. "I'm gonna bleed out—"

"Sure will, if you move."

Keller returned her attention to the interface, using her left hand to enter the command codes for the core wipe—which didn't work here, either. She swallowed her disappointment and moved on. She'd have to delete the most interesting sectors manually, using one of the techniques she'd learned while stripping war-dead freighters near the ruins of Arcadia.

She waved the gun at the competitor again. "What were you trying to do?"

"Screw you," the woman said.

"If Ramsay wanted the new episodes of *Alien Attack Squad*, all she had to do was ask," Keller said, bringing up the computer's root directory. The most recent files went first—all the precious new data from the planet, the records from Ash's pod, and Sharma's analytics. She felt a pang in her stomach—she'd never even gotten to read them.

After that, she deleted all the executive-privilege directories: the list of weapons they'd discovered in the wrecks, the Company ansible directory, the maps of Auroran-owned wrecks near the Lost Worlds. She followed up with files flagged for captain's-eyes-only, memos from Solano's office, ansible news meant for citizens only. Len's cache of *Alien Attack Squad* vids. Holos of the six of them celebrating the full inventory of the *Mumbai* weapons cache with her treasured Neversink bourbon.

She skipped over the names and faces of the men and women they'd lifted from *London*'s eviscerated corpse. Their bodies, held in coffins in the darkest part of *Twenty-Five*'s ample cargo bays, would never come home, but she couldn't in good conscience remove them from history.

Keller's notes went. Her lists. Sharma's database, and the physicals she'd taken of the crew. She found the file labeled *To Ashlan—Letters*. With a knot in her throat, she deleted that, too.

The competitor spat out a few strangled swear words, and hauled herself toward the door, her hand bloody, pain-pale, and shaking.

"In here! She's in here!" she shouted.

Keller panicked for a moment and thumbed the charger on her boltgun. The fear and thrill of it crawled up her arm and settled, warm and unwelcome, in her consciousness. When nobody responded, she took a step closer to her prisoner.

"Shut up! There are eight of you onboard, tops, otherwise we'd all be getting carbon monoxide poisoning. And they're all down trying to raid the weapons stash, aren't they? Or sitting in my chair, trying to get in the front way? Nobody's going to hear you."

*Don't get distracted.*

It was Ash's voice, whispering somewhere underneath her skull, behind her ear.

She shook her head. Maybe she *was* getting carbon monoxide poisoning.

Footsteps clattered above her, and a sick solemnity settled in her belly. She was going to have to take care of the rest of the list in one fell swoop—until she'd seen the celebration files she'd forgotten about *Mumbai's* computer core, wrapped and ready for transport in the lower cargo bay. She couldn't save any of it. She needed a new plan.

She wrapped her hand around the warm grip of the boltgun, thinking of the last time she'd nearly died—on the tug, during the Vai advance. A cracked cooling brace on the tug's engine had nearly killed Keller on her first tug run. She couldn't ruin *Twenty-Five's* engine brace—but the computer had one, too, for

when the processor ran hot, like it was now. That would do the
trick. It would force Ramsay's people away from where Keller
needed to go. They'd need to run the ship's environmentals on
manual. They could fix it easily—

—but she'd be gone, in the meantime.

In a pod.

On her way to Ash.

Awash with sudden hope, Keller crossed to the core housing,
flipped open the sealer on her multi-tool with one hand and
slipped it under the core's safety box. She had to lose her bead
on the prisoner, had to swing the boltgun around so it dangled
by the trigger ring, had to use both hands to slide the box away
from its housing. The wounded competitor saw she was no longer
pegged, and hauled herself toward the door, screaming. Keller
let her go; she needed both hands for what came next, and if she
wasn't fast enough, nothing would matter.

Casting aside the safety box, Keller surveyed the cooling
setup. Her tug's engine brace had decomposed over a period
of two days lost and listing, galvanized by cheap Company connectors hooking the fan to the core. This computer had a very
similar rig.

Keller didn't have two days; she needed the break to happen
in two minutes. She aimed the boltgun at the plasteel connecting
tubes, firing quick, low-power bursts. The tubes shattered, pop-
ping away from the main core. She felt a blast of frigid air and
nearly cried.

The boltgun charge depleted too early, as she'd feared—so
she grabbed it by the barrel and started smashing the cooling
works with the butt, causing a deafening, screaming noise that
could be heard in the hall.

"Step away from the computer, Kate."

Ramsay's familiar voice, behind her.

Keller withdrew the gun from the core, sliding her thumb

over the charge indicator. It was dead in her hands, dented, lacking the signature hum. It would have to do.

"I have an itchier trigger finger than you," Keller said, "and you know it."

Ramsay stood blocking the door, carrying a boltgun of her own. She'd changed; instead of the familiar blue Aurora jumpsuit, she was in mercenary black, a jacket and tight, dull pants, decorated with a green armband and unfamiliar citizens' tags at her throat. Her hair, hands, and chest were streaked with the silver sibilance of celestium residue; it confirmed Keller's guess that she hadn't been lying when she said she was working on the injection system.

The first thing anyone took—salvager or competitor—was the valuable, irreplaceable beating heart of any ship: its fuel. *I should have seen this coming.*

"How long?" Keller spat.

Ramsay's shoulders seemed straighter; her manner less deferent. Keller took a step to the left to block Ramsay's sight line to the core, so she couldn't see the smoke.

"Does it matter?" Ramsay said.

"You tried to *kill* me."

"No. I just spiked your coffee. I didn't want anyone to die. You killed that man. He had a *family*."

"So did I. You were a part of it." Keller's stomach flipped. She tightened her hold on the boltgun; behind her, the coolant fan spattered and spun its last, and she heard the first few labored turns of the boltshot core. All she had to do was keep Ramsay distracted for a few more minutes. "Was it money they gave you? Did they make you a birthright offer?"

Ramsay's jaw worked. "I can explain, but you need to come with me."

"Where's the rest of the crew?"

"Let's *go*, Kate." The other woman's face set like flint.

"I'll go with you," Keller said, her stomach twisting. She inhaled, searching for the taste of burning metal in the air. Nothing yet. Too slow. "But first, you need to tell me where the *hell* Ash and the others are."

"Sharma's on my ship, *Phoenix*. She's safe. The others—"

Keller's hand felt sweaty on the damaged grip. "The others *what*."

"They killed themselves," she said. "Blew up their own shuttle rather than come. I never knew Ashlan had such a flair for the dramatic."

*She's lying*, Keller thought, but there was plain truth in the face she'd trusted, the woman she'd spent nearly every day with for the past year—and her body reacted, twisting underneath her, drowning in a dark ocean of grief that knocked the breath out of her lungs and loosened the muscles at her knees. She caught herself on the wall before she fell. Her finger squeezed at the trigger, shook against the dead gun, as if she could will the thing to fire with the dragon's rage clutching her shoulders. *This is my fault. I let this happen.*

"You awful—"

"I didn't kill them, Kate. I didn't make that decision. I tried to help. You can make a different choice."

The heat was spinning up now, clawing at her back. Despite the grief, she needed to keep Ramsay busy, keep her talking just a little while longer. *For Ashlan.*

"And what does the deal include?"

"You don't even know how special you are," Ramsay said. "What you can do. Who you *are*."

Keller's throat closed again when she tried to respond. She opened her hand behind her back and found the heat she was looking for—the sweet, bitter tang of death burning at the heart of a shuddering ship. *Just a few more minutes*, she thought. *I just have to keep her busy for a few more minutes. That's all.*

"I told you," she repeated. "I'm not executive material. We both know that."

Shadows moved behind Ramsay; voices whooped. The bitch had men and women clearing out the storage rooms closest to the core access point, stripping *Twenty-Five* of everything that mattered, that had value, anything that could be used or stored or sold. They'd probably gorge themselves on her whiskey stash tonight. *Bastards.*

"But you want more. I can give that to you," Ramsay said. "The research at Bittersweet—I was part of the team that picked it apart, see, deciphered it after we bought Wellspring, figured out the Auroran connection. It was insane. Insane and beautiful. It's going to make my company a market leader. And unless you enjoy being Aurora's vulture, used until you're broken and cast aside, just like everyone else, you'll come along."

"You're risking a Company war. A bad one. Aurora's not going to lie down when they hear what you did to us."

"Yes," Ramsay said, smiling. "They will."

The heat curled at the back of Keller's neck. "This is about the weapon."

"Of course it's about the weapon. It's about the weapon and who can protect us when the Vai return. You remember what it was like. You watched what happened to Arcadia. You watched what happened to the Lost Worlds."

The disbelief curdled in Keller's chest. "This isn't about *them*."

"We were never going to win. Not like that, not arguing amongst ourselves, not letting *the market* decide who was the leader."

"It's over. The Vai retreated over the White Line. They're gone."

Ramsay's eyes lit with a quiet, terrible certainty. "And what is the White Line?" she whispered. "Why don't the probes we send return any data? What's going on? It's not good for us, whatever it is. Keller, there's just one way to make sure humanity survives.

Do you really think Solano cares whether you live or die? There are a hundred more like you coming up. A hundred more who would *do* more to get ahead. Come with me."

Keller breathed in a tendril of smoke. "I told you before where I wanted to be. What—an hour ago? Two? Was this why you asked?"

"You said you wanted to be *up here.* Doing good work."

"I said I wanted to be on *Twenty-Five,*" Keller said. "And you fucking killed her, so go to hell."

A confused, deep disappointment crossed Ramsay's face, but she dropped the gun to her side and stepped back into the corridor. "Fine. Go with your ship. I have what I need. Just know that I tried to save you, *Kate.*"

Behind her, Keller heard the crackling of the circuits frying.

*Here we go,* Ash whispered, long ago and far away.

"You're forgetting one thing, *Alison,*" Keller said.

"And what is that?" Ramsay crossed her arms.

Keller took a long, sweet breath. It smelled of death and burning data and shattered dreams. "You're forgetting that this is *my* ship. And that, on *my* ship, I don't need a weapon to beat you."

"What are you going to do, try and—" Ramsay stopped mid-sentence, finally catching the scent of frying electronics, her eyes going wide. "*No.*"

Without the cooling brace and heat sink attached, the core behind her had been heating up all this time as it spun and ground, frying the environmental motherboard. When this had happened to her tug, Keller spent two exhausting days running herself ragged from manual interface to manual interface, keeping the backup systems in check until rescue showed. Ramsay would have an easier time of it, but enough of her crew would have to be diverted to allow Keller to make her next move in relative peace.

Fire sparked and flickered, lighting up the cabin.

"Have fun," Keller said, before the entire ship was plunged into darkness.

This time, Keller welcomed the acrid stink of her dying ship—*Twenty-Five*'s last breath spent to keep her safe, to keep Aurora's secrets safe. Smoke billowed out of the core, and she threw herself back at the hole in the ductwork. Ramsay moved as if to follow, but a sudden, terrible light flashed up and sucked at the remaining air in a destabilizing rush, and what was left of the ship's autonomic systems started screaming. She heard Ramsay's voice shrieking orders as Keller took the turn toward the cargo bay. She knew her ship. She knew every step. Every bend. She didn't need something as prosaic as light to get her to where she needed to go.

Fire would take the core—the last of Aurora's privileged data and the final six months of her life. It was a decent exchange. The sacrifice would give her enough time to draw the last line between Aurora's secrets and the competitors who would have them, to justify the sacrifice of her crew, to honor them in the way she hoped they would have honored her. Keller knew she might die, that she still might fall into the hands of Ramsay's outfit, but she still needed to do what she could to make this right.

She would draw the line. She would stand. She thought of Joseph Solano and the citizens' tags still on her collar.

And yet, as she hauled herself through the darkened maintenance duct toward her uncertain future, the same questions dogged her certainty:

*Why not kill me? Why am I even alive? Why am I special?*

# 13

Ash's next memories were half hazy, barely in focus, shaky, and feverish. She was warm, lying on soft pillows, and people in white and blue came and went, moving over her without speaking, like ghosts or shadows. For a little while, she was too tired to care if her new world was death or rescue.

When she finally felt coherent enough to move, she lifted her head, locating herself squarely in a medbay on a Company ship, lying in the same sort of hospital bed that she'd occupied in those first incoherent days after Bittersweet. The ceiling was dotted with the same black-circle renderbots she'd seen on *London*. She was connected to familiar hookups: intravenous port, heart monitor, brain monitor. Someone had started an IV feed of some sort of greenish-yellow, unlabeled fluid into her uninjured hand, and she wondered if that was the reason everything was surrounded with a fuzzy, half-unreal halo. The other half of the room lay behind a heavy curtain. She checked for the autobandage at her shoulder and found just scabbed, rough skin, stitched and healing.

*They came for us.*

She felt grateful, at first, a feeling that was swept aside by a crush of fear. *How many years is this going to cost me?*

Ash clawed at the blankets, attempting to sit up, feeling the quiet rumble of a stalled grav-engine in her legs. She tasted the blessed, metallic tang of well-filtered atmospheric mix. Her things—the important ones, Len's tool set, her pants, the multitool Keller had given her—were sitting on the nightstand like a minor miracle, presided over by the toy unicorn, staring sightless and worn from atop the pile.

Her vision twisted as she reached for the unicorn, and she fell back into her bed. Scrollwork, black and burgundy, slipped from the corners of her vision like someone writing on her retinas. She clamped her palm over her eyes, bringing blessed darkness.

"Be careful," a man said.

She dragged the hand away. Someone had been sitting nearby the whole time, writing with a stylus on a tablet just outside of her drug-slagged vision. He was in his late fifties, dressed in an immaculate Aurora-blue suit, with dark curled hair tied back in the kind of businesslike chignon that had been popular two decades ago, an extravagant diamond info-implant right above his left eyebrow, threading down into his ear, the kind of implant Kate had always said she wanted but could never afford.

"Hey," she croaked, waving her hand. "Hey. I can't pay for this. Let me walk out. I can't afford this kind of treatment."

The man was planet portly, with the tattoo of a birthright citizen under his ear. She was sure she'd seen him before. "Of course you can't." He paused. "That's why we have citizenship accounts. But we're grateful for your fealty in a tough situation, Ashlan, so we're providing bandages and the bed at no cost. I just had to approve the adjustment myself. See you myself, actually."

She blinked. Tried to place his voice. "How many years?"

"Don't think about that right now. Do you know who I am?" he said.

She shook her head. "I feel like I should."

"Confusion is part of the disease, I'm told. I'm Mr. Solano."

Ash felt dizzy. "You got our message."

His face slotted in as recognizable. She'd only ever seen it over the two-dimensional ansible feed, softened and flattened by the distance. In person, she could see the dark circles under his eyes, the flush to his cheeks. He looked human. "We did, yes. Very smart of you. Are you well enough to answer some questions?"

Questions of her own rushed to her lips. "Have you found out what happened to—"

He raised his hand. She fell silent. He put down the stylus and leaned back in his chair, just like the doctor on Bittersweet when he'd given her the bad news the first time.

"We found *Twenty-Five* in the asteroid belt an hour ago— picked to the bones, the engine scragged. There'd been a computer core meltdown. No survivors, or none that we can find. We think the pirates might still be on the planet, so we'll be sending a party to check. You and Indenture Natalie are our best sources of reliable information. So. Tell me what happened."

"Ms. Ramsay," Ash said, and then was caught by a coughing fit that, violent and involuntary, shoved air out of her frostbitten lungs. "Sir, I need to be on that search party, I need to find Kate—"

"Ramsay, your executive officer," prompted Solano. "She was a pirate."

She hauled in a painful breath. "They're not pirates. She was working for another Company this whole time. She took Sharma, the experiment—"

Solano waved his hand again, stopping her. "Are you sure that is correct?"

Confusion. "You don't think I had something to do with it?"

"Did you?"

Heat rushed to Ash's face. Anger. "Kate was my—my best friend, I would have never—" She gulped a breath. "We fooled Ramsay into thinking we'd died with our shuttle. Then we called you. Two people against an entire cruiser was not a good bet, sir."

Solano didn't respond right away. "What was your last memory aboard *London*? Do not lie to me."

Natalie, warm and close, her hair smelling of frost. In the air, ketones and piss. "Frostbite." *Visions. Falling.*

Solano picked up his tablet and spun it to face her. He flicked it on. The tablet opened to a video taken with a standard Company tactical camera, the kind grunts like Natalie clipped to their helmets. She saw herself strapped to a stretcher, her eyes open, fighting, her hands like claws, screaming "Glory, glory, Kate, Kate, cannot connect, glory." The rescue operator turned around long enough to see Natalie on another gurney, her mouth covered with an oxygen mask. The video came to an end, and Solano narrowed his eyes and remained silent.

"I—" She swallowed, a sour note dangling at the back of her throat. "I can't explain that."

"Why not?"

Ash felt her stomach churn. She searched for her glass of water, swept it up, and drank it in one gulp, as if it could give her courage. "I don't know. I was out of it. It was freezing. Sir, I want to be on the team that looks for Captain Keller."

Solano's face flickered with disappointment, and the corners of his mouth pressed into an unhappy line. "Of course, that's out of the question. Your cit account balance disqualifies you from that kind of work. And there's the matter of that," he said, tapping her image on the tablet, "not being hypothermia. That's celestium sickness. Dr. Cantrell confirmed it. How desperate were you? Were you working with another Company to get around the rules?"

Her heart sank. "No. I would never. Sir, I—"

"Misrepresentation is cause for departure, indenture."

"I—I didn't know," she stammered.

He shook his head. "That was a lie. Like Ms. Ramsay lied."

"Not like her."

"You don't think so? Let's say that you're not a traitor. You still knew you could snap at any moment, and destroy Company property or personnel? What about that is *different*?"

"I care about Aurora—"

"I don't think you do." He pushed up out of his chair, standing over her. "You care about yourself. You can claim to love your captain, your fellow indentures on *Twenty-Five,* but to put their lives on the line for your own selfish needs, Ashlan? That's not *love.* That's treachery. We'll bring you back to Europa Station when we're done here, and you can find your way from there."

Her stomach cratered, and she pushed herself up, dragging her stone-heavy legs over the side of the bed. "That's a death sentence."

"Citizenship isn't for everyone," Solano said. He turned for the door. "Thank you for your service."

Her head swam. Panic kicked up under her belly button and slipped, a roaring hurricane, up her throat and into her limbs, her brain full of the dank tunnels of her childhood, the sickness, the hunger. She'd die there, at the humming, beating heart at the center of whatever station they found for her first, accruing the debt Christopher had died to free her from. She got to her feet to stop him, hanging on the nightstand, her knees knocking, grabbing on to whatever she could to stand up straight. Her hands felt the soft, yielding cotton flesh of the—

—*miracle.*

She swept the unicorn aside, reaching into the pants pocket where she'd stashed the isolette's memory chip. The overhead light glinted off the metallic contact points like small stars.

"You can't let me go," she said. "I have information you need." Solano kept walking.

"I'm the only one who knows how the weapon might work. Natalie wasn't there." *Forgive me, Natalie.* "I have hard data."

Solano turned. "Indenture, I am hardly a unilateral despot. This decision has been made by the board of directors, and—"

"So, *unmake* it," she breathed, cutting him off. "Bring them the hard data. I can—" She licked her lips, trying to stop another desperate lie. Failing to do so. "I can tell you how it works. Without me, you'll be dead in the water. Let's make a deal. I'll give you the hard data on the weapon and you keep me in the Company. I want citizenship."

The CEO nodded his head, and then extended his hand. "Let's see it, then."

"I want assurance you'll make me a citizen," she said.

Solano's eyes widened in leery surprise. "You have a debt. I can assure you only that the value of the information will be put against that debt."

Ash limped over and placed the card into his palm. He turned it over and over again, and then slid it into his jacket pocket. "May I remind you, indenture, that everything you have is Aurora's, and that you are in no place to make demands. But I will certainly take a look, and talk to the board," he said, and then with a few sharp clicks of his heels against the metal floor, he was gone.

Ash picked up the unicorn. Stared at it. It smiled at her with its glinting glass eyes: she looked into its silent, wide-open red mouth.

*Dumbass*, it said.

She tossed it aside and swore.

"Keller tell you to use language like that on an open channel?"

It was Natalie's voice, scratchy and low after treatment for the frost. Ash crossed the room, pushed open the curtain and found Natalie lying on the bed, her skin still pale from her ordeal on *London*. She did not smile when she saw Ash but lifted one hand up in a slow greeting. When Ash came closer, Natalie tensed, drawing her knees close and balling her fists. Ash saw it and stopped farther away than she would have liked, her heart fluttering nervously.

"I should have seen that coming," Ash said.

"Yeah," Natalie said. "You should have."

"Feeling better?"

"Like I've been trapped in an ice cube for way too long." Natalie coughed. "They tell me I'll be up and rolling in an hour, though. Modern medicine, hurrah."

Ash paused. "They didn't tell me how you were."

"Yeah, well." Natalie looked away. "I didn't want you to know."

Ash felt heat rising, past her shoulders, to her cheeks. "I'm sorry."

Natalie picked at her blanket. "You knowingly put us at risk. You went out there every day and you didn't care for one blasted second that one bad hallucination could have killed us all. And we were a gunshot's breadth from dying on *London*. We got through that together. And you still didn't tell me? You know what? *Screw* you, Ash."

"I needed the cure," she said, the excuse rolling out even as she knew it was a bad idea. She felt hot and sick all over. "You would have done the same."

"No. I wouldn't have. You don't fuck over your team. Ever." She pushed herself up on her left arm. "Do you know how scared I was? One moment we were chatting about our families, and then you were talking gibberish, screaming at some ghost only you could see—I thought you were going to kill us both. I had to knock you out. Twice."

Ash bit her lip. "I don't remember. I'm sorry."

"No, I don't think you are." Her eyes filled with anger. "None of us mattered to you. Just Ms. Keller."

"That wasn't—"

"That's who you were talking to the whole time. I just wrote it off as delirium from the pain, but no, it was her. You thought *she* was there? Wasn't that it?"

Ash bit her bottom lip. "She was there."

The words dropped like a bomb between them.

"I need some time," Natalie said.

"Fine," Ash said and stood still, stuffing her own anger back in the dark place where it belonged. Anger wouldn't get her anywhere. She turned for her side of the room. "Have some time. Have all the time, actually."

Ash crawled back into her bed, sudden exhaustion pressing into the space behind her eyes. She could almost feel the celestium buzzing in her veins, harmonizing with the rumble of the ship's engine, the hiss of the life support system, the beeping of the machines. She drifted for a few moments, feeling like she was back on *London,* clutching Natalie's small shoulder in the guttering light of the torch, the skeleton's jaw clacking together, speaking of *Glory,* and she was flooded with a feeling of lust and shame as powerful as it was terrifying.

*Glory.*

Whatever that meant.

"Do you think she was telling the truth about the Vai coming back, Ash?" Natalie said.

Ash opened her eyes and pushed up from the bed. Pain tightened a lasso behind her ears. "Who?" she said.

"Ramsay."

"I hope not."

The younger woman kept her eyes focused on the ceiling. "I'd kill them all, if I could. Wipe them out like what they were aiming to do to us. No qualms. I'd just do it. And that should scare me, but it doesn't."

"I'm sorry," Ash replied, feeling helpless.

"Don't be," she whispered.

She heard quick, determined footfalls and brought her eyes to the door. Two men entered. One was an olive-skinned executive, wearing blond hair in a chignon like Solano's, a silver-white tattoo, and heels. He stood just inside the door, observing. The other was a young black-haired birthright wearing a Company ID with the name "Dr. Jie Cantrell," a pasted-on smile, and a citizen's tattoo. There was an insidious sort of friendliness to him, a desperate taste of earnest corporate bullshit in his face—*Fear? Is he afraid of me?*

*Should he be?*

He pursed his lips and extended a syringe in her direction. "Europa 5242-B. Ashlan, is it? Your arm, please."

She extended her soft inner elbow to the stranger and watched him fill the chamber with her blood, feeling a quiet emptiness at the center of herself, an emptiness that felt every painful ache and dark measurement of the loss of the rest of the crew. She hadn't heard her Company uncitizen number, the one that identified her to the dole, since her rescue from Bittersweet. *What's the use of fighting it, now that they know?*

*I'm an uncitizen now. I can't fight it.*

"I'm Dr. Cantrell," he said, his eyes on the syringe. He tapped it a few times, then slid the syringe into a testing chamber. "I work for Dr. Julien in R&D. I'm a follower of Reva Sharma's early work, so it's fantastic to look at a victim of celestium sickness up close."

The disgust Ash felt was flooded out with a momentary confusion. "Her . . . early work?"

"With the first victims of the madness on Arimathea. Wasn't that why she was on *Twenty-Five*? To study you?"

Cantrell flipped her wrist and checked her pulse with thin, arrogant hands. It felt like Bittersweet again: having to allow this, having to let him do it, having no choice in the matter. "I suppose so," she said, slowly. It was news to her, and surprising. "Are you . . . continuing that work?"

The computer continued its noisy analysis for a few seconds longer, then fed back results Ash couldn't decipher.

Cantrell's face fell. "Why no, that can't be right." He tapped at the interface. "You've only been with us for a year. What are your symptoms?"

*I see her. She talks to me. She's probably dead.* "I see things that aren't there. Sometimes . . . dots, spirals. Sometimes people. Dead people. My hands shake, coordination's an issue. Can't always judge distance."

"Shaking hands, sure, that's normal for the first year, but—" He pointed to a diagram she didn't understand. "You're not in the early stages. Your neurons are degraded to the point that I would have expected you to have had celestium infiltration for ten or eleven years. And your lungs are clear. But you say it's been a year?"

"And some months."

Cantrell exchanged a wary look with the executive at the door, who nodded

The doctor then brought the blood test up on the monitor nearby. It showed red and silver geometries, grains of sand sloshing together like the Bittersweet desert; it looked nothing like Ash's experience of blood, the muck and the tang and the ruddy fear of it. "You know how it works, don't you? They did tell you?"

*It fucks you up,* Christopher said, just over her shoulder, *and then you die.*

Ash said nothing.

"You take a breath; the celestium settles into your lungs and binds to the walls, then is carried into your bloodstream with any new oxygen, and then from there into your body, your brain. You find it a lot in mining companies like Wellspring, shitshows that don't provide adequate lung protection for indentured workers. And you certainly have celestium in your blood, but you didn't get it from breathing it in. And there's something else there, too, something beautiful—"

"That's all I need to see," the executive said, and then pushed off the wall. His violet eyes were shining, and he crossed immediately to Ash, pressing his face close to hers, yanking her eyelids up with a hot finger. His breath smelled like cinnamon. Ash tensed.

"Remarkable," he said. "Oh, you're right, Doctor. That's not celestium. That's Aurora's *future*."

"I didn't think it was celestium, no," Cantrell said.

For once, she pushed back, overwhelmed. "Just . . . stop. Please. Stop touching me."

The corners of the executive's mouth turned up a little more, folding into thin, rubbery cheeks. Ash had never seen teeth that white. "That's *true*. I shouldn't touch a future citizen, should I? We're prepared to make you an offer, indenture," he said.

Ash's heart started pounding out a frenzy in her chest. She broke into a sweat across her forehead that stung her eyes, and she felt dizzy simply from the bare hope of it.

"Your current cit account, including your most recent medical care, stands at twenty years. The information on the card brings it down to fifteen," the executive said. He noticed and paused to let her take in the number, to let her shake, to let her blood roar in her ears. *Asshole.* "You can stay an uncitizen, but after the data you provided, Mr. Solano and the board of directors would like to offer you a better deal. We want you to undertake a full indenture while we're still here at *Rio*. We will need to study your condition to develop treatment for it. The period will last up to a year. At the end of this period, you will be a citizen. There are conditions—"

"Yes," Ash said. The word came out before she could control it, springing from the same deep place as her thoughts about Chris, Kate's smile, the love of warm blankets and hot tea and hope.

"Mm. Let me get through the offer before you decide. Because of the medical involvement and the need to involve R&D, this will be a full indenture. You will wear a monitor. It binds you to strictures far more stringent than the ones that you signed for Bittersweet. You will give every *yes* that is asked of you, to every task that is asked of you, no matter how daunting, immediately and without fail, in any department we choose. Or else, your life may be on the line."

"And you'll find a cure?"

Cantrell and the executive exchanged glances. "That's part of the goal, yes," the executive said.

"Put me on the search team for Captain Keller, and I'll do it," was all Ash could say, even though Christopher was in her brain, screaming *Slavery*.

"We can start there," the executive responded, "but at some point we're going to have to get you in a lab. I'll stay with you, for observation. That's really all I can promise."

*It's a year, Chris. I might make it.*

The executive said nothing more; he whipped out a tablet, made some changes, and turned it around. Ash affixed her signature with a shaking hand. Behind him, she barely saw Natalie, sitting up in her bed, pushing off the covers, shaking her head, her eyes wide—

—and Ash averted her gaze, thinking of Kate.

"Thank you, Mr. . . ."

"Indentures," Cantrell said, "I'd like you to meet Aram Julien, *Rio*'s associate director of development. He's going to brief the two of you on what happens next."

"I'm in a hospital gown," Ash said, feeling suddenly naked.

Cantrell produced two newly stitched, hard-pressed Aurora expedition uniforms. "No, you're not," he said.

Five minutes later, Ash felt much better in a snappy blue Aurora field jacket, striding down familiar corridors, listening to the sound of her heels on the deckplates, Natalie by her side. The antigrav pulled at her legs and pushed the blood through her heart in the way a planet's gravity ought. It was almost like things were normal again, even if the skin of her wrist felt hot and tight against the plastic of the new monitor.

*Twenty-Five* had been a stocky, safe cargo hauler with insides full of corpses and scientific equipment, sporting the aesthetic appeal of a half-crushed box of crackers. *Rio* was a testament to the Company's power, built to be seen, to shuttle around notables from the administration on one deck while facing down violent blockades on another. It was sleek where it didn't need to be and ostentatious in its simplicity. Like *London, Rio* was riddled with new haptic interfaces in every compartment, and when Ashlan stopped to gawk at the new and improved pod bay, Natalie lingered behind, grabbing at her elbow.

"Why did you sign that? I was trying to tell you, it's not a good deal—"

"It's *citizenship*," Ash said. "In twelve months. Not fifteen years. And you were a soldier—you did a full indenture. They gave you healthcare—"

Natalie's eyes were dark, and her face deadly serious. "Yeah, but . . . not like this. Remember when we were out on that last run together? We talked about the benefits I got—the savings account, the credit toward my contract? Ashlan, your deal isn't *fair*. They can ask you for every task. Every single one. And they didn't give you any idea about what those tasks will be. Ash, they can ask you to *die* for them. And you can't say no."

Ash's stomach twisted. "They said they were going to give me the cure."

"No, they said it was a goal. A goal, not *the* goal. You don't even know what they found. Frankly, I'm a little scared of how fast Mr. Solano seems to have moved on this. They know something you don't, and they leveraged you."

"So *now* you care."

Natalie narrowed her eyes. "You make it *really* tough to be your friend, Ash."

Ash sighed. "I'm still here. That's what matters." She ran her hand through her hair, the noise of the shuttlebay, the people running to and fro, the shouting, all of it suddenly too loud. "And, God, I can do anything for a year. I made sure of that. How long do you think *Rio* is going to be here?"

Natalie grabbed her hand. "Depends on what they find below. The fact that they didn't tell you, that they don't know, should have tipped you off that this was a *bad deal*."

"Indenture Ashlan," called the executive from down the hall. "Catch up."

And she had so much to say to Natalie, so much to explain, but the new monitor on her wrist was cold and tight, and she'd made a bargain, hadn't she? Ash swallowed a knot of acid confusion. "It's all a bad deal, Nat, that's all people like us ever get," she said, squeezed back, and took off down the hall.

She felt Natalie's angry eyes boring into her back long after she wanted to stop caring.

# 14

Compared to the *Rio* recon team, the salvage engineers on *Twenty-Five* had been a circus troupe.

The shuttle kissed dirt right in the center of the settlement and emptied itself of five soldiers and the research doctor in record time, with Ash playing the part of the woozy caboose. By the time Ash unclipped her safety web and her boots hit the sulfur-splashed earth, Natalie and the others had already started setting up the command post nearby. She stepped away to look around, raising her hand to her forehead to block out the golden light of the late afternoon sun.

Beyond the boxy prefab buildings, the fields that once fed the colonists—corn, wheat, amaranth—were long dead, choked by craggy bloodsap brambles and trees covered with glittering fractal moss. To the left was the dead maglev train, a series of broken cars and smashed-up engine units, and to the right was the main storage barn, its gray doors shattered and jagged where they had burned in some unknown assault. The colonists had tried to personalize the place, painting the plasteel dorm exterior a soothing green, hanging windows with curtains and ragged tinsel that flickered in the tendrils of the quiet sulfur wind.

Solano had given Natalie command of the soldiers in place of a citizen officer, and Ash watched her work with a guilty, nauseous envy. The younger woman worked with an effortless, fluid curve to her body, shouting orders to the others. She sent two of the soldiers trotting toward the barn with a nod of her chin and had the other two help her set up the local ansible a few meters away, where it had clear line of sight to the wine-bright sky. The uniform fit Natalie like she'd never left the military department, never tried to be anything but a soldier, never switched to salvage. Like she *belonged*.

Ash sighed, pulling on her field jacket where the too-small tailoring pinched her wrist.

"Your friend is going far, you know."

Ash jumped. Dr. Julien stood just behind her, smiling with just the corners of his mouth; under the massive trees his carefully maintained citizen's body looked even thinner than it had on *Rio*, and the golden afternoon light just highlighted the craggy, gray tones in his ship-pale face. Ash thought he might have been handsome, once. "You mean Natalie?"

Julien nodded. "That's what I hear from above."

"She's . . ." Ash paused, and then decided on a neutral word. "Something."

"Do you think you can . . ." Julien said. He trailed off and waited a moment before pursing his lips, dropping that line of inquiry and pulling out a syringe from the medical bag hanging from his shoulder. "This is trihexphenidyl," he said. "Dr. Sharma developed it to cure Parkinson's and treat celestium sickness, and we gave it to you on the ship when that's what we *thought* you had. I'm not sure if it'll *keep* working, but it's a place to start. Your arm, please."

Ash sighed and pushed up her sleeve. A quick pinch later, and she watched the tentacles dragging at her peripheral vision fold up and clear away with mild surprise. She blinked, expecting encroachment. Nothing. She felt clearer.

"Feels better," she said.

He straightened. "Good. Let me know when your symptoms come back, and we'll check your levels then."

"What do you want me doing?"

"I want you to stand here," he said, "and wait."

Ash felt heat flood her cheeks, and she looked around, gesturing at the busy soldiers, the search-and-rescue map being laid out on the table under the command post tent by—that one, Marley, and the other, Laren. "That's just silly, sir. I'm good in the field. I have overwatch experience, I can mark off quadrants for S&R, I can be *useful* here, and—"

Julien leaned in, his voice going dark and kind, like a particularly patient schoolteacher. "Look, indenture, between you and me, I understand how difficult a transfer to full indenture can be. So, I was instructed to remind you if you asked: You are to accept all orders without fail, without question. That's what Mr. Solano wants." He paused. "It's why I didn't ask you to introduce me to your friend back there."

Ash swallowed the tight, screaming ball in her throat and nodded.

Julien squeezed her right shoulder and moved off toward Natalie, leaving Ash steaming. She shook out the tension in her shoulders and then shoved her balled-up hands in her pockets, trying for some control of her ragged breathing, her sudden roiling anger at Julien and the contract and her useless body. She tried to redirect, to calm herself down, to focus on the sounds around her: the rushing of the wind in the trees, the choking, soaring calls of the local birds, the quiet shuffling noises coming from the barn—

—no, that couldn't be right.

She blinked, then stared at the dark maw of the barn, trying to concentrate. *I'm not a canary,* she said to herself, *I'm a valuable participant in research. We're here to find Kate.*

Laughter on the wind, from a throat stripped of its kindness by the Bittersweet mines. *You're a fucking canary, love.*

Christopher.

The muscles in her jaw tightened like fraying ropes. If she was still hearing voices, the drugs weren't working, no matter if her vision was clear or not. She coughed and tried to put the hubbub of the yard behind her, focusing instead on the quiet darkness of the barn. She felt a second of doubt before she heard the shuffling noises again. She took a step forward, and then another, slowly, thinking that *No, it's just the sickness*, before she saw the darkness move, fold over on itself, dart past on two legs.

Someone was inside the barn.

Ash took a step even closer, squinting, tilting her head. She saw a dark presence, black on sable, stooped and bent, pushing something heavy closer to the door, a box or a crate—or was it just her broken eyes?

"I think someone's inside," she called.

The noise of camp setup ceased. Natalie hopped down from the box she was standing on and unholstered her boltgun, charging it with a quick, frightening whine. She and Julien were next to her in breathless seconds, the other soldiers flanking them, and the air around them was suddenly tight and hot and serious, filled with a humming spread of boltguns ready to fire.

"Come on out," Natalie called.

Whatever had been moving was not moving now; the figure had retreated into the dark cloak of the unlit barn, or had never been there at all, and the confidence leached out of the soldiers' stances. Julien rocked back on his heels, the doubt radiating off his loosening shoulders. He sucked in a sibilant breath through his perfect birthright teeth. "Maybe the indenture was—"

"There," Natalie said.

This time they all saw the shadow. The figure fluttered behind the left side of the barn door, hands and legs and a head covered in dirt and darkness. Ash heard a sob, a cry, and recognized the gravel-caught rasp of someone whose airway had been destroyed by gas, by particulates, by inhaling an atmosphere humans were never meant to breathe. She'd heard it a hundred times below the surface of Bittersweet.

The person inside was *very* sick.

She opened her mouth to tell the others, but Julien swung his open hand toward Ash, pressing two fingers against her lips. "Stay back," he whispered.

"Come on out, now," Natalie called, her body taut, her fingers white and tense near the trigger of her boltgun. "Let's be friends, we're—"

"You won't take me, not again," the voice gasped.

An abyssal second passed. The wind slipped through the trees. A bird chattered.

"We don't want to—" said Natalie.

"This is for *her*, you bastards," said the ghost.

Ash heard a muffled crash, the sound of plasteel against earth. A crate fell into the space between the broken doors, its contents spilling out onto the ground: a fist-size marble the color of the twilight sky on Earth, spilling out of white quarantine swaddling like a dragon's egg dropped from a nest, rolling to a stop against Ash's toe. The marble began to shake. Deep inside its razor's-edge border, as if galaxies away, blue light kindled, grew, spun, knit together in a violent pirouette, in a whispering hurricane.

Without her pod between her and the Vai weapon, Ash felt rooted to the spot, paralyzed with fear, a crawling scream forming behind her teeth. The soldier nearest to her—Marley—breathed out a *shit, shit, shit,* and the gun began to shake in his hands—

"Kinetic! Go go go!" Natalie screamed. "*Blue screamer!* Dome evac, half mile! A-three, now, now, now!"

Ash knew that protocol.

The first step was *Run like hell.*

The blue light ached at the edges of the weapon, shivered there, and it took a millisecond, two, and a hundred years to do it—

The world spun to the side and Ash took off, hurtling past the dorms in what seemed like the easiest direction, crashing into the bloodsap brambles at the edge of the forest, feeling the alien air alight in her throat. Behind her, she heard crashing noises, haphazard and reckless, smashing sticks and leaves and hollering. A rumble crackled under her breastbone, shuddered up through her feet when they hit ground; some of the soldiers were lifting the shuttle off the ground.

Behind her, Natalie screamed. "You won't get off the ground in time! *Dome* evac, you *fucking—*"

Ash ran as fast as she could, her breath burning. She heard Julien cursing nearby, alive and barreling into the forest with the rest of them. Natalie was telling them to *go,* that the weapon had a range of a *half mile,* and Julien was absurdly fast, nearly catching up with her, nearly passing her—

—when the shuttle fell out of the sky.

She stumbled to a halt, turning, her breath stolen by the fireball unfolding into the wine-soaked sky—

*"Fucking run!"* screamed Natalie, barreling out of the bushes behind her.

Ash took off again. She could see Marley behind her, a bobbing blue streak with a strained, frightened face, just within sight range. Behind him, she saw a brilliant alien light, a cloud of lights and mist. It was blue like the depths of the ocean and the bright stars of the early morning, and it slithered after Marley, around leaves and through bushes, torch-bright and violent in the gathering gloom.

Natalie stopped where she was, her face desperate. Ash ran up to her, dragging her by her shoulders back toward the slavering forest—

"We can't leave them," she said.

"We *have* to," Ash said.

Marley threw himself forward, screaming. The blue light twisted in the air behind him, coiling its way toward his hands and head. He fired bolts haphazardly while looking back, as if he could slay the light like he could slay a body. The bullets disintegrated into puffs of silver brilliance, hanging in the air like fairy dust against the ancient alien forest. For an insane half second Ash was reminded of the fireworks she'd seen on the holiday holos, of the hundred dead ships glinting in the light of the Sebastian sun, and she knew, as much as she knew anything: he wasn't going to make it.

They ran.

The blue lights sped up their oscillation, spinning faster, as if they were alive, as if they could smell Marley's fear and delighted in it. Ash tripped over a fallen branch and grabbed for Natalie's arm. The younger woman caught her, and threw her forward into the bushes, following Julien.

She looked back once. Marley wasn't fast enough. The lights wrapped themselves around his limbs. "Go," he gasped, and then threw himself into a last desperate sprint, his arms pinwheeling. The caterpillar beams snaked up to his mouth, leaving burning swaths of blackened skin behind. The light coalesced in his chest, pressing against his ribs and skin from inside. His eyes widened with some indescribable, terrified thought. His mouth opened, and the lights took him apart in a swift, hideous twist.

One moment, Marley was there; a bright second later, he was gone, strands of winding blue light where his bones should have been. Ash's muscles knit back together and she ran, almost involuntarily now, shoving herself forward through the trees and brambles, the caustic breath of alien air stinging her throat and branches whipping at her arms and cheeks like the devil himself was after her.

"What's the range on this thing?" hollered Julien.

"Half mile!" Natalie screamed.

"I can't run that far!"

"You have to!"

Natalie picked up the pace, nearly reaching Julien. Ash pummeled herself onward into the darkening forest as the trees around them alighted with alien azure bouncing from one trunk to the next, catching up to them faster than they could run. Ash's lungs were on fire and her muscles were cramping with the effort, but adrenaline pushed her on, and she caught up to the others.

The three of them made it some distance into the forest when their retreat came to a tumbling halt. Natalie's foot caught underneath a fallen tree, and she came down hard, cracking her head on a nearby rock. Ash aimed for a tree and put her hands out, using it to stop her forward momentum; as the shock of it ran up her palms and wrists, she whirled, scrambling back over to Natalie, falling on her knees beside her.

"Ashlan!" screamed Julien.

"Just go!" Ash screamed back, and the young doctor turned and barreled in another direction, disappearing into the blackening evening. Natalie was awake but stunned; blood flowed down her face from her temple, and her eyes stared, dull, at Ash, and took a moment to resolve. "Ash, go—"

"Get up," Ash yelled, moving to grab Natalie's hand, attempting to yank her to a standing position, even as her eyes lolled back, disengaging, going blurry.

The clearing filled up with alien blue; Natalie's chin tilted up. Reflected in her eyes was a gathering of blue threads, whirling, hovering, covering them in a blanket of quiet menace. Ash tried one more time; she dragged Natalie to her feet, and this time, the younger woman stumbled, then barreled forward again, Ash at her heels.

Ash felt the tendrils before she saw them; they were indescribably hot and viscerally beautiful, moving with a swift grace in a twisting, turning braid that never resolved and never ceased. Ash looked over at Natalie; she tried to yell something in her direction, let her know she'd been caught, but she could not. The storm had taken away her words. Finally outside of the exclusion zone, Natalie slowed, turned, stopped. Tears streamed down the young woman's face, and she stopped just one moment to give Ash the Auroran salute.

"Run," Ash called, the gesture opening her mouth to the crashing flame, the stunning, howling pain of the threads twining up her neck and her chin, forcing her mouth open, thrusting down her throat—

—and then nothing.

# 15

*Twenty-Five*'s environmental alarms howled keen and bright as Keller climbed down the aft maintenance duct, careening toward the pod bay as fast as the thin air and darkness could carry her. There was a skinny, hungry desperation in the familiar sound. She'd never thought for a moment she'd thrill to hear it.

The ship shuddered as if it were alive. Keller stopped dead in the pitch darkness, shoved against the side of the tunnel, feeling the guilt like a bolt to the stomach.

No. Not guilt.

*Shame.*

This was all her fault.

She dropped away from the heat, away from the flames, hoping that the training she'd given Ramsay and the others had paid off. She'd drilled them on fire response at an exhausting, incessant pace during the trip here, knowing that uncontrolled fire could kill ships in seconds. The protocol would have a convenient side effect: With everyone dealing with the emergency, Keller could grab a pod and go.

*Go where?* Ash's voice, again.

*Rio's coming, if it isn't already here, and Aurora needs to know—*

*Bang. Bang.* She heard hard footsteps on the deck above her. Shouting. The clattering of feet heading for the fire. She fished the bolts out of her pocket and hurled them away toward the habitat ring. They skittered off with a jangling clatter and fell down the habitat duct with a dull crash. It might buy her a minute or two as they went to investigate, but then, that might be all she needed.

Keller pulled herself toward the cargo bay, choking down the shame. She knew how things worked in the real world. She'd seen moleculars take apart entire fleets; she'd seen hungry corporations snacking on their bones, through dropped promises and subverted ceasefires. She should have known. She should have guessed. She shouldn't have gotten *comfortable*.

Yanking the bolts out of the hatch to the cargo bay as she'd done in the core access room, Keller pulled the hatch into the tunnel. She sat on the edge of the bay, swinging her legs into the open space, four feet above the floor. Above her, a single backup light gleamed, casting the cargo bay in bare, gray twilight. She clutched the sides of the hatch with sweaty fingers, swinging her body into the cargo bay with as little sound as she could manage. The low gravity made it an easy landing.

The traitor's locusts had already been here, but they weren't done. They'd left their tools and their dollies strewn about like they were coming back to get them. She jogged over to Len's wall interface and brought up the pod status, swearing under her breath.

Her perfect escape was foiled. The pods were already gone, and both pod airlocks were being used for boarding umbilicals.

A howling drop in air pressure dragged at her upper body, spinning up from the center of the ship, spiking at Keller's belly with sloshing nausea. She choked down sudden panic, and heard a terrible, sucking roar somewhere far above; she guessed that Ramsay's people were using the grav-engine to suck the fire out the secondary exhaust filter into the darkness of space.

Exactly as Keller had taught her to do.

*Which gives me twenty seconds before they get back to what they were doing. Thirty. Maybe.*

She looked around. Crates. There were plenty of crates. Big

ones. She'd stocked up, expecting a profitable salvage run. The invaders had been in the middle of loading the hard-earned Christmas list on dollies—in particular, the greenhouse kinetics in the largest cases, the ones it had taken Natalie three days of painstaking, suit-sweaty work to defuse. They were rare. Rare and dead. If she folded her legs, she could hide. They'd probably find her, but they might not. It was a gamble.

Keller heard the crashing of feet on the ladder and angry voices in the corridor.

*This is the stupidest plan in the history of stupid plans,* she thought.

She threw open the top of the two closest crates. The first held three defused greenhouse bombs nestled in quarantine fabric, heavy as the kettlebells in the gym she used on Europa and just under the size of her head. She kept them as swaddled as possible as she shoved them into the next crate, the one holding the green B9s they'd picked up the second week in the spinfield. Natalie would scream at her. Natalie would tell her that she was crazy, that they didn't really know how this shit worked. *If the Vai show up you could be dead in seconds, get your hands off of that.*

But Natalie wasn't here.

And neither were the Vai.

*Small blessings,* she thought.

A woman's voice. "We're not going back to HQ?"

"Not yet. That R&D cit says we're not done."

"You don't think Aurora's picked that corpse clean?"

Laughter. "I think there's plenty left for us."

With a swallow of revulsion, Keller yanked the first crate closed and locked it, then slid herself into the one she'd nearly emptied, drawing the top closed and clicking it into place. The round, cold weapon that was left pressed into her belly, and she gathered herself around it, holding it between her chest and her knees like a baby to keep it from rolling around, turning herself into a trembling human quarantine blanket. The footsteps grew close, and she shivered and went still, remembering too late that she hadn't gone to the bathroom in a few hours. And that she had no idea how long she was going to be trapped.

*Shit.* And then: *Oh, God, I hope not literally.*

She bit her bottom lip, five seconds away from terrified, screaming laughter.

Next came the crashing sound of boots on the deck, the hollering of enemy voices, the mechanical whir of self-propelled dollies. The dolly her crate was on jerked to the left as someone fired it up and pushed it out toward the umbilicals.

"This thing's unlatched," the first voice said.

"So fucking *latch* it," said the other.

Her hand went instinctively for the multi-tool in her pocket, ready to defend herself with the cutting edge of the knife, but all she heard was the double click of the crate's latches falling into place.

The person pushing the dolly made an abrupt right, and Keller's shoulder hit the side of the box and wrenched with a sudden, *wrong* pain. She bit her bottom lip to keep herself from crying out. Keller ached, then, the blank greenhouse bomb pushing, impossibly cold and viciously round, at her belly and her muscles and her bones. As the gravity fell away, she realized: this was it, she was leaving *Twenty-Five*, possibly forever.

She could tell the moment they hit the full gravity of the enemy ship by the breath that was knocked out of her chest, and she counted—*forty steps, two lefts, and a lift*—before the dolly came to a rest.

Even the air smelled different here.

The stevedores worked around her for an interminable time, lifting boxes, chattering and grumbling. Her leg muscles cramped and groaned. Time passed in monotonous skeins until she felt an ache in her stomach, felt the hot stink of a lack of oxygen, a desert in her mouth, unwelcome pressure against her bladder.

She set her jaw. *I'll piss myself over my own dead body—*

She shoved her nose against the seam where lid met body, then took long, quiet breaths of sweet, recycled air, listening to the engines. The grav-drive on the competitor vessel spun with a light, sweet soprano, a marker of a newer Kimbright-Hawn or a late-model Hansen, which meant this Company had cash to invest. The spin rate ran longer than *Twenty-Five*'s, which meant the bones of the ship were heavier, which meant—a cruiser? A hauler? Which Company felt they needed a cruiser to take down a ship as small and unimportant as *Twenty-Five*?

*You should take it as a compliment,* she heard.

Ash's voice again.

*Great,* she thought. *I need to pee so badly that I'm hearing things.*

Ash's tough, sweet laughter. *You were hearing things before.*

Keller heard Ash's voice nearer, now, as if the woman had slipped into the box beside her, as if her lover's soul had slipped into the dead weapon she cradled and caused it to speak. It felt warm, almost welcoming, like something had kindled inside at her presence.

*The moment Solano got on the line, I should have figured out how important that weapon was going to be. I got distracted by the shinies, by the thought that—that we could maybe, that Ash—*Keller gulped down the desert behind her teeth, unable to finish. She closed her eyes, black against black, and tried to sleep.

When she woke, it was quiet outside. The stevedores were gone for the first time since her arrival on the competitors' ship. Keller pressed her fingers against the top of the crate, feeling the ache of her cramped muscles. Whatever thirst-driven psychosis that had conjured Ash up and slipped her into the aching dysphoria of the situation slithered away, and she was suddenly afflicted by a starving clarity, carrying a wrenching empty knot where the rest of her life had been.

She placed her palms against the top of the box and pushed up, feeling a solid, curving resistance at the box's standard latches, seeing a slight curve of light through a seam. The box had been placed underneath another, but the weight was light, and Keller was sure she could dislodge it by kicking hard enough—if her cramped legs would play along. She forced herself to relax, to listen, to breathe; she heard nothing but the spin of the engine and the soft croon of the unfamiliar ship systems around her, but no footsteps or human voices.

*Time to go.*

Keller twisted her body so that she was lying on her back. She pushed her foot as hard as she could against the top of the box, fighting off the blinding ache of a leg cramp. The latches stuck. She grabbed the dead boltgun from her waistband and held it again by its damaged barrel; straining the latches and hinge by pressing her knee against them, she slammed the butt of the gun over and over into the hinge until the force of it made her hands numb, until she was convinced someone would hear her, until the hinge slipped apart and she could push the lid far enough to shove her hand out, flip the latch, and open the crate.

The box above her clattered to the floor with a piercing racket. Keller blinked away the pain of the sudden light, and then peeked over the edge of the box.

Keller was in a large cargo bay. This ship was no freelancer; it was Company quality, newer than her own had been. The deck shone in the brassy way of newly installed plasteel, devoid of deckplates dented and darkened by years of shuffling feet and rolling dollies. She hauled herself to a sitting position, then attempted to push herself up and out.

The attempt failed.

Keller felt a moment of addled panic as her body refused to

work, as her arms cramped, as her legs filled with blood, as she fell back, numb, against the bottom of the crate. She stretched one limb at a time, feeling the serrated, needlepoint agony of her blood speeding up, feeling returning to unused muscles, trying not to whimper. When she felt like her legs were hers again, she swung her feet over the side of the box, climbing down the stack of crates with the confidence of a small child on the playground, coming to an ignoble stop as her foot slipped and she hit the deck, face-first, with an audible crack.

Picking herself up, wiping blood from her already broken nose with the orange armband she'd taken from the man she killed, she looked around for shelter. A bathroom. She needed to pee. She needed to clean herself up, to get rid of her Auroran clothes. She felt the bawling need for water in her bones, the angry complaint of an empty stomach. She had no idea how long she'd been in the box.

*Too long,* whispered Ash.

She slid the damaged boltgun into her belt and limped to the cargo bay door, on the verge of the unknown, peering into the empty hall. She knew she should turn left, head for the pod bay, make an attempt at escape.

But Sharma's zero-point theory echoed in her brain, bright and loud.

A proper boundless energy solution had the power to change everything. It meant an unbelievable amount of savings for the Company that owned it, and a huge push toward an end to the scarcity that had defined space travel since humans had thrown themselves away from Earth two hundred years before. It meant batteries that never died, tools and boltguns that didn't need to be charged, the easy ability to power entire stations, fleets, colonies. Entire planets.

And if that Company could use it to replace the corporate reliance on celestium—why, that would be a freedom beyond anything Keller had ever imagined. How far could she go, if she never needed to return to port? What would happen to the indenture system, to the need for people to earn their way in the world? It could reshape the entire scope of human industry and culture. It meant wars that never had to happen for resources that would never run dry—

*No,* she thought, her mouth a desert. *It means wars that never end.*

*Wars that have already begun.*

She'd been imagining the weapon as Aurora's all this time, but the scientists who had died on *London* hadn't had the time to truly understand what they were looking at. It had belonged to someone else before this. If she didn't do something about that, it would continue to change hands. People had already died for it, and people would continue to die for it. They would never stop fighting for that kind of advantage.

*Well, whoever Ramsay is working for, they can't have it. I have to get this back to Aurora,* she thought. *For me, for Ashlan, for all of us. For everyone.*

*How do you think Aurora will be any different?* Ash's whisper.

Hovering near the cargo bay doors, on the verge of the unknown, Keller had her first quiet doubt.

She didn't like how it felt.

# 16

For the second time that week, Ash stood unsteady in alien darkness, trembling and astonished to be alive.

Her world had receded to a black-blood silence, the bare yellowing behind the trees the last evidence of the turn of the planet from its star. As if loosed from a spell, she stumbled forward against one of the bulky trunks, coughing, the pain of the molecular weapon still incandescent on her skin. Natalie struggled up from where she'd fallen, crossed the distance between them, and threw her arms around Ash's shoulders.

Once again, Ash shook in Natalie's tight grasp. She couldn't speak. She couldn't move. She had been so certain that she was going to die, so sure that the alien forest would be the last thing she saw. Her knees buckled. Natalie helped her to the ground, then sat herself.

"I should be dead," Ash whispered. She couldn't manage more than those few words before her lungs demanded to be filled again, and all she could do was suck down sulfur-tinged air. Ash licked her dry, unburned lips. She touched her shoulder, her neck, where she'd felt the certain crackling of her skin to black; her blue expedition jacket was tattered and burned, but her skin was as olive and unbroken as ever.

"How did you *do* that?" said Natalie.

"I . . . ran. I was fast enough." Ash's words stumbled, caught on her recalcitrant tongue.

Natalie kept her close for a few seconds longer, then released her, looking from Ash's shoulders to her torso to her eyes. "No. *I* was fast enough. That wasn't it. It *killed* you."

"It was going to. Going to pull me apart." Ash felt the panic spin up again, threatening to scramble into her shaking limbs and stay there.

"But *how*—"

"I don't know. Stopped by itself. Changed its mind."

Natalie shook her head. "That's impossible."

Pain squeezed at the center of Ash's chest, and she grabbed Natalie's hand, crushing her fingers, as if she couldn't believe the other woman was real. She felt like she was back in the tunnel on Bittersweet, dirt shoved down her throat, crawling in the darkness, her world pushing in around her. "We can't think about that right now. The shuttle—"

"It's gone," Natalie said, slurring her words. "They're gone."

"They might have—"

"They didn't listen to me." Natalie's voice broke.

Ash's vision sharpened as she calmed, and she drew her hand across Natalie's head injury—a bloody mess at the hairline just above her temple. The cut was shallow; the blood made it look worse than it was. "Hey. You hit your head."

"I'm fine." Natalie set her jaw and attempted to rise, wavering. "I'm not the one who ate a screamer and lived."

Grateful to put her attention anywhere other than the burning residue of her encounter with the weapon, Ash steadied Natalie's shoulders with her hands.

"You've probably got a concussion," Ash said.

Natalie made a face. "Don't have time for that."

"We have plenty of time. You're the one who told me that the detonation of a molecular means that the Company waits at least an hour before sending a rescue team. And I've got my monitor, so they'll know I'm still alive, at least. We have, what, fifty-six minutes?"

"You're slurring."

"So are you."

"It's fine."

Ash looked down at her hands. In the boozy aftermath of the adrenaline shot of near death, she hadn't noticed that her hands were shaking again. She'd have to tell Julien the half-life of this trihexphenidyl crap was—

*Oh, hell. Dr. Julien.*

She looked around into the darkening forest, then reached into her pack and took out a bandage, pressing it against Natalie's forehead. "Here. Keep pressure on the wound and stay here. I need to find Dr. Julien."

"Think he made it?"

"He was ahead of you," Ash said.

Natalie coughed—a welcome, human sound against the dusky, crackling chirping of the alien wildlife, even as the cough worried Ash. "I'll try to raise *Rio* on my local while you're gone—though, if the shuttle took out the ansible, we might just have to wait in the black until they feel comfortable breaking the molecular quarantine. Could be a few hours."

Ash smirked. "Weren't we just playing this game? 'Sit around and wait for *Rio*'?"

"Yeah, well, we're good at it." Natalie's fingers lingered against her shoulder, and for a moment, Ash wondered if there was forgiveness in them.

"Go get him," she said, pushing Ash away, leaning back against the tree. She reached for the talkie at her belt as Ash turned back to the forest, picking her way through the brambles and bushes. Julien's path was easy enough to follow—the disturbed leaves and the footprints in the loamy black soil were all easy enough pointers to the degree of the man's panic.

She called his name as Natalie's position was swallowed by the creeping branches behind her. The forest returned nothing but the dusky sound of wind in the trees and tiny creatures in the bushes, singing down the sun. The sulfur taste grew as she walked farther, fetid and slippery, coating Ash's tongue with a foul taste she couldn't spit out. As the forest tightened around her, she marked her path by worrying bark off the trees, until she saw Julien's jacket—his blue executive's jacket, his golden citizens' tags, his name in white stitching—impaled on a shattered trunk, and the bag of medical supplies he'd been carrying opened to the sky, syringes and bottles and autobandages scattered.

"Dr. Julien!" she cried. Then, even though she knew she shouldn't put a citizen's first name in her indenture's mouth: "Aram!"

Nothing.

Ash inhaled again, testing the air; on the tongue of the sulfur air was the faint smell of flame. Her lungs burned, and her body labored to keep up. If she went much farther, she'd find herself out of oxygen. He had to be close.

A small, loud voice in her hindbrain began to panic.

*All right, calm down,* Ash told herself. *You're either on the outer range of the atmospinners or the madness is kicking in, and either way, you don't want to be alone when that happens. That poor guy is gone.*

She dropped into a squat, gathering the medical supplies from a puddle, wiping the water on her pants leg, and was going for a second syringe of trihexphenidyl when she heard the whine of a boltgun safety going off.

She felt a press of metal against the back of her head and knew exactly what it was: the round, tough, business end of an Aurora duty boltgun.

"Stop." A man's voice, dark and shaking. "Turn around."

The voice was Julien's, ragged and frightened and just as slurred as Natalie's. She lifted her hands behind her head and turned. Adrenaline kicked in. She felt frantic, wanting to breathe, wanting to run, unable to do either. Julien's face was bloody, dirt-stained. He'd fallen, or tripped, or slammed straight into a tree.

"You were going to take my stuff and leave me here?"

"I wasn't going to do that," Ash said, keeping her palms open, near her ears. "I came looking for you. I thought—when you didn't respond, I thought it got you."

Julien's eyes were dark and desperate. On the ship—even ten minutes ago—he'd seemed cool, cosmopolitan, executive. Now the fear in his eyes betrayed how young he really was, how out of his element he was in the threatening embrace of the alien forest.

"How did you survive?" he said.

"I ran. I just ran. I outran it. Like you did."

"That's not what happened," he said.

"I swear, on my contract—"

The gun whined, and he raised his voice. "No. That's *not* what happened. I saw it *eat* you. You were glowing—I could see right through you, like I could see through Marley, could see the light gobble up your bones—and then you just—you just *lived*."

Ash still felt the incandescent afterburn of the weapon in her throat. Above them, Ash heard the rustle of feathers, the flapping of wings, the crack of a branch breaking. "I don't think you saw what you thought you saw."

"What are you?" he whispered. "Are you Vai?"

"That's insane."

"It would explain the test results. You know, I was at Grenadier," Julien said. In the near dark, Ash could see his Adam's apple bobbing. "With R&D. I was there. I *saw* the final massacre, the shit loosed on the 121st. The Vai mechs waded right in, dropped them. And the 121st, they—" His voice shredded for a moment. "They died just like Marley. Glowing. Screaming."

"Dr. Julien, please, *please* put the gun down, Natalie's waiting for us and she has a bad concussion, she could use—"

He cut her off. "Those monsters just *strolled* by, mowing down the soldiers. And you know what? The weapons tore through the mechs, too, and then they just kept on going. Like you, just like you."

"But they died," Ash said, her mouth going dry. "Natalie said—"

"They died when our reinforcements showed," he said. "Using suicide moleculars. But until then? There was nothing we could do to stop them. The greenhouse gassers did *nothing* to them, even as they killed everyone else. I know what I saw then, and I know what I saw now, and I swear on the birthright blood in my veins that *you are one of them*—"

Ash took a tentative step back, nearly stumbling on a thorny bramble. "You're sounding crazy. Let's calm down. Sort this out."

His hands tightened on the gun. "The only place you're going is the brig."

"Natalie's hurt. The others in the shuttle—you saw the shuttle fall—there might be people still alive—"

He pressed his lips together, clearly conflicted.

"We can figure it out together," she said.

"If you don't kill me out here," he replied.

"There are people *hurt* out there, Dr. Julien, I'm not going to kill you. I *need* you," Ash said, her voice going ragged and annoyed, unable to keep herself from blowing her top. She stepped forward.

He pulled the trigger.

The bolt missed, swishing past her ear, burying itself in the tree behind her. She fell to the side, arms pinwheeling, stumbling into the muddy puddle, the cold liquid dragging at her knees. She tried to get to her feet, but the young citizen had already turned and was tearing farther into the forest, the boltgun still charged and whining in his hand.

"Stop," she cried, stumbling after him. "You won't make it. There's no oxygen out there. You'll suffocate!"

Julien didn't stop. A gust of sulfur wind came from the west and ripped down Ash's damaged throat, causing her to catch herself in a bent-over, sobbing sort of coughing fit, placing her hand on a tree and doubling over in pain. When she was done coughing, she looked up. The doctor was gone, and the forest flickered on in darkness, alien leaves twisting in an inhuman breeze.

She left him his coat.

She squinted in the darkling night, searching for the path back to Natalie. Lights had returned to her vision, swirling, blocking her path. She shoved the syringe of trihex into her pocket and shouldered the medical bag, then trudged down the path of broken branches and leaves that led back to Natalie and the settlement.

By the time she got back, the younger woman had found her flashlight. She gave Ash's approach a weak smile, dropping the grin when she realized that Julien wasn't present. "Guy's dead?"

"He shot at me and took off into the forest," said Ash, offering Natalie a shaking hand.

Natalie grabbed Ash's lower arm, struggled up to her knees and did a queasy half dive for the medical bag. "What was he thinking?"

"Thought I was a Vai."

"What the hell?"

"He saw the weapon fail, and, I don't know . . . jumped to the craziest possible conclusion."

"That isn't the *craziest* possible conclusion."

Ash ignored the salvo. "He'll have to circle back around to the rally point, eventually, and I've got his medkit, so we need to get back and see if there's anyone left alive."

Natalie's jaw set. "There's nobody alive," she said.

Ash wanted to protest, but she saw the look in Natalie's eyes, and simply slipped her arm under Natalie's shoulders, supporting her as they walked back to the settlement.

It didn't take long for the slight tremolo of Ash's fingers to become a disabling tattoo, and by the time they reached the abandoned shacks that had once belonged to the farming hub's indentured workers, she knew she needed one of Julien's mind-clearing trihex shots. In the late twilight, the only light extending from the opposite side of the compound looked like a basic flashlight, and it beamed bare and white from the common barn, barely reaching the run-down shacks and dorms that had once served as housing for the Aurora indentures.

The clearing burned.

The shuttle had come down hard in the center of the clearing, obliterating the ansible and the command post. The twisted remains were burning lethargic and bright, and she could smell an awful, screaming stink of charred metal. She narrowed her eyes and searched for the bodies of the young soldiers who came with them. Nothing.

Of course she found nothing.

Natalie rested her back against the native wood slats of the house while Ash crouched on the dusty ground, rifling through the medical bag. She gave a small white pain pill to Natalie, then yanked the syringe of trihexphenidyl from her pocket. She applied it to the inside of her arm, gritting her teeth at the pain of the needle breaking skin. The lights flickered away. She felt cleaner. Brighter.

*It's not a cure,* she reminded herself. *Two doses in less than an hour can't be good for you.*

Natalie tossed back the painkiller Ash handed her; her knuckles were white where they grasped at the wall for purchase. She looked back around the corner of the building, narrowing her eyes. "There's—that's a flashlight. In the barn. Was that light on when we left?"

"I don't think so," Ash said, looking herself. Behind the fire licking at the edges of the clearing, threatening the darkness of the forest, she could see a bare white light moving in the barn. "If they're Vai, we're screwed."

"Yeah, the fuckers are in there," she said, rising to her feet. "Time for recon."

"Wait." Ash snapped the bag shut and stood. She didn't feel like she had the heart to mention to the bloodied, concussed Natalie that if the Vai were behind this attack, *Rio* might not even be there to call in a few minutes. "I don't know," she said. "That crate was *pushed* over—"

She was cut off by the sound of swearing.

*Human* swearing.

Natalie pushed herself up again. Ash intended to ask her companion if the sound was yet another hallucination, but Natalie had her war face on, and months of working together had taught her to shut up when the younger woman was trying to analyze a situation. Ash ducked, crouching in the dirt. A human figure emerged, silhouetted with light. He was alive—*alive*—and moving boxes around.

"We need to retreat," she whispered.

"Wait." Natalie had her eyes narrowed, and the look on her face was that of someone attempting to solve a tough puzzle. But then her face went bright, and her eyes wide, and she popped up like a field antenna, taking off through the briars and the brambles, careening toward the barn after a destination Ash couldn't see.

"Natalie!" she hissed, but Natalie was undeterred, a shout tearing from her throat.

"Len!" she called.

# 17

Ash grabbed at Natalie's sleeve as she took off toward the dark figure in the clearing. The fabric slipped through her fingers like water.

The man—it *was* a man, skinny and crooked, with a familiar stoop to his shoulders—was limned in light from the burning shuttle. He turned at Natalie's approach, and the light caught his face. It was Leonard Downey: alive, right there in front of the burning shuttle, smeared with soot and dirt. *Alive,* when the soldiers had died, when *she'd* nearly died, when *Natalie* had nearly died. *Alive,* like her.

An initial jolt of happiness ceded to a crowding of questions, and not all of them pleasant. The questions twisted and curdled: *How did he get here? How did he survive the screamer?* He had to have been over a half mile off, walking from town, maybe, recognizing the presence of friends, running to see them. The alternative was too awful to consider, too sick to bear: a version of her friend who would be in league with Ramsay, who had been inside the barn, who had pushed over the box with the screamer on purpose.

A version of Len who would kill for profit.

Ash closed her eyes, refusing to believe it. That kind of bad guesswork was what got a canary trapped.

Len's boltgun was raised soldier-tight in the direction of the quick-footed Natalie. He coughed against the back of his other hand. His dark-eyed, terrified gaze watched the younger woman down the weapon's short barrel. The whining sound broke up the reunion, and Natalie drove straight to a questioning halt.

"Come on, man, it's me," Natalie said.

He blinked and licked his lips. He held the gun for a few more seconds, his hand shaking, as if he could not quite decide if Natalie were made of smoke or flesh. Then he switched off the gun and dropped it to his side, the tension leaching out of the air with the loss of the charge.

Natalie yelped and crossed the last few steps, enveloping him in a hug that was too tight and too long to be friendly. He returned it, kissing the top of her head, his hands tight around the small of her back.

"Nat," Len said, his voice muffled where he spoke into the cushion of her jacket. "I thought you were dead. I thought they'd killed you."

"No way," she said. She pulled away, then cupped his chin with the curve of her palm. Len leaned into the gesture, and the firelight caught the tears in his eyes. "Me and Ashlan, we're hard to kill."

Len's voice adopted a sharp edge. "Ash's here?"

"And *Rio*. We can take you home."

"Where is she?"

The sharp edge to his gravel-caught voice caught Natalie cold, and her face tilted toward the fire. She paused. Tensed.

"Stopped to tie her shoe."

Len's face fell. "Don't fuck with me, Natalie."

Natalie's jaw worked, and she stepped back, putting some distance between herself and the engineer, her hand going back to hover near the boltgun at her waist. "No. Don't fuck with *me*. What's your problem, Len?"

His arm traced a wide arc over the burning wreckage, the dark barn. "Are you working with them?"

"What?" Natalie's hand tensed. Her eyes darted around the square, the burning shuttle, the dead screamer sitting in the dirt, emptied of its horrors. "You mean *us*. This was *us*, Len."

"I *saw* you with them," he whispered. He coughed again, the sound shattering into the crook of his arm.

Natalie blinked. "You were in the barn when the weapon went off?"

"Yes, I—"

He realized what he'd said far too late. A dark disgust crossed Natalie's face; she drew her gun with a fluid flicker of one hand. Len mirrored her, and Ash heard the whine of boltguns painting the air with promised bloodshed. She swore under her breath and dove for the medkit, opening it up, trying to find something that might double as a weapon.

"You *killed* them," Natalie whispered.

"They were in crates! Crates! Like they were defused—I didn't know! I just meant to scare them off. They had guns, like the people that took Sharma—"

Natalie snarled. "We were wearing Aurora blue. Aurora *fucking* blue!"

The gun shook in his hand. "That word again, like it's supposed to mean something to me. Aurora! What the hell is *Aurora*?"

"Be serious, Len!"

"Never been more serious in my life," he whispered.

For a moment, the only sound was the low, aggressive hum of their weapons.

Ash's world twisted to the left. She felt dizzy, upset, broken. *This wasn't what was supposed to happen.*

Keller. *We don't always get what we want, do we.*

Ash picked up the medkit thermometer. It had a cold, round end, and although it was too small to resemble a gun barrel, she knew Len wasn't a soldier, and all she needed to do was end the standoff. The cold, the pressure, the shape—the very thing that worked on her in the forest just fifteen minutes before would probably work on Len. She slammed her boot heel into the wall and strode around the corner with self-inflicted, half-true confidence, coming up behind Len, pressing the thermometer to the soft triangle at the bottom of his skull.

"Put it down, Len," she growled.

"Ashlan. Come to finish the job?" Len said, still looking straight at Natalie, whose face warred between sheer relief and angry panic.

"This is gonna end one way and one way alone," Ash said, "and that's with you putting down the gun so that you can talk straight with your family."

Len closed his eyes and flipped his wrist, letting the gun drop so the body swung harmless by its trigger ring, dangling from his outstretched thumb. Ash reached around and took the gun from him, shoving the weapon in her belt, and then nodded to Natalie.

Natalie lowered her boltgun in a slow arc. Her voice was full of heartbreak. "Why'd you do it, Len?"

The engineer's skin was touched with gray, his jawline covered in stubble, his hair streaked with rust. He looked defensive. "I thought they killed you. And then—when you came back, when you were there, I thought—" He coughed again, phlegm clogging in his chest. "I thought you were working with them."

"Them? Look at my *fucking* uniform," Natalie repeated, grabbing a handful of her collar. "You killed your family. Your *brothers*. How the hell can you not *remember*?"

"I just don't!" Len trembled, his voice dropping to a fevered whisper. He expelled an exhausted breath, and his shoulders deflated. "You had guns. A shuttle. There are—holes in my memory. A lot of holes. I remember you. Ash, and the doctor. I remember Captain Keller. I remember my parents, the apartment in New Orleans. But I don't remember how we got here. I don't remember *why* we're here. We had to have come here on a *ship*, for a reason, but all of that's gone. And when you don't know what you don't know—"

Natalie took a step forward, her fist coming up. "Oh, I'll make you remember, you son of a—"

A memory tugged at Ash's mind, and she stepped forward, her arms out, placing her body between Natalie and Len. "Wait. Let's hear him out."

"You *believe* this asshole?" Natalie said, her voice full of heartbreak.

"You weren't there," Ash said. "The weapon—it messed with my mind. I wanted the doc to shut it down, but she wouldn't."

Len ran his hand through his hair. "Right. I heard things, too. I don't remember what, but I remember how I felt. I was *scared*. I don't get scared."

"So how did you get away?" Ash said.

"I stepped outside to take a piss and figure things out," he said. "And that's when I saw them. Five of them, wearing black, hauling guns, and so I lifted my talkie to comm someone for air support, and that's when I realized I didn't know who to call. And you had just left, so I thought it might have been an evac—"

"I would never—" Natalie started.

"No, listen. The doc could have hauled out the back, but she said she wouldn't leave the weapon. That it was too important, that someone had to get away so they could tell Aurora about what happened. So I put the card in the unicorn and ran, so if I was captured, they wouldn't get the data. I knew that one of you would get the *Alien Attack Squad* reference, at least."

Ash shook her head. "She tell you why she wouldn't leave?"

He breathed out. There was a dark shudder in his halting breath, a muted wheeze. "No. They just firebombed the place. They knew exactly where to go, what to do, how to hold the weapon, even brought their own quarantine isolette. So, you'll understand why I thought it was you—"

Natalie spat on the ground, then turned for the barn. "It was Ramsay who screwed us over. You remember Ramsay?"

He nodded slowly. "So she has the weapon."

Natalie's jaw clenched. "Whatever Company she's working for, it has some sort of connection with Manx-Koltar. Ramsay didn't make her move until we fixed the ansible, and Solano put a *damn move on* when he found out. From what we could piece together on the *London,* some information was released from the buffer that . . . changed things. For her. For Solano."

"Solano. He's . . . the boss?"

"You don't remember *anything* about Aurora, do you," Natalie said, but didn't wait for an answer or a comment, just walked over to where the screamer husk lay on the dark ground. She squatted and polished the surface with her thumb. "Like I thought. One and done. Let's call *Rio* and tell them the situation's clear."

"It's not clear," Len said.

"What do you mean?" said Ash.

"Look inside," he responded. "That's what I thought you were coming for. The weapons."

Natalie exchanged glances with Ash and stood, walking into the barn with her flashlight on. Ash nodded at Len, and Len shoved his hands into his pockets, entering the barn in front of her. They made it three steps in before Natalie raised her hand.

"Nope. Both of you, stay right over there. Don't even get near these things."

The barn resembled what Ash had once thought a colonial farm might look like: packed to the brim with bales and crates, maglev carts, broken equipment and scattered tools, all covered with the thinnest layer of burgundy dust from when the atmo-spinners on the outside of the hub had begun their inevitable failure.

Most interesting were the ten weapons crates piled haphazardly and just inside the door—the kind of weapons crates they'd had on *Twenty-Five.* Natalie stowed her flashlight in her belt and stood, unlatching them one by one, looking inside. Her frown grew deeper.

"Screamers. One-use screamers. Hundred-and-eighty-degree

deployment, half-mile range. All of them have the same fucking screamers in them. And they're fucking *live*. What the hell do farmers need with this many kinetics?" Natalie said.

"Farmers don't," Ash said. "But these are on the Christmas list."

"What were you doing in here?" Natalie asked.

Len pointed to the corner, where a plain cot was set up next to an open first-aid kit and a large tin of ready-to-eat settler meals. Next to the cot was a scattering of tools and what looked like the heart of an ansible, divorced from its comm tower and controller. "I was working on the ansible. I didn't know who I was going to call. Just that I had to call someone, if I was going to live."

Ash crossed her arms. "And what happened after the attack? Did they know you were missing?"

"Yeah," he said. "I couldn't find you guys, couldn't stay in the city. When I got to the shuttle, it was gone. I found a ranger station on the edge of town that was running its own solar equipment. Connected to the colony systems. That's how I found out the atmospinners were still rolling out here, so I thought there might still be food, too."

"Was the maglev working?" Natalie said.

Len paused. Coughed. "I walked the track. Twelve miles."

"Without atmospinners."

"I'm not going to assume I came out of it all right," he said. He coughed again. His hand came away spattered with red blood.

Natalie closed her eyes and turned away.

"Nat," he said, turning toward her, "you have to forgive me."

Natalie placed the top on the crate and pushed it back to a stable position, rolling her eyes, moving on to the next one, checking the interior with her flashlight and her munitions-steady hands. "Fuck off. Before I shoot you. Because I sure ain't forgiving you. How many years are you going to have to give to pay for those lungs, Len?"

Len narrowed his eyes. "Did you hear me? I was afraid for my life."

"You could have stayed in town," she said.

"I'll have to put a few more years on my account, yeah. But, Natalie—"

"You kill all of those people, then you kill any chance you— you and me—"

Ash stepped between them. "Stop. Both of you."

"Says the *fucking* liar," Natalie said. She was shaking. Incandescent.

"He's *family*."

"He's not acting like it."

Ash sighed. "We're all just going to calm down for a minute," she announced. "Natalie, take a walk. Len, once both your tempers are back in control, we'll figure out what to do next."

Natalie stuck her head back in the crate. Len's eyes misted, then he turned back to Ash, blinking quickly. "I knew you'd—"

"I didn't do it for you."

He paled.

"I *want* to believe you," she said, then pushed off, walking over to the machine. She squatted, then poked at the innards. It was Aurora-standard and missing a few parts; nothing Len couldn't fix with spit and glue and luck and a few more days. "But there's a problem, Len. You *lived* through that screamer—"

Her voice caught on the words *like me,* on the terror they implied, and she did not say them.

"Oh. That, I can explain," he said, picking up his flashlight and pointing it to a dark corner of the barn. He tilted his head, and Ash followed, and Natalie, too, picking up the rear, an angry, walking thunderstorm. He kicked away a piece of plywood. It covered a machine-cut hole in the ground, dripping tiny roots in a well-packed wall. Natalie leaned over and hauled the plywood completely aside, revealing a set of metal stairs clambering down to a second set of crates and, like a urinal in a ballroom, a metal, card-locked door embedded in the wall.

"You escaped the screamer's dome dispersal by going *down,*" Natalie said. She sounded oddly touched. "You were listening to my stupid lectures."

"I found the ansible parts there. I'm thinking we should check out the door, but I didn't want to go down without backup," he said.

Ash wanted to say, *No, we need to wait for the Company, they can sort it out, we can't go below*—I *can't go below,* but Natalie was already heading for the stairs, her jaw set in quiet assurance.

"Come on," she said. "You need a crapload of credit for your cit account, Len. Let's go find out why a bunch of farmers had enough Vai shit to kill an entire squad."

# 18

Len and Natalie clambered into the basement, their boots making a loud clatter on the dusty metal stairs. Ash found herself hovering near the top, her knuckles white with a sudden, clawing fear.

"You coming, Ash?" said Len.

"Just a second," she managed.

She'd spent enough time underground to pause at the soaking humidity of the room, the tight-packed dirt floor, and the rotting joists in the ceiling, made of local wood. There were crates here, slicked in moisture and mildew. She'd lived in rooms like this. She'd lost Christopher to a room like this. Going back into a room like this was the last thing she wanted to do.

From her perch at the top of the stairs, she could see the shine of the steel door in the blue-edged light, and the two engineers squatting nearby, poking at the lock.

"Typical gene-coded citizen bullshit. Auroran as hell, though, and that means we can use the Christie hack on it," Natalie pronounced, then slid a slim tool she'd once called an uncoupler into the works. Ash blinked at the resulting sparks, but Natalie looked like she'd been expecting them.

"You never tried to get in?" she asked.

"I was curious," said Len. He peered over her shoulder. "To be honest, though, I was more concerned with getting the ansible running."

"Yeah, I know how that goes," muttered Natalie.

Ash took a deep, shuddering breath of the sulfur-scented air, then descended, one step at a time, keeping her eyes trained on her toes. She made an attempt to banish the irrational fear to the place she'd put everything else. *It's no different than being in space,* she reminded herself. *You go outside the room, you suffocate. No different at all.*

It somehow made her feel worse.

Len nodded. "This was where I'd found ansible parts—in the crate over there. It's all high-level electronics, spaceflight components, nothing an ag-center should have really needed. Oh, and baby blankets."

"Baby blankets?" said Ash.

"Laid right out on top."

"Like they were hiding what was inside."

Len tilted his head. "That's certainly one explanation."

Natalie swore at the lock while Ash crossed to the crate, flipping open the lid. She couldn't identify the parts by sight, but she could tell some weren't Auroran. Some were painted with half-faded InGen logos, while others sported the far too familiar Wellspring moon and fountain.

The textiles in question were nearby; they resembled the rough, uncitizen-issue blankets of her childhood. These were printed with Auroran logos and embroidered with rough black thread in a mean attempt at personalization: stick-figure children with simple, black-thread smiles, and below them, the words *Arcadia Birthright Orphan Wellness Center 1.*

She shivered and dropped the blanket back on the crate just as Natalie crowed her victory over the lock. Len pushed the door open, and a rancid stench rushed into the storage space. Len gagged, while Natalie pinched her nose, stumbled to her feet, and shone the flashlight into the dark space beyond.

It could have been any waiting room for any Company, with prefab plasteel walls and plain white paint. Ash saw chairs installed against the near wall, and a thick metal door on the opposite end with an unfamiliar locking system. In front of that was a plain white receptionist's desk, the kind that were shipped on supply runs in their flat-packed dozens.

Behind the desk was a dead receptionist in a black jumpsuit, his jaw akimbo, his bony hand still wrapped around a dead bolt-gun.

"Waiting for *Rio* is a shitty game with way too high a body count," Natalie whispered.

They shuffled in place for a moment.

"Let's find out what he was guarding." Natalie broke the silence, brandishing the uncoupler and heading toward the door. Len's eyes lingered on the body, and he picked up the flashlight, moving to join her.

Ash turned back to the dead man, feeling a strange compulsion to ensure that he was dead of a clear and explainable cause, that he'd been shot or stabbed, or that he'd fallen asleep from some kind of gas exposure, that he had no jagged crack in his rib cage. She couldn't tell until she was entirely too close for comfort.

"He still has a heart," Ash said.

"Figuratively?" asked Len. "Or, um, you don't mean . . ."

He trailed off, like he didn't want to know the answer, and Ash obliged him. She drew a finger across the desk, tracing a line in a thick layer of dirt. Her nail caught the corner of a half-buried flimsy, and she shook it free. It was a shipment manifest for medicines and isolette supplies, topped by an unfamiliar black logo: an arrow crossed with a palm branch on a field of stars.

"This should be working," Len said.

"Well, it's not." Natalie's voice was tight and angry. "Just give me the uncoupler."

"It's not either of us," he said. "It's the nonstandard wiring."

"Gimme. And hold the light steady."

Len adjusted his grip on the flashlight, and Ash's eyes were caught by a sudden glimmering around the dead man's neck—a plain silver chain with a pendant dragging at the bottom. Curious, she trapped it between two fingernails, fishing it out from underneath his black jacket, managing to avoid his rotting skin.

She flipped it toward the light, and recognized a twin of the necklace Natalie had left on the captain's body: some variety of female saint, holding arrows in one hand and palm branches in the other. Ash turned it over to check the lettering, and found the logo on the manifests below, and block-letter capitals: *SACRAMENT SOCIETY*.

"It's not going to work," Len muttered, breaking through Ash's reverie. "You're thinking about gene-activated circuits. That's a tri-d pattern lock, and it's wired into a system on the other side."

"So we should be able to fuck up those circuits and—"

Len sighed. "You can take down the lock, but the door still won't open. You need the pattern it wants to recognize."

"And it could be anything."

"Absolutely anything."

Ash ran her finger over the pendant, feeling the rough pattern of the woman and her strange load against the pad of her thumb. "What about an oval, say, the size of your thumb?"

Len tilted his head, shone the light into the lockworks to check, then nodded. "Yeah. That'll do it. Why do you ask?"

Ash reached behind the man's neck, undoing the clasp. It popped with unexpected ease, and she crossed the room in two quick strides, sliding the pendant into the open mouth of the lock. The red light flipped to green, and she heard tumblers moving behind the door.

"Because he was the guard," she said. "He stayed here until the end. He probably did that for a good reason."

Len tried the door handle, and the door opened with a deafening creak. Ash and the others walked onto a small metal balcony set at least one story above a massive dirt cavern. Long and deep, the massive cathedral ceiling was supported by prefab rafters

that curved like the ribs of a dead whale. The whole place was lit
from below in shades of sunshine and blood.

The light was coming from dozens of pulsing isolettes—
similar to the ones they'd brought to Tribulation, but in different
sizes and colors, arranged in lines like benches in a mess hall.
Empty protein wrappers lay scattered hither and yon.

Ash paused just inside the door, letting a sudden assault of
dizziness settle into her bones, battling a sudden, blank dread.

"Wait," Natalie said. "Are those *InGen* isolettes? *Awesome*. I
haven't seen those since we salvaged Aucrin Station. I keep on
telling R&D we need to reverse-engineer their signal-blocking
code."

And then she was down the stairs in a shot, with Len behind
her. Loath to let either of them see her waver, Ash picked her
careful way down the staircase. Isolettes were as crucial for salvage work as they were for medical purposes, and she recognized Aurora's bright blue light among the other colors—purple
and orange, chartreuse and ocher. Each isolette was connected
to snakelike power cords that bunched together and ran underneath the lines to several unfamiliar generators and—probably,
if she was remembering right—a server. They whirred along as if
there had been no Vai attack, no war, nothing to see and nothing
to worry about.

"Guys," said Natalie, her fingers trailing across the plastic
covering of one of the InGen Company isolettes. "This is the
*Christmas list*. The entire Christmas list."

Feeling weak and dizzy, Ash walked toward the first row
of light-splayed isolettes and peered inside, lingering just long
enough to recover what was left of her equilibrium. Here in Au
roran isolettes, purring and clicking and breathing, were unfamiliar Vai molecular weapons in configurations Ash had never
imagined. She saw pulsing red cords, breathing fire that did not
catch; moon-shaped crescents with razor-sharp edges that crackled

with an absinthe glow; crooked assemblages that resembled guns and crosses and computers and goats; smooth white capsules and rough silver boxes; acoustic squares that could crush bodies like drink tubs, all contained in boxes spitting angry light like an intensive care for the devil's newborn children.

Len shook his head. "What's the Christmas list?"

Natalie's mouth twisted at that, and she went to speak, but Ash jumped in first. "If this were the Christmas list, none of us would have gotten within light-years of this place. We'd be picking through mech guts on Glaive," she said.

"Right. It's obviously not Mr. Solano's." Natalie waved at the isolettes. "Half of these are from other companies—InGen, Rimworld, even some from Bay-Ken. Aurora would rather go belly-up than partner up. With anyone."

"Still, though. This must have taken years to arrange," Ash said, surveying the expanse, its flickering lights and fat cables tied together like taut muscles. "Like, 'back when the colony was founded' years. That's the only way they'd get away with this kind of construction project."

"Unless *everyone* noticed," Natalie said.

"*Everyone?*" Len said.

Natalie paused in front of a InGen isolette, peered in, and shuddered at what she saw there. "If the entire settlement was in on it, I mean."

Len blinked. "That's a huge accusation. The level at which you'd have to suborn an accountancy to hide such a massive conspiracy—it's just mad how hard that would be."

Ash looked back down to the necklace still in her hand. The cavern reminded her of the great halls in the catacombs of Bittersweet, carved by decades of indentured workers with mining lasers and massive machines, curled back vein by vein and stone by stone. She still felt the rumble of it in her dreams.

Some of those new halls had been sealed off and devoted to

projects with dramatic names. One of them had taken Christopher, had sent him back with tremors and hallucinations and dreams of death. And still she hadn't thought of asking.

No. She'd *thought*. She'd just been too scared.

"They knew," she said, finally. "You don't excavate a place like this and chalk it up to earthquakes. But they were all indentures. When the alternative is losing progress on your indenture, you learn to stay quiet. You learn to stop asking about the weird shit."

Len nodded, suddenly solemn. "The people that knew, then. Why didn't they come back?"

Natalie hummed. "We're assuming they got away when Manx-Koltar showed up. They probably died in the war. They obviously had accomplices elsewhere that left clues about Tribulation—otherwise, Ramsay wouldn't have bothered us, right? But she didn't know shit about this place. We're the only ones who know." She paused, and her eyes went wide. "We're going to be so rich."

"If we get out of here alive," Len said.

"I'll make an inventory." Natalie's voice held an eager, almost religious reverence. She looked around, picking up a crumpled paper from the floor while Len fished a marker out of his tool belt.

Ash turned back to the weapons, fighting off the beginnings of a headache and a faint whispering of anonymous voices. She wondered if the others could see the weapons breathe, or if that was her own celestium damned problem. The one closest to her was a pulsing, shimmering golden crescent, laid out in an isolette with the bulky curves of the transport crates she'd seen on Bittersweet. She leaned in, and the voices grew louder. They were joined by nervous visions, of flickering colors in the darkest parts of her mind, screams that stank of sulfur and loam and blood. Memories. *Bittersweet.*

She staggered back, caught in a wave of fear and exhaustion.

"You all right, Ash?" Len said. He stood next to Natalie, six feet away.

"Fine," she lied, swallowing against a dry throat. "Just some memories. This one looks like it might be from Wellspring, that's all."

"See if you can get in," said Natalie.

Ash placed her fingers on the interface, which popped up on contact, and was comforted by the familiarity. She couldn't forget this orange color, this familiar, stabbing memory: the color of the Bittersweet sun reflecting off the desert sand, the shade of refined celestium, the moon and fountain that was emblazoned on every Wellspring uniform, stitched in orange above every indentured heart.

She'd used this interface to label hundreds of canisters of raw celestium on Bittersweet. The full metadata was easy to find: *Unnamed Crescent Weapon. Origin: Baylor-McKenna 8-A sample 124. Found unused at Bittersweet. Ship to: Main Lab. Director: Dr. Reva Sharma.*

*Wait,* she thought.

Blood rushed to her head, throwing her into a dizzy swirl. She felt anger—no, not anger, something else, a deeper kind of pain, the same sort of inchoate agony she'd felt when Ramsay first played her hand, when she'd clutched at dead Christopher while the fighters wailed above, when she'd still thought that decency was something to be found and cherished.

Ash's head ached with sudden dark conspiracies.

"The doctor," she said. "What was she doing before she joined up with *Twenty-Five*? Before you came to help with the wreckage at Bitter—"

She looked up. The others weren't listening; they stood over a set of isolettes bathed in white, two stark, silent statues clothed in glaring light. Something was wrong. They never acted like this, never lingered so long in quietude. Len's hand was shaking where it barely held the marker; Natalie's covered her mouth. They stared dizzily into an isolette, their faces white from the glaring light. Ash pushed off the table where she was and walked closer.

"It's an inversion cube," Natalie finally said. Her voice was measured, calm. Too calm. "Starts inside. With your nucleotides. But that—that—"

"That," whispered Len.

"Ash, don't," Natalie said, putting her hand up to stop Ash, but Ash was too close, and she saw the beating human heart, and all the thoughts in her head screeched to a quick, nauseous halt.

The heart was lying next to a half-breathing, coal-black square molecular, impaled on a piece of surgical equipment glistening in the wet confines of the quarantine box, the chambers contracting and expanding like the thing were still nestled close inside someone's chest. The flaps of the artery were ragged and torn, as far from surgical as Ash could imagine. The whole thing was fitted onto a clear tubed apparatus that fed blood into blank black notches carved into the weapon's exterior.

She followed the passage of the blood into the weapon and out again, back to the heart, and back to the weapon; sickened, mesmerized, she stayed there until Natalie grabbed at her arm and forced her gaze toward the next one.

The next isolette was similar—and the next, and the next— weapons of death hooked up to evidence of it, slammers and sounders and screamers being fed with clotting blood, bags of it, fed into sickened, exhausted human body parts. She saw beating enlarged hearts, shivering, shrunken kidneys, cirrhotic livers and, most horrific, entire circulatory systems that looked like they'd been ripped from human hands and torsos and legs, laid out in the careful, recognizable treelike pattern of what had once been life.

Farther down the line, the biological matter—Ash couldn't bear to think about it as tissue that used to be men and women, as parts that used to be people, not in an Auroran lab—became less and less recognizable; the tissue took on a grayish discoloration, and Ash, with her limited knowledge of battlefield medicine, was no longer able to recognize the organs, the circulatory patterns—if nerves were what they were, muddied and slippery with fluid.

"The man who killed Captain Valdes talked about samples," Natalie said. "Is this what he meant?"

"What the hell is this one?" Len whispered.

"Check the interface. She's labeled them all. See for yourself," Ash said, and then moved toward it herself. These were the blue-and-gold rounded buttons of the Aurora ships that had been her home, given her friends, granted her hope, helped her build a future from a world she thought was dust. One more quiet betrayal, in a life that had far too many of them.

*Inversion Cube, Black. Origin: Wellspring-Bittersweet 10-B. Never used. Undergoing Secondary Gene-Twisted Tests. Director: Dr. Reva Sharma.*

Ash had seen dead bodies. She'd seen rockslides split open a woman to her intestines, had seen the surprised, twisted mouths of the poor space-burned victims on the ships she'd been tasked to salvage. But tragic as it was, the rumble of an earthquake, the impact of a cruise missile, atmosphere venting from a half-breached hull: those were unlucky, elemental, inarguable for miners like her, ordinary people caught in the teeth of extraordinary times.

This kind of death was much different. This was intentional, purposeful; this was a butcher-surgeon intimate with a knife, and a murder victim on a medical table. These were the dark years of Karner-Albion and General Spaceflight and the failed experiments meant to place humans on heavy-grav worlds, the horror stories from her history books. These were the Lost Worlds fighting back, their last breath a nuclear scream against the Vai.

These were the dark centuries, the fallen governments, the

tyrants who did not answer to shareholders. This is what she'd learned about back on the station, in the nighttime Wellspring vids at her mother's feet.

"What the hell does the doctor have to do with this?" asked Natalie.

# 19

Lit only by her flashlight and the humming, bloody transgressions that surrounded her, Natalie moved down the line of isolettes, checking each one for identifying information. Ash followed, and read *Sharma*, and then *Sharma* again, and *Sharma* a third time. One or two displayed the name of another doctor—an Aster Jessen—but most of the isolettes with accessible data belonged to experiments run by *Twenty-Five*'s missing doctor.

A quiet panic began to build in Ash's chest.

*C-6 Hornet, Gold,* she read, *Origin: Cluster 2827A. Possibly used. Undergoing Nervous Connection/Neuroglia/Meninges. Director: Dr. Reva Sharma.*

*10-A Cutter, Green. Origin: Wellspring-Bittersweet. Never used. Vascular System/Antigens AB and 0. Director: Dr. Reva Sharma.*

"What the hell are meninges?" Natalie said.

Len stopped in front of an isolette where a golden, apple-small sphere nestled against a chunky, cirrhotic liver. He snorted in disgust.

"Ash, this can't be right," he said. "Wasn't the doc already with *Twenty-Five* when Captain Keller got the salvage contract for Bittersweet? She was on Cana cleanup, right, and then Gethsemane shuttle duty? She was nowhere near here."

Ash took a deep breath, tasting mildew and loam and hating her suddenly dry throat. She drew her hands into fists, pressing her nails into her palms, hoping the pain would stop her from panicking.

"I don't know," she gulped out, fighting an abrupt, embarrassing dizziness. "Dr. Sharma was on some other captain's crew before the attack on the mine. Captain Keller noticed our team hadn't been triaged, and went back down into the tunnels to search for us. The doc was the only medic willing to go. That's how they met."

"Wait, the only one?" Natalie blinked, confused.

"We were hollowing out a new set of tunnels that week, and we didn't have the struts up yet—not that the struts would have helped." Pain yanked at Ash's back molars, and she realized she was clenching her jaw. "Wellspring didn't want Aurora filing a wrongful death claim if the tunnel collapsed on their heads, too."

*Wellspring didn't want them to find Christopher,* Keller whispered somewhere in her amygdala. *That's why he was on tunnel duty that week.*

*We don't know that.*

*Yes, we do.*

Natalie's eyes widened in disgust. "Wellspring was going to write you off. Why didn't you tell us?"

"Well, why don't you talk about Cana? I mean, *really* talk about Cana? I just—" The words evaporated as Ash fought a wave of angry fatigue. "I just wanted to move on with my life."

Natalie nodded slowly, getting the hint. "But she was on *Twenty-Five,* afterwards?"

"Yeah. Mostly. Dr. Sharma turned the cargo bay on *Twenty-Five* into a hospital deck. She saved our lives. And then it was all training on Europa. I saw Captain Keller a couple times— she was having the grav refit done and running my sponsorship paperwork. But I didn't see Dr. Sharma again until *Twenty-Five* left for Tribulation."

*Why are you lying?* Keller whispered. *I came to see you nearly every day.*

Ash balled her fists tighter and concentrated on breathing.

"Which was months later," Len said. "That's enough time for a trip out here—"

"Let's be real, Len. You can't place *yourself* on Europa Station right now," Natalie snorted.

Ash looked down at the weapon in the isolette to her right, blinking away the bright swirl of it, letting the light burn into her retinas—anything, really, to keep the hallucinatory Kate Keller locked up tight in whatever closet the trihex shots had originally put her in. It was bad enough Ash was barely keeping it together, dealing with this stupid panic and this shuddering room full of nightmares. She didn't need Natalie realizing she was having symptoms, too.

"Just check the confirmation dates." The words rushed out of Ash's mouth. "Aurora's isolettes will have them. Wellspring's, too."

Len frowned as Ash ducked back around to the WellCel machine she'd originally been using. The interface ID was still active, and with a few quick motions, she brought up the date the experiment's information had originally been entered.

"Holy shit," Ash said. Her stomach flipped.

Natalie whistled. "This is—"

"Dated a year and a half before the Gethsemane massacre," Ash finished.

"Not possible," Len said. "Gethsemane was first contact. That was the first time anyone had ever heard of real aliens, let alone their goddamned murder weapons."

"Unless it wasn't the first time," said Ash.

She locked eyes with the others, all of them caught still and cold with the heresy she'd just uttered. Ash's heart thudded in her chest, and she took a step back, her stomach a tight, nauseous knot.

"It would explain why the war got so violent so fast," Len said, his voice low. "If the war was already going on, and Gethsemane was an escalation."

Natalie moved to another isolette. "Does it matter? The Vai wanted to kill us. We defended ourselves."

"You ever wonder why they wanted to kill us?" said Len.

"They're aliens. I don't know. Do I look like a philosopher to you?"

Len narrowed his eyes. "Don't fall back on this 'I'm a dumbass soldier' bullshit, Natalie, not to me. You're better than that."

"Don't treat me like a child," she snapped.

Dizzy and uncomfortable, Ash let them fight. She closed her eyes, trying to remember the dreamlike, terrible days around the massacre at Gethsemane. She remembered watching the community uplinks in the miners' lounge, the sweep of silver alien mech-wings and the first glance of weapons that spat black fire and golden death. She watched the drone footage of the massacre site with Christopher, held his hand as the headlines uttered the words that changed her world. She'd felt small, insignificant, and terribly confused.

*Aliens are real.* She'd never seen an Auroran communications associate hyperventilate during an ansible transmission before. *Auroran settlement at Gethsemane destroyed by alien attackers. Aliens attack Barricade Station. Aliens attack Grenadier. Aliens attack Cana.*

And, inevitably: *Aliens attack Bittersweet.*

"Ash," Natalie said. "Are you okay?"

Ash opened her eyes, wiping cold sweat away from her upper lip. "Fine. So she knew?"

"She knew." Len had moved away toward the front of the room, and indicated the three lines of isolettes near the door they figured led to the administrative wing. "She was here before Gethsemane, at least, and for some time afterwards. She could have come on any of the colony supply ships. But the planet was under interdiction after the war. The only way to get back would have been a work ship. *Twenty-Five*."

"So which Company was in charge of this bullshit, do you think?" Natalie said. "There's an awful lot of crap from InGen here."

"You assume that CEOs were running this, but these people were like us," Len said, his hand making a quiet arc over the rest of the room. "When you're doing salvage, you work with what you have, right? This is all salvage engineering: Manx-Koltar parts with this Wellspring bit, this Armour framework paired with an InGen logic board. They were working with what they could get."

Natalie shook her head. "But then—dozens of people must have been complicit. Hundreds, even. I mean, you'd need executives who could sign off on shipment deliveries in all of these companies. The indentures who ran the maglev had to know. And, come on, these farmers must have noticed different procedures. Like you said outside. The level of collusion would be unprecedented."

"So is the Sacrament Society," said Ash.

She fumbled in her pocket for the necklace. She turned her hand palm-up, then let the necklace slither into the palm of her hand. It shimmered in the shivering, gory light. She looked down at the saint standing on the skin of the earth, the arrows, the palm branches.

"Shit," said Natalie, closing her eyes. "We can't even tell the executives about this, can we? Until we figure out which ones are traitors."

"I doubt they see themselves as traitors," said Ash, thinking of businesslike Sharma on *Twenty-Five*, scanning her broken ribs, telling Ash she was *home now,* that *everything was going to be fine*.

Len sighed. "Dr. Sharma was always so nice to me."

Natalie stared at him. "Yeah, well. Everyone's nice as fuck until market share's on the line."

"Look," Len said, shaking his head. "I get that you're mad at me for what happened upstairs, Natalie, but I'm done fighting with you. I'm going to try to open the door to the administrative wing while you calm down. Maybe that's where we'll find this 'Main Lab.'"

"Take your time," muttered Natalie.

The engineer nodded and moved off, and Natalie looked back down to the interface, her body a nervous, angry perpetual motion machine. Her fingers moved, thin and shaking, bringing up more data, more dates, more history. The light from the silver weapon below caught her unkempt hair and her sour face.

"Nat—" Ash began.

"You think you know people," she said, after a moment, not meeting Ash's eyes. "You think you work with someone for six months, a year, stand by them in the black and the cold. You think you know them."

Ash hesitated. *She means Ramsay,* she thought. *And Sharma. Not me or Len.*

"You know the captain," Ash said. "So let's think about what she would do."

Natalie tapped her finger against her chin. "She'd wonder about the profit advantage from running such a massive, dangerous experiment, which means the people in charge of this madhouse thought the outcomes were worth some pretty severe risk. So, if we're sticking with Auroran thinking, because Dr. Sharma's Auroran, what's the first thing the manual tells you to do when you find another Company's technology and there's no mutual return treaty?"

Ash thought back to basic salvage training. "You reverse-engineer it."

Natalie nodded. "Right. The only major thing we know about Vai moleculars is that they have some sort of biological trigger. We only have battlefield experience to go on, so we don't know if it's skin contact or something else. Hell, maybe you fart on it."

"And the profit motive?" said Ash.

"Oh, shit, yes. Imagine the profit if you were first on the market with weapons that could kill the Vai."

She took off, and Ash followed her down the line to an older Auroran isolette. It held a Vai weapon connected to a smattering of striated, variegated tissue, ending in what looked to Ash to be some sort of artery. The whole setup pulsed with a silver fluid that resembled the liquid celestium shipped out from the Bittersweet refinery. The weapon was a sweeping gold crescent, small enough to fit in her palm. It had hard lines and spoke in a sweet voice, slipping behind her ears and into her mind as if it were standing behind her, a comforting friend.

She blinked and swallowed and tried not to listen.

*It's just my illness,* she said. *Just panic. That's all it is. I'm underground and nervous as hell that the ceiling's going to fall in and I'm stuck in the nads of a massive conspiracy. That's all.*

"I don't *exactly* know how this one works," Natalie said, "but this crescent form usually means it'll evaporate any organic matter within a particular radius, kind of like the blue screamer, but worse. I'd bet you a bottle of the captain's whiskey that this is a test to figure out which part of the body makes the weapon work: the circulatory system, the nervous system, lymph nodes—"

Ash swallowed acid. "They're assuming the aliens have any of these things."

"It's a big assumption, sure," Natalie said. "But, you gotta remember, science is science out here or in Vai space: for a bomb, you need a charge, a payload, a detonator. A trigger. Kinetics, well. That just takes an impact. Vai moleculars just have . . . well, think of it as a Company-specific trigger, but with blood. Or genes. Or spit. Or the alien equivalent of that. We just don't know."

Ash nodded. "Which is why the Vai need to be present for it to go off."

Natalie looked at the weapon with grim determination, and then started to unseal the top of the isolette. "Time to do some science of our own. It's a molecular, so I should be able to unhook this one without setting it off, and we can look at the guts of the experiment and what it's trying to do."

Ash grabbed for Natalie's wrists. "No way. Not after what happened upstairs."

"I know," Natalie said. "It's a molecular. That was a kinetic."

"We can check when *Rio* gets here. They have specialists."

The other woman snorted. "I *am* a specialist."

"You have a *concussion*."

Natalie narrowed her eyes and lowered her voice. "You're one to talk. Something something *degraded neural pathways*, Ash."

"Just tell me what to do."

The younger woman bit down on her bottom lip and paused. "Fine. Okay. What we need to do is test the attachment point to see if the arterial's permanently fused, or whether we can remove that adhesive, there."

Ash moved in closer as Natalie pressed the disconnect switches, sliding the top of the isolette open and exposing the inner workings of the experiment to the dank air of the cave. Everything seemed intact. The battery-powered nodes were still pumping silver liquid from the arterial to the weapon. And the weapon hummed, it sang, it—

She heard kind whispers.

*Shut up, Kate,* Ash thought.

Keller's ghost did not respond.

The crescent weapon shimmered, soothing and gold, as if it were a jewel or a bar of soap or a stone glistening on the side of an alien river. Ash hesitated for a moment, reached in and pressed her index finger to the curve of the plastic equipment near the arterial.

The weapon lit up, starbright, and whined. Light poured through her fingers in gracious beams.

*Sweet sister,* the weapon said.

Ash snapped her hand back. "Um."

Natalie blinked, reverent and horrified. "Do it again, Ash."

Ash responded by slamming the switch that slid the isolette top back into place.

"Do what again?" Len said, arriving back with a microspanner cradled in his hand. His eyes darted from Ash to the still-whirring isolette. "You didn't fucking *open* that, did you?"

"Dr. Julien was right," Natalie whispered. "Fuck. Fuck!" Her hand came down hard on the bench, causing Ash and Len to jump.

Ash's stomach ached. The dizzy terror returned in seconds, storm-surge sure. She backed up, eyeing the staircase that led to the sulfur air. "I'm not a light switch."

"No, you're a Vai," Natalie spat.

"Wait a minute." Len put a wide-splayed hand between Ash and the door. "Nobody's going anywhere until someone explains this to me."

Ash gulped for air, pushing at him. "Let me by, Len."

"She's a fucking *Vai,* I made a joke about it in the forest, shit—"

Len kept his voice reasonable. "That's a pretty big accusation."

Natalie ignored him, and focused on Ash with bright, angry eyes. "We know you're different. You *walked away* from that blue screamer. The doctor on *Rio* saw nanotech in your blood. Maybe the reason none of us have seen a Vai is because they can't be seen, because they *look like us.* Fuck, maybe the Sacrament Society are the good guys—"

Len clearly believed none of it. He dropped his hand, watching Natalie like he might if she'd been holding her boltgun and pointing it at him. "Okay, guys, this is bullshit. We're done here. Let's go upstairs and wait for *Rio*."

"Tell him," Natalie spat. "Tell him what *really* happened."

Ash stumbled over all of the things she wanted to say. "Don't make me."

"Tell him, or I will."

Ash eyed the door and thought about running, but Len had softened a little, and she was tired of lying to him. "I—" She balled her fists again. The pain felt sweet. "I thought it was celestium sickness. I've had it since I left Bittersweet. I thought I had years to go, that I'd become a citizen. Get treatment. I didn't know it was anything more until I got to *Rio* and talked to the doctor there."

Len's face darkened into disbelief. He rubbed at the stubble on his chin. "While we were working together. Did the captain know?"

Ash bit her lip rather than respond.

He stepped away from her, dragging his hands through his hair. Ash's eyes caught on the stubble of Len's brown beard, the terrified, sharp line of his jaw. "I need a second."

"Len, I'm sorry."

"Yeah," he said, "me, too."

A yawning silence descended.

"*You're* the trigger," said Natalie.

The ordnance engineer was a sudden flurry of motion, moving back over to Ash, stepping in front of her, shining light into her eyes, staring at them like a bad impression of a Company physical. A sudden headache flared behind Ash's forehead, and she pawed at the flashlight. "Stop—"

"Vai moleculars are always on, just waiting for their trigger. If that's what they were trying to do here—figure out how to trigger the *London* weapon— " She shone the flashlight at Len. "This could change everything, Ash. We figure out what happened to you, and we could stand a chance against the Vai."

"No," she said, immediately

"We could bring the war to them," Natalie said. "We could win."

Ash closed her eyes and tried to think about what *winning* would look like. All she saw were bodies. Hearts. Livers. Blood. Stones, fallen from above, crushing Christopher's chest, blood pooling at his neck. Marley, taken apart by light, breathing one moment and gone the next. Natalie, bloodstained and snarling.

"You don't *win* a war," Ash whispered, stumbling backward, away from the offending light. She looked around for an exit, for the staircase leading to the dead receptionist's room, for the sulfur air.

Len reached forward and grabbed at Ash's wrist, to stop her, but he was speaking to Natalie. "If what Ash is saying is true, the only way to save Ash is to bomb this place. Make it look like the shuttle crash took it out."

"*Save* her?" Natalie slid the flashlight back into her belt, and the beam cast harsh, dark shadows on her face. "What about saving Aurora? Or do the two of you want to start over somewhere else? Are you just dying to go back to the dole?"

"You're so damned young," he said, gravel in his words. He grimaced, rubbing at his temples. "There'll be a war, all right, but it'll start right at home. You have no idea what it was like before the Vai, before the intercompany treaty. You two were still on the dole for the last Company war. You don't remember what it's like for humans to kill other humans. You like weapons, Natalie? Well, this is the fucking arms race of the century, and we're all going to be meat on a bayonet. I know that's not what you want."

Natalie's shoulders stiffened, and she said nothing. Ash couldn't breathe.

"You don't want that," said Len. His eyes were dark and haunted. "Any of it."

"You didn't tell me," she said.

Len looked away. "This is *Twenty-Five*. Nobody talks about anything."

*The Company war.* Ash shivered. Wellspring had always won the Company wars. Company wars had meant bonus days at the wellness center, ice cream on the promenade, and afternoons in the park. It wasn't until she was on *Twenty-Five,* working the wrecks, that it had occurred to her that war was terrible.

*I have to know,* she thought.

Natalie was talking, now, and Len, too—but she heard louder voices in the margins, in the isolettes, in the tussocks of alien clay shivering above, and they wanted her to *listen.* Ash ran her hands over the edges of the isolette, pressing the disconnect switches. She heard the top of the isolette loosen with a click and a hiss, and the sterile walls gave way once more.

She looked down at the beating heart, the ragged place where the human tissue met cloudy plastic tubing. The heart slowed. The machine ground to a halt. The blood moving through the Vai weapon became viscous and still. The isolette was of Wellspring make, as familiar as the plates in her childhood apartment, her first orange jumpsuit, the chained hope she felt upon signing the indenture agreement.

*I have to know if I'm the trigger.*

Dirt and stone became fear and shame and anger, dripping down the walls in lurid reds and yellows. The ground below her rumbled, reaching in bone-rattling shudders up her legs and arms and throat. The weapon sang as she slid her hand against its smooth golden curve, lifting it from the isolette. The blood vessels it had been connected to gasped once, twice more, and putrid, silver-clotted blood puddled on the bottom of the box.

Like the screamer, the weapon seemed to exist not just in her hands but right under her skin, in her ears, in her mind. The heat was uncomfortable, but it did not burn her fingertips. The light was as bright as a supernova, but her eyes were bathed in blessed black. The weapon whined in its desperation to burst apart. It whispered without words, showed her vast, burning vistas, alien stations ablaze, spoke of revenge, wailed in mourning for the hundreds and thousands of ancestors, milk-white eyes stilled and gone. She saw herself above all of it, her body long and white, her fingers thin, her vision expansive, and she felt a searing pain like she'd never felt before. Death.

*No, more than death—*

"Okay, Ash," Natalie said. "You can put it down now."

"I don't think I can," Ash whispered.

Natalie's hand twitched near her gun. The strain made her voice tighten. "Put it down."

Ash pushed her hand back into the isolette, and her stomach cramped with the effort of letting it go, a spasm of loneliness flooding her fingers at the very thought of it, and when Ash placed the golden crescent back in its hell-sworn bed, she felt an ache like the aftermath of a gunshot to the heart.

Satisfied, Natalie turned around and stalked off to the door of the administrative wing. Len hovered for a moment, his face a rictus of fear tinged with dark sympathy, then hurried to follow. "Come on," he said, and turned away.

The crescent was back in Ash's hand before she knew what she was doing. The weapon sang, dazzled, swirled on her palm. She closed her hand around it, feeling truly warm for the first time in weeks, and when Natalie told her to hurry up, she slid it into her jacket pocket.

*Everything is fine,* it told her, *now that you are with me.*

It chilled her to the bone.

# 20

Keller stepped into the body of the enemy ship as if she belonged there. Beyond the door was a bright corridor, decorated with scuffed lines of paint running down the center of the deck, military-style. The gentle, sloping curve made her think *big*, made her think *cruiser;* the shades of orange and green on the walls made her think *merged conglomerate.*

She waddled forward, holding her bladder, looking for a bathroom. With every step, the architecture became more familiar. The ship had updates and a sparkling paint job, but its bones were Armour Shipwrights, the kind they'd sold to smaller companies on both sides during the last major Company war, the kind she'd salvaged over Cana back when colonial corporations were working together instead of stabbing each other in the back.

*And if this is an Armour cruiser, two intersections and a turn should get me to a junction, which means there'll be a main sewage line running behind there, and a bathroom—*

She hurried, hearing voices, and ducked into the head just as two indentures walked by, slamming the door, holding her breath. She saw two stalls, and one of the doors was closed.

"Ms. Diallo? That you?"

Scratch that. One was *occupied.* Keller dragged herself into the unoccupied stall, closing the door behind her, yanking down her pants in a near desperate motion. She'd never been so happy to find a bathroom, even if it was one of the zero-gee ones, even if she had to whack away half of the vacuum equipment just to use it.

Even if there was no water.

She peed, hoping beyond hope that the person in the other stall didn't notice she was wearing blue pants.

"Ms. Diallo?" the voice repeated. A man.

"No," Keller said.

"Can you get her?"

She reached for the cleanser, saying nothing.

Rustling. The door to the other stall opened. The person sharing the bathroom lingered, then spoke again.

"Are you okay in there?"

Keller pulled her pants up, but stopped just before buttoning them, her hands hovering for a moment before she yanked her pants off. She didn't like the plan coalescing behind her eyes.

She didn't like what she needed to do. She didn't like any of it. She'd have to do it anyway. "No," she said, then gulped down more guilt. *No, more shame.* "I'm, uh, actually feeling pretty sick."

*They wouldn't put Sharma in a brig,* Keller thought. *They'd put her with the weapon, in a lab. A lab or a medbay. But I don't remember where the medbays are on an Armour-type. C-deck? B-deck, by the engines?*

"Do you need me to call Dr. Richards?" the voice said.

Keller cleared her throat. "No, I'll walk. Where's their office again?"

The man paused. "*Eir* office." His voice had picked up a hint of suspicion. "So, yeah, I'll just call Dr. Richards for you."

Keller winced. "Just, uh—just remind me where eir office is—" She swore to herself. "Ah, shit. I'm sorry."

"I'm sorry, I don't recognize your voice. What are you doing on this deck? What's your name—"

He didn't get a chance to finish his sentence. Keller opened the door to her stall with a vicious yank and barreled forward as hard and fast as she could. The man—a few inches shorter and broader than her, blond, an indenture—barely had a second to react before Keller pushed him against the wall. His head cracked against the plasglas mirror, and he hollered in pain. Keller kneed him before he could recover. He swore at her, doubling over. She pushed his head back into the wall, and this time, he fell to the floor, insensate, a sack of forest green.

Keller pressed her fingers to his neck.

*A pulse.* She exhaled, relief shaking her shoulders. *Still alive.*

She stripped the enemy of his clothes, apologizing under her breath: green pants and a jacket, plus the same orange armband she'd seen on the man she'd killed. She buttoned the too-short jacket over her Aurora-blue shirt, tied the armband around her biceps, then hooked her arm underneath the man's shoulders, dragging him into the stall and closing the door on him.

She turned to look at herself in the mirror, straightening her hair and frowning at her broken, skewed nose, then locked the bathroom door behind her. She stiffened and walked forward, trying to look as normal as possible. Two men came up behind her; they were dressed like executives, in tight, long skirts and high heels. Absorbed in their briefcases and flimsies, they gave Keller little attention as she ducked into an open office door.

*If I'm right, there should be a crew boss office . . . there.*

The boss's office was empty, but there was plenty to rifle through: tools and manifests hung neatly on the walls, and a tech's jacket hung idle and wrinkled over the back of a chair. It looked like Len's office might have looked, if Len at any point had ever heeded her requests for him to clean up. She opened the desk drawer and picked up a faded credit chit from a Baylor-McKenna Company store.

*So this is Bay-Ken, or used to be,* she thought. *Makes sense. The green. Bay-Ken and . . . who else? Which other Company used orange? I should know this.*

The room boasted an older wall monitor at the back and a

haptic holograph on the desk; Keller had been right about the upgrades, the ship had been subject to more recent technological installations. Keller skipped the haptics and went straight to the familiar wall monitor, tapping her fingers against the slick black interface like she was still on *Twenty-Five*.

The OS was precisely what she expected from an older Armour install, and a moment's quest found the query window, where she searched for the ship's status. The computer obliged with a low, dark drone, returning the kind of basic information that would be available to any low-level requester. The ship's name was ACS *Phoenix*, and it belonged to Baylor Wellspring Consolidated, an unfamiliar Company with a very familiar logo.

Baylor's slanted sigil overlay blended with the stylized fountain of Wellspring Celestial Holdings.

Ash's old Company.

The shock wore off quickly. It made sense, really. A merger. Two companies that hadn't made it out of the wreckage of the Lost Worlds on their own, coming together to survive, purchasing a couple of Armour cruisers and going after big-ticket items to reestablish market share.

"Like a legendary zero-point battery," she muttered.

*You've probably got five minutes before the man in the bathroom wakes up*, Ash said, behind her. *You should probably figure out where they're holding Dr. Sharma.*

Adrenaline kicked Keller's body into sudden, stabbing overdrive, and she whirled. As if Ash had never died, as if this awful day was any plain Tuesday after dinner in the *Twenty-Five* mess, Ash was perched on the holodesk, one heel on the low support bar beneath her, the other crossed at the knee, her black hair swept up away from the nape of her neck. She was staring at Keller like nothing in the world was wrong.

Keller tried to speak and found that words failed her as much as her heart.

"You're dead," Keller croaked.

*And you need water,* Ash said.

The dead woman wore the orange uniform and tight-spun ponytail of the Wellspring indenture she'd met on Bittersweet, with the Company logo on her chest. This hallucination was her first memory of the woman, was Ash the day she'd met Keller on Bittersweet—the broken ex-miner with the celestium-streaked hair and the shattered heart. "This is all in my head," she whispered.

*I'm not kidding,* Ash said. *They're going to find that man, and then you're out the airlock with no suit. Get a move on.*

"What—what are you?"

Ash smiled in the way she always did—with crooked yellow teeth, infuriating, endearing. *Your own thought process, mostly.*

"So, I'm hallucinating."

Her lover's ghost shrugged. *Could be the fact that you're really fucking thirsty.*

*Could be something else.* Keller felt a jolt of unease. "I need to find Dr. Sharma."

*Yes. Before she gives up the zero-point device.*

"She would never collaborate."

Ash hopped off the holodesk and crossed the room between blinks. She hovered in front of Keller, smelling of death and metal. *Look at me,* she said. *I'm not sure you can trust what your brain is telling you.*

Keller's heart ached. "I don't care. Stay with me."

She pushed Ash's bangs back, to smooth back her hair as she'd done months ago, first in the danger of the mess but then in the quiet of her quarters, in the storage cabinets, on the bridge. But there was no heat in her skin, and no comforting human touch—all Keller felt was a draft of canned air from the environmentals in the corner. The spell broken, Ash and her crooked smile vanished like smoke out an airlock.

"I wish we'd talked about it," Keller said to the empty air.

Keller heard low talking in the corridor, and quiet, casual laughter, and she turned her back to the door, swiping some flimsies from the desk for her cover in case anyone looked inside the office, then returning her attention to the deck plan on the back interface. Once the group in the hallway passed by, she turned back to the interface and requested engineering specs: the power draws, the locked doors, all the quiet little numbers that told a captain all the stories she needed to know about where people were and what they were doing.

She smiled to herself.

There was only really one reason to lock a medbay.

She took one more look at the deck plan, memorizing it, before wiping the request clean, fixing her armband, and setting off into the hallway. She walked forward, toward the engine ring, hiding behind her bangs, holding the manifest in front of her as if she were just another nameless tech on the way to somewhere more important.

She passed a gaggle of stevedores in the hallway, then the same two executives from before; their eyes slipped over and through her. *Just another indenture,* whispered Ash.

She held her breath as they passed; she swung herself into the ship's central spine and climbed down to the engine ring, trying to hold back giddy sobs of relief.

Dropping two floors, Keller turned right and found herself in front of the medbay with the locked door. She whipped out the multi-tool in her pocket, looked both ways, and tried to remember the last time she worked an Armour door. The door clicked after a few breathless moments and slid open.

Keller was staring straight at an exhausted and stunned Reva Sharma.

# 21

Behind the door leading out of the cathedral of death, Ash found narrow hallways, stale air, the faint smell of loam and organic decay and more empty ration bar wrappers. She kicked one aside, watching it skitter to the wall. She was starving, but she knew she couldn't possibly eat, not with what she'd just seen. The very thought of eating made her stomach lurch. She covered her mouth to keep her last meal where it belonged, letting Natalie and Len take point, the symptoms of her unknown illness warring with the wear and tear of the last few months. The weapon in her pocket whirred and sang, and she drifted off for a moment, the world going blessedly foggy.

A quick tug on her sleeve brought her back. Len and Natalie were waiting for her to fall in before heading through; the sphere burned and glittered in her hand, a warm, jealous presence. *They can't know I have you. It's just for now. Just until I know what's going on,* she thought.

*Can't connect,* the voices answered. *Can't connect.*

*Connect to what?*

It hummed. *No routing to node.*

"Ash," Len said. His eyes went, nervous, to the motion of her hand. "You don't look okay."

"Sorry," she said. "I'm sorry."

"Clear," Natalie said, moving into the hallway.

Len went for his flashlight. This part of the compound was a tight, long corporate hallway that led to another scoured-out tunnel. The lights guttered above, connected to whatever solar power backup that had kept the rest of the facility running all this time. The gray walls were decorated with tasteful black-and-white landscapes. Just like the uncitizens' dorms on Wellspring where she'd grown up, there was just enough decoration to be palatable and enough blank wall to remind you to whom you belonged.

To the right were a set of office doors decorated with plain wooden slats displaying unfamiliar officials' names. The plain styling seemed to speak of every Company Ash had ever known yet implicated no Company in particular. Many of the doors were open, revealing bare desks with broken computer terminals, glass shattered against floors and walls, plastics and circuitry spilling out over thin gray throw rugs.

A few offices still had bookcases against the walls and pictures on the desks—family pictures, taken on temperate planets, featuring men and women with the healthy builds and white tattoos of birthright citizens. She thought of the picture of Christopher on her vanity on *Twenty-Five*, now less than dust.

One office had a set of ancient file cabinets, the drawers open and blackened, the ashes of flimsies and actual paper scattered all over the floor. One office seemed to have been Sharma's; Ash saw pictures of the woman ten years younger than she was on *Twenty-Five*, holding hands with another middle-aged gentleman and standing near two handsome teenagers. Next to it was a note, in Sharma's handwriting: *My Family*.

"This was a bugout," Natalie said.

"Not an assault?"

"No," she said, pointing at the terminal connections below the desks. "These were firebombed. On purpose."

Ash walked into Sharma's office, circling the desk, opening the drawers, scanning through: empty, aside from a few crumpled ration bar wrappers, someone's experimental printouts, and scattered flimsy pens. She lifted the printouts, paging through, but didn't recognize any of the scientific terminology.

Natalie popped up behind Ash, a dirty index finger pointing to the date. She'd seen the same thing. "The doc left the planet to fend for itself," Natalie said, reading the chart over Ash's shoulder. "She left them all to die and left in the shuttles. That was her we heard in the record, wasn't it? Back on *London*?"

Ash struggled to bring up her memory of the woman's voice, but found it drowned out by the horror of the dead captain's beating heart, the aching, desperate cold. "I think so."

"She left them all to die," Natalie repeated, scowling. "And M-K *knew*. They harbored Captain Valdes's killer."

"Hey, they might know just as little about this as Aurora does," Ash said. "Nothing. We're still just guessing as to who he was."

"You're presuming that Aurora is completely innocent," Len said, and the two women quieted, staring. Len shrugged at this, his face grim. His hands slipped into his pockets. "What's necessary during a war effort becomes a war crime afterwards. And you don't think people *aren't* going to kill each other over zero-point tech? It might have been the best decision she could have made. If she couldn't get back under the radar, maybe, or if she couldn't find her coconspirators."

"Tearing out somebody's *heart* is *necessary*?" Ash said. "What the hell, Len?"

"When you're up against the wall, *necessary* feels like it has a different definition. War is just like salvage: you've got a problem in front of you, so you have to figure out a way around that problem," he said.

Natalie looked at him with a hard-edged respect. "We need to talk about this."

Len pushed off the wall. "Later. Let's find something more useful to do. A look at some real equipment will tell me more about this mess, and if there were shuttles here . . ."

He moved down the hallway, whistling, following the painted floor into another corridor and around a bend.

"Jackpot," he said.

Ash rounded the corner and nearly slammed right into Len's back. Natalie skidded to a stop, her eyes wide.

The space was a pod bay, excavated from the earth itself like the other rooms and sized big enough for three four-person shuttles. The walls and floor were decorated with yellow safety patterning, with a closed hatch in the ceiling just big enough for the firebombed Armour shuttle in the corner. The south wall was decorated with tools, the north with stacked storage boxes, the east with flimsy logs hanging on clipboards. If it hadn't been for the twisted black wreckage and the six dead bodies rotting on the floor, Ash might have thought that the people who worked here were expected to return at any minute.

The soldiers no longer looked human. They'd been savaged with some sort of serrated weapon before they died, their black mercenary jackets ripped and torn. Dried blood lay in quiet, branching puddles around their hands, their stomachs, their heads. Their eyes, rotten holes, lay as open to the local insects as their shattered jaws. She turned away in seconds, wandering instead to the inorganic wreckage of the shuttle, the smashed interior, the burned, twisted plasteel hull. "This would have been a pretty big fire," she said. "Do you think they died because of that?"

Natalie squatted near the bodies, kicking aside another empty ration bar wrapper. "No. They're not burned. Three women. Two men. Not sure about the last." She pointed to the body closest to the door. "That one was thrown against the wall. His back was broken. The one closest to the ship has wounds on his chest. They're deep enough that they punctured his lungs."

She gulped, then pointed at a third. "This one had a broken neck. But he suffered before that. And they got a few shots off before they died."

"A mech?"

"I've never seen a mech do this," Natalie said.

"Hey, more clues," said Len, who was bent over a large, half-burned storage box, ignoring the bodies. He fished out what looked like a pod gravity stabilizer and waved it at them.

"Engine parts are clues?" said Ash.

"Yeah," he said, dipping back down. She heard crashing noises; metal against metal. Len was not being careful. "The parts in here make me think they had an InGen retrieval pod, maybe a Wellspring pile driver. All of them could have fit through the hidden bay doors above and broken atmo. This," he said, picking up an unfamiliar silver box, "is for that Armour Ace 4400."

"Valdes's log said two shuttles got off the planet. You think . . . ?" Natalie said.

Ash cleared her throat to get the stench of fire and death out of her lungs. "I think it's too much of a coincidence. What else did you find?"

Len paused. "You two keep on. I'll look for clues in here. I'll meet you around the bend when I find something."

Ash pulled back into the hallway and continued exploring. The next doors belonged to labs: microscopes and machines, some shattered, most with their power cords ripped away from the wall, as if they wanted to destroy them but not the source of the power that was keeping the rest of the experiments alive. The smell of decay became stronger; Natalie pressed a glove to her mouth and muttered to herself.

Natalie pushed open the half-closed metal door at the end of the hallway. It swung open, revealing a smell that was weighty and wet, rotten and stale. The lights flickered but stayed on long enough for Ash to see a long silver table in the center, several cabinets with their doors open and contents strewn across the room, a large pile of smocks and blankets in the corner, discarded ration bar wrappers, and fat cables running from a large, flickering computer system into a hole in the ceiling.

Above the table hung large machines that resembled the laser cutters she'd used to section celestium from stone on Bittersweet, and a standard intravenous injection machine she'd been hooked up to in Aurora hospitals. To the right were four isolettes, all carrying circular molecular hullbusters connected to lumps of flesh that might have once been kidneys.

But none of that stank like the thing at the center of the room.

Natalie covered her mouth, and a disgusted, strangled noise caught heavy on Ash's tongue.

There was a white, smooth thing on the bed, laid up and tied there, covered with a white linen smock. It took her a moment to recognize fingers, legs, arms, the blank orbs of what could be eyes, the dark braided lines of bones and disintegrating muscle. This was a dead body, dead for months, disintegrating at a different pace than the soldiers on the pod bay floor. It was clearly not human.

*Glory,* whispered the weapon in her pocket.

Natalie dragged herself up and reached out toward Ash's left hand, lacing their fingers together. She looked miserable. "What the hell is that?" she whispered.

The dead figure was vaguely humanoid, in the fashion of a bird or a gazelle; the floor was covered in a putrid, sticky slime, and the elven, clawed fingers had long since rotted to bone. She couldn't tell how long it had been dead. Ash forced herself to walk around it, observe the slack jaw with its sharp silver teeth, see the graceful and articulated bones of its long-dead hands.

"It's a Vai," she said. "I mean. It has to be."

"Nobody's ever seen one."

"What the hell else could it be?" Ash said.

Natalie moved toward the dead thing, taking in its bony fingers, its empty eyes, the remains of its life-starved, desiccated flesh. "No, you're right. It makes sense. Basic Auroran engineering, right? If you're trying to figure out how something works, you're going to want the original model it's based on."

"Nat," Ash said, "has it occurred to you how big this is?"

"No shit," the younger woman whispered.

"If Sharma was using Vai in her experiments here, as well as humans? When the Company was telling the rest of us that nobody had ever even seen one, let alone—let alone this?"

Ash flashed back to the war propaganda she'd seen while on Bittersweet—the commercials encouraging uncitizens to apply for citizenship through the military program, the bloody footage from the battlefields over the Lost Worlds, the sobbing news anchors after the first contact massacre at Gethsemane. She remembered footage of the lethal silver teardrops that were Vai fighters, of the stunning war machines on the Cana plain, of the blue-green flicker of razor-sharp Vai weaponry taking apart a Bay-Ken cruiser. She remembered the carelessness of their desire to kill. The sheer destruction they'd brought on bodies and bones. The fatal, silent ease of their suicide lines.

But of Manx-Koltar and Aurora above Tribulation, there were only stories.

The stories said that the Companies turned back the alien onslaught, but they'd never said exactly how. *The strength of our alliances,* the plutocrats said, *the backbone of our industry and the leadership of our executives.*

*The smell of our bullshit,* whispered Kate at the back of her head.

Natalie shook her head, tapping her finger against the table. "I don't get it," she said. "I just don't understand. How did this one get captured? They kill themselves rather than be captured."

"Some of the experiments outside are dated before the war," Ash said.

Confirmation flickered over the younger woman's face. She drew a thin breath between her teeth. "You don't think they started killing themselves because of this one, here?"

"It's possible." Ash skirted the table and sat down in a rolling chair nearby. Her shoulder ached with the motion. She tested the power button of the flickering computer system with one index finger and felt the comforting, telltale rumble of Auroran-based computer system starting up. "Maybe the Vai were just trying to rescue their friend."

Natalie narrowed her eyes. "That's naïve."

"I'd do it."

"Yeah, it's also likely that old Solano's gonna go full equality on the entire Company and give *kids* citizenship." Natalie's voice had taken on a hard, sarcastic edge. "The Vai care about killing us, and nothing else. You can't compare anything they do to human thought, to human life. That's a massive logical leap, Ash. You make logical leaps like that in battle, and people die."

*No routing to node,* the crescent spun from her pocket. *But you are with me. You are with me.*

Ash felt her stomach churn. "But they're sentient, right? They must have—I don't know, feelings. Families. Friends. They have to care about something. Or else, what was it all for?"

"You are fucking *wrong*." Natalie looked away, dropping a curtain on the conversation.

Ash swallowed a sour retort and dropped the line of inquiry, focusing on the machine in front of her. This computer had been carefully ignored in the bugout—had been kept connected to the backup generator system that was powering the rest of the facility. The screen flashed as it connected to the renderbots in the facility, loading with a simple circle, silver on black, with an infinity sign turning and glistening in the center.

The Sacrament Society—whatever they were—hadn't spent much time on the operating system of the computer. This one sported white-on-black text and simple iconography with a keyboard interface, nothing like the complicated, beautiful haptic graphics and slick operation of the postwar Auroran fleet. She tried to open the main drive to search for ansible messages or security logs, but the system asked her for a passcode.

"Hey, let me," Natalie said, and Ash traded places with her. Ash rested her hand on the back of the chair, distracted by the dead alien. Natalie wriggled her fingers and set to her first guess. *Invalid,* said the interface.

"It's weird that this computer isn't firebombed like the others," Ash said. "It works fine."

"Well, if you think you're coming back . . ." She trailed off, then opened a salvage window. "You leave a back door, you leave a server. We know that *someone* got off the planet, right? That there were at least two shuttles."

Natalie entered a nine-digit number and the computer's main menu flashed into being. She smirked and started looking for the security logs. "This was definitely Reva's console."

"Wait," Ash said. "How do you know her passcode?"

Natalie smirked. "Six months with anyone who isn't a hacker, and it's obvious. Sharma's smart, but I'm not sure she had a proper computer tech here."

"Do you know *my* passcodes?"

Natalie snorted. "What do you think?"

Ash rolled her eyes, then moved away from the computer screen, letting Natalie scan the file system. She searched the room again, supporting herself against the cold-packed earth, noting the room's flickering lights, scattered flimsies, layers of opaque dust. She tried not to look at the dead body, its crooked arms, its thin, knobby knees, its broken ribs, its predatory, skinny claws.

*Less a medical bay than a morgue,* she found herself thinking, pushing off from the wall, fighting her typical dizziness as she leaned over, picking up pill bottles and printouts.

*Kerithromycin. Bescinol. Korithstat.* Not medications she recognized.

*The Effect of Half-Life Hemolytically Soaked Celestium on Human and Vai Physiology.*

*How to Remove the Human Heart for Use in Experimental Processes.* There were diagrams.

She gulped and dropped those flimsies on the floor. *Definitely a morgue.*

"Ash, I've found some logs," Natalie said. "Local storage. She, ah, taped whatever experiments she did here. Her autopsies. I think someone tried to wipe them, but they left the cameras on when they bugged out. The last file was automatically closed out when there was no more drive space."

"They had a haptic recording system? Like on *London*?"

"Want to see the last couple minutes of this horror show?"

Ash wanted to say *Hell no,* but kept her mouth shut. Light swirled up—a red-orange holographic grid that dredged up shivering, unwelcome memories of the *London* bridge in Ash's unwilling mind. She eyed the renderbots in the ceiling—earlier, bulkier versions of the panopticons that watched over *London* and her hospital room on *Rio,* recording and remembering and reporting whatever they saw. The renderbots drew feet, hands, a knee-length coat that might, in life, have been white. The ghost was a woman—dark hair, tight bun, compact frame. More than familiar. She was family.

*Sharma.*

The doctor was bent over the dead alien, using an unfamiliar tool to pull back muscle on its dead, claw-bent arm. Ash winced and stepped forward to see—the white skin was still mostly intact, and she could view the doctor's work directly on the corpse itself. Ash had seen Sharma's face like this so many times: the uncanny concentration, the bright, wide eyes, the businesslike mouth. She'd always been able to work well under pressure, Ash knew, but until this point she hadn't realized just how well.

Orange sketch-soldiers carrying boltguns ran down the corridor outside, and she heard shouting from a distant speaker. Ash jogged to the door and stuck her head outside, following their path. They hung a right into the shuttlebay, and before she could say anything, she heard crates falling and tools scattering over the concrete surfacing, then Len swearing up a storm.

"It's just a recording!" she yelled. "They've got this place wired up like a ship!"

"Figured that out, thanks!" he hollered back.

A young woman wearing a long, orange-dark coat ran down the hall from the offices and slipped right through Ash on her way into the morgue. Ash blinked away the orange light that lined the hologram as she passed.

"I'm busy, Dr. Jessen," Sharma muttered.

The woman was Natalie's age, and had a familiar bearing. Ash noticed her WellCel citizen tags and tried to remember if she'd ever seen her from far away on Bittersweet. *Maybe. I don't know.* "Problems," she said.

Sharma kept her eyes on her project. "Bribe the governor, then."

Jessen straightened, offended. Her voice adopted an arrogance Ash recognized at once as a Wellspring birthright tactic. "Shut up," she said. "We've got Auroran cruisers inbound, coming fast. They saw our ship on the long-range. Allen and our Manx friends have already fragged the ansible, but Command still wants a demonstration."

This hijacked Sharma's attention. "Absolutely not."

"The device is finished. You're go for launch."

"Finished but not *tested*," The doctor flexed her left hand and looked down at it. "We've never tested it on a living human being. We haven't tested it on a living *Vai*. And we can't get our ships out of the way in time."

The girl put her hands on her hips. "This isn't doctoral research, Reva. It's war. We don't have any more time and I can't tell you how screwed we're going to be if *Aurora* gets hold of this tech. You have to set it off."

"And if the secondary node calls in reinforcements?"

"We *want* it to call in reinforcements."

Sharma was silent. "This was not what I signed up for."

"We can end the slaughter, Reva."

"With more slaughter. It doesn't have to be a *weapon*."

The younger woman tilted her head. "If you really believed that, you would have campaigned otherwise at the beginning of all this. But you didn't. You agreed with the directorate. Did all those indentures die for nothing?"

Sharma was quiet for a moment, and then slid her arms behind her back—Ash had seen Natalie use that stance when speaking with Keller. "If you say we're ready to set off the device, then we'll be ready."

"Good," Jessen said, her voice going soft for a moment. "Reva, you should be very proud of what you've done here."

The doctor did not smile. "What's the plan?"

Jessen peeked out into the hallway. "Allen and his people will take care of the Aurorans and clear a path. We'll put you on one shuttle, the Heart on another, the secondary node on a third with the frag team. The rest of us will evac to the city and hope for the best."

Sharma looked surprised. "No. I need to go with the weapon."

"And lose you, too?"

Sharma bit her lip. She was nervous. Ash had never seen the doctor nervous. It gave her a strange, uneasy feeling. "I need to make sure it works."

Jessen stepped forward. "It will. Just follow the plan. Don't doubt yourself now."

"I know."

"It's us or them."

"I *know*."

"The team is sedating the other Vai, and the quarantine locker will be on the second shuttle. You have to get on one or the other in ten minutes or we have to leave you behind." She sighed. "Don't make me do that."

Jessen passed through Ash on the way back into the hallway, causing orange light to block her vision. She blinked away the sudden headache. Sharma's ghost wavered where it was, then placed her hand on the expanse that looked like it might have once been the alien's forehead. The doctor stroked it with her thumb, as she would a sleeping child, and then leaned over and kissed it, light and sweet, her lips lingering against the dead thing's cold skin.

She then crossed over quickly to the computer and sat. Natalie jumped up like a popped hull breach, waving her hands, as if the orange light was a cloud of stinging insects.

"Ew. Okay, that's really weird."

"What's she doing?" Ash said.

"Erasing logs," Natalie said, looking over the hologram's shoulder. She raised her fingers and tried to follow Sharma's fingering. "I think. I can only see her keystrokes, so it's just a guess."

Ash turned away and walked back to the bed where the alien lay. She looked at its long legs, its folded-in hands, the darkened, chylous eyes. Terrible thoughts wove together in dark patterns behind her eyes. "The Sacrament Society was responsible for the Battle of Tribulation," she whispered. "*Sharma* was responsible."

Natalie's hands stopped in mid-air. "Manx-Koltar killed *London*, yeah. It's war."

"War between companies. When we were supposed to be fighting the Vai."

"Doesn't mean that Sharma was responsible."

Ash pressed her fingers into the side of the bed. "But you remember those bodies, right? The ones in the last compartment, the Sacrament operative in the black coat, the scientists. We couldn't figure out how they died. What if someone triggered the weapon, and that's how they died? The scientists, the rest of the crew?"

"The Vai did it," Natalie said.

"What if it was someone like me?"

"Impossible—"

"You saw me with the crescent."

Natalie said nothing in the few moments that followed, then shook her head. The younger woman's face reflected the pallid light of the monitor. "I don't know," she said. "The most reasonable guess is still a Vai attack. I just know—"

The rest of her sentence was drowned out by the rattle of gunfire and shouting from down the hall. Ash's hand went to the gun at her waist—*Len's* gun, confiscated an hour before.

"He's not armed," Ash said.

Natalie hurtled into the hallway, taking point. "Right flank, Ash."

Ash followed, her adrenaline spiking; she felt for a moment like she was in the pod again, like she was a live bomb, shivering, unready, unable to make the connection, ready to go off at any second. *Calm down,* Keller said behind her eyes—and she focused on following Natalie's sure stride, turning, coming to a screeching halt alongside her, flanking, spinning up the weapon at a room washed in orange light—

"Holy shit," Natalie said, relaxing. Her shoulders drooped, and her voice went husky. She wiped the back of her mouth with the sleeve of her jacket and shoved the gun back in its holster. "The log's still on. We forgot the log was still on. I am a dumba—"

She stopped mid-sentence.

Ash grabbed at her arm.

The cameras in the room stuttered and strove, working overtime to properly render the fight occurring in front of the trashed

Armour shuttle. Five soldiers in power armor fought a demon from hell. No—not a demon, Ash realized. A Vai. The orange light painted the Vai's rawboned body and clawed hands with an infernal tint, lit its whirling eyes and sharp teeth, its wide, roaring mouth, the broken chains hanging on its legs.

The Vai smacked the humans away like toys, a gyroscopic nightmare, clawed through their armor, used its fingers to pierce them through the chest, twirl them like rags, fling them to the ground. They fell, one by one, their breath failing, their blood painting the walls, and as they died, their silent forms evaporated like rainfall in the heat of the summer. The Vai, remaining, screamed the sound that gave the creatures their name—the *vvvvaaaaaaaiiiiii* noise of a dying star, the grinding, heartrending sound of a planet ripping apart.

The renderbots closed their lenses and went silent.

"Jee-sus," Len moaned, emerging from where he'd hidden behind a stack of storage crates. "I thought you—I thought it—"

He wrung his hands, in the motion he used when he was trying to convince someone that he wasn't scared, and his eyes focused not on Ash and Natalie but on the alien figure in the center, limned with orange, huffing quietly, recovering its breath. He worked his jaw, picking his way over the moldering bodies on the floor toward Ash and the door. "Can I have my gun? I need to take a walk, I need to—" He gulped, looking down at the corpses, and said nothing more.

Ash offered Len the butt of his boltgun. He grabbed it and exited the room, turning back toward the cathedral. Her attention was on Natalie, who stared, wide-eyed and vacant and shaking, at the recording. She was still holding her own weapon, clutching it so hard her knuckles had gone white. Ash walked up to the younger woman. "Go with him," she said. "Take a break."

Natalie stood stock-still, a blank statue. "It's still here," she whispered. "The other alien."

"What do you mean?"

"It's still *here*." Natalie looked around the room. "It has to be. Do the math. Three shuttles. Two got out. One's still here. And the recording's *still going*."

The recorded Vai shook quietly where it stood and examined a gash where flickering orange blood dripped to the floor, evaporating into dust and faint traces of dead glitter in the real world. The renderbots closed their lenses and went silent.

Ash reached for Natalie's arm. "It's been over a year. It can't have survived."

Natalie narrowed her eyes. "Okay, sure. And I bet you think it's that priss-face Sharma and her scientists leaving the food wrappers everywhere?"

"You don't think—"

"*Think* is bullshit on the battlefield. Think is death. I need to *know*." She swallowed. "We need to clear this room. Shit, you don't have a gun. Get behind me."

Sudden panic kindled in Ash's throat. "Okay."

Ash followed, slow and sure, as Natalie padded her way toward a pile of debris. This side of the room contained the lost detritus of engineers who had evacuated in a hurry: generators left on, their fuel long ago having run out, spanners cast every which way, tool racks turned over in fury, and ration bar wrappers forgotten in the corner, next to a pile of linen smocks.

The pile moved.

"Nat," Ash said.

Natalie responded with a terse nod. The woman was engrossed, her eyes narrowed, looking down the sight of her bolt-gun. Ash ducked forward, pushing the pile to the side until her breath caught, until she saw it, until both of them swore and stumbled back, until the orange recording of the bleeding, screaming Vai reflected on the pathetic body below—an alien, but barely recognizable as the same one, wrapped in linen and sallow and shaking, as if it were bracing against a cold wind or hiding from something terrible.

*Hiding from us,* Ash thought.

The alien barely moved upon seeing them. It was starving; Ash recognized the way the skin stretched over dark bones from seeing severe debtors in the lower echelons of Wellspring Station, walking past them quickly, her mother's hand tight and painful on hers, before she'd joined them. Either way, the alien was nothing she'd ever seen before. Its mouth worked, the jaw weak, revealing a set of variegated, sharp teeth. It had a face—eyes and a nose—but she would be hard-pressed to call it anything like human. Near the alien's hand were empty syringes with familiar labels.

"Don't get closer," said Natalie.

"That's *trihex,*" Ash said.

She breathed in; she could detect no smell, no sign of rot. She leaned over to pick up one of the syringes, and the alien moved: the antelope-horn fingers first, then a ragged, strained breath in the torso. The alien's eyes opened, milk-opaque, focusing. Like a tidal wave, Ash's mind was filled with *burning ships, inhuman screaming, a crown of stars above an unfamiliar planet, blood on her hands, fear, fear, human figures in monstrous guise, loneliness, loneliness, staggering loneliness and terrible hunger, don't hurt us, don't hurt us —*

Ash screamed, clawing at her head.

In a quick half second, Natalie was up, her gun primed and wailing, flanking Ash. "I've got you."

"Don't," Ash screamed.

"You saw what it did to the others, sir," Natalie replied, her hands steady, calling her *sir* like she were back at Cana and Ash was a citizen, leveling her even, half-glazed stare at the alien. It uncurled, made a high, sibilant noise, and reached out its hand toward the women, a ration bar wrapper open and crackling in its thin hand.

"It was hiding from us. It's *scared*," Ash said.

"It should be," Natalie responded, her eyes like flint.

"It's a witness to what happened here," Ash said, "and I think it was just talking to me."

"You're sick," Natalie said. "Sir, I need to put it down. You have no idea what these things did to my unit."

"Or what the Sacrament Society did to them first."

"Sir, I respectfully disagree."

"We don't have enough information."

"It's the enemy, sir; that's all the information I need to know."

"Stop scaring me, Nat." The words came out as final, as Keller-like, as *commanding* as Ash could make them, and she pulled herself up, her shoulders back, fighting the nausea that had been a constant companion since she woke up after *London*. She ran her hand through her hair. "It's in no condition to hurt anyone."

"Um, I think there might be some shuttles descen— Holy *shit*," Len said. He appeared at the door, paused, gulped, and the three humans watched in almost reverent quiet as the Vai staggered to its knees and pointed straight at Ash. Its hands were thin, seven-fingered, topped with tearing claws; one claw was set with a thin line of tiny diamonds. Along the alien's right side was a set of ill-healed wounds, ragged skin set in nasty blue scars. It keened again but did not open its mouth.

"It likes you," Len muttered.

"Um," said Ash.

It extended its hand.

Orchestras sounded, somewhere far-off, hits of angry brass. The sighs of the dead. *Fear.* The weapon in her pocket told her what she needed to do.

"Do you hear that?" she said.

Len exchanged worried looks with Natalie. "We don't hear anything. Come on now, step back—"

Ash looked back at the alien. She took a few tentative steps forward instead, opening her hands in what she hoped was a pacifying gesture.

"What were they doing to you?"

The alien continued to speak, adding an octave—a ghosting, ethereal, questioning note far above the first note, in a register Ash couldn't quite hear. The lids of the milk-white eyes narrowed, looked around the room one last time, and with a smooth motion the Vai grabbed Ash's arm, plunging the diamond claw into the soft flesh of her wrist. The world went blurry and bright in the shocking pain, turned on its side and back again, and beyond the hollering she vaguely recognized as Natalie's voice, she heard a new song.

*Baby. Baby, it's all coming down around us. It's all coming down. We have to leave now. We have to go, or everything's gone.*

"Christopher?" she gasped.

# 22

Sharma sat at a haptic console, looking hunched and hungry. She was half hidden behind a representation of the *London* weapon, turning round and bright, shining like a diamond lit for display in a museum. The doctor's own dark eyes were the opposite—dull and striated with red, rimmed with sleepless exhaustion.

Keller's identity took a moment to register, but when it did, the doctor jumped to her feet, brushing off her hands on her filthy blue pants, as though looking good for Keller still mattered. Sharma was wearing an ill-fitting green shirt, like Keller had seen on the executives in the hallway, but the pants were Auroran, the pair she'd been wearing when she left for the planet's surface a day earlier, now streaked and soiled with red Tribulation dirt. She crossed the room to stand in front of Keller, her face bright with surprise.

"You can trust me," Sharma said.

"I need water," whispered Keller.

"Just stand there," Sharma said, "and tilt your chin down. You'll look like security." She pointed at the ceiling with her other hand. Keller followed the motion with her eyes, checking for cameras. She didn't see them, but this was Ramsay's world, and she'd assumed a hundred things about Ramsay that turned out to be wrong. She could assume nothing.

The doctor crossed the room—methodically, like the request was ordinary—and filled a beaker from a dispenser spigot. Keller kept her chin tucked, looking around. The lab was small but tiered, set up around what looked to be an operating theater. In the center was a metal bed, flanked by haptic devices she couldn't quite explain. A grand gathering of cables met underneath, ran aft, and rose toward the ceiling, separating where the bulkheads met, threading into the wall. In a place like this, Keller hoped to see medical trays full of surgical tools she or Sharma could use as weapons, but the surfaces were clean.

"You're working for them." Keller fought a deep and dark disappointment.

"No. She *thinks* I am, but no. This isn't my first trip into the glorious lands of corporate espionage." Sharma snorted, and returned to Keller, handing her the beaker of water. Every cell in Keller's body screamed for it, and she lifted it to her lips. The liquid was cold, sweet, and welcome, with a metallic tang that betrayed its recycled origins. It tasted like heaven.

"I'm so glad you got away," Sharma said.

Keller took another gulp of the water. "*Got away* is a pretty charitable description of what's been happening. How's *Twenty-Five?*"

Sharma grimaced. "Scuttled. With a spinal lance, so you couldn't escape. Ramsay told me you were still aboard. I thought I was going to be stuck doing this alone."

"Doing *what* alone?" Keller wiped water from the corner of her lip and sucked it off her finger. "Getting off this bucket?"

Sharma hesitated. "Not quite. This racket—Baywell, they call themselves now, when they're trying to be a real Company—isn't as put together as it looks. She didn't know about the weapon until you did, so they have just as much information as Aurora does. I know more at this point than both companies combined, so that gives us room to make a more considered move."

Keller finished off the liquid in the glass and handed it back to Sharma, feeling marginally calmer. "Is Len on the ship? He'll know this cruiser type."

The doctor hesitated. She looked away, and something like shame flickered in her eyes. "I don't know if he's alive."

"What happened?"

"He left to relieve himself, before I was taken. He's not aboard—or at least, I haven't seen him, if he is."

"Alien planet with possible hostiles, and you let him go out *alone*? Didn't you listen to your training? My orders? What the hell were you thinking?" Keller fought a hot, terrible anger, and raised her voice, ignoring her better angels.

Sharma leaned in and snatched up the glass. "I was thinking that he didn't need to pee in front of me." She sighed. "Things are complicated. We can talk about that in a moment. Alison thinks you're dead, and she needs to continue to think you're dead. And since she's on her way for an appointment, you can't be here."

"*Complicated?*" Keller's voice gained a register.

Sharma snatched at Keller's shoulder and turned her around, propelling her toward the wall. "She's on her way. I'll have to be nice to her, so both of our lives are about to get quite disgusting. Walk toward the back wall. Slow. Steady. Keep your chin down. Get in the drawer."

"But the cameras—"

"There's nowhere else to hide."

Four large drawers were built into the bulkhead—a morgue, which they didn't have on *Twenty-Five*. Sharma slipped the latch and pulled out the top drawer to reveal a dead body, corpse-cold, its skin tinged with malicious blue and a blackened, congealed bolt-burn right under a broken sternum. His face was a gnarled, inhuman death mask, but she remembered him. She'd be remembering him for the rest of her life.

*The man I killed.*

Keller's guts rebelled. "Not in a million years."

"I can't do this without you, Captain. The other bodies are

worse. They burned during the core fire. It'll be tight, but it's better than the alternative."

Keller groaned, feeling a deep revulsion wrest control of her spine. *It's going back to the crate. It's worse than being back in the crate.* "You don't understand. I can't."

"Then all is lost." Sharma's voice was hard metal, her mouth an apologetic twist. "Then Ash and Natalie died in vain."

Keller gulped down vomit and acquiesced with an angry gulp, using her hands to hoist herself onto the platform, putting one leg on each side of the dead man's body, and pushing herself into a plank position. Her calves screamed.

"You won't fit that way. Lie down," Sharma said. "Hurry."

"You were my *least* favorite crewmember, Dr. Sharma," Keller hissed.

"I know."

Keller caught the mixed odor of death and formaldehyde as she let herself rest on the dead body, gulping down sudden acid in her throat.

The drawer was cold storage, and the man was dead ice. She shivered, and Sharma pushed the door closed with a brisk finality that startled Keller. Her world shifted into darkness, into pollution, into keeping her stomach from sending up what little was left inside. She pressed against the platform and pushed herself up as far as possible, breathing in thin streams through her mouth, trying not to vomit, trying to direct her attention back to the sounds outside rather than the dead man below her.

Sharma had just arrived at her chair when the swift flutter of the door sounded. Keller heard hard-heeled executive's shoes making their way across the room.

"Where's the guard that was just here?" *Ramsay,* Keller thought, and her stomach seized.

"I believe he went to find some lunch." Sharma's voice was nonchalant.

Silence.

Keller distracted herself from the stench of death and chemicals by imagining all the ways in which she could break Alison Ramsay's filigree nose.

"Fine," Ramsay said. "Let's get this over with."

"I didn't think you would go through with the procedure yourself, Ms. Ramsay." Sharma stressed the woman's last name, adding the citizen's honorific, as if Keller didn't know who it was, as if she wouldn't already hear that voice in every single one of her nightmares for the rest of her days.

Ramsay's tone was naked annoyance. "The analysis I asked for?"

"It's here. Like most Vai devices, this one functions on low power until it comes into the presence of a Vai or Vai cognate." Keller heard a flimsy being pushed across a table. High heels clicked again, crossing the rest of the way to the doctor's desk. A few seconds passed in silence.

"This was worth waiting for. It really *is* an elegant way to kill."

"It's a battery. Not a weapon. And it doesn't kill. Not exactly."

Ramsay sighed. "Can you make it work against Aurora?"

Sharma's voice was incredulous. "Zero-point energy isn't enough for you?"

"*Enough* is never enough," Ramsay said. Her voice wore a smooth, nasty edge that made Keller shiver. "We need to be competitive again."

"Then don't set it off anywhere near your side. The device is faction-agnostic," Sharma said. "It doesn't care who owns the local power sources; it'll draw power from all of them."

"And it can't be changed."

"Not unless you're Vai, I imagine."

Ramsay sighed. "Understood. I'll take the injection now."

Keller tried not to breathe. She smelled death, rot, sour blood.

Her stomach roared its emptiness; the sound echoed against the raw metal of the drawer.

"Alison, I'm a doctor," Sharma said, after a tense moment of silence. "I am *your* doctor and you are asking me to go against my oath to do no harm. Do not force me to do this. Taking the captain's blood to make this was bad enough, but forcing me to—"

Ramsay's voice brightened. "I'm not forcing you to do anything. I want this."

"That's not how this works." Sharma clearly did not believe her.

"So you're negotiating. All right, let's negotiate. Aurora never saw your worth. Your research and ours—it dovetails perfectly, like we were always meant to work together. Baylor Wellspring is prepared to provide you with equipment, personnel, and a carte blanche fiat to pursue research on Vai technology. You're a birthright now, yes, but imagine what it would be like to have *founding* status. What it would mean for your family. We can give that to you. Or—here's your other option, let me get the picture—"

Silence. Kate heard the rustling of a duty jacket, the click of fingernails on a computer surface, and set her jaw against the ache of her legs and her desire to scream.

"No," Sharma said, her voice hoarse.

"Aurora won't find her until it's too late. There are always jobs at Bittersweet for children." Ramsay's voice was calm and quiet and dangerous, like the echo of broken machinery. "Your granddaughter is small. She'll fit in the new veins they've found in the wreckage."

Chair legs scraped against the decking. "Don't touch her."

"As I said. We're negotiating."

The room was quiet for a few long seconds. Keller heard the thump of Sharma's slight body as it fell back into the chair, and the angry animal huff of her acquiescing breath. "The research is important, and you're right. Baylor Wellspring is a good place for it," the doctor said.

"I'm glad you see it my way."

Keller wanted to scream. *No. No.*

"I thought they'd send someone less important for this," Sharma said.

"Someone on the junior staff? What, the power to bend worlds, to remake the galaxy, to silence the Vai themselves—and you think I'd just waste that on some mewling birthright? This gift is mine."

"This isn't a gift." The doctor's voice was modulated, comforting, careful, like this was still *Twenty-Five* and Ramsay had come in for one migraine pill too many. "The original test subjects on Bittersweet went less than a year between their initial dose of Vai blood and the first terminal symptoms. Christopher Durant succumbed within a year and a half. Ash was already screwing up out there at eight months. She had a couple of *really* close calls. And I have no idea how any of it works. You're head of Baylor Wellspring's R&D. You know the scientific method. You know this is madness. Suicide."

*Christopher Durant.*

Keller knew that name.

Ramsay snorted. "Durant was ours before you even touched his body, Reva. I know what I'm asking you to do."

"This will kill you. You will die."

"You're going to save me."

"I don't know how," Sharma said, her voice pained.

"I believe in you."

Sharma huffed an exasperated sigh. "I'm just saying that you can't rush science this complicated like this lab is a machine shop pushing out screwdrivers."

"I understand what I'm asking you to do."

"No, you don't." Sharma spat the words. "This is alien nanoscale technology, and it's so far beyond our current science that any promise to save you is a promise I may not be able to keep. Ash's illness functioned like celestium sickness, yes—but that's just because Vai blood contains celestium. It was poisoning her directly, from the inside, not just through the mucous membranes. On top of that, the nanoscale material that lives inside is inexplicable. It'll take years to figure out the basic physics behind it, and you just won't have that much time."

Ramsay's voice was warm, like she was smiling. "It's not inexplicable. We both saw her react to the weapon in the pod."

Sharma sputtered. "The battery was using the pod to charge itself. That is all."

"Come on, Reva. I saw the footage you took. She *reacted*."

"You will die."

Ramsay raised her voice. "You will save me. We worked together long enough that I know you're going to try."

"What if I don't?" Sharma's voice was quiet. Challenging.

"Like you said." Ramsay's voice matched Sharma's for volume. "You're a doctor."

Keller felt her legs starting to cramp again in the silence that followed. She bit her lip to channel the pain.

"I'll need nanoscale engineers, then," Sharma said, soft and slow. "The best you can get. You'll have to give them similar founders' deals. Genetic scientists. Surgeons—a hematology background is preferable. I want people who worked with Vai tech before. I can give you names and numbers for their citizenship buyouts. It'll be expensive, but I can't do it alone."

"We'll get you what you need," Ramsay said.

Sharma's voice adopted an edge of defeat. "Then roll up your sleeve."

Keller heard the crackling of a sterile pack opening. Her stomach turned in the stink, and the swallowing, resonant sound seemed to echo off the morgue drawer walls and fold back in on itself.

"All right," Sharma said. "It's done."

Ramsay's voice lost some of its sun-bright steel. "What am I supposed to feel like?"

"Nothing, for now."

"When will it start working?"

"Immediately, but you have to give the nanotech time to replicate. The celestium will take a month or two to poison you to the point that you notice, but the nanobots should start working immediately. I've hypothesized that the weapon's effective range has something to do with how much of the technology is active in your system. Again, that's just a hypothesis. I didn't get enough time to really study the effects in the field, thanks to you."

"So the Vai set the weapon off at the Battle of Tribulation."

"That is also a hypothesis."

"And now I can, as well."

Sharma didn't pause this time. "You are the only living Vai cognate, now."

"Well." Keller heard the executive's heels on the ground again. "As long as we're ready for what's ahead, everything will be fine." Her voice had a familiar sharp point to it.

Sharma's voice went soft. "That's the plan."

"We're going to do great work together, Dr. Sharma."

"I'm sure."

Keller heard footsteps once more, and the door opened with an airy swish, clicking shut like a toast at a funeral. Keller heard Sharma rise, then walk closer. The doctor fussed with the latch before yanking the door open and sliding the drawer back into the light. Keller took hungry lungfuls of clean, processed air, swung herself off the drawer and the corpse with an angry, woozy purpose, then staggered over and retched into a nearby disposal chute. She knew anger was clouding her judgment. She knew Sharma was in a terrible position. It didn't matter. Nothing mattered.

All she wanted to do was nail the doctor to the wall.

"You knew what was wrong with Ashlan," Keller said, wiping her mouth on the back of her sleeve, a fist forming. "You knew what was wrong the whole time. You could have saved her."

Sharma looked tired. "No. There's a treatment for celestium sickness, yes, but not for this. I'll need funding for a cure, and funding is funding, no matter where you get it."

"The cure. Which you'll give to our *competitor*."

Sharma crossed her arms. Her shoulders tightened. "It doesn't matter. I'll make sure it gets out."

"It sure as hell does matter. Ramsay can use the weapon now!"

"It won't matter. Kate—" Sharma tried to push Keller into the position that was best for the cameras. Keller was having none of it; she knocked Sharma's wrist away.

"Don't *Kate* me. We're not friends."

The doctor's jaw set. "It *won't matter,* because you're going to steal the weapon and return to Auroran space with it. *Now.* Before Ramsay's abilities kick in."

Keller blinked. "I— What?"

"I estimate your ability to fully operate the device at somewhere near to fifty percent, seeing as you've been exposed for at least three months. You won't be able to disable *Phoenix* entirely, but nobody's going to be able to stop you from just walking out with it."

Keller's mouth swung open. "*Operate* it?"

She'd never seen the doctor give bad news, never seen the woman disappoint a patient, but Keller imagined it had to look something like this. Sharma's mouth turned into a frown, and she reached into her pocket, taking out her ubiquitous penlight, switching it on, and shining it into Keller's eyes. Keller tried to swat it away, but Sharma was too fast for her. Her vision went star-white.

"Are you hallucinating yet? Hearing voices?"

Keller went ice cold. Remembered Ash's ghost sitting on the desk in the crew boss's office a few decks below. Smiling.

"No," she whispered.

"So you have."

Keller's mouth hung open. "Dr. Sharma."

"I suspect the indenture started seeing visual artifacts—flashes, dizziness—shortly after her Auroran onboarding. It lines up with some of the mistakes she was making in the field. Celestium sickness is part of my field of study. I noticed. She would have seen bright lights, at first, bright lights and black dots. Does any of this sound familiar? What did she tell you?"

Betrayal shocked Keller's body. "Why didn't you tell me that you knew?"

Sharma was quiet for a moment, and then she uncrossed her arms. "Until we found the weapon, I was just monitoring her condition. Tracking it. Just because there's no profit advantage for a corporation in treating celestium sickness doesn't mean *I'm* a monster. I couldn't tell you."

"We could have helped her together."

"I know. But I'm a Company doctor subject to reporting regulations. I justified it to myself by saying that if she never came to me—if *you* never came to me—that I wouldn't have to report on it to the indenture health department. I didn't want to ruin her life if I was wrong, or add years to her indenture. Captain, I didn't understand it was more than celestium sickness until Ash came into contact with the weapon."

"And you didn't tell me?"

"I couldn't, Captain. You were rearranging Indenture Ashlan's schedule so she'd be able to get away from her routine blood tests. You were not following Company protocol."

Keller felt a burning, embarrassed anger prickling in her cheeks. "You know how much that shit costs on the indenture account."

Sharma sighed. "I do. Which is why I went along with it until I could no longer. I was going to show you the results of the test, the danger it posed to all of us, to force the issue and get the weapon back to where it belonged." She sighed, her hands moving to her hips. "But then, you listened to the indentures over me, and we went to the planet, not Europa."

Keller shoved the extra questions down her throat. "It *is* a weapon."

"Oh, yes. And it should *never* be used."

"By Baywell? Or is *Mr. Solano* trustworthy enough?" The words had sharp edges; they were meant to cut. Kate felt a quiet pride when Sharma winced.

"No. I serve humanity, not just Aurora."

"What's that supposed to mean?" asked Keller.

"It means I'm on *your* side, not hers. Did Ashlan ever tell you about her fiancé?"

Keller flashed back to the cavern where she'd found Ashlan and dead Christopher during the Bittersweet rescue: the thick stink of stone, the dark stains of blood on the ground, the dead bodies like scattered leaves. She shuddered, drawing the stolen coat closer around her shoulders. "She didn't really talk about him."

"From what I can put together, Indenture Christopher was trying to get both himself and Ashlan out of their contracts, so he joined a medical experiment that Wellspring was running, one that paid twice as much as mining but required a severe total-body contract for the duration. What he didn't know was that the experiment was based off some alien technology that Wellspring had salvaged from a battlefield. An alien body that hadn't evaporated."

Keller's eyes went wide. "Shit, really?"

"The head scientist on that project was . . . sympathetic to my own research group, and asked me to quietly consult. Implanting

the alien nanotech in human flesh was obviously successful, at
least for Indenture Christopher, but he was never able to be put
on the battlefield. He was the reason the Vai attacked Bittersweet. He and his fellow bioweapons perished in the attack."

"The Vai attacked Bittersweet because it was a major celestium depot," Keller said. "It supplied half the fleet."

Sharma shook her head. "No, but you'll be forgiven for thinking that. It's true that Cana, Bittersweet, and Arimathea were all
wartime centers of celestium production. That they were Wellspring's. Not just mines, though: mines and refineries, shipping
points, main offices. Scientists. Weapons labs."

Keller felt dizzy. "Your connections?"

Sharma paused. Considered her words. "Why do you think *we*
were dispatched to help with the rescue?" she said. "This kind
of technology can't be trusted to a Company that makes its profit
margins by starving its indentures."

"So one of your *connections* on Aurora's board sent us because
of you."

"Yes. Christopher had no idea how sick he was. He thought he
had celestium sickness, but when I did his autopsy, I found that
if a rock hadn't fallen on his head, he would have been dead long
before his citizenship came through. I'd never seen the sickness
so bad in someone so young. It matched nothing we knew about
the disease. But I still didn't make the connection, didn't realize
that Ashlan must have contracted the nanotech infection outside
the Wellspring weapons lab. It's only when I looked at Ashlan's
blood work and compared it to Christopher's that I realized I was
dealing with a different illness."

"Without her permission."

"I had to."

"You could have told me."

Sharma shook her head. "I couldn't trust you then."

Keller exhaled. "I'm your captain."

"No. You loved her."

Keller closed her eyes. "You could have trusted me."

"She was *dying*. You both knew it. And there's no trust in the Auroran medical system. There was very little I could do without turning her over to Mr. Solano and sparking a major health-related fraud investigation that would have put both of you back on Earth and on the dole for good. *Stateless*. I still have *ethics*, Kate. Is that what you wanted for her? Is that what you wanted for *yourself*? Blame me for making sure the two of you could have at least a little happiness, if you have to blame me for anything. Here, let me show you what you're up against."

Sharma stepped back. She walked to the wall and called up her interface, taking a few seconds to bring up a video. It took Keller a moment to realize what she was seeing: a close scan of human blood, rushing not through a vein but swirling in a test tube.

"Look," Sharma said.

Keller narrowed her eyes. In between the obvious erythrocytes, tiny silver machines slipped and swam, attaching to blood cells, clumping together, unnatural metallic clots that swirled in unnatural directions. Keller took a deep, uncertain breath, and shivered again.

"This is Christopher's?"

"No," Sharma said, pausing. She clasped her hands. "It's yours. This is the sample Alison took from you while you were unconscious."

Keller felt a rushing noise at her ears and a quiet dizziness. She knew that slippery silver surface; the Vai metal always looked just a tad wrong, like spit running down the side of a building on a hot day. Like death. "The hell . . . ?"

"Nanotech."

"It looks Vai."

"It is."

"Damn—"

Sharma shut off the display. "They'll be everywhere by now. Your blood, your brain. I think they're alive."

Keller's world spun. "I didn't even *know* Christopher."

Sharma nodded. "But you were . . . close, with someone who did."

In the back of her mind, somewhere in a lost, faraway memory, Ash nestled into the crook of her neck and breathed, warm and trusting, against her ear. The memory made her shiver.

"You knew? We tried to hide it."

The doctor's mouth twisted. It wasn't a smile. "It was a logical leap. The alien nanotech is carried inside the body through blood and bodily fluid, much like one of the blood-borne pathogens eradicated a century ago—hepatitis, or HIV, for example. But it also has qualities in common with another sickness we once called meningitis, which can be spread through more casual contact."

Keller blinked away sudden dizziness. She felt nauseous and faint and hot. "Then you should have it. Why not Len, or—or Natalie?"

"The nanotech goes dormant outside a living body. As far as I can tell, it dies fairly quickly, for lack of a better word, outside a host body." Sharma looked away. "All it took for you and Ash was a kiss. But it could have as easily been a shared cup of coffee."

It was as if the ship was tearing away around Keller, as if the air had been replaced with boiling oil. "Stop. Just stop."

"She didn't know."

The nausea ceded to rage. Hot bile poured into Keller's veins, and she stepped forward, her hands forming fists beyond her control. "But *you* did."

Sharma stepped back. Raised her hands. "I made the wrong decision, but what's important right now—"

Keller advanced again. "Oh, *I'm* about to make the wrong decision."

The doctor kept her hands raised, her palms facing Keller. "What's most important right now is to separate that weapon from any person or Company who wants to use it to destabilize our fragile and necessary peace."

Keller's lip curled. "And *I* have to do it."

"You've been infected much longer than Alison. She'll be the only one who can fight you. All you have to do is walk up to the gunnery, take out the guards, pick up the weapon and get off the ship."

"Is that all," Keller deadpanned.

"It's a better plan than the one I had before. *Medellin* will arrive in a few hours; it will have diverted from a nearby system when I did not send an update notice. Specifically *Medellin*, not *Rio*. Our people are on both ships, of course, and we'll deal with whatever you can handle, but *Medellin* has a framework that can make the weapon disappear. And that's the point, Kate, to make it disappear. Nobody can have this. Can you imagine? Can you imagine the lives it would destroy? You can back my play, Kate, or you can lose everything."

Keller shivered. "Don't have much of a choice, huh."

"That's it," Sharma said.

"I don't even know how it works."

Sharma took a considering breath. "It's a zero-point battery. I wasn't lying about that. But it's unusable in human contexts, because it does something with the energy it holds inside involving the brain's electrical impulses. The human memory."

"How do you know?"

"This." Sharma weaved her fingers together and sat on the large medical table in the center of the room. "I had a personal comm device on me before I was taken to the *Phoenix*. I was flipping through some photographs I'd kept there while I was waiting for Len to get back from the toilet. There's a child in them. I seem to know her. I'm hugging her, at least . . . she's perhaps four, five years old. And I can look at her, and I know she likes rainbows, I know she enjoys cartoons . . . but I don't know who she is. She's a stranger."

"That's your granddaughter," Keller whispered. "You talked about her all the time."

"Yes." Sharma looked distant for a moment, then snapped into business mode, straightening her back. "I imagine, sometimes, that I love her very much. I'm theorizing that exposure to the weapon through the isolette erased her memory from my mind. Imagine what it would have done if we'd seen it full-on. Imagine what a *Company* could do with it, especially if they were able to reverse-engineer these capabilities."

The worst part about it was that Keller could imagine what a Company could do. A workforce with no past to worry about had no future beyond what was presented to them. If she couldn't remember Neversink or *Twenty-Five,* if she forgot the crisp taste of recycled air, the crack of ice melting on the lake, or, for God's sake, forgot Ash—

She took a deep breath. Thought of Ash.

"What do I do?"

The doctor turned and walked toward the door, crooking her finger for Keller to approach. She opened a drawer and came out with a piece of silver-white fabric about the size of a small tablecloth, folded it up and gave it to Keller. "They've been getting ready for something like this, Kate. This is a new kind of quarantine weave Baywell has developed to block Vai molecular effects toward soldiers in suits. It should do the trick of blocking the battery's signal long enough for you to get your pod launched and back to Aurora."

She then pointed toward the lock. "Just get the device, then get to *Medellin.* Up seven levels, then a right, then out, down a corridor twenty feet. I believe they have it connected to the main battery in the hopes it can power some of their Vai moleculars. I believe Ramsay plans to use them on our Auroran friends. If I'm right, all you'll have to do is touch the damned thing, and it'll be yours. You'll walk out with it and nobody will be able to stop you."

"And what are you going to do?"

"Leave me here. It's actually best that you do. She still needs me to cure her, so I'll have at least six safe months before I need an evac."

"And I'm going to forget?"

Sharma shook her head. "I don't know."

"You *don't know.*"

"It won't matter."

Keller's jaw worked. She shivered. The implications bounced around her head like an unsecured grenade in the back of a station tram. Her hand shook where it had slipped into her pocket and circled the cold steel of the multi-tool but did not move. "Earlier. You said *our people,* but you didn't mean Aurora," she prompted.

"Yes. I told you I served humanity," Sharma said. She hopped down from the table and reached behind her neck, grabbing at a silver necklace, drawing it out from underneath her dirty shirt. It was a medallion of sorts on a tarnished chain, like she'd been wearing it continuously for years, in and out of showers and battle zones and hours asleep; Keller only saw a glint as Sharma shoved it over her neck and under her shirt, and then drew her long hair over the name of the stolen coat. She recognized the chain as the necklace that Sharma had draped at the back of her neck since she'd onboarded on *Twenty-Five* over a year ago.

"This is how they'll know you on *Medellin.* Welcome to the Sacrament Society," she whispered.

# 23

Kneeling on the floor of the pod bay, flanked by the living and the dead, Ash was clear on only one thing.

Her memories no longer belonged to her.

The silver blood slipped into her veins and coursed hot and bright there, and within a few heartbeats, the voices sang under her skin. She felt the Vai peel back her skull and grab her neurons like a bouquet of roses. The voices chorused in inhuman sibilants at first, then in stuttering phrases, then, finally, coalesced into words she could understand.

*Connecting. Connecting.*

Ash was on fire, watching her life flash before her eyes. The voices rushed through her prefrontal cortex, sorting through her entire life like a person searching through a box of printed flimsies: huddling with her mother in the Wellspring tunnels. Signing the indenture documents as a teenager. Her first bleary view of brown-haired Keller. The attack on Bittersweet, the blood in her eyes, Christopher protecting her from the falling rocks above. And then all the memories were of him: Christopher smiling as they pressed their thumbs to the indenture agreement. Christopher brushing celestium dust from her cheek. Christopher playing cards. Wearing his orange sweater. Drinking coffee.

*Stop. He's dead.*
*The words ripped from the darkest place in her body.*

*Dead. Deleted. Gone forever.*
The alien spoke in Christopher's voice, multiplied by a thousand.

The alien's eyes went glassy, abalone-pink, and Ash swayed, nearly bowled over by the black terror crowding her brain like an overloaded circuit. The Vai removed its claw, and Ash was finally able to see the circular indentation in its wrist in the same place that Ash's human body displayed small, corded sapphire veins. The gap was deep, protected by a round edge of gems that shone with blue fire and a thin protective sheet of gossamer gold. Below it, she could see the river of the alien's bloodstream, the celestium-silver sweep of it, the thrumming of its pulse; it was calling her. That was the only word she had for the experience, the way like called to like, the way her blood was thrilling to a sense that was both familiar and completely new.

*Connecting. Connecting.*

*I think I know what you want.* Unable to hold steady, she reached into her pocket to grab her multi-tool, flipping up the knife. She made a small cut in the pad of her index finger and slid her finger into the lacuna. The alien's fingers interwove with hers, feeling quiet and salty, and its claw slipped back into her arm, into the dark purple of the veins leading to her heart, and they held each other there, hand in hand, blood in blood.

*Primary node: Ashlan. Secondary node: Christopher.*
*Connection made. Network established.*

A gate swung open in Ash's mind. Her senses exploded like an overclocked boltgun: loneliness, shaking loneliness, her own and that belonging to the thousand voices shattering her mind. She felt wet tears on her cheeks. She still inhabited her own

body, still lived in its marrow and muscle and gristle, but her
mind was full of memories that weren't hers, voices that spoke
in spiraling, chittering glitter. Her mind bilocated. She knew she
was Ashlan Jackson, but she also was a thousand others; she was
*together* with a thousand others, married to a new consciousness adopting her blood, in her brain, in her mind, all of them
saying *Welcome, sweet sister, welcome.*
It was almost too much, like her head had been shoved into a
rock spinner and her body left to drown, and—

—then Len yanked her arm away from the alien, pressing his
wadded-up jacket against the spattering cut in her wrist. The
real world popped back into existence with a sobbing disconnect.
Natalie's boltgun whined too close to her ear. Ash was suddenly
aware of a thousand little details in the hangar bay: the pattern
of the blood spatter on the floor, the sweat collecting like stones
at Natalie's temples, the pinot-noir moss crawling up from the
darkness.

The Vai crowed like a starving child. The sudden loss of the
thousand voices felt like a tornado at her very core. She shoved
the jacket away, craving the tidal-wave sound of the *together*,
reaching for the alien, for the hive consciousness that was so
close, for the *glory* she'd just experienced. The alien screamed,
bright and *alone* and terrified.

"I have a shot," Natalie shouted, the boltgun wailing and
steady in her hands.

"No." The word was incandescent on Ash's tongue. She scrambled forward, trying to cover the distance between her body and
the alien's—*theirs, them, plural*—and succeeded only in ripping
herself away from Len, blood spattering on the floor behind her
as she pulled herself closer, closer—

Nat's voice tore. "Move, Ash."

"No."

"Ash, for fuck's sake, I will shoot you—"

Len pinwheeled between them. "Calm the fuck down, just hold off—"

"Goes for both of you," Natalie spat, but she was looking at Len, now, and the gun was shaking in anger or fear or both. Ash, her hand still blood-slick, used the distraction to reach for the Vai, sliding her finger back into the lacuna, into the rushing silver inside.

"It won't hurt me," she said, and was—

—swept away by the *reality* of the silver, by the intense and shuddering understanding that as long as she lived, Ash would never be *alone* again. This was home. This was *together;* it was the closest word the Vai had to two bodies sharing a thousand souls, two bodies sharing memories and thoughts and intentions—

There were things Ash had to know. *How did you get here?*

*Give yourself to the silver,* she heard.

*I don't know how.*

The instructions were argent glitter. *Let go.*

*It was an honest mistake,* Ash thought, as she was swept further into the bright arms of Christopher's whisper-song. An *honest mistake* to think the Vai were the bodies they presented and not the silver inside—cousins to the nanocreatures that lived in her own blood and the silver substance that kept them alive. An *honest mistake,* to think that consciousness worked on the same basic template everywhere, that the Vai had the same relationship to their own bodies as humans did to theirs. Christopher showed her memories of an alien ship, as dense as flesh itself with flashing light and bulkheads that breathed and computers woven into the nanocreatures' very consciousness, where Vai rushed through tight corridors the size of her wrist in organic silver, a circulation as alive as lightning. He showed her the nodes: specially grown secondary interfaces with useful hands and feet, organic machines that humans called *bodies* and *mechs,* interfaces that would serve as the home for the Vai making new colonies on worlds inhospitable to the silver. These bodies that would build new nodes, new factories, new horizons, would connect them to the master node on the homeworld that was the source and summit of all that was Vai, were the very things that terrified human children and caused Natalie to cry in her sleep—

*Like a computer network? Your species is a computer network? You download into these bodies?*

*You are alone. You cannot understand.*

*I can try.*

*It is horrible. Horrible. We did not know.*

*Did not know what?*

Ash heard the slightest hesitation before the memories shifted. The *together* showed her an alien ship, organic and red-slick, the tight veins where the bright silver Vai coursed in their thousands. Then she saw the *download room,* where the secondary nodes filled with bright silver, the Vai in their veins causing them to rise from their slumber ten years before they reached the colony—because history was happening here in deep space, happening to these ten thousand Vai in the veins of their ten vessels, ready to interface, to speak, to trade, all of them understanding the shattering importance of this moment.

*First contact with aliens.*
And then: fire. The hull of the ship, holed.

*Why did they have to do that? Why did they not download?*

*That's a breaching pod,* Ash told the *together. There was no other way to for them to get on board.*
Ash recognized the intruders immediately, their gangly two-legged bodies in familiar blue-black carapaces, their stubby fabric-covered fingers and alien machinery. *Humans. Auroran humans.* Their blinding, sickening flashlights. She'd seen this before when her body was broken and bloody, barely breathing, on the floor of a mine. This color. This light. *But this was no rescue—*
Wait.
One of them was Reva Sharma.
*I know her.*

*We did not know they were alone. We thought they were together.*

*You mean you thought they were interfaces. Nodes. Like you.*
Christopher offered the speaking-claw. [*Christopher, the secondary node,* she thought, *the one that is many in front of me.*] The alien intruder hesitated, then entwined its fingers with the fat, stubby ones of the secondary node. The intruder's blue carapace felt hard to Christopher, unlike any kind of secondary or tertiary node they'd ever encountered, but it yielded to the claw, nonetheless, as everything did.
But it all went wrong. A puff of air slithered from the alien's wrist rather than words of welcome. A spatter of warm, red, *wrong* blood, dead blood, silent blood. And more, and less, after that: a new sound [*screaming,* explained Ash], and then utter silence, the blank whispering gallery of a singular human brain.
The word for it was *alone,* they'll learn.

*Alone.* A terrified howl.
And then a stuttering cracking sound like khilar trees bending
in a storm, like bones breaking—
Ash knew that sound, too. *You mean gunfire. They thought you
were attacking, when you did to them what you did to me.*

*This is where we learned about death.*

She felt the next memories like gunshots to the gut, a wild blast
of pain and confusion. The weapons were primitive, but functional, and the ship went dark as the *gunfire* scrawled holes in
the secondary nodes and they fell, broken, to the floor. Vai were
spattered everywhere, chylous white and silver, outside their
ships, desperate to upload, unable to upload, and soon the red
steel-stink of the *monsters,* too, because Vai had just learned of
*death* and *war* and *being alone* and it is terrifying and wrong and
monstrous and they are returning it directly to the invaders—
*They killed you.*

*They made us alone.*

*I don't understand the difference.*
At the end of the slaughter, only two nodes survived, licking up
the silver, tasting the voices that sang in their throats, hearing
them cry *glory* as they reintegrated. And they thought they were
doing well, until the humans yanked out the Heart at the center
of their ship. The Heart: the beautiful screaming scrollwork
thing Ash knew as the *London* weapon, the weapon that was not
a weapon, the thing that was going to power the Vai colony and
connect them back to the master node. The mainframe. *Home.*
The silence was murderous. The humans took them aboard a
vessel that did not sing, and since then
they'd had to sing for themselves and—

Someone slapped Ash back to her own skull, once, twice, three times. *Len,* a dark, close blur smelling of dirt and sweat. Trapped in her skin, sucking down dust and blood at the back of her throat, she tasted the silver there, the knowledge of life eternal, of a thousand things she should not know but now did.

"—and you are not in command here, Natalie. Look. She's here. Ash, talk to Nat," she heard Len say. "Tell her it's fine."

"S'fine." The words came out of Ash's mouth, half muddled. She felt submerged, slow, confined to tight, recalcitrant skin. "Doesn't hurt."

"Bull*shit,*" said Natalie.

"If she *says* it's not hurting her," Len said, "then you need to believe her—"

"It's *killing* her."

Ash looked from one to the other. How long had she been under? "We're the killers. We taught them about death," she said, trying to put human words around a concept that suddenly seemed too awful for human words to describe. Blood pooled and clotted in the wound in her arm where the alien's claw dug, crooked and white, into the soft bed of her wrist. "We *tortured* them. Kidnapped them. Aurora did. Dr. Sharma. Took their way home. *We* were in the wrong."

"Ask it what it wants," Len said, his voice hushed as if he were witnessing a miracle.

Christopher was waiting for her when she closed her eyes again, and they told her they—

—simply want to go home.

That easy?

We did not know what being alone truly meant. Anguish.

*What do you mean?*

Ash was in a cage with the other vessel, the tertiary node, on an alien world. Ash recognized ragged, damaged prefabs, failing atmospinners. For a moment, she thought it might be Tribulation, but no, she looked to the sky where the master node's bloodships were trying to reach them, at the shattered atmospheric dome there, at the black sky, the ragged blue Auroran flags fluttering in a poison wind. Rubble. Bodies and blood, all of it wine-colored, human, drying in the sun.

Nearby, she saw a sign, pockmarked by burns: *Gethsemane Town*. She knew the master node was close, heard the bloodships in orbit above sending down weapons that will make the aliens on the planet retreat and re-upload. There was no need for war. *It's not the same for us*, Ash thought. *We get—we get deleted. Do you understand? We get deleted.*

Anguish. *They did not know. They do not know now. Only we know. We have to go home to let them know. We have to go. Now. Baby, it's all coming down around us, baby—*

Ash's nausea spiked, and she—

—saw stars, choked on sudden vomit in her throat, Len's fists a hard tattoo on her back. Ash clawed herself back, swallowed her pain, swallowed the realizations that crowded against her forehead, let the hangar twist back into existence before she spoke.

"They were at Gethsemane. They were being held there as prisoners. Gethsemane was supposed to be a rescue, not a *massacre*."

Natalie's face was painted with bright tears. "They sent down *bonecrushers*."

"They didn't know we could die." Ash's mouth was dry, coated in blood, in living silver. She felt faint, felt dragged back toward the *together* in an inexorable, welcoming whirlpool.

"That doesn't make any *sense*."

"They don't die. Not how we die. The bodies, they're—" Her body started to shake, big, shuddering tremors she couldn't control. "They think we download into our bodies, like they do. They don't understand."

Natalie shook the gun. "How can it not understand? All those people? *Four thousand people,* destroyed in minutes? What about Cana? Thessilane? The Lost Worlds? Bittersweet? It doesn't matter how it started, Ash. When lives are on the line, it doesn't matter what is believed. It matters what is *done*."

"This changes everything," Len said.

Natalie's lip curled. "Doesn't change a thing."

Len clambered to his knees. "Ash. You can tell them about us. You can tell them to stop. You can do what nobody else could have even thought possible—you can broker peace with the Vai, and right here. Right now. You can talk to them."

Hope hung incandescent and sobbing in Ash's throat, and then fell, like a punctured balloon. "No. They're *alone*."

Natalie spat her next words. "There's no peace with the Vai. Even this *peace* we've had is just—just the absence of war, just the lack of it."

Len looked toward the door, wringing his hands. "Let her try, Nat."

Natalie made a grudging noise of assent.

*Come back,* Ash heard, and she—

—fell back into the warmth of *together.* Christopher nagged in his chorus, a child tugging at her leg, a supervisor screaming from the other room.

*Aurora.* They showed her Sharma again. The picture lacked photographic detail, like a human memory caught broken and cluttered by the ravages of time, but Ash knew who it was.

*We made a mistake,* Reva Sharma said, looming above her. Ash

was still looking at her through the eyes of the secondary node. Pain lanced through her body. Hers, and theirs. It was too clear, too bright, more than a memory. *But it doesn't have to define us.*
*The blood nanotech these aliens use—do you know how many diseases I could cure if I just had time, how many uncitizens I could save? Do you know the core of their ship might be a zero-point battery? How we could stop scarcity? Feed everyone?*
The other woman had a familiar face; smaller, younger.
*Are you sure this is a good idea?*
*A good idea? To save people? I have some connections on a Wellspring base. Bittersweet. If we bring them into the program, we can sign up some indentures for medical trials.*
The younger woman slots in. Jessen, from Sharma's recording, all orange lines and sketched-in detail. *I mean, will the creatures be missed?*
*Just two of them, lost on a colony ship far from home? Aurora would write that off. We have to fix this. Make our sin a sacrament. Something beautiful from all the blood.*
Christopher tried to scream but—

—the alien's claw slipped out, and they fell, weak and rattling, back into the pile of rags. Len's face was close to Ash's, his breath smelling caustic, like insomnia and engine oil. It seemed strange to not know what he was thinking.

"Let me go." She felt a rag, clammy-painful against the dark gap in her wrist.

"You can go back one more time," he said. "You're losing too much blood, and I don't know what this silver shit is doing to you. We're not going to let you bleed out."

"It's okay," Ash whispered. "I'm in the *together* now."

"Len, this needs to stop," said Natalie.

And she felt herself, still in her own body and in the alien's, bilocated and brilliant, floating, burning hard and sane like no human had before. "No. One more time. Please. They don't have linear minds," Ash said. "There's no such thing as *one single Vai*. They—it's the wrong word, but I don't know how else to describe it. They're like files on a server. They download into bodies to interact with worlds that aren't made like theirs, just like we use suits to work in vacuum. They have an entire technology built around it—nanotech and biotech, network and energy maintenance. We weren't killing them, in the war. They were just *uploading.*"

She gulped down more dusty air and opened her mouth to continue, but Natalie, red and shaking, cut in before she could speak. "My unit. Killed nothing. Died for *nothing*. None of it was real."

"They made mistakes," Ash said. The words were like water in her mouth. "But we made mistakes, too. The biggest ones. The doctor was on the ship, Nat, when the science team botched first contact. The Vai were trying to be friendly—"

"They're lying to you," Natalie spat.

"Listen. We kidnapped an entire family line. Disabled the Heart of their ship so they couldn't upload. It was like—if we wandered straight over to an entire colony and sucked it right up. That's why they attacked."

Natalie looked down at her gun. "Blood for blood."

"No, they—"

"Our lost for their lost." Natalie raised the gun again.

Dizzy, Ashlan tried to get to her feet as Len attempted to apply an autobandage to her cartwheeling arm. "No. That's not what happened. They didn't know they were killing us. They didn't know we could die."

Natalie's voice grew stronger. "Can you hear yourself right now?"

Len managed to get Ash to stop moving long enough to slap the autobandage on her arm. "Not yet," Ash said. "There are a hundred thousand people in this body right now, Natalie, so put the fucking gun *down,* so I can try to make peace. We can stop any new war, any conflict in the future right now, we just have to get in a ship and get them beyond the White Line, back to their people."

"And I suppose you'll want to bring the weapon back, too." Natalie's index finger flickered. "Mm?"

Ash put herself between Natalie and the alien, whose chest moved up and down, shallow, mother-of-pearl eyes spinning blank and sick at the ceiling. "Yes," she said. "It's not really a weapon. It's their connection to their world, their only way home—"

This time, she didn't need Christopher to bring up the memory. She had the *together* in her veins now, and she could be back there in a second, back in the pod, the darkness crawling up her arm once more, the cold air dropping into her heart and taking root in her veins.

She remembered everything now. How the weapon had scrambled behind her eyes, dragged out the memories, one by one, and thrown them into a darkness from which there was no exit. A device, a machine, an engine whose very purpose was to connect Vai with their source destroyed humans by doing the same.

A machine that had been changed by the Sacrament Society to work against the Vai, that had taken Len's memory of Aurora and God knows what else. She tried to clutch at her lost memories in the blank reverie, throwing herself again and again against the wall—she hadn't been trying to hurt herself, she'd been chasing them, all the things she'd forgotten, her parents and her home—

Natalie tilted her head. "Step away, Ash. I won't ask you again."

"No," Ash said. "There must be peace."

She could see Natalie swallow, panic alight in her throat.

*We did not know death. What a gift you have given us, this word, this concept, this horror, this sobbing, sucking blank slate. We are dead every moment of the day.* Not the cold loneliness of an empty bed or the silent press of a family lost but *the howling void where a hundred thousand voices should sing, the fore-mothers, the children, the generations who lived all at once.* Ash understood. *Christopher is not dead, he can never be dead, be-cause time was space, space was emotion, emotion was memory, memory was speech, everything lived at once—files that lived within them, the decisions that were made because of them, the potential that grew from them, the servers that would grow and germinate, the glorious colonies all feeding back to the master node,* alone *or* together, *they were the same— all we want—*

—is to go home," Ash finished. "Anything less is genocide, anything less is death for Aurora and every Company and Earth and *everything* we are."

"Now it's a victim?" Natalie shook her head, and her gun shook. "Millions dead, Ash, and you're calling *that* the victim?"

"Natalie," said Len, taking one step forward. "Come on, let's take a walk."

Ash shook her head. "Would you just listen for one goddamn second? There's something else—"

"*There is nothing else!*" The words clawed their way from Na-talie's throat. "You weren't there! You weren't at Cana! You didn't see what they did, you didn't see the bodies, how many people they killed! And now you say it meant nothing? My friends' deaths meant nothing? Now you say that *we're* the evil ones? Whatever it's doing, it's just using you! You can't believe anything it says, Ashlan!"

"Put down the fucking gun, Natalie!"

A twitch of Natalie's finger.

A single gunshot.

A dark crater erupted on the alien's forehead, and the thing fell back against its pile of rags and meal bar wrappers.

Ash screamed, losing her balance, her head empty, her blood cold, falling like a clump of quiet, deathless earth back against the concrete floor. The alien's shining eyes went dull and the long limbs limp. Milk-silver blood flowed out into the linen smocks in which it lay. Ash clawed at the rags, the *together's* legs, its hands, trying to hold it, trying to take it inside herself, trying to do anything to make the *alone* a little less diamond-keen. She shook the dead body, screaming, placing her lips against its shuddering wrist, trying to drink in the life there, tasting astringent metal and the ache of death. She understood Reva's kiss, her reverence, everything she'd done after leaving Tribulation. This was the corpse of a civilization, thousands upon thousands of files dead, and she was choking on it—

"You killed them all." She turned back to Natalie when she came up breathing; the younger woman's eyes danced over Ash's silver-coated lips in disgust.

"I did the right thing," she whispered.

"You—I told you it was genocide—I told you," stammered Ash. "All of them, you've killed all of them—there's not just one—they don't live *just one life*—"

Natalie swung her dark eyes from the dead alien to Ash. "No. You're sick. You're *terminal.* You're not thinking. Take the alien beyond the White Line? In what? What did you expect? Were you going to ask Mr. Solano for a subcruiser? A crew?"

Len's mouth worked in silent surprise as Natalie continued. "Let's say you were right, and that we let it live. Then that *thing* gets brought up to *Rio,* and what do you think is going to happen? Don't tell me you wouldn't want it alive, if you were Mr. Solano or any of the other CEOs. The single greatest market advantage any Company has ever had. It's better off dead."

"You killed them."

"I did you a favor."

Tears welled in Ash's eyes, and she lay against the dead *together*, searching for the voices and coming up only with dead, screaming silence. "Anything that happens from here is your fault, Natalie, your fault, anyone who dies, any planet that burns."

"You have to figure out whose side you're on, Ash, and by that I mean—do you want to live?" Natalie said. "I want to live. I want to be a citizen, and you want to be a citizen, too, even though you're a dumbass who can't even negotiate a contract or see her own fucking worth. I just saved your life. With *that* gone"—she pointed at the alien corpse—"they'll still need you."

At some point, a thousand years ago it seemed, Ash had cared about citizenship. Now it was different; she reached for the crescent in her pocket, and the voices she heard weren't real, but they were at least something more than *alone*. Keller's ghost was something more than *alone*.

"Get out," she spat.

Natalie's face flickered with a moment's uncertainty, before settling back in to a cold, chosen confidence. "I'm going to meet the executives. You'd best smash up the computer if you want that monster's death to mean anything." She turned on one heel and strode out.

Ash found that she could not stand, that the world had gone blue and gold and her body numb. Her knees buckled. She fell to the ground, hitting the concrete floor with a painful shudder, her sickness rushing back in a great wave, her hands barely supporting her weight. When her head stopped spinning, Len was still there, right beside her, his hands helping her to sit, pressing a bottle of water into her lap, telling her that it was going to be okay.

It was a useful lie on the best of days, but Ash did not imagine she would ever have a day like that again.

She hauled herself to her knees and tried to push him away. "You should do what she says."

Len sat instead, moving close so his shoulder rested an inch from hers, so close Ash could hear the angry clatter of the small bones in his back as he settled in. He tilted the bottle toward her, the clean water sloshing around inside.

Ash was suddenly all too aware of the blank twist of desert in her mouth, and she snatched it up, tossing him the cap, gulping down a few angry, lukewarm mouthfuls. Down the hall, near the lab, she could hear the clanging of boots, the clamor of excited Auroran voices. "Oh, Arbiter," one of them breathed, "it's— it's—do you know what that is—"

"Go with her," she said. "She'll need you."

"She needed me before she—" His eyes flickered toward the dead *together,* worried at the metal decking with his thumb. "Before. They'll make her a citizen now, and I'll never see her again. Ash, I'm sorry—"

She closed her eyes. "It's not your fault."

"No, listen. I knew she was broken, Ash. I didn't help her. She said she was fine, and I believed her. I could have—I would have—"

Ash handed him the bottle. Something small and horrible and angry rattled in her chest, growing louder by the moment. *You can save us,* it hollered, *you can save us,* but she couldn't, could she? She couldn't save any of them, not the *together,* not Kate, not herself. She couldn't even walk out of here on her own power.

"We're all broken," she said.

He forced out a quiet, incredulous laugh. "A *planetoid* collapsed on you, Ash. You walked out, and you kept on walking. That would have destroyed anybody else. It would have destroyed me. But you—"

"Len—"

"Just listen to me. You don't give up. You never give up on anything—or anyone. You try, and you try again, for me and for

Natalie and for—" His voice went hoarse, and his eyes tipped back over to the dead *together*. "For *them*. You're not broken. You're not even close. Don't you know how much I admire you?"

Her head twisted with surprise. He was looking at her with such compassion, and tears in his eyes—brown eyes, the color of soil and salt and earth, of the deep darkness of a home she'd never known.

"Maybe I did," she whispered, "but now?"

"Well, that's bullshit," he responded. He reached for her hand, and she let him take it. "No. Now *we* help *you*. What do you need?"

*What do I need?*

She almost didn't answer. She looked from him to the pile of dead skin and bones that hid the reality of *together*. *Need* was a broken word, a fairy tale from a time in her life before she'd entered this room. She'd needed things, once, like love and air and food and light, but sitting here in the tomb of the silent *together*, in the lair of ashes and lost promises, even breathing was difficult. What was breathing, if she was to rattle about in her own head like a lost child for a blank eternity? She should have died underground years ago, on a death-bound planetoid soaked in corporate sin. She wanted to sit here and let the smothering earth above finish what it had begun.

She forced air out, in, back out again. Dragged it in. Pushed it out. She did not want to move ever again.

But the *together* deserved better.

"You were right. I need to go there," Ash said. "Beyond the White Line."

He blinked. "The Vai is dead. What's the use?"

"If I can talk with them, I can talk with the others," she explained, her hand working around the fabric of her jacket. She held it tight, like it was real. Like anything on this dull, quiet world was real. "I can talk with their primary node. But there's a problem. Once I walk out there and give myself back to Aurora, I'll never see daylight again."

He blinked. A knowing quiet settled on his shoulders. "I still have friends in *Rio* engineering. We'll get you out. We'll get you there. You're strong. You'll make it."

She wiped a tear away. "I'm not," she said. "That's where you're wrong. I didn't walk away from Bittersweet. They carried me."

His arm tightened around her shoulder. "Hey," he said. "Hey. We carry each other."

She felt something sticky and hot on the palm of her hand, and when she lifted it to see, she found the alien's milk-silver blood a film on her fingers. The memories of Christopher, of Keller, of the thousand voices, were already fading again, back into her faltering human mind and her shaking, sick body. She turned her head to rest against Len's shoulder, and his hand rested light and secure against the back of her head, and he stayed there as she cried.

She cried for the dead aliens, for all her kind and her kin, even after new voices shouted their names in the hallway, and Len slid his arm under her shoulders and took her down the hall toward her uncertain future.

# 24

The soldiers who met Len and Ash at the door to the admin wing wore the bright collar tags of new citizens and the dark blue tactical jackets of seasoned veterans of the Vai war. They were young, like Natalie was young, with strong bodies full of the shaking memory of trauma. Ash shoved her hand in her pocket to put her fingers around the weapon, and it assured her of its presence and attention with a comforting hum.

*They're not enemies*, she assured it. *And you can't help them upload. Shh.*

*Glory*, the weapon responded, and hummed hot and bright in response.

Slipping her hand around the weapon felt like the *together*, felt like the thing she'd wanted all her life, the thing that Natalie had wrenched away from her with a single shot. Explaining what she was missing now—explaining how *glory* felt—was like trying to drink the ocean or explain the depth of the universe.

She mourned as she walked.

Rio's ordnance staff moved from isolette to isolette with flimsy clipboards, cataloging the weapons and checking the isolettes for security flaws. A few days ago, the sight might have left her overjoyed; the entire Christmas list, packaged up and placed as payment against her desire to live. Now, it made her feel sick.

A group of well-dressed executives idled on the landing, their polished high heels and diamond-cut jackets glistening bright and violent against the jagged stone walls. Natalie, whose dirt-streaked face, blood-filthy hands, and rumpled jumpsuit provided significant contrast to the executives' stainless outfits, spoke in an animated fashion with a well-coiffed Joseph Solano and a thin-looking Dr. Julien, wearing a silver coat and slicked-back hair. At the sight, Len's shoulders stayed compact, keeping small, low, and silent beside Ash. Julien saw her coming, and he went red, looking away. He was still afraid. His reaction did nothing to quell the nausea spinning up from her stomach and the memory of the *together.*

Ash squared her shoulders and lifted her chin. *Executives. Shit.* She looked like an uncitizen and smelled even worse. Ash took a stabbing breath and rubbed her bloody hands on her pant legs as they approached, but the silver substance had already dried, and came off in small flakes. Bodies. Death.

Natalie squirmed in her shoes rather than look back at Ash.

". . . a spectacular find," one of the executives was saying. "A record for any salvage outfit anywhere and done under such difficult circumstances."

Mr. Solano cleared his throat. "Indeed, Mr. Stephenson. I'd like to talk with our success stories, please. Get your departments ready to ship all of this to *Rio;* Dr. Julien, get prepped; you'll be taking our heroes back to *Rio.*"

The executives moved off to survey the carnage; Julien turned away and started making calls. Solano hopped down the stairs, approaching them rather than the other way around, the way it should have been. Natalie waited, her hands clasped behind her, her gun cold in her holster, silent. Solano extended his hand to Len, who shook it, and then to Ash; she refused it with a shake of her head.

"I'm far too dirty to touch you, sir."

Solano gave her a cursory glance, up and down. Disapproval flashed for a moment in the form of pursed lips, before the executive's face fell back into practiced calm. "Yes, I can see that. You've been through a lot, I'd imagine. Well, we'll make sure all of you get a nice, hot shower on *Rio* before we put you back to work."

Ash straightened. "The weapon's gone. Sir, after what I just saw, I think we need to set up an expedition to go behind the White Line. Immediately. We can't wait."

Solano cut her off, opening his hand over the expansive cathedral. "*We* have to ensure and expand Aurora's future. *You* need to fulfill your contract."

"Mr. Solano, I need to explain to you what I just saw—"

He crossed the space between them in two quick steps and cut her off again with a cold, half-paternal hand placed on her shoulder. Ash felt a trickling unease building in the back of her throat. "You signed a contract, Ashlan, that says you will give every *yes* that is asked of you, to every task that is asked of you, no matter how daunting, immediately and without fail. Or are you holding back again?"

Ash looked over at Natalie. The other woman shuffled her feet, still silent.

In the cavern filled with the faint, sure promise of so much death—humming, singing, whispering at the edges of her sanity, sounds cartwheeling around exploding stars the entire concept of citizenship shattered against Keller's absence, the absence of the *together*, cold and quiet. Citizenship? The cure? Alone in her shattered mind? All she could see now were quiet days filled with the silence of a stalled world. Cold winters and ashes, the inexorable and malignant slide to a screaming death, and a thousand aching years in between. All of it spent alone—and *alone*.

And yet.

"This is important enough to sacrifice my citizenship, sir," she said.

Solano tightened his hand on Ash's shoulder. "I know you *think* it is, but let citizens in the know make the decisions. You'll be briefed on *Rio* as to your new responsibilities. We have a lot of work to do, and it will be wonderful work. I promise you, Ashlan. If you obey, without fail, we will find her."

*Find Kate.* Her vision blurred. Tears. Ash felt faint. "Of course, sir."

"We just need to find out what you can do first, for the sake of the Company."

In her memory, the *together* was singing hymns of *glory* in oranges and reds, shades of fire in her veins, a phoenix pyre for Keller and the hundred thousand colonists who had died in the shuttlebay. For the death of worlds, of battlefields, of civilizations, of grand starships traversing the darkness between stars, bringing control or death at the tips of her fingers. *What I can do. Fly pods? Operate mining machines?*

Somehow, Solano was still talking. "Captain Keller would be proud of you. You'll be helping us become a market leader. We'll be able to expand our influence throughout the Outer Reaches and maybe into the halls of the Inner Worlds itself," Solano said.

His words finally made sense.

"You want me to use the moleculars," she said.

"Your presence will be enough of a deterrent, for now, I believe," Solano said.

Ash's stomach bottomed out, and the words started tumbling from her mouth before she could stop them. "I'm not a weapon," she said. "I don't care what I signed. You don't know what happened in there, you don't know what *she* did." She stabbed her finger in Natalie's direction. "And if you did, would you care? Oh, you'll start with the aliens, and that'll be justified because of the war, what they did in the war, and you won't for one second think that wrong can run both ways. And then you'll justify using it on humans, using *me* on humans, and my blood after I'm dead, because I've seen this bullshit before. It's this whole project, it's Wellspring sending me into the tunnels all over again, every single inch of it—and I can't live like that. I can't, Mr. Solano."

She was breathless at the end of it, breathless and shaking. Solano's mouth twisted. "You'll live any way we ask you to. You have Auroran lives to pay for, indenture."

"You were the one that sent me down here without doing enough research," Ash said. "Those lives are on your conscience."

Solano cast a glance at the stairs, then beckoned Natalie closer. "You *negotiated* for that privilege."

Len moved to her left, a worried presence. "Ash, maybe we should talk about this."

Ash wrenched her shoulder away from Len's touch, losing her balance. It was hard to keep stable when there were so many stars exploding in her peripheral vision, she thought, so many orchestras screaming angry, low bass crescendos underneath what everyone was saying. After a moment with her hands clutching her head, driving down the noise with angry whispers, she was able to speak again.

Mr. Solano stared at her.

"What happens to me when I get back on *Rio*?" she asked.

"Ashlan, stop," Natalie whispered.

Ash pointed at Natalie. "Don't you even *talk* to me."

"Dr. Julien, attend to your indenture," Solano snapped, rubbing his temples. He waved Natalie to his side; as the younger woman stepped down, she lingered the brand-new citizens' tags on her collar, but did not smile. Her eyes flickered over to Ash for the barest of seconds before she turned her back.

"What if I said I could make peace?" Ash said. "That I could stop a second Vai war before it started?"

Ash heard an uneasy silence and pressed, anger pushing spittle past her lips. "Is it because the war was *good* for you? Because despite all the people that died, Aurora still fucking *won market share*?"

Solano was already halfway across the courtyard.

Julien stepped forward and cleared his throat, his eyes looking nervous under a curtain of straight blond hair. "Come on, indenture, ah . . . let's get you to the shuttle."

Ash stepped forward, forcing herself to put one foot in front of the other, forcing herself to follow Julien. They passed up the staircase and into the barn, where a group of ordnance engineers scanned the crates containing the Vai weapons with a resolute haste. They passed through the door into the town square, still bathed in midnight, where groups of indentures in dark blue coats set up floodlights and battled patches of burning brush. They murmured together, pointing toward the dark, enveloping forest in the direction Ash had stumbled just hours before, when everything had been so different. *They knew,* she thought. *They were ready for this. How were they ready for this?*

Len coughed, then stepped up beside her. "Ash, what did he mean? What the *hell* did you sign?"

She could say nothing to that, but she allowed herself to bend, leaning on her friend's warm shoulder to steady her stride. She let the moment fill her heart; she and Len, walking together, the last real members of her salvage family. It wasn't *together,* wasn't even close, but her *alone* brain was desperate for it.

*Friendship,* the weapon whispered from her pocket. *A new concept.*

She wondered if there was silver inside, coursing through living veins, lonely, waiting—

*Together,* it whispered.

She removed her hand—somehow—and walked toward the shuttle.

The shuttle was located near the tree line, and the hatch opened in a slow and familiar way, cutting off Ash's response, revealing the interior: tight and beige-blue like the shuttle she'd piloted during her year in Aurora. Julien stopped at the door and Ash piled in, Len following behind, both going through the old, familiar motions of sliding into seats and drawing the safety web around their hips and shoulders.

The shuttle was an upgrade from the kind of jaunter she'd piloted on *Twenty-Five,* as she'd expected from a *Rio* launch. The pilot was already hunched over his interface, fingers adorned with the corded haptic caps, running through his preflight check with businesslike aplomb. He wore a full helmet, obscuring his face.

"Next stop, *Rio de Janeiro,*" Julien said, his voice bright, as if he were taking Ash to get ice cream. Too bright. His eyes were trained on her. "I hope you're as excited by the research we're going to do as I am."

*Yeah, well,* she thought, *I hope I still scare you shitless.*

She tried to make herself less angry by studying the haptic interface: it functioned as it was supposed to, unlike the one she and Natalie had found on *London.* The pilot's very thought process hovered over the front window for everyone to see in an easy, curving arc, jagged power readings coming through in soothing blues and greens. She surprised herself when she found she could still follow it.

And why not? Pods and shuttles had been her entire life for the past year. She'd found a talent for it. Fuel injection percentage. Environmental interference. Vertical grav intake. Being in the cockpit felt like greeting a long-lost friend. How long had it been since she'd been behind the controls of a pod or a shuttle? The time she'd gone out with Natalie to retrieve the Vai weapon from the wreckage of *London,* she decided. It was what, a day? A fortnight? Thirty hours? Two days? She was starving.

It seemed like years since she'd set out for a normal day in the pod. *Eons.*

Ash watched the pilot mutter to himself, clawing shapes in the air like a deranged magician. It was just as well she was being sidelined. With her brain the way it was, she would never be used to the haptic interfaces, she thought; she was all buttons and switches and shoulder-mounted mining lasers, the last breathing remnant of the human world that existed before the Vai. Maybe she had died back there on Bittersweet, beside Christopher. Maybe all of this since had been some sort of sick purgatory. A holding pattern for hell.

Ash coughed, clearing her throat. "Did you know that they didn't have a concept for war, before they met us?"

"What do you mean?" Len said.

"Cruelty. They learned that from us."

"Please be quiet during preflight," said the pilot, his voice muffled.

The engines whirred to life. Ash let the heads-up blur, looking past it for the last time to the planet beyond. The red trees of Tribulation lived on, blithe and oblivious, their leaves shivering in the sulfur wind. The shuttlecraft shook and sputtered through the too-familiar motions—the sound of the grav-drive spinning up, the tight pull on her shoulders and feet as ship's gravity reasserted itself. The familiar feeling tore at what was left of her composure, and suddenly she was dizzy again, leaning forward in the safety straps, sobbing. The universe tilted on its axis, shaken free of Tribulation's gravity at last. She felt nausea, stomach-clenching pain, a screaming loneliness.

She felt a hand on her knee.

"Doing okay?" whispered Len.

"Yeah." She opened her eyes.

"I call bullshit."

"I'm fine."

He snorted. "You know what she used to say. Space plus bullshit equals death."

Ash thought of Keller standing on the bridge of *Twenty-Five*, bathed in blue and yellow light, her hair half tied up with wisps by her ears, her hip canted to one side, and for a moment she could not breathe. Keller had tried so hard to make her stance look like an executive's but could never quite manage. There was something provincial there, uncouth and unpolished and utterly fascinating. The vision caused a hard, terrible lump to form in Ash's throat and stole her words away. She reached into her pocket to hold the comforting warmth of the weapon. It hummed.

"I've got six months, Len," she said.

He blinked, uncomprehending. "Until citizenship?"

"No. Six months tops."

Len said nothing. His hand left her knee and went up to take hers, lacing through her fingers, holding them tight.

Below them, the settlement spun out like a distracted, drunken top, the city with it, its dead green dreams gasping against the inevitable. She watched the back viewscreen until she could no longer see buildings, and then turned back to the stars. They shook and whirled and cried. She heard whispering. The *together.* *Christopher. Kate.* They sounded as real as Len. She needed it to stop before she decided to claw her eyes out.

"Dr. Julien," she said.

"Mm?" He looked up from a tablet.

"Do you have any trihex shots on you?"

"No, I'm sorry," he said. "We're starting you on a slate of new meds when we get you settled in to molecular development, so just try to hold on until we get to *Rio.*"

"New meds?" Ash's breath caught. "A cure?"

Julien looked distracted; he looked back toward the viewscreen, the HUD, the shuttle's rumbling trajectory out of Tribulation's stratosphere. The air barreled away; stars began appearing in ones and twos, then hundreds. Here were the constellations that had just begun to become familiar over the last few months—the ones Kate had named the Drunk Executive, the Ration Bar, the Ballerina.

"Well," he said, still typing. "R&D has had literally *three hours* to work on it, so no. But we do have some promising antipsychotics, for now, at least."

The shuttle rumbled beneath Ash's body. The pilot made minute movements of his fingers, tilted his hands to adjust the shuttle's path. "The cure's still on the table, though?"

Julien hesitated, his face falling into an emotion that barely resembled sympathy. "We know what you're up against. We're going to do our best."

*Bullshit,* Christopher whispered.

"Hey, look outside." Len had his eyes narrowed, staring past Julien and the pilot to the faraway spinfield. Ash started to make out the familiar curves of the battered hulks, and then of *London*'s, of the thousand glittering pieces of metal that twirled endlessly in the void in front of the curve of the ship's hull.

Behind them were new shapes, dark blue against pitch black, catching the Tribulation sun on their familiar curves. They were Auroran warships like *Rio*, meant to slice through the hulls of Vai vessels, to defend, to protect, to stand against the darkness. She'd never seen so many gathered in one place.

"Holy crap," Len said. "That's *Hong Kong, Medellin, Cape Town*—"

Julien leaned back in his chair. Now that they were out of the atmosphere, he unbuckled his safety straps and stood. He lay his arm on the top of the chair. The motion drew his jacket back, revealing that he carried a personal boltgun.

"This is a big find," he said. "Tribulation is about to become a popular place. We'll need to defend it."

Len gave a nervous chuckle that turned into a rattling cough. "We're expecting a battle?"

"Mr. Solano is always hopeful that any intercompany dispute

can be resolved in a peaceful fashion," Julien responded. "What's that thing they teach you in school—that ancient phrase from the Democratic Age? 'Speak softly and carry a big stick'?"

Ash watched the ships approach with a growing sense of dread. The cruisers' rail guns, their armor, their overpowered spinal lances—none of it would matter a damn if the Vai showed today. Once the Vai learned the secondary and tertiary node were truly dead, along with their portion of *together*. So *many* dead. They would come.

And if Ramsay showed too, what would happen then?

*There's no department called molecular development,* she thought.

*There might not have been three hours ago,* Christopher whispered back.

"After the cure is administered, will I be able to control the weapons? Or are you going to do this to someone else once I'm cured?" *Or dead?*

He looked back to the spinfield. "We'll talk on *Rio.*"

Len squared his jaw and shook his head.

Ash's mouth felt dry. "Dr. Julien, please."

Julien stared into the viewscreen. His shoulders tightened. "You signed a contract. That contract limits what I can tell you."

Frustration made her itch. Ash dug her fingernails into her thigh to keep herself from hearing Christopher. "This is my life, Dr. Julien, and you're a doctor."

He was quiet for a moment, then he put the tablet aside. "Celestium sickness is one thing. It's almost prohibitively expensive, but it's eventually curable, with enough investment. This is celestium-bonded alien nanotech, and it's . . ." he said, low, with a tremor in his voice. "Well, it's so expensive we don't even have figures for it yet. And I've studied Sharma's work, but I'm not Reva Sharma. All I know is that it's beautiful and terrible. The power of a thousand suns in your fingers, but such a trade."

Ash looked down at her hands: dirty, streaked with the alien's blood, trembling. Calloused. A worker's hands. A weapon's.

"A trade. My life." The words came out crumbled, like boots on bone, like gravel.

"But you're going to do such wonderful things, Ashlan," he said. His eyes were wide and earnest. "You're going to pave the way for a whole new approach of seeing human life in space. *You'll* do this. You're going to be the founder of a brand-new Aurora. We're going to be able to get so many people off the dole, found so many new colonies, make new lives for hundreds of thousands of people. I'll fight for that."

She took a ragged breath in and held it. Stars exploded in her eyes. Her thinking felt congealed, like she'd dropped a milk-shake on the deck and forgotten it for days, like she'd come back two days later expecting to drink it. To distract herself, she examined the haptic interface again. If she hadn't walked into the Sacrament lab, she might not have recognized that the whole setup stank of Vai power. That every new ship on Aurora had it, and every new ship in every decent Company. She'd thought it was a normal development of Companies collaborating after the war, but now she wasn't so sure.

The pilot made a few, slight course changes with his left hand; the numbers in the destination field shifted and the nose of the shuttle angled to the side. She felt the pull of the grav-drive at her shoulders. Ash narrowed her eyes, checking the coordinates with the trajectory, imagining the destination as she had whenever she'd been behind the controls.

Their trajectory was not correct.

"Why aren't we going to *Rio*?" she asked.

Julien looked up. "Hm? We're going to *Rio*."

"We're not," Ash said. "That trajectory is taking us to one of the three ships on the fore-end of the formation."

The doctor looked over at the pilot, and then checked a few

readings on his own interfaces. "You're right," he said. The pilot kept on, silent, his left hand tilted, his right hand raised as if conducting an orchestra. *Speed and tiller, pitch and yaw,* she thought. She'd recognize those motions anywhere, on any haptic or standard interface. The pilot had diverted on purpose.

"Hey," Julien said, clumsy, stumbling, attempting to tower over the pilot's seat. He put his hands on his hips, took a breath, and made an attempt at being an executive. He came off like an ill-traced hand drawing in a children's book. "I think you're on course for the wrong ship, pilot."

"Our orders are clear," the pilot said.

His voice sounded familiar.

Julien pulled up his chin and squared his shoulders. "We're going to *Rio.*"

The pilot traced sigils in the air. *Autopilot.* He slipped off his haptics—first the left hand, then the right, laying them carefully on the console. Then, lightning-fast, he, grabbed Julien's sidearm, and with a quick flick of his wrist, shot Julien through the head.

Blood spattered the copilot's side; the doctor's body spasmed and fell back over the chair, his face frozen in surprise.

Len screamed.

"I'm going exactly where I want to go," the pilot said.

# 25

The medbay door shut behind Keller, leaving her standing sick, alone, and confused in the green corridor outside the room. Her fingers pressed against the metal of the doctor's necklace, lying flat and cool against her breastbone. The doctor's mission was believable. Admirable. She even meant well.

It didn't change the fact that she'd betrayed Keller as well.

*Move, you stupid asshole,* she told herself.

*I'd never call you that, you know.* Silver-streaked Ash, her ghost-white smile hanging from her lips like a casual afternoon in the mess, slipped in next to her as if summoned by pure anguish.

"Not now, Ash." Keller's throat closed in grief.

*You have no control over when I appear.*

"Obviously."

Ash laughed—cruel and soft. *Move, you stupid asshole,* she whispered.

She had to keep her rage under guard out here. She heard human voices down the hall, and she adjusted her hair, slipped the quarantine weave under her shirt, fixed her jacket, and started walking.

Keller thought about going straight for the escape pods without stopping for the weapon. After all, if it hadn't been for the lies, Keller would have been inclined to trust Sharma. The doctor could have waited for Ramsay to walk in, or opened the morgue drawer, presenting Keller to the enemy captain like a holiday dinner. She hadn't. That was something.

But there were too many lies. Not just falsehoods—outright

lies, wholesale omissions. The reasons Sharma came to work on *Twenty-Five* in the first place. Sharma knowing about Ash's illness and doing nothing to ease her suffering, treating her instead like a test subject, an experiment. And Ash was an indenture, sure, and as a citizen, Sharma had been well within her rights.

But *rights* didn't always mean *right*.

She'd do her part to get the weapon away from Ramsay and her cronies, but that didn't mean she had to bring it to the Sacrament Society. There was still a perfectly good asteroid field outside.

The decision made, Keller adjusted the flimsies on the clipboard she'd grabbed in the medbay, pretending to be entirely engrossed in them as a group of techs appeared from spinward. She winced; she'd apparently picked up the cargo manifest from *Twenty-Five*, broken down into delivery dates, profit structures, departmental needs, shipyards, colonies, even a line for her whiskey stash. Every line of it cut like a knife to the back.

Keller brought the clipboard to her chest and swung herself into the spine of the ship. The closer she got to the bridge and the gun batteries and *Phoenix*'s beating heart, the more she'd have to rely on her limited disguise and pure dumb luck. It made her nervous.

The ghost swung in behind her, climbed beside her, as if this were a normal day on *Twenty-Five*.

"If this used to be WellCel, you can tell me how to behave so I don't trip any behavioral wires, hmm?"

The ghost hummed. *Sorry. I can't.*

"You can't? You grew up in this culture. Plenty of Wellspring people about. How do they stand? Do they smile? What's the protocol for meeting an executive? Hell, is there a secret handshake?" Keller pulled herself up another level.

*We never talked about it when I was alive. You were scared of bringing up bad memories, remember?*

Keller swallowed a tight knot. "I regret that."

A young, towheaded tech with Wellspring indenture tags swung into the spine from the hatch above. Keller tucked her chin, turned her face away and kept climbing as he passed. He paused, and she grabbed the last few rungs, climbing onto the first deck before he could get a good look.

The bridge deck was decorated with a strange, lavish friend-liness, painted with vivacious orange curlicue phrases Keller didn't stop long enough to read. She stepped toward the forward battery with her chin tucked and her stride long, as if the deck were her own and she belonged there.

The area was full of people of every rank and the buzz of ex-cited conversation. Executives stood in loose groups, chatting, while men and women in heels—not executives, but some other level she couldn't match to her Auroran experience—walked with clarion purpose from room to room. People in tech jack-ets like the one she was wearing gathered around open access hatches with tools and frowns, reinforcing plasma conduits for the main battery. Beyond them, just around the bend, was the dark outline of the battery hatch.

*Just be yourself.* Ash's ghost appeared from behind, looking a bit out of breath.

"They're prepping for battle," Keller whispered.

Ash inclined her head. *That makes the most sense, yeah.*

*It doesn't make sense at all. If they were here for the weapon, why stay? Why aren't they on the way back to their HQ?*

*Don't you think there might be more where that weapon came from? Isn't that why Mr. Solano was on the ansible and not one of his VPs? Never underestimate the clarity of corporate greed, Kate.*

Keller worked her jaw and put one foot in front of the other, ducking between two groups with her eyes on the door. *If there were more weapons to steal, we would have known about it. Or we wouldn't have been there.* One *would have, or* Two. *Ships Solano trusted, with all-citizen crews. It's not like* Twenty-Five *was even near the top of the salvager food chain.*

Ash shrugged. *Selling yourself short, as usual.*

*Never.*

The ghost laughed. It sounded out of place and made Keller feel uncomfortable. *And on the most important things, too. You believed your crew could log the entire Christmas list in one deployment, but not that you and I had a future? Come on, Kate. It's your own fault I died thinking you hated me.*

"That's not true." Keller turned and snapped, and Ash vanished in a smoky instant.

Faces—real faces—looked up. Keller's stomach hit the deck as she realized she'd spoken aloud. The faces examined her jacket, her pants, her armband, her mouth. She flushed, muttered an apology, and turned back to the battery.

"Wait," she heard.

One of the executives turned, stepping in front of Keller to block her progress down the hall. Her clothing resembled Aurora's, but her red hair was twisted in tight braids that fell loose around her shoulders, a style that no Auroran executive would have been caught dead wearing. She wore the Baywell version of birthright tags at her wrist, and a set of green tattoos on her neck. An emerald ring flashed as she extended her palm to stop Keller where she was.

"Excuse me. I don't recognize you. Your name, indenture?"

Keller guessed from the immaculate jacket and high heels that the executive didn't go belowdecks often, and cleared her throat, hoping words would follow. She looked down at the jacket for the name, trailing her gaze back up to the executive's face. "Cameron."

"From the cargo crew, right." The executive pressed her red lips into a thin line, her disbelief evident. "Your shoes are laced wrong. Your pants are wrinkled and dirty. And you're speaking out of turn on the battery deck, where you don't belong. Explain."

Keller shoved the clipboard at the executive. The flimsies caught the light. "I'm sorry. I—did not have time to prepare. The enemy ship was filthy and . . ." Some of those weapons were meant for the battery, she remembered. "The gunners need this list of Vai weapons we picked off the Auroran corpse as soon as possible."

The executive plucked the flimsies from Ash's hand, scanning them. To her right, the techs had averted their eyes, making themselves as quiet and small as possible.

The tension leached out of the executive's mouth as she handed the flimsies back. "Drop this off and fix your uniform. If this happens again, you'll go home. Clear?"

Keller's back unknotted. "Yes, sir."

"Go on."

Keller took off, walking brisk and straight-backed to the main battery, her breath stuck in her throat. Dizzy, adrenaline pumping, she didn't even turn around to check if the executive was still looking at her. She stopped at the battery door—painted dusty green, with Baywell's orange logo—and thumbed the comm.

"Yes?" A man's voice.

Keller's voice squeaked from stress. "Cameron from cargo." *If it worked on the executive, it might work here.* "Bringing up the list."

"The list? What list?"

"Vai manifest. I was told to bring it up."

A moment passed. She heard the muffled pop of the hatch lock, and the door drifted open. "All right, let's see it."

The main battery was a rangy, thin room extended along *Phoenix*'s forecourt curve. A large visual interface dominated the room, fed by young people lying prone in haptic chairs, their fingers and foreheads covered in shining silver metal. They shook and thought and worked, their eyes rolled back into their heads, their bodies thin and starved and stuck in syncope. They looked curved and gaunt and weak, as if this were a hospital ward and not the most important war room on the ship.

Someone had hung a star at the center of the battery.

No, not a star. *The weapon.*

It lay sparkling in a familiar isolette, larger, spherical like a moon and argent like a supernova, just big enough to carry and just bright enough to make the clear lights in the ceiling seem like rudimentary torches. It was beyond beautiful.

Wires led from the isolette in question to the front targeting computers, connected to an empty chair laced head to toe with haptic wires.

She moved toward the weapon.

"Hey," someone snapped. Keller stopped, turning her head.

A burly indentured tech rose from where he'd been working on an open panel near a targeting computer. He had a well-cut black beard and wiped an oily substance onto his overalls. He looked her over, his gaze lingering on her face before dropping to her boltgun. His face was dark and unwelcoming, compared to the bright light in the room.

"Indenture Cameron," he drawled.

"Here's the list," Keller held it out.

The man paused, then perused the flimsy with a confused stare. Keller looked from one side to the other, trying to figure out how she was going to get around him to the weapon. "You know," he said, "I thought there was only one of you on this ship."

"I'm his sister," Keller said, attempting to be dismissive.

"No," the man said, after a moment. "Pretty sure you aren't."

She met his gaze.

He broke, diving for a nearby comm panel. Keller whipped out the boltgun she carried, almost forgetting it was chargeless, then jumped forward to chase him. She threw herself at his legs when he got too close to the computer, feeling the thick fabric of his pants in her grip, and he yelped, coming down hard on his knees. Keller stomped on his leg. He hollered in agony. Keller felt a crunch and a snap in the man's ankle and a shaking, cracking pain in her own shoulder.

He dragged himself forward and made a wild grab for the comm panel, but Keller climbed through the pain in her shoulder to grab the waistband of his pants and yank him back. He struggled. She brought down the butt of the gun on back of the man's head, repeatedly, until she saw blood. The man grabbed at her twice, three times, and then went limp.

She scrambled to her feet before she could see if he was still alive, pointing the shaking end of the dead boltgun at the young people in the battery chairs.

Lost in their haptic dreamland, scanning the sector for enemy cruisers, they hadn't sensed a thing.

Keller turned back to the isolette. She was shaking too hard to operate the keypad, so she slammed the butt of the gun into the familiar Auroran controls until sparks flew, until the gaunt men rose from their seats like fairy-tale skeletons, until the lights of the isolette flickered and failed. The men roared, clambering forward, calling at her to stop.

She ripped off the top of the isolette and reached inside. Something ancient and giant and horrible exhaled around her, and the world went dark.

# 26

Adrenaline hit Ash like a blow to the chest, and she slammed the safety release on her straps—but this was a shuttle, where would she go? The pilot raised his visor. He was familiar. He was more than familiar.

"Please, sit down, indenture. I assure you," Jie Cantrell said, calm and assured, "that man did not have your best interests in mind."

Len stayed seated, shocked and stock-still. Ash couldn't breathe. The kind, excited doctor who had treated her after her return from the *London* icebox was the last person she'd expected to see under the pilot's helmet. She crushed her nails to her palm in her right fist. The pain told her she was still alive. *Don't panic,* said her old miner's hindbrain. *You'll just die faster.*

"He—he—you killed him." She gasped for oxygen.

Cantrell flicked the barrel of the gun at Ash's chair. His voice was ice. "Sit down, strap in, and shut up. It's dangerous to be up and about while the shuttle's in flight."

Ash fell back, left hand grabbing at the safety straps. Her body felt like rubber and her hands felt wrapped in heavy insulation, and she clutched at the fastenings, nervous, three or four times, before succeeding.

"You didn't have to—you didn't—"

Len's wide eyes fixed on the doctor's dead body. Cantrell checked a reading on the haptic interface that only he could see, his eyes momentarily glassy. "You don't want to have to do these things," he said, "but there's a crisis on, and we do what we must."

"What—what crisis?" Len had finally recovered enough to stammer out a few words.

"The Vai weapons crisis. The fight *you* started. The blue screamer was a very convincing demonstration, by the way. Everyone's on their way, and they all seem rather panicked. Some of Dr. Julien's colleagues basically had to be held back from piloting a shuttle on their own to go get you, Ash, during the molecular waiting period. They wanted to stick antipsychotics into you until nothing was left but drool and reprogram your motor cortex. And it changed the Society's timeline. We've had to rethink our entire approach, and without our top administration. But then, no plan survives implementation, as they say."

"*Our?*" repeated Ash.

Cantrell stuck his fingers under his uniform collar and fished out a familiar religious medal on a chain. It dangled there in the light of the console, hanging from his thumb, before he let it fall onto his chest. "Our."

Ash's heart beat a tight, frightened bass line; her hands twisted together, her knees shook and knocked. She couldn't calm her breathing. Beside her, Len's face faded into a gray shade of green.

"The cancer at the heart of Aurora Company is real, and has been for some time," Cantrell said. He placed the gun on the dash, and slid the haptic interface back onto his left hand. "It's a lot like the cancer at the heart of Wellspring, the science that led to the cataclysm you barely lived through, Ashlan. It's the cancer at the very heart of our society. We must fight against it. The things they have planned are wrong. We must stand up and fight the things that are wrong, no matter who you are. Don't you agree?"

"He didn't deserve that."

She couldn't stop shaking—she felt like an earthquake that would never end, violent aftershocks slipping into her hands, shaking her jaw. She could not breathe. Julien's hot blood oozed onto the decking, running in a rivulet toward her boots, in the zigzag pattern dictated by the grav-drive functionality.

"Did he? Do any of them?" Cantrell adjusted the interface with a flick of his index finger. "All right. Listen. The plan is to shuttle you through medical elsewhere, where we'll implant an interference card that will make it difficult for Aurora to track you. By the time they realize you're gone, you'll be safe with the Sacrament Society."

"*Safe.*" Ash bit off the word. Her thoughts wandered through a fog as thick as any station smoke spill.

"You can work with us. You'll have a place. A voice. In the Society, there's no such thing as citizen and indenture." Cantrell made further edits to the interface. "We're all equal."

"You talk equality, and at the same time you're treating me like I don't have a choice in the matter."

The destination coordinates disappeared, but Ash could still extrapolate where they were going from what she knew about the vectors: the newest Auroran cruiser, *Medellin,* packed with traitors and parked farther along the x-axis toward the Tribulation sun. "I'm sorry. But it's not a *difficult* choice, is it? To go with us? You're loyal to the truth. That makes you precious. There is no Auroran plan to give you the cure. Julien was truthful about that, at least. If they cure you, they'll lose their best chance at market share. If you walk into molecular development on *Rio de Janeiro,* you'll die there."

Ash's fingers curled; her hand formed a fist. "I'm going to die anyway."

Cantrell sighed. "But you still have time. And you still have so much to do. Don't you see? You're the missing piece to Dr. Sharma's research, the key to all of this. In a way, you'll be the most important person there."

"People keep telling me that." It was hard to speak; it was like her brain itself had shaken loose from its moorings. "And I'd be inclined to believe you, except for the fact that I've seen your work. You know, like Captain Valdes and his missing heart. Or the time Dr. Sharma and the lot of you walked onto a Vai colony ship and committed genocide and taught an entire race to *hate*. *You* started the war. You kidnapped those aliens. *You* are the reason all of this began."

"And we're willing to give our entire lives to fix it."

She choked spit down a dry throat, heaved in a breath and continued. "You're *willing*? I already have."

"And it doesn't have to be in vain." Cantrell looked back out to the stars and looming, black *Medellin,* and through the fog Ash thought of Reva Sharma in her medbay, quietly stocking the shelves. Cantrell's voice softened. "Dr. Sharma told us you were brave. That you were brave and good, and I'm glad to see that she was right."

The world turned around her, addled and upside-down, pointing her woozy feet at the floor where Julien's blood soaked the decking and his shocked, blank eyes looked up to the ceiling and the stars beyond. She found herself looking at him with the eyes of the Vai, through the dead nanotech that congealed in her veins, dragged at her throat. All the people Julien had been— the child, the teenager, the man, maybe the husband, the father, the possibility of a future—all gone in a millisecond, ruined by a bolt. A *together* of a sort, murdered. She choked down nausea and grabbed at her safety straps for comfort that did not come.

Going with the Sacrament Society would be just as much a prison as going anywhere else.

*Run,* she thought, *I need to run, but where? Where could I go?*

Her blood ran hot, banging pots and pans and neutron bombs in her ears, a full percussion section of panicked thoughts. *Medellin* loomed even larger; a curved, onyx mass that was patently Aurora and much less comforting than Ash would have liked.

"Don't make me do this," she said.

Cantrell paused for a moment in deliberation. "*Make* you? Once you see what I've seen, you'll *want* to. You were an uncitizen once. We want to take down the corporations that see human lives in trade for product and profit, that decide you're worth something because of how much product you put out. We want to save the stateless, make indenture illegal. Don't you want that, too?"

Ash felt a dull, febrile roar in her ears. She thought of Gethsemane—the dead colony, the human bodies, the crumbling, splintering feeling as the human hands dragged her away from her home. It felt like Bittersweet. She weighed the aliens against her human family for clarity and found only indistinct shadows. "I'm nobody. I can't do any of that."

"Let me explain," he said.

"She said no, asshole." Len moved to rise and unhook his safety restraint.

Cantrell turned in his chair and snatched up the gun, swinging the barrel toward Len. "The fact that you're not involved doesn't restrict you from earning the good doctor's fate, indenture, so sit your ass down."

Len closed his mouth and sat down.

Ash's eyes went from Len to the gun to the dead man, and she couldn't even think for the vertigo, the orchestra that played havoc with the world around her, the whispers in her ear that accompanied it. *Run, run run run run—*

"*Now,*" Cantrell said. "You think you're nobody. Watch."

Cantrell flicked a finger. Video popped up in the upper-right-hand quadrant of the viewscreen, laid out over the advancing hulk of dark *Medellin.* With some shock, she realized it was her, hovering around *London* in her retrieval pod; she recognized the swift rise and fall of her panicked chest, the dark, dead exterior, the way she'd done her hair, even as the wide, high angle of the camera distorted the image. She watched herself use the pod's arms to retrieve the isolation chamber with the weapon in it; she watched the computers in the pod flicker and go dark, watched her frantic attempts at fixing them.

She expected the camera to go down, too. The camera persisted. The tiniest green light flickered on next to the lens; alien-green, like nothing she'd ever seen before. It was just enough light for the camera to log her unhooking herself from her harness and standing, banging one fist on the wall, shouting, sobbing.

"How did you—"

"Get this vid when the rest of your pod was down?" Cantrell said. "The camera is based on some Vai optical circuits Aurora picked up just after Gethsemane, the same circuits that power the HUD and half the new haptics we have," he said.

"Dr. Sharma put it in?" Ash said.

"She did."

Onscreen, she clawed at the plasteel window. She imagined Keller on the bridge of *Twenty-Five,* shouting orders. Natalie running pell-mell for the second pod. Len hauling himself around the ship, preparing for battle or an issue or a death or whatever came next. Ramsay, hearing the alarm, pulling herself exhausted from her bed.

"Watch here," Cantrell said. "This is where you finally access the weapon."

He fast-forwarded; on the screen, she finally stopped throwing herself against the wall of the shuttle and had collapsed on the ground, sobbing over some faraway anguish, then going quiet, like Len had been quiet on the surface of Tribulation during the test. She pulled herself up, then, into the chair, and reached out toward the Heart. Light slipped into her veins, as if poured from her own heart; green light, gold light, blue light, slithering into every capillary. She held out her hand and the Heart trembled in its quarantine chamber, falling dark and silent.

"You operated it," said Cantrell. "Hundreds of subjects on Bittersweet, and you're the only one that can communicate with it. You know how it works, don't you? Quantum entanglement across the light-years? That's how it was used the first time, at Tribulation."

She started to shiver. "I didn't operate it," she said. "It *took* something from me."

It was Cantrell's turn to look surprised. "What do you mean?"

Len raised his hand. "I'm told I work for Aurora. I don't actually remember that."

Cantrell blinked. "That makes so much sense," he said. "And that's a small price to pay, isn't it, for such a future?"

Ash felt as if a great landslide was building inside her, an earthquake that had shaken loose from the gravity of her heart as surely as their shuttle had from the planet. The landslide was the roar of a thousand people, a thousand screams, an echo running in her blood from her heart to her toes and back again. It said: *You are going to die, and the only thing you can control is how.*

"Save you," she said, "save you from the great Company war. The one that you'll win with me at your side. Nobody'll ever see it coming, because nobody knows you exist."

Cantrell cleared his throat. "We're not a Company. We're impartial."

"Nobody's impartial!" Ash said. "You want it as badly as Mr. Solano and Alison Ramsay! Just because you didn't walk in there and kill Captain Valdes for his stupid sad heart yourself doesn't mean you're not as culpable as your friends who did! Is that what's going to happen to me? Heart, lungs, liver, intestines, stomach—what else, my spleen? All you need is my blood. Plug me in and go. Isn't that right?"

Cantrell's mouth opened and closed like a fish. "That's not what we want."

"It's what I'd want. Lungs don't fight back."

"Do you plan to fight back?" He looked amused.

*Medellin* sat in the window, coming closer every minute. The tendons in Cantrell's thin wrist bulged where he held the gun. Underneath his collar Ash could see the white tattoo she'd never have, the inked-up hope she'd never get for herself. Len's eyes flickered over to the fingers on Cantrell's left hand, the ones capped with the haptic interface, the ones driving the ship. He was staring at them like he stared at new engines—willing them to divulge their secrets, running checklists in his head. He was planning something. She needed to give him space. A distraction.

She had a distraction in her pocket.

"No. I'll . . . tell you what I know," she said, after a few nervous seconds.

Cantrell sighed. "And what is that?"

She slid her hand into her jacket.

"You had a hard time figuring it out because you never were able to understand the Vai," she said. "You saw the mechs and you figured there were aliens inside with hearts and livers and kidneys. And that's true. To a point. That's not exactly how they work."

"And?" Cantrell said, raising his eyebrows.

"All a Vai needs to do is touch a weapon to set it off."

"That's all?"

"Mostly. I think you need to talk to it. The moleculars are somewhat intelligent. They connect to the local Vai node," she explained. "Except that the Vai node was slaughtered twenty minutes ago, and even before that, it had been divorced from its mainframe. Anyway, the weapon talks to you. You talk back. It responds to commands given by any local Vai. Or . . ." She paused. "Or, I suppose, the closest thing would be me, right?"

"Talk to it," Cantrell said, clearly skeptical.

"Like you'd talk to a friend."

"How do you know?"

"Because we're *together*." Ash fished the whining crescent out of her pocket; it felt like a beating heart, a straining violence, a quiet desire for death. It twirled heat up her arm in anticipation of what she might have to do, spoke in delicate whispers of blood and energy. She pulled it out. A soft golden shimmer lit the cabin, and Cantrell jerked back, his eyes wide.

"Great *fucking* Arbiter," he whispered. "This is everything we've worked for. Everything we've dreamed."

Len took Cantrell's momentary distraction as a chance to slide his arm toward his safety release.

Violent-white, sibilant, curved like a knife, the golden crescent rested in her palm. It trembled, warmed in her hand, and in some sort of language she'd never heard before, called out for *alone*. The percussion pressing against the back of her eyes graduated to a crescendo.

*We're going home,* it said.

"You don't want peace, do you, Mr. Cantrell," said Len. It was more of a statement than a question.

By now, *Medellín* filled the viewscreen, a black hulk blotting out the stars; she could see the lights on the bow, blinking stubborn and sure against the freeze. The Aurora curves should have been comforting; instead, they twisted her stomach. She began to shake, and she clutched the weapon close to keep it from falling. The thing warmed in her hand, until it was almost too hot for comfort. It told her, in sibilants against the back of her neck, that it loved her.

"We are so close to everything humanity ever dreamed of, everything we've been working for. An equal society, built on the zero-point energy the weapon provides. Don't you want to go down in history as the person that made that happen? A society where people don't have to be indentured? Hungry? Without debt? Where all people can live as equals, and do what they like?"

"And how many people am I going to have to kill to make that happen?" she whispered, thinking of the tall man who had taken Captain Valdes's heart in vain, who had perished along with everyone else. "How many people did you kill on Tribulation? God, your own people—the spies on *London* and *Mumbai* and the M-K ship?"

Cantrell blinked. "We didn't kill anyone at Tribulation. It was the Vai, they—"

"Dr. Sharma reverse-engineered the Heart in that lab on Tribulation. That's what the Vai call the device you're all looking for. She changed it so that when they showed up, the Vai wouldn't upload. They'd *all* die. And she did something to the humans, too. Something awful. Not like we weren't already doing a good enough job of being awful already. And, of course, it took her a year to get back to the battlefield to retrieve it without tipping off the hand of anyone at Aurora. There's one last thing I don't know: Who was the trigger?"

"What?"

"If the weapon was usable on its own, you wouldn't be chasing me. You need a trigger. It can charge without one, sure. But to set it off? To—I don't know, to delete everything—you need a trigger. Who was your trigger at Tribulation?"

Cantrell blinked. He wavered, for the first time that afternoon looking a little less than smug. "I have no idea what you're talking about."

"Was it Aster Jessen, the other doctor? Did she die like I'm going to die?"

They were so close now that *Medellin* felt like an entire planet, an inviolable, unbreakable wall. Ash could see the details on the sleek black hull and the hatch to the cargo bay opening on the inside. Once they got there, she'd be rushed out, pushed somewhere, installed like she was some sort of part, ordered to work and told that was equality. Indenture. Slavery. It was her payment for being born into the wrong life, for the generations before her who never saved enough to become citizens. If she allowed the shuttle to land, she would be a citizen as long as she lived, and her hands would destroy in the name of the Company or the Sacrament Society or whatever other group stole her away.

Her children would be citizens, as she always wanted: children not of her body but of her blood, young birthright soldiers with their bright faces being turned and changed, celestium in their veins, nanotech slipping out their fingers, orchestras in their heads, watching the world come apart, willing sacrifices to a war that would go on forever.

"I won't do this for you. I won't do this for anyone. The only thing I'm going to do is take this shuttle beyond the White Line and find the *together* and make peace," said Ash.

Cantrell's face reddened. He was done being polite. "Come with me willingly, as a war hero, or you can come as a prisoner. Either way, we're going to *Medellin*."

"No," she said. "We're not." Ash thought she would feel frightened, but with the Vai crescent in her hand, all she felt was anger and a strange kind of loud, humming power that filled her fingers and her arms and her head with noise.

"Tell her I was going to come to Albany," said Len. "To meet her dad. I wanted to go to that little place she talked about by the river, the one with the coffee and the mango ices."

"What?" said Cantrell.

"I mean, I'm dying," he said. She could hear the rattle in his chest. "I was dying the moment I walked those ten miles, breathed that air. I can't pay for it. I was dead the second I didn't stop Natalie in the hangar. I can't live with it, Ash."

"You said you wouldn't give up," she said, reaching for his hand. "You said we carry each other."

"So don't let me down," he said.

Before she could protest, Len pressed down on the release

tab; the safety harness flew back, and he was up in a split second, throwing his body toward Cantrell. The doctor fired. The bolt burned Len in the soft mass of his stomach, but he kept on barreling forward anyway. Len slammed Cantrell with a tough right hook and pressed him against the bulkhead, grabbing his right wrist and clobbering it against the molded metal, attempting to get him to drop the gun. Cantrell was clearly the better fighter; he slammed his heel onto Len's foot, loosening Len's grip long enough to push him off, swinging the gun around one last time.

"Do it!" Len called.

"You'll die!"

Cantrell responded by firing again, hitting Len in the shoulder. Len staggered back, bleeding.

"Tell Natalie I love her," he gasped.

Cantrell fired the boltgun at close range. Len fell against the wall, clutching at his gut. His hands came away covered in blood. Cantrell advanced, the gun spooling up for another round. Len closed his eyes, blood flowing from his mouth. Ash stumbled forward. The weapon told her what she should do.

"Stop this," Ash screamed.

*Glory,* came Christopher's quiet voice.

In her hands, the crescent shook and shuddered; small portals opened at the top and the bottom. Green light poured out. She expected particles—chasing, swirling, like they had with the blue screamer—but this time the light multiplied, slithering into the corners and the shadowy places behind the seats, slipping up the gun barrel, filling Cantrell's open mouth with bright blood.

The light bent backward and found her very pores, drilling into her eyes, silencing her heart. Pain sliced her skin like a thousand knives at once, carving lines in her belly, separating muscle from bone. Her blood slowed to a trickle. The world pulled away from her. *This is it,* she thought. *This is death.*

*Upload,* Christopher sang in her mind, long ago and far away.

Cantrell leaned back, clutching at his chest, then his throat, then the air in front of him. He began to peel apart, slivers of his skin stripping away, floating in front of his frightened eyes. Panicked, he threw himself toward Ash, screaming with a shredded larynx, his slivered fingers attempting one last grab at the weapon. And then, like the end of a twisting firework, the floating slivers burned with hot white light and consumed what was left, leaving a faint cloud and the acrid scent of burning oil.

Len looked over his shoulder. Ash pleaded for the weapon to stop, screamed at it to end, but the process continued. Len's eyes shone red and streaked with white light; from his fingers erupted skeins of silver thread. He opened his mouth to say words that couldn't come out, reached out to her, and with a shredded cry, evaporated.

As hastily as it had taken hold, the light let her go, and Ash could breathe again. Her blood shielded her, saved her, like it had in the forest.

She clawed her way into the pilot's chair, sober and sobbing.

*Run,* she thought.

# 27

Swaddled in the darkness of the living star, Keller tasted blood, then night, then silence. The temperature crashed. Memories flickered somewhere dark and deep: Auroran ships burning so hard they could be mistaken for stars, andan trees swaying in the breeze on Neversink, the astringent smell of *Twenty-Five* when it was new. All of it danced and sang and disappeared, and then only blank silence remained.

The moment took forever and lasted less than a second. It crushed her so completely that she could not breathe and filled her lungs with the musty breath of an ancient and dire need. She was intoxicated, sent whirling, subsumed. Even the Tribulation sun suffocated beyond the window, sacrificed to the black hole at the center of the battery.

One by one, the computers rebooted.

The orange Baywell logo graced the grand interface over the targeting computers, filling the room with charring light.

Keller stood, coming back to herself, her hand still wrapped around the weapon's warming curves. It was beyond cold. Her joints howled with pain. The men in the battery room lay where they'd dropped, taking in shallow, broken breaths. Their eyes were focused somewhere past the bulkhead, somewhere past the stars, their faces in rictus, like they were witnessing the bloody end of the world. She checked her chronometer: it hadn't even been ten minutes, but then, she'd expect a ship like *Phoenix* to have more efficient solar chargers than Ash's pod.

She stumbled toward the door, the weapon whispering *glory*

in her hindbrain. It had been waiting for her, she knew, thrilling her blood, sending a stab of yearning, longing, lust into her fingers and toes. She felt cleaner. It felt like sleeping next to Ash, if Ash hadn't been dead. There was a word she wanted so badly she could taste it, digest it, eat it: *together.*

"It's a mindfuck, isn't it?" A familiar voice.

Blinking, Keller watched Alison Ramsay swing in from the darkened corridor, blocking the door. Still swirling in the aftermath of the weapons fire, Ramsay looked less like another human being and more like stark lines and howling anger and stinking, charring black. She was holding a boltgun in her right hand.

Keller stumbled to a sick and dizzy halt. *Boltguns. I'm so sick of goddamn boltguns.*

"How are you awake?" she asked.

"A *literal* mindfuck," Ramsay said, tapping the barrel of the gun against her temple. She advanced, three short steps. "See, Dr. Sharma was right on both counts. It's a zero-point battery, sure, but it's not just sucking the energy from *Phoenix,* is it? No, it's going much further than that. Congratulations, Kate. You're a killer, just like the rest of Aurora."

Keller stepped back, trying to keep some distance between them. She checked the gunners' bodies again, watched their chests rise and fall. "They're not dead. They're still breathing."

"Are they?" Ramsay gave the living dead less than a cursory glance. "Does it really matter if they're *breathing*? That *thing* just sucked the memories straight out of their minds. All the years that were left. All the electric signals in their brains, bouncing neuron to neuron, or did Dr. Sharma not tell you that was the way it worked? You took *everything* they were. Everything they were going to be. Congratulations, Kate. You're a Vai. Just hand it over."

Keller felt something wet dripping from her nose; she wiped it and found blood smeared on the back of her hand. She was loath to believe anything that came out of Ramsay's mouth, but the young men hadn't moved.

"Your boltgun is dead. You'll have to punch me to death."

"It's not a boltgun."

Smirking, Ramsay turned the weapon toward the veins of starlight spreading across the floor, so Keller could see its ancient, deadly lines: it was old, made of bright, burnished silver metal, with a stock and a hammer and a cylinder for projectile ammunition. She had seen something like it before in a museum exhibit about pre-corporate Earth.

Keller felt the weapon respond to her twisting, sudden fear, rumbling and building in heat. Of all the dangerous, stupid things to bring aboard a spacecraft, this was one of the worst. She stepped back. "That's a bullet gun. You're crazy. You brought a bullet gun and you're threatening me five feet from the *hull*?"

Ramsay ran a thumb up and down the handle. She flashed white teeth in the burning light of the reboot. "Don't worry. As close as I am, it'll be quick."

The dark terror in Keller's chest was staunched by a rising, red anger. "And you call *me* a murderer. That the kind of thing they teach you, growing up in Wellspring? Or are you a Baylor kid?"

"Wellspring? No. I'm just as Auroran as you." Ramsay laughed, and it sounded like broken glass. "Maybe this'll help explain things. I didn't grow up on Brown's Station, like it said in my file. I had that changed. We all had that changed, every single one of us that made it out. No, I grew up on Gethsemane."

A thick liquid, gagging and metallic, slipped down the back of Keller's throat, warring with bare shock. "Can't be. Everyone at Gethsemane died in the massacre."

"War propaganda," Ramsay said. She slipped her thumb behind the hammer of the gun and cocked it; it made a stunning snick-click in the broken silence, and Keller jumped. "There were three shuttles for the executives and their families. None for the rest of us, of course, but that was Auroran evac protocol at the time. Execs first. That's how Aurora taught me that nothing is truly yours until you *take* it. Baylor Wellspring understands that."

"You're a *birthright*?"

"No, I was a *farmer's kid*," she said. "They were going to leave me behind, just like those poor assholes on Tribulation. So, I *took* a spot for myself. With my father's gun. *This* gun." She held it up; it caught in the light. "You have to fight for what you want, Kate, or else you're just a dead body burning at the end of the world. Everyone talks about teamwork, about rising through the ranks, about *earned citizenship*—don't you know that you're living a lie? They gave me citizenship to shut me up. You'll never be as *equal* as the birthrights. They're never going to give you half of what you deserve. Are you willing to sacrifice everything you are for *executives* who don't give half a shit about whether you live or die?"

Keller's breath came more quickly now. "That's not how it is."

"You wouldn't have hidden Ash's medical records if you really believed that."

"There were extenuating circumstances—"

Ramsay's eyes were wide and frenzied. "Nothing is rightfully anyone's, *Kate,* not unless you can hold it. All these planets, these asteroids, this infinite emptiness. The executives came out here and they took it all. We didn't wait for someone to come along and grant it to us. That's the way things get done, the difference between us and them, and the faster you realize that, the faster we can get on with changing the world."

The orange light of the reboot ceded to white; the ship shuddered again as it started to come alive. Behind Ramsay, Keller could see the door, the flickering lights, a sleeping human form slumped against a wall, head lolled. She flicked her gaze back to her former XO, fear dancing in her chest. The weapon tried to calm her, to tell her that *glory* awaited, that it did not understand this *fear,* that she did not *need* it.

Ramsay heard it, too. She raised the gun. "That has no place in the arms of a coward."

Keller smiled. "Fine," she said. "If you think I'm a coward, take it."

Potential energy zipped up and down her spine, crackled in her hands, slammed toward her feet as she struggled to stay down. She met Ramsay's confused eyes for a half second, then took off into a pell-mell zigzag run. The sound of the gunshot came as soon as Keller's second step. It hit the wall in front of her with a discordant report, ricocheting back into the room, desperate to bury itself somewhere in body or bone.

Ramsay fired again as Keller ducked through the hatch back into the corridor, the weapon cradled in the crook of her arm. The lights were low, guttering, still reestablishing a connection to the main computer. She escaped being hit in the back of the head by tripping over a pile of unconscious Baywell indentures. Ramsay screamed her name, firing again, the bullet hitting the shoulder of a sleeping tech. The tech bled but did not move. Keller pulled herself up, feeling alternatively terrified and invincible.

Up ahead, she could see the spine—the lights blasting from below, the people shouting, trying to figure out what the hell was going on above. *So, I didn't take down the whole ship,* she thought, *just a level. Reva was right. I'm not strong enough.*

She swung into the spine, hooking her feet around the ladder, then muttered a prayer to nobody in particular and loosened her one-handed grip, sliding down the ladder like she'd been taught in training. Ramsay appeared before her, shooting once and missing, then swearing, losing the bead the farther she got from Ramsay. She climbed in herself and slid down the ladder, closing fast.

Keller stopped back at the cargo level, swinging around to shove herself between the ladder and the wall, anchoring herself with her left arm, the arm that cradled the weapon. Ramsay matched her speed and smashed at Keller's right knuckles with her shoe as she passed, bringing up the gun one last time. Keller caught Ramsay's wrist, her muscles straining to keep her from bringing the gun any closer, and she met the other woman's triumphant gaze. Below her, she heard the clatter of troops on the move. If she didn't win now, it wouldn't matter.

Ramsay hissed, "Just—give up—"

"No," Keller said, slammed on Ramsay's left shoe with her heel, then brought her knee up to knock her foot from the ladder. Ramsay's eyes widened as she lost her balance, which gave Keller enough give to make a violent strike against Ramsay's wrist. Ramsay's eyes went dark and frightened, and she pinwheeled. Keller shoved her one last time and Ramsay fell, screaming, into *Phoenix's* faraway belly.

Keller threw herself through the nearest hatch as techs started climbing in from above. She heard the sickening crunch of Ramsay's body hitting the floor. She looked in once to see her former XO unmoving, bent at an unnatural angle on an aft hatch, and choked down puke. She heard juddering footsteps, boots against metal, shouts to *get her get her get her get the bitch,* and so she turned in the opposite direction, barreling away in the alien-lit darkness.

For a few seconds, the recycled air caught in her throat, and she thought she was going to get away with it. The shouting Baywell troops were behind her now, but she was faster, and she hurtled ahead, weapon in hand, until she turned a corner and skidded to a halt. A line of green-clad people blocked her path down the hallway, helmets down, eyes barely visible. Their boltguns were alive, whining and straining, pointing in her direction. She skidded to a halt, trapped, afraid, and in the guttering light, she felt not fear and panic but a quiet, brilliant assurance that climbed into her veins and sailed through her heart. She grasped the weapon and held it to her chest.

Keller wondered if this clear, clean assurance was what the Vai felt when they went into battle.

If it was what kept them from hating themselves.

"I'm sorry," she said.

The soldiers advanced, left foot first, the leader screaming for her to *drop it, bitch, drop it*. The lights around them guttered and died.

"You drop it," Keller whispered.

The weapon breached light from her fingers; it swirled and slipped and turned, and she felt heat running up her spine and around her shoulders. This was warmth like she'd never felt before, warmth like Ashlan's skin and her mother's arms and a lover's kiss. It was the closest thing, since Neversink, that she ever came to feeling calm. To *together*.

Her blood sang. *Glory*.

The lights crashed around her.

The men toppled at once, their bodies collapsing together, their guns falling against each other like harmless sticks, lying on top of each other like cargo. Shaking, hating herself, Keller picked her way through, then followed the guides on the wall to the hangar. When Baywell indentures came to stop her, she told them to step aside. That she *didn't want to hurt them*. That she was a weapon now, a monster. They fell, too, their eyes open, staring beyond as she passed.

She was sobbing as she wrapped the weapon in the quarantine fabric, and sobbing when she cracked open a pod airlock and climbed in, setting the grav-drive in motion. The system whined its welcome in an unfamiliar, content tone, as if her world had not already died, as if this were just another day in the tug, as if Ash would be there at the end to smile at her and tell her things would be all right. She lay her hands on the interface, feeling the mundane comfort of switches and buttons.

This would either work, or Keller would die gulping down vacuum, her lungs rupturing from the inside out. Either way, she wasn't going back.

Keller's mind was too full of blood and glitter and remorse and triumph to concentrate, so the pod jerked to the side and slammed into the bay door as she left. As the pod burst from *Phoenix*'s main bay and rolled into the sunshine, the ship came fully back to life, and she saw fighters behind her, spit from cruiser bays like marbles dropped from the hand of a child.

Adrenaline powered her hands. The weapon powered her soul. She was not out of the woods by a long shot.

But she had a ship.

And she was a captain.

# 28

*Medellin* loomed like a cold gray death sentence; it gobbled up the viewscreen, the dark teeth of a cruiser transport bay spinning closer with every second that passed.

Ash could still taste incineration in the air, could still feel Len's sacrifice as an electric charge, could still remember the bright orchestra singing the humanity out of her fingers. Her body howled with pain, nerve endings echoing the memory of a death she deserved but never received.

Ash pulled herself into the pilot's chair, hearing her dead friend's voice echo inside her skull. His favorite phrase; Kate's favorite phrase. *Space plus bullshit equals death.* Her hands shook as she picked up the pilot's haptic interface. She repeated it like a mantra, over and over, slipping on the gloves, the helmet. All she could think of was Len's face. All she saw was the golden light taking him apart. *I can't live with it, Ash,* he'd said. *I can't live with it.*

Bastard. *And you thought I could?*

The haptic interface pushed at her thoughts and caught the back of her brain, clumsy and unsure compared to the glossy certainty of the Vai moleculars, but unmistakably, eerily similar. It felt like she'd just downed half a bottle of vodka on leave—fritzy, half melted, but up and stumbling off to a party nonetheless. She took three deep, hard breaths to banish the grief from her chest. The shuttle shimmied in response and the engine thrilled to a crescendo.

Her eyes blurred with tears.

The shuttle responded, executing a too-quick, half-cocked turn, shifting toward the twinkling battlefield. *No, not there,* she thought, *somewhere safe,* but the shuttle hurtled bold and bright, the destination the broken husk of *London.*

*London,* the last place someone with her Vai blood could hide, with her memories of the *together* and her ability to tear to bloody, broken shreds anything she'd ever known. Anything she'd ever loved.

She could go to *London.* Could wander to the bridge and sit in the captain's chair. Take off her helmet and let the cold creep in. Let the ghost ship finish what it started.

*Len didn't sacrifice himself so that you could end up a god-damn suicide,* Christopher said.

And then he was there, seated in the copilot's chair with his feet resting on Julien's still, slumped body, there with his kind smile and his tired eyes and his stupid floppy hair. She thought of the mines again, of celestium glittering sweet and silver in the rocky sky. The shuttle listed to the side and she blinked away the tears, trying to concentrate on the approach vector.

"I don't want to die," she said.

*Don't you?* he said. He lifted a hand, indicated the battlefield around them. *The shuttle's pretty sure that's what you want to do. Fucking haptics.*

The comm sounded, five blaring, clear notes. The source said: *ARS Rio de Janeiro.* She ignored it, and careened past a set of dead fighters, their cockpits cracked open like empty boxes. "Nobody else is going to die for me."

*That's not your decision to make.*

"Isn't it?" she spat.

Debris hit the top of the shuttle with a resounding smack, jarring her teeth, slamming her world to the side, then up, then into a shattering spin. She swallowed puke. Her vision swirled, unable to reconcile telemetry with her celestium-soaked brain.

The after-strike confusion was so much like the attack on Bittersweet, the way the ground swayed as if the entire planet was being knocked off course, the crush of her entire world down to the body of a dead man and an hour's worth of oxygen.

"If I hail *Rio,* if I tell them about Julien, about the Society . . ."

The interface helpfully accepted the local connection to *Rio*—

"No, no, shit! No, I'm not ready."

She tried to shut down the connection. *Too late.*

"Shuttle Seven, this is *Rio* actual. Pilot, why have you diverted?" Solano.

Ash swallowed thick, sour spit. She felt thirsty, aching. "Because I'm not coming back," she said.

A thin, dark moment passed before Solano responded. "Ashlan, put Dr. Julien on, please."

"He's, uh, he can't," she stammered.

"Put him on."

*London* was growing larger by the second. "None of this is my fault," she said. "I didn't want this."

Solano paused before responding. She could hear the quiet hum of the *Rio* bridge. "That's not exactly true, Ashlan, now, is it?"

Her voice wavered. "I wanted to live."

"You remember that your choices brought you here?" Solano said. "Specifically, the choices you made every day to save your own life at the cost of your shipmates' safety?"

"I didn't mean—"

"Of course you didn't. Nobody does. You understand why we had you sign that contract, now? Turn the shuttle around and come in."

Her hands shook. The shuttle shuddered around her. She remembered the forest, Marley's eyes, Len's bones, the stink of it, the sick whisper of *glory* that remained, even now, haunting her brainstem. They'd be alive if she hadn't hidden her illness.

They'd be alive. "If I come in, you're going to make me use those weapons. You're going to make me a weapon."

"Yes, Ashlan." He paused. "That's the only way."

Her voice wavered. Tears blurred her vision. "You're *Mr. Solano*. You have a fucking *Company* at your disposal. Figure out a different way."

"I understand that you must be feeling confused, so let me give you the whole picture," said Solano. "You'll want to bring up the tactical map, and perhaps that will help you understand."

All she had to do was think about the map, and it popped up, painting bright lines against the debris field speeding by. Behind her were the four Auroran cruisers, lined in blue, receding quickly. Behind *London,* though, limned in orange and green, was the enemy—Ramsay's unknown ship, accompanied by three new ships whose designs she knew very well.

Ships like those had brought her to Bittersweet.

"I thought Wellspring filed for dissolution," she stammered.

"Everyone did," Solano said. "But we just discovered Wellspring also entered into a silent merger process with Baylor-McKenna and a few others shortly after the war. They registered their articles of incorporation with the war council five days ago, probably to be ready for something like this. I just got off the comm with their admiral, and they have confirmed that they have the *London* weapon, and a way to use it. Without you, Ashlan, every citizen and indenture aboard our ships will die."

The implications spun out in her head, bloody and broken, her stomach twisting. The shuttle lost speed. With articles of incorporation filed, this was no longer piracy. This was war. She would be able to stand against the very people whose policies killed Christopher, who took Kellor.

"They have someone like me? A trigger? Are you sure?" she repeated.

"We have no reason to doubt, and every reason to prepare," Solano said. "And we don't have time to waste."

She looked over at the copilot's chair, where Christopher sat smiling in the ruddy darkness, his eyes filmed over, his head half open, his brain spilling out. The pressure on her chest felt like he'd been that day—heavy, dead, permanent. There had been so few survivors of the Bittersweet attack; what was the chance that someone else had made it out of the mines from the medical program?

But she hadn't been in the medical program; Cantrell had told her she'd contracted the disease from contact with Christopher, and she'd been with—

*—she'd been with Keller.*

"Sir, it's Kate," she said. Hope was raging, sudden and true, at the very core of her body. "Captain Keller. It's Captain Keller over there. That's who they have. It has to be. We can't attack. We'll kill her."

Solano's voice had gone hard. He seemed done with explanations. "Return to *Rio* immediately, indenture."

"I can't. We can't." She grabbed at her safety net and yanked to make sure it was fully deployed. "I know you don't understand. I know you can't, but please, this is the way it has to be. She'd die rather than use the *London* weapon on Aurorans. I know Wellspring ships. I can get to her. She'll be trying to escape, I know her, she will. We get onboard, we find her, we bring her back."

"I said, *return.*"

She swallowed sheer panic. "No, sir. I won't kill her for you."

"Indenture Ashlan, you are under contract, return to base."

She closed her eyes. Thought of Len. "I can't live with it, *Joseph*," she said, and cut him off.

When she opened her eyes, the shuttle was screaming ahead toward the dead husks once more, and Christopher was gone. *London* came up fast in her window, black and blue and dead,

darker than frightening *Medellin*. She swallowed bile and tried
to calm down. Keller had always repeated that salvage was a state
of mind. Len had always said that a good salvager could find a
way to work with what was on hand.

Ash was about to put that advice to the test.

She braked, almost too late, and the shuttle hit the port with
a sickening crunch, throwing Ash forward against the harness
hard enough to bruise. She felt a savage, jolting pain in her bad
shoulder as she unhooked herself and crossed the cabin to the
survival cabinet. She pulled out a breather and a vacsuit, grabbed
Cantrell's gun, and, for the second time, evacuated into *London*'s
dead halls.

*London* was a puzzle coming together around her, an autopsy
that finally made sense. The dead bodies, the scorch marks on
the walls, the lowered hatches: the Sacrament Society in the
guise of Manx-Koltar, trying to recover what they thought was
theirs. The engine room lacked power, but it hadn't locked, and
she wrapped her feet around a handhold to give herself enough
leverage to crack it open. She shoved herself inside, slammed her
feet against the wall and pulled up to close the door behind her.
There was just enough air in the chamber to hear the clang of
the bulkhead seal.

The engine room was smaller than she expected for such
a large cruiser, bathed in the guttering light of whatever consoles were left and far too quiet for her liking. It was as drab as
*Twenty-Five*'s and almost as tiny, packed full of instrumentation,
a dizzying, starry-sky array of questions and answers and status
updates she'd need extra time to understand. Machinery ground
its teeth in the quiet behind her.

Ash turned away, pulling on the wall's damaged main hatch.
She was rewarded with access to *London*'s innards. It took her
about ten seconds to diagnose the situation: the injection and delivery cables were coiled in on themselves, corroded, torn open

by an explosion—and, following that, decomposition and evaporation. There was very little fuel left, and she didn't even know
if it would get her out of the Tribulation system, let alone all the
way to the White Line.

She screamed again, bringing her fist down against the wall
twice, three times, until the pain made her feel human, until her
suit read damage.

*Space plus bullshit equals death,* said Len, *and this is bullshit
behavior. You still have one last place you can go.*

*The planet? That's death.*

She heard his dark belly laugh. *It'll keep your blood away
from the companies. What other future do you think you have?*

Ash turned back to the hatch too late—she stuck her head out
into the corridor just as a group of Auroran combat engineers
in heavy armor and navpacks burst into the spine three decks
up. She panicked, grabbing a sliver of floating metal and slipping
it into the lockworks to cause a jam. They saw her and floated
closer, leaving fluffy blue chemical trails behind them.

Ash counted four, gathering around the lock. They spent ten
seconds trying to pick the lock before the commander brought
out a mining laser from her backpack. The commander was slight
and young-bodied; she flicked on her helmet lights to reveal a
familiar face, dark-haired, young, exhausted. Her lips moved as
she shouted unheard words to the rest of the team and dragged
herself over to the porthole.

*Natalie.*

Of course Solano would send Natalie.

The suit lights made her former friend's face look jagged, un-
friendly, wan; she put her glove against the glass and mouthed
something at Ash.

Ash gave her the middle finger.

Natalie banged on the door.

The decision to draw Cantrell's gun on the murderer of the

*together* was a quiet, sure one, settling onto her shoulders like a weighted blanket, smothering her future in a rolling dark fog. It was just one more thing she'd have to live with. She was accruing those like dole debt.

The hatch rolled open. Fumbling with the suit gloves, Ash lifted the gun just as Natalie burst into the engine room with her three blank-faced suits. Ash heard the sticky whine of line-of-sight comms being established.

"Where's Len?" Natalie said.

# 29

Natalie's face was angular and death-blue in the light of her face-plate. She pushed past the other three combat engineers, leveling her flashlight first in Ash's direction, then around the rest of the engine room. The light caused a sudden, nauseous dizziness to rise into Ash's throat, and as she raised her open hand to block it out, she saw the bright blue citizens' tags on the front of her former shipmate's suit.

She tightened her grip on Cantrell's gun in response.

"We don't have time for that," Natalie said, indicating the gun with a twitch of her flashlight. Her voice sounded businesslike and bright in Ash's helmet speaker, as if nothing had happened between them on Tribulation, as if they were still equal, as if Natalie hadn't put a bullet between the eyes of any future she and Ash could have together. "We're here to take you home. Where are the others?"

Ash's stomach twisted. She turned back to the fuel canister, making another attempt to yank it from its housing. "*Twenty-Five* was my home." She paused. "*Ms.* Chan."

Natalie sighed. "Don't be dramatic. *Rio* is home now."

"For you, maybe."

The younger woman stiffened in her suit. "I'm doing what I can."

Ash tried to loosen the canister one more time, then gave Nat's crew a quick once-over. They wore citizens' tags, too, and blocked the only way out, using their armored combat suits and darkened, anonymous faceplates to their advantage. Cantrell's boltgun would do very little to deter them from taking her down if she made a wrong move. "And that involves bringing armed soldiers to find me?"

The other woman's lips flattened into an annoyed line. "Your shuttle went rogue with hostiles nearby. My people are a standard precaution. And even if that wasn't true, you can't just break your contract and wander off. Where are the others?"

"I'm not the one who broke my contract." Ash craned her neck, looking for another way out of the engine room, spying only a locked maintenance tunnel blocked by the debris of a shattered console. She swore under her breath.

"Ash, come on—"

"*Seven years.* Not so long, you think, not when you've just spent quite a few years in a mine, ripping celestium from the walls. But it's not *actually* seven years, is it, Ms. Chan? It's eight, or nine, or nineteen. It's how much soap you buy and how sick you get. It's how much the boss likes you, and damn your soul if he doesn't. It's bonuses that aren't, not really." She paused, shaking, then tried—and failed—to yank the canister from the wall again. "It's getting shot on a dead colony planet by a freelancer and your CEO telling you that the hospital bed is a *treat.*"

Natalie sighed. "You signed that contract. I told you it would be a problem."

"I didn't have a choice."

"You could have refused it," Natalie said.

A bright anger took hold of Ash, and her hand went white-knuckled with the tight pain of keeping her handhold on the open engine. *I don't have time for this,* she thought, but the words came anyway. "You grew up an uncitizen, too. Earth sure, but you still thought *war with the fucking Vai* was a better life than the one you had. But you were a soldier, with guaranteed citizenship. And Christopher, well—" Ash's throat closed around his memory. "He died for *his* better life. I don't know why I ever thought I had a chance. Not if this is what *family* becomes when they pin cit tags on your jacket."

Natalie took a step inside. "Where is Len, Ash?"

"He—" Ash felt sour. She closed her eyes. The lie she meant to tell stumbled to a halt on her tongue. The last trihex shot had long since worn off, and her veins burned with the scalding ache of being *alone*. The voices sang to her of *death,* of *deletion,* of Auroran ships twirling in jewel-steady flame, of Len's body burning. Red flashes filled her vision, bringing back Len's last cry, the sobbing way light had shoved its way down his spine to the very tips of his fingers, and she fought tears.

"Ash," she heard. Then, louder: "Ash! Where is he?"

She opened her eyes. "He's dead."

Natalie stiffened in her suit. "How?"

"Cantrell, he—"

"The R&D doctor?" Her voice was clipped. "Was it him? Where the hell is he?"

Listening to the clicking silence inside her suit, Ash thought about answering in the affirmative. It would be easy to pin Len's sacrifice on a dead Jie Cantrell. But Natalie would want to see the body, wouldn't she? To know for certain that Len was gone, to feel the dull ice underneath his dead skin, to make her soldier's farewell? She couldn't give either of them anything like that.

And they both deserved so much more from Ash than a *lie*.

Ash fumbled for the bag and the cold weapon inside, and she withdrew it, revealing the husk of the depleted crescent weapon to the other woman.

"We had to," she said.

Natalie's eyes grew wide inside her helmet. The moment stretched and festered between them. "He—" She licked her lips. "You *what*," she said. It was not a question.

Ash struggled for calm. "Dr. Cantrell was working for the Sacrament Society. He killed Dr. Julien, and he was going to betray

Aurora by handing me over to the Society's people on *Medellin*. He shot Len, and Len—" Her throat closed. "Len was going to die anyway. From the long walk he made to the ag-center. You guessed that. You know how much his care was going to cost. And he knew what they were going to do to me, and what would happen to everyone else because of it. I had to. It was the only way."

"Don't you dare blame this on *him*," breathed Natalie, pink-faced with anger and quietly incredulous.

"It's my fault, but—"

"Indenture, you are under arrest for—"

Ash met her eyes. "I'm not going back with you."

"The hell you aren't."

"You'll shoot me first." Ash felt spit on her lips.

The engine room interface flickered. Natalie's eyes went wide with curdling hate, and all Ash could think of was Len's silent scream, Cantrell's twisting, voracious mouth, the thousand ways that Keller would die in Ash's exhausted dreams when she finally found a safe place to sleep again. *I can't live with it, Ash.*

Natalie's boltgun whined, still charged and hungry. "You *murdered* him."

*I can't live with it, either,* Ash wanted to say, but she felt reckless now, invulnerable in her burden, coasting on starving adrenaline and a sick, desperate hope. She stepped forward until the breastplate of her suit was one yawning inch away from the barrel of the other woman's gun. *I can't live with it.*

*And I'm going to make sure you can't live with it, either.*

"No. But you did murder *them*," she said.

She wasn't really talking to Natalie, now. She hadn't been, not since the second trip to Tribulation, after they'd promised her friend the blue tags glinting on the front of her suit. Ash was talking to Ms. Chan, an Auroran full citizen, and behind the honorifics and the faceplate was every chin-tilted citizen she'd ever met, every man and woman who chose to ignore that their world was built on spreadsheets and blood, on manipulation and broken promises—because it was convenient, because it hurt, because confronting it brought them to truths their lives could not sustain.

"It's war."

Ash swallowed. Her dry throat felt uncomfortable. "It was genocide, Nat. An entire colony of Vai," she said. "Vai innocents. Civilians, colonists. They'd been tortured. Is that all right, now that you're a citizen? Is it justified now, that it's them and not us? Me, and not you?"

The boltgun still sang in Natalie's hands. "You're lying. You lie. Lying is what indentures do. No more words; move into the corridor. You're under arrest."

Ash took one step forward and felt the jarring impact of her suit against the other woman's gun in her fingers, her legs, her toes. She wondered if the bolt would feel like that, once it punched through her suit and buried itself in her breastbone. If she'd die from that ache, or if the ache of the airless cold would take her first. "If that's what you believe, Natalie, but I'm still not going anywhere."

Natalie's eyes went lambent with some angry, wet emotion. "Are you trying to make me shoot you?"

*Am I?* Ash shook in her suit, savoring her dry throat, her desert lips, the ache in her back, the erratic, broken-machine beat of her heart. The words came out before she could stop them, and she closed her eyes. "You'd be doing me a favor."

"Ash. *Please*. Don't make me do this."

"Make you. Like you were *made* to kill an entire colony. I understand, and I'm sure Len would, too." Ash whispered. "He'd get it, wouldn't he. He'd understand why you were so eager to get so much blood on your hands. He'd understand why your citizenship is so much more important."

She heard Natalie's hissing, angry breath. In the darkness of what was left, Ash thought of Christopher's smile, and the dirt under his fingernails. Of the crooked way Kate crossed her arms. Of her mother's eyes, limned by liquor, lost somewhere on the Wellspring dole. And, finally, she thought of the bright *together,* of the humming warmth of a thousand voices. She held on to that, grasping at that great, golden memory, and waited for Natalie to pull the trigger.

"Get out," Natalie said.

The bolt never arrived.

When Ash opened her eyes, she was alone with Natalie. The engineer was crying openly, a skewed group of wet trails lit bright blue on her skin. Her men were gone.

"Is it true, what I did?"

Ash nodded, unable to speak.

Natalie processed that information, her mouth working soundlessly behind the faceplate. Her eyes dropped to where Ash was still holding the dead crescent weapon. "It's war," she whispered, then looked up. She gulped down air as she spoke. "We do things. In war. That we're not proud of. Just like you. Like—you can control this, can't you?"

"No." Ash blinked away exhaustion and black scrollwork and the faraway screams of the dead in her veins. "It's not *control.* It's more like—like I'm talking to it. Requesting. Asking. Back in the forest—do you remember, after I died? I told you that Dr. Julien thought I was Vai. And we thought it was ridiculous."

Natalie nodded. "And it's not."

"No," Ash said. Her skin prickled and itched. Her veins burned. "But they're inside, I think."

Natalie bit her bottom lip, hard. It was a common spacer move, meant to reroute pain or discomfort from inaccessible places elsewhere in her vacsuit. "So if you die, this secret dies with you. Fucking *hell,* Ash."

Ash turned back to the broken engine, sliding her gloves along the sides of the fuel canister, finding purchase there. She yanked, and it refused to move. "I don't know. I have to hope so. On my way here, Mr. Solano mentioned that Baywell is *sure* they have the weapon and a way to use it. That trigger has to be Kate. There's no other option. So, if you're not going to kill me, I'm going to take this leftover fuel, rescue Kate, and then take her to the White Line, where we can end this."

But Natalie was shaking her head, already on to a new thought. "If it's the captain, she won't cooperate."

Ash slammed the top of the canister in frustration. "She won't need to. This is Wellspring. They'll—" Her words caught. "They'll core her. Or torture her, or worse. And imagine what Aurora's going to do to me since I signed their damned full indenture. And even if you don't care about that—even if you're perfectly fine with screwing your old family in favor of that asshole *Joseph Solano*—with the Vai colony dead and the weapon lost, the Sacrament Society will be desperate. They were already desperate enough to kill Dr. Julien."

Natalie shook her head. "But if Baywell has you and the captain—"

"Then Baywell has market share, and it'll be bad. But there's no arms race, no Company war. At least—not in the beginning. You'll have time to prepare for a bigger Company war. But imagine this fucking arms race, Natalie, if I go with you. Imagine the new war that starts tomorrow, that spills out from Tribulation like a fucking plague. You didn't fight the Vai so you could just turn around and shit on humanity. I know I won't stand for it. Len wouldn't. The peace he died for will die, too."

Around them, the light from their helmets bounced off the walls of the engine room, off dead consoles and the traceries of frozen blood and quiet ice. Natalie subsided into an aching, trembling silence, which ended when she flicked her gun to neutral, sliding it back into the holster.

"It's a mess out there, Ash. Even if you can make it past the Baywell ships, you can't survive in open space in a shuttle, let alone fuck off to the White Line," she said.

"I can, with enough fuel and the right burn sequence. That's why I'm here," Ash said. She pushed off, sailing over to the injection system, shutting down the remaining engine works protocol by broken protocol. "Are you going to stand there, or are you going to help?"

Natalie hesitated, the indecision clear in her eyes. Finally, she exhaled and stepped forward, fishing out a multi-tool. She called up some industrial pliers and slipped it around the canister bolts, yanking with a few violent tugs, loosening the connectors easily enough for Ash to shake away the tubing leading to the rest of the engine. The canister hung there, indecisive about falling, and Ash grabbed hold of the bottom to steady its drunken curve.

"Thanks," Ash said.

Natalie snorted. "Don't thank me yet. Your plan is still pretty thin. Baywell's got four ships out there, and they've all got pod and fighter decks."

"And they'll be watching *Rio* and the capital ships. I fly well. I can slip by."

"And if you can't find Captain Keller?"

"Then I'm—" Ash had sorted it in her mind; she hadn't put it to words. The plan was, as Natalie had said, thin. Her brain seemed blank, inchoate, full of bad ideas, and the worst one of them all was also the only one that seemed remotely sensible. "I'm going to remove myself from the equation."

"Not acceptable," Natalie said. "No. You can find Dr. Sharma. There must be treatment for this. A cure. You have to live."

To *live*. *Life* had always been hunger and struggle, even with

Christopher, even when that struggle was punctuated with the warmth of his arms. On Bittersweet, those little moments of happiness slipped through her hands like stars wheeling above, cold and out of reach. She'd thought it was enough just to see them.

But then came *Twenty-Five,* where she'd loved again, where four strangers had become a crooked little family. They'd taught her to trap happiness, to keep it inside her body, to make it her own.

All of that was over, now.

Ash coughed away nausea. Her arms felt weak, and her legs ached, her muscles tight and exhausted. "I'm dying, Natalie. I have been for some time, and I'm asking you to let me go. Nobody should have the Heart. Nobody should be able to use it as a weapon. It's too powerful." Her voice broke. "If you loved Len at all, you'll let me go."

Natalie blinked quickly, then turned her face away. "Did he say anything about me? Before—" She licked her lips, gave up, and looked back. Tears pooled above her eyelashes. "Before."

"He loved you," Ash said. The words felt muffled, quietly apocalyptic, like a bomb exploding underwater.

"But not enough to stay," she said.

"*You* could stay," Ash replied, and for a moment Natalie wavered where she stood. Considered it. "You could come with me."

Ash sucked in a breath and extended her hand to Natalie.

She looked like she was considering it, too, until suit alarms went wild. Natalie swore, her moment of indecision left behind, then raised her wrist and brought up a holographic interface showing the battlefield outside. The space above her arm blinked into bright fire. The battle had begun, with both sides using conventional kinetics, torpedoes and fighters and human lives. Explosions bloomed in the black between the two sides.

Baylor Wellspring's four starships had taken up a spherical formation above and below Aurora's, trapping them at the very center. Aurora, on the other hand, had drawn their ships in a tight formation around *London*, oscillating in all directions to avoid targeting sensors, large burning satellites around the dead shipwreck, outflanked and outgunned.

In the bare, formidable darkness between the flashes of artificial light, she could see Natalie's lips form a thin, determined line.

"You're not going to make it past that line in a shuttle," Natalie said, after a moment.

"That's what I have."

Somewhere, metal tore from metal in a splintering, screaming shear. Sparks came from a junction above.

"No, I mean, my team will take your shuttle. You take our troop transport. It has a railgun. You'll be able to defend yourself. And if they think you're in the shuttle, we can give you a little more time. If you're going to break their line, you're going to need it," Natalie said. "You're probably going to want to swing around wide, then flank around the back. Looks like they're doing a center push."

"You're going back to Solano?"

"You're going to need someone on the inside of Aurora. Someone who knows about all of this. It's gotta be me."

Ash nodded.

Natalie hollered orders at the other engineers, who were hanging angry and confused outside the engine room door, then waved them out and down toward the spine of the ship. They objected—Ash heard her hollering about *follow my orders or I'll have your credits docked, you assholes*—but they eventually left. When they were gone, she turned back to Ash.

"I'll come for you," she said.

Ash shook her head. "I'm not worth it."

Natalie snorted. "I'm not doing it for you. I'm doing it for Len."

*London* shuddered, the telltale shiver of a missile impact

somewhere on the top deck. Ash thought of the bridge, of the broken, rotten body of poor Captain Valdes. "And for the colony."

Natalie bit her bottom lip. "It's not—" She paused. Something terrible settled behind her eyes. "And for the colony."

"Go," whispered Ash.

"Don't forget. Space plus bullshit, Ash," she said, and was gone.

Ash gulped down a frog in her throat, tasting tin-stained re-cycled air, and shoved Cantrell's gun in her bag. She hoisted the fuel canister, examining the fuel level tally on the front. She might get one long burn out of it. If she could set a course for the White Line—if it were straight enough, if she were lucky enough—it would have to do.

It would have to be enough.

The ship shuddered as a Baywell missile gave it a last coup de grâce somewhere near the bridge, and then all that was left was her own breathing, and the guttering lights on her low-battery suit.

It was time to move.

# 30

Five minutes of oxygen got Ash back to *London*'s spine and to the cargo deck below. *Twenty-Five* had pillaged this section first, hauling out boxes of personal items, undelivered farm equipment, toys, guns, and computer parts. The light from the Tribulation sun poured into open compartments she herself had created from a Company pod far above to better access the science deck. Staring into the broken deck above felt like staring into a different life. A different universe.

*Was it all really just a few days ago?*

Stopping just after the cargo deck hatch, Ash looked past the shattered hull and the shredded gray metal ribbons that stood at attention there, jagged strips of seaweed standing sentinel against a raven-black ocean. The Auroran troop transport was docked at an airlock nearby, the rail gun a malignant glint in the starlight. She palmed the entrance, hauling herself into the back, then fell into the pilot's chair. This ship, at least, had no haptic interface.

*Small mercies*, she thought.

Ash brought the vessel online, and the system chimed its cheery salute as if her world had not already died, as if she were going on a simple salvage mission, as if someone would be there at the end to hand her a coffee and a protein bar. Releasing the hold on the airlock, Ash pulled the transport away from *London*, driving toward the whirling, pivoting starships and the blood-red marble of dead Tribulation.

The great cruisers passed in tight circles in front of *London*, moving fast. They exchanged fire; arcs of white and red sailed across the expanse, causing too bright explosions against the darkness, hothouse flowers swallowed in seconds by choking nothingness. She held tight on the tiller, calming herself, telling herself that there was no way they could see her at this scale. Behind her, Natalie pulled away in Julien's shuttle, ducking debris, hauling away for *Rio*.

Ash pushed the nose of the transport under *Mumbai's* nose, using the ship's corpse to block any followers that might have already painted her as a problem. A torpedo flashed by, nearly clipping her gun; panic grabbed her throat, and she yanked the transport to the right. It took a moment to realize the torpedoes weren't heading for her, but for *London* itself. She held her breath as they made impact, shattering the ship's broken hull into glitter, pulverizing what was left in a bright orange cataclysm. Baylor Wellspring was trying to destroy Natalie's shuttle.

*Go. Now,* whispered Christopher's ghost. *You can't help her now.*

*You're back.* She felt a quiet thrill in her chest.

*I'll be with you until the end of your days,* he said. *I promised you that.*

Ash snorted, reset the altimeter and gunned for the Baywell line, ducking through the debris to block targeting sensors. The battle was a cipher within a storm, an ill-scrawled ebony ink note in a dead-dark room, a confusing chiaroscuro sweeping by in breathless, brilliant arcs. She figured her best chance was to circle backward and approach from the rear, where—

*Shit! Shit!*

Wrenched from her plans, Ash nearly wheeled straight into a group of Baywell fighters, dragging the transport straight up, whirling, the enemy ships a wheeling kaleidoscope. Expecting them to follow, she dove back into the debris field, bringing the rail gun around in a heavy rush. Instead of engaging with her, though, she watched as they careened down toward an apex she could not quite see from this distance, bent to attack a bright and burning point, sailing hell-bent away from the Baywell line at incredible speed.

She slammed her gloved hands against the bulkhead nearby in frustration. The last moments of her salvage career had been spent barely missing things. Putting her shipmates in danger. Barely able to distinguish fantasy from reality. Barely able to control her own reaction time.

This time, she was ready.

She gunned the grav-drive, reached into the transport's med-kit, and stabbed herself with a stimulant. Then a second. A third.

A cold, terrible sigh took hold of her heart. The world slowed down around her. She felt more awake than ever, connected to the universe in a way that transcended the connection she had with the *together*. She felt focused. Sharper. Somewhere, her mind screamed that she was *just high*, that her body couldn't survive this, that an overdose would kill her, that her heart would burst and shred in her chest.

But Ash knew like she knew the Tribulation sun would burn for another hundred million years that she no longer needed a body that didn't belong to her. She did not know what to do with hands that she did not control. She could not live with blood that flowed with alien memory, with a mind that could disassemble the atoms of another human being with a thought.

Len's terrified face flashed before her eyes. She'd felt his every decomposing atom, every shattered bone. His death had given her a great and terrible knowledge that every victory, every flag planted, every enemy killed, was hollow. She could not live with what she had done. She could not live with what she could do. She could not live with being the last one left.

She could not live without Kate Keller.

More Baywell fighters screamed by, ignoring her.

She adjusted her trajectory. "What the—?"

There were now six fighters trailing away from the Baywell line, but they weren't engaging with the Auroran ships. Instead, they focused on the shining thing with the screaming velocity, like whatever was there was more important than *Rio* and *Medellin* and *Hong Kong* put together. She magnified the area in question.

"A *Baywell* pod?" she said aloud.

It was pod-size, for sure, with the same kind of worker-bee accoutrements she was used to using herself, and it was wobbling slightly, listing to the right, as if the pilot wasn't quite experienced. The pod didn't look like it was attacking any Auroran property; in fact, it looked like it was being *chased*.

Christopher slid into the troop seats behind her. She felt his presence like a quiet curse. *Why would they be going after their own?* he said.

"This is the absolute right time to show up with a rhetorical question—"

She heard his kind laughter. It felt terribly out of place. It had always been out of place. It made her ache. *It's not rhetorical.*

Alarms sounded. One of the fighters had figured out who she was and had painted a target on her tail. She waited until she'd come close to a piece of rubble, then dropped two hundred feet and reversed thrusters, letting loose with the rail gun. The fighter tried to stop but caught a bolt in his engine, and barreled straight into the piece of rubble. The cabin sheared in two, then exploded.

When Ash could breathe again—could think again—she brought up the view on the Baywell pod. It was listing in a staccato motion that reminded her of watching Keller at the helm.

*I know someone who drives like that,* she thought.

She turned on the local comms.

"—and that's right, get near me and I'll fry you—"

*Kate?*

Hope kindled like dynamite in every length of her body. The ships outside were moving again, taking up a new formation against the sleek Auroran cruisers: hulking old WellCel things, a Bay-Ken freighter with a brand-new spinal lance, a nascent, terrible alliance come to bear, a Company war beginning, human against human, blood against blood. Lives yielded to profit, like they always had been, always would be. Ash looked down at her hands, sweaty on the tiller, red-dark in the cabin's light, then hit the line-of-sight comms, sending a direct beam toward the enemy pod. *If I'm wrong, I'm dead.*

The shaking transport, the taste of eternity at the back of her throat: it all fell away.

"Kate," she said.

"Auroran vessel. Auroran vessel. Disengage." Keller's voice, high and bright with the kind of starving glee that only came with a dose of adrenaline. "I'm an Auroran citizen. Unless you *want* to blow me up, in which case you might as well get fucked by your own fucking rail gun, because that's how pissed they're going to be when they find out you—"

Ash stammered. "Kate. I'm here, it's me, it's Ash."

Silence. A sob on the line. "Can't be."

Adrenaline pushed its way into Ash's fingers, and she swerved, half drunk with it, toward the Baywell pod. "I'd know that driving anywhere. Look thirty degrees portside. I've got a rail gun and I'm coming alongside."

"You know," Keller said, "when Ash told me about the hallucinations, I didn't know they'd be such bullshit, right? And this is what you freaks want, people *dying* to kill, actually dying—"

"I'm not a hallucination."

"How can I tell?"

The words ripped from Ash's throat. "Because I fucking love you, you total *asshole!*"

When Keller spoke again, her voice wavered, as if she hadn't used it in a while. "Do you have a heat shield on that thing?"

Ash checked. "Yeah."

"I don't. I've got the weapon with me, Ash. I was going to enter a heavier mass value into the shuttle computer, get drawn down into the atmosphere. I'll be dead before I hit the ground, and with any luck, this bastard won't survive reentry, either. I was hoping"—another sob—"that you had a better plan."

Ash slammed down on her velocity and drew around to point the back airlock at Keller's pod door, to match her trajectory. The Baywell fighters re-formed, trying to flank the Auroran transport, letting loose a scattering of railfire meant to puncture her hull. She yanked to the side, then back again, returning with her own gun.

"I have the beginnings of a really shitty plan," she said.

"I'm good if I keep breathing."

Her mind was too foggy to do the math. *Is there enough food, is there enough air, is there enough fuel, do I even care about any of that*— "Get in a suit," Ash answered. "We're going to the White Line."

"I don't have a suit."

"Then hold on to the weapon and get ready to jump. Don't hold your breath."

"Don't hold—shit, *shit*, you don't mean—" Keller's voice rose three octaves.

"Get ready. We only have a few seconds."

A group of Baywell fighters swerved, aiming their fire toward Keller's engines. Her pod was hit and it lurched to port; the engines flamed and swirled. The comm link dropped, and Ash worked her hands over the interface, desperately trying to reestablish it. Her hands were shaking. *Bad idea,* she thought. She grabbed another stimulant, stabbed it in her leg, and depressed the plunger.

For a moment, she felt as normal and as focused as she ever had been before Bittersweet, before the madness crept into her bones, before her blood ran thick with celestium and nanotech and the memory of an alien civilization. She kicked the engine into gear and hurtled closer to Keller's pod. The fighters fired again, this time making a fire-bright impact on Keller's engines, causing the pod to spin. *Of course. If she has the weapon, they can't get close without risking a loss of power. And neither can I.*

She yanked the controller into a matching spin and yaw. The shuttle pitched, vicious and stark, the harness digging into her shoulders so hard they'd bruise. Ash leaned over and slammed the handle on the transport hatch.

"Now," she screamed into the comm, hoping the damned thing was back up.

"I love you," she heard.

The top of Keller's pod snapped open with a puff of air. Five seconds. There was Keller: bright in the sun, beautiful, her hair spread out around her like a mermaid's, her arms wrapped around a light so violet and beaming there seemed to be nothing else in the universe. Four seconds. Her eyes wheeled until they met Ash's, and then rolled away, unconscious. *Three seconds.*

Keller sailed into the cockpit.

Ash closed the door with a bone-shuddering slam. Two seconds.

She ripped herself out of the safety harness, repressurized the cockpit, and set the transport on autopilot to the planet. One.

Keller was cold as ice but breathing; she was unconscious, covered with the red, veiny blotches of broken blood vessels. She'd held her breath, and was carrying a silver-white blanket in her arms. Ash tore off her helmet and gloves, tasting blank machine air, reaching down with a trembling hand to touch Keller's cheek. Warm her up. She took out an emergency blanket, wrapped Keller in it, then grabbed the last stim, jabbing it into the other

woman's arm. The woman's real arms, her skin, her clothes—
they were real, she was real—

—and the *device* was real.

Keller's hand loosened and opened, and the weapon rolled toward Ash.

The shuttle started to shut down around her. The pod's exterior cameras crashed, one by one. Her nose ran; when she wiped it, blood stained her fingertips. The temperature plummeted twenty degrees.

It was a yellow-gold sphere with a light like a thousand summer days—*no*, the glare of a thousand snowy mountaintops—*no*, the warmth of her mother's home or a guttering sunlamp in a Bittersweet lounge, purple like a sunset, black like the night, heavy like the bottom of an ocean.

It was calling her in a chorus of a thousand voices, calling her home, calling her beyond the White Line.

She picked it up.

*Glory*, it sang.

The universe rolled to a stop as Ash stared into the depths of the *London* weapon, as it rolled from the protective fabric, as it started dragging the light and the heat and the life from the world around her, as it tried to connect to the master node hundreds of thousands of light-years away. Her nose bled. A great need slipped into her mind, grasping at her memories of the *together*, probing at her veins, thrilling to the nanotech, calling to her.

She thought it would speak of battlefields, of blood, of mourning and revenge. Instead, the shaking, shuddering world of the transport gave way to a foggy memory—dancing together in the mess to the sounds of *Twenty-Five*'s engine, to Keller humming an old spacer's song, feeling the thrill of it as she pressed her lips against her neck, the two of them in their own world. And even that slipped away into the gathering darkness, those memories being sucked down, down, into the Vai matrix, into *together*.

Keller's hand came out of nowhere, clawing at Ash's wrist, and she tumbled back into reality. Keller shoved the isolation fabric at Ash. Ash unhooked her helmet, dropped the fabric over the weapon, slammed the helmet over the fabric, then hit the seal.

"Isolette on the cheap."

"You're not a hallucination," Keller whispered.

"Nope," Ashlan said, breathless, gulping down cold, tin-stinking air. She tasted blood on her lips and wiped her nose with the suit sleeve. "You weren't sure when you jumped?"

Keller's eyes jumped back to the exterior. "Didn't need to be sure. I wanted it to be true." She hauled in a breath, then coughed. "They've been trying to stop me, not destroy me. They know what's onboard. That'll give us some room to move."

Ash grabbed the tiller and pulled herself back into the pilot's chair. How long had it been? *Five seconds? Ten? Minutes?* The transport had broken away from its straight line to the Baywell line's left flank, hurtling instead toward Tribulation's pockmarked moon. She yanked the ship back on course and looked over her shoulder at the woman she had thought she'd never see again. Her heart twisted, mended, and broke in one moment.

The transport shuddered with the impact of railfire.

"Shit," Keller said, crawling into a sitting position, using the back of Ash's chair as ballast. "I think that was the engines."

Ash bit her bottom lip. She was sweating. She grabbed the tiller and swerved to port. She felt a sickening crunch against her hands, and a shudder below her feet "It was. Check it."

Keller pulled herself into the copilot's seat and punched up the maintenance interface. "Broken injection seal. It's not good."

Ash felt a dark, screaming panic. "We just need to punch through, burn for the White Line—"

"Impossible," Keller said. "We'll get one burn, tops, and no correction burn. I get the math wrong, and we suffocate or starve. And they'll be able to follow us. We need another option, and fast."

"Kate, we have to—"

The other woman shook her head, and when she spoke again, it was in her tight, no-nonsense captain's voice. "Another option."

Ash heard the silence of the cab, the rattling of the hull. She remembered a sulfur sky, alien air rolling in on a dead farming town like a bastard tide. "We'll go to Tribulation," she said. "There are beds. Rations. Weapons." She tasted bile at the back of her throat. "Crates and crates of blue screamers."

Keller entered a firing solution into the keyboard before her, as serious as Ash had ever seen her. "How long do you think we can hold them off?"

"Years," Ash said. "But it won't be years. It'll be six months, tops. For me. A year for you. That's all the time we need to make things right."

Kate blinked. "Six months? You don't mean—"

"All we have to do is hold off. Defuse all the weapons, and hold off." The plan, inchoate in Ash's throat, was terrible and screaming.

"How?"

Ash grabbed Keller's hand, tightening her fingers; her lover's hand felt warm and dry and real, a fever dream fashioned into flesh, and she fought tears so strong they threatened a flood. "I'll tell you later," she said, and brought up the battle on the transport's main HUD.

"Later."

The fighters around them—unsure Baywells, and tailgating, hungry Aurorans, now, sweeping in from the side—were recovering from exposure to the *London* weapon, coming online one by one. Behind them were the cruisers, turning toward the transport, the eye of the entire battlefield on the small opening. They all knew what it meant now, knew who was on the transport, knew *what* was on the transport. Knew how that changed the game.

"Is it nice down there?" asked Keller.

"It'll be fine, as long as you're there," Ash said, her voice a winding laugh. "You can tell me if it's like Neversink."

"Where?" she said. "I've never lived on a planet before— Shit! Gun! Make a hole." Ash yanked the tiller to the ceiling, too busy to ask her what that meant.

There was no gravity here, but she could imagine she felt it pushing on her chest as she pointed the transport toward a break in the Baylor Wellspring line. Keller splayed her hand on the railgun controls, spraying railfire, causing explosions on the fighters. Aurora swirled in where Baywell careened out, though, firing at their maneuvering thrusters.

"Aurora, hard to port. You don't remember Neversink?"

"Never what? Got it," Keller said, firing again. An Auroran ship bloomed into death, and Ash punched the engine to its highest velocity, twirling around until she could see Tribulation. They shoved forward, a bright silver kite, the other ships falling in behind them like a deadly tail. Keller swung the railgun around and scattered fire, knocking another Auroran ship to the side, but her eyebrows furrowed, and her lips tightened in stress, and she shook her head.

"Baywell's too fast."

"We'll make it," Ash said. "I can go faster."

"Even Len couldn't make this thing go faster. It's not meant for speed."

*Len.* Ash felt the familiar knot in her throat, the yawning loss. "We don't have any other options."

"Yes, we do."

"Prayer?"

Ash could see the knot in Keller's smooth throat. "That thing." Keller pointed at the helmet still in Ash's lap.

Ash felt a ringing in her ears. "No."

"I'm not strong enough to control the weapon," Keller whispered, her eyes reflecting railgun fire, her fingers causing it right back. "I can detonate it a hundred meters, tops, like I just did when I jumped. That's not enough for any of these assholes. But your nanotech's been integrated for a year. You can do more."

Ash's world spun. *She wants me to—* "No," she said. "Fuck no, not even for *you.*"

"It's the only way."

Ash yanked the transport left to avoid spinning rubble and a shining, dead Vai skimmer, then right to avoid a short torpedo. She felt like Natalie, standing behind the trigger, staring at the starving *together* on the ground. She thought of dead civilizations and dead ships and dead planets. "On the planet, on the shuttle, with Len, when I—" She couldn't speak. "It's not an option. If we die, it all dies with us. You haven't fucking seen *genocide*, you didn't see it explode in your brain, you don't know what you don't know."

Kate's mouth turned down. "We don't have a lot of options, Ash."

"*No*," Ash spat, but she thought back to being in the shuttle with Natalie, facing down Ramsay's treachery for the first time. Ramsay had been quick to accept their refusal, so quick, but Ash hadn't known at the time what she was looking for, hadn't thought for a second she'd passed on the bloodtech to Keller—

—and if she could fly right, fly straight, fly better than anyone else in this damned graveyard, she could be on-planet in ten minutes, breathing air, holding Kate's hand, kissing her, *together*—

The temptation was almost too much.

Railfire reflected in the viewscreen, painting fireworks on Keller's jaw. "We don't have a choice, Ash. Just detonate it once. It'll destroy Baywell's evidence, destroy whatever research both sides have. It'll bring down *anyone* who knows."

"You never knew me at all if you think for one fucking second that I will do that, even for you, even for *us*."

Keller grabbed a stabilization rail and dragged herself to a sitting position. Ash spied a glint of metal around her neck; gravity dragged at the pendant and it fell out, dropping against Keller's breastbone like a molecular taking a claw to her heart. Horror curled in the quiet places in Ash's mind, hacked away at her last dreams of happiness. Her world tilted. "You're one of *them*."

Keller clutched at the necklace. "I— What? Dr. Sharma gave this to me when she told me to go to *Medellin*."

"How long have you been screwing all of us?"

"I'm not! She gave it to me! On the Baywell ship!"

Distracted, Ash wasn't fast enough to dodge a bolt impact, and they felt the juddering explosion of one of the thrusters being blown out of existence. Ash, shoved into the safety harness, took the brunt of it on her bruised shoulders, while Keller was thrown against the side of the transport. Ash thought she might have hit her head, but Keller pulled herself up, dazed, hanging on to the copilot's harness. The HUD painted a guttering future on the side of her face: they weren't going to make it. Ash swore. The ship's controls were damaged and logy, half fried by the blast, and the targeting computer was burned to a crisp, with the engines to follow.

"We're doing manual atmospheric entry," Ash shouted.

"We won't make entry at all if you don't detonate!"

Six fighters followed them—Aurora's and Baywell's, firing on each other while jockeying for a better position to stop her transport. They fought each other at short distances, using railguns and small spinal lances that sizzled Ash's cameras to death and jolted their small universe once, then twice.

Keller hollered in pain. "Please! Or everybody dies! I *saw* it, Ash! They're never going to stop. Not Baywell, not Sharma's crew! They've all seen what that thing can do, and they don't *care* how many people they run over to get it! To get *us!*"

Tribulation came up fast. Red. Angry. Accusing.

A thought occurred to her. "You said Sharma was there?"

"She was there."

The helmet warmed nearby, and Ash imagined the delicate filigree of the weapon spinning, starlike, behind the polarized faceplate. The decision came on like a shock to the chest, like a long-simmering poison that had turned her organs and her bones and her heart to darkness—like sleep, like prophecy. All she had to do was ask, and nobody would be left to know what was in her veins. What could be. What would be, if she didn't make this choice.

Keller was right. Ash could stop all of it.

She could end the war.

And all she had to do was trade her soul.

"Kate," she whispered. "If we do this, there's no coming back."

Keller's hand slid, warm and human, into hers. "We don't have to. Not as long as we're together."

A projectile sailed past Ash's window and she scrambled to catch her breath—*no, no, don't breathe so hard, air is precious*—and hit the transport hard to starboard. Fighters sailed in gracious, sharklike arcs, dropping and twisting and firing and exploding in patterns of gory glitter that splattered the ship with clanking, iced-over debris.

Ash looked back at the battle, the weapon making excited humming noises. Beyond them, the cruisers fought on. Aurora seemed to be losing; *Cape Town*'s hull was shredded, and *Rio*'s aft wing, where she'd stayed in the hospital months ago, was open to the stars. Ash thought of the unicorn toy that had repeated everything she said, and the nurses, and her stomach churned with guilt.

She unhooked the safety harness and slipped out of the chair, the weapon warming in its improvised, failing helmet isolette. *Glory*, it whispered, the excitement slipping up her arm and into her mind, connecting her to Keller's fear and Solano's lust and the memories of those who had died in the battle like she was an ansible terminal and the entire galaxy was whispering in her ear and *glory* was reuniting with the master node, with the *together*, with what was left of *together* in the weapon that was the Heart of a long-dead ship, the echo of a defeated civilization.

*I can't live with it, Ash.* Len's voice, just twenty minutes ago, when he was still alive.

Or maybe he *was* still alive, somewhere in the lost *together*.

Or maybe she was already dead.

She thought of him as she kept her breath as shallow as possible, fighting off the encroaching fog that came from the stimulants wearing off. She wondered if this blank, overwhelming emptiness was what Len felt when he turned the blue screamers on the people he thought were enemies. She wondered if he felt sorry when he died.

Sorry—or *relieved.*

Keller turned the transport into a planetary orbit, bringing them to a bruising stop. The fighters screeched to a halt, trying not to bounce off the atmosphere, spinning off back toward the battlefield.

"Now—before they come back—"

Keller threw her the helmet, and Ash tore open the seal. The grav-drive wailed underneath their feet and Keller prepped for manual entry, gripping the control wheel, flipping the throttle levers. Ash placed her hand on the weapon again. It slipped into her mind, a supernova, a lover, a tale of revenge, a deep rumble that made her think of ancient forests and canyons cut deep into the prismatic stone of an alien planet. It waited for her to speak.

"Just stop this," she whispered.

Keller looked out the front window and gasped.

Ash closed her eyes. *One minute. One minute fifteen. One minute thirty—*

The transport politely rebooted.

Kate slid out of her chair and retched.

Ash could not see the stars for the debris. She scrambled to aim the transport's cameras at the battlefield around her, to better see what she had done. The fighters spun out into the darkness, their pilots' eyes glassy, staring ahead, their minds blank, their memories sucked into the black hole in Ash's hands, their engines as dead as the sky around them. Some of the pilots who had once been chasing them had unclipped their safety harnesses, screaming, clawing at their lost memories, and now stared at their hands like they had just been born. Some of them had hit the hatches on their fighters and spat themselves into space, not understanding what was going on, struggling for a few seconds before going calm. Others stared, shaking, into a desperate nothingness. Others smiled, lost somewhere beautiful.

The lucky ones.

The guns on the great cruisers had gone cold. They themselves had joined the great dead hulks in the sky above the planet, tiny, pulverized moons playing a silent testament to the greed of man. Grav-fuel and glinting, crumbled hull fragments floated in lazy spirals. She did not want to imagine what would be happening on the cruisers. Thousands. Tens of thousands, glassy-eyed, turning, twisting, sweeping through the corridors, trapped inside their memories, dying in increments. The silence of strangulation on a dozen grisly moons. Baylor Wellspring would come for them. Aurora would come for them. But it would be too late.

Keller sobbed behind her. "I'm sorry. I'm sorry, Ash, I'm sorry, I didn't know. I didn't *know*."

"You knew."

"Ash, please. *Please*."

Ash ignored her. For a moment, she wished she could forget, but she was a weapon now, and weapons could not forget.

She turned the transport back toward Tribulation, kicked the engine into gear, and vomited in her suit.

# 32

The transport dropped like a rock through the Tribulation atmosphere. Ash tilted her chin toward the receding battlefield, taking in every moment of the last descent she'd ever make; around her, the burgundy sky knit together from snatches of black space and the flame screaming around the windows of the transport. It was morning again in the hemisphere when the transport broke through, and there was just enough celestium left in the tank to land them in the ruins of the agricultural center, just outside the Sacrament Society lab.

Ash ripped off the harness and stumbled outside, clawing off her suit, dragging down mouthfuls of sulfur air. She looked every inch the cancer-ridden uncitizen she was now. Kate followed, casting aside the Baywell jacket, her legs unsure and wobbly, and her body covered with red pinpoints right underneath the skin. She reached for Ash's hand, and for a moment, Ash almost refused it.

Weapons did not love.

She could only imagine how inhuman she looked, her hair tangled, her eyes wild, holding the weapon that had killed an entire battlefield in the hollow of a shattered Auroran suit helmet. But Kate looked like hell, too, spittle at the corner of her mouth, shaking, her eyes darting like the scrollwork was taking her vision, too, and her hand was warm and tight, and suddenly, Ash felt like she could breathe again.

In the days that followed, they pulled themselves into a semblance of a life. They slept in a bed that had once belonged to someone else, and sat at night on the colony's dormitory porch, watching the blank burgundy sky and listening to the avians sing down the sun. They kissed in the heat of the afternoons and talked until they were hoarse, beating back the shivering fear with the call of warm skin.

But this wasn't retirement.

There were five Aurorans left on the planet, blank and gibbering under the death-sodden sky—scientists, of course, from the newly named molecular department. She and Kate dragged them to the dormitory below, put them in beds, fed them a paste made of water-soaked ration bars, found IV bags, and made saline solution.

She and Kate inventoried the conventional weapons, the screamers, the moleculars—all of it was straight or dome dispersal, quite possibly to protect the Sacrament lives below the surface, and now, to protect the lives of the so-called survivors. They pulled apart Sharma's lab. There was medicine—stims and painkillers, at least for a while—and food, although weapons only ate when they were forced to eat, when Kate would plead with her to *shove something, anything, down her throat.*

They expected retribution to come, for fire to rain from the sky, for shuttles to land, full of violence.

But nothing came.

A day passed. Two. Three, and still they lived. Ash found herself up before dawn doing maintenance on the atmospinners with some of the parts from the lab's shuttlebay. Kate set up a perimeter of crescent weapons that hummed, bold and ominous, whenever she checked them, just in case someone arrived when they were elsewhere.

Only then did they feel comfortable descending once more into the black cathedral of the old laboratory.

Solano's men had partially restored Sharma's server and left enough computer equipment to get her medbay running. Being around the weapon made both women unsteady, backward, prone to drifting off into blank, terrible reveries, so they kept it in an isolette in the bugout bay, unless they had to take it out for research.

And there was so much research. Medicines to learn about, blood tests to take, numbers to crunch—how long they had, how many months they could expect, how quickly they'd lose their ability to walk and their ability to speak and their very mind itself, how many months they could stay wrapped around each other in this groggy parody of the thing they'd wanted for so long. They spent two days trying to remove Ash's monitor, to no avail.

On the fourth, Ash found the Vai's diamond claw—hacked off, like someone had seen it and wanted to take it as a trophy—and slipped it on a string, tying it around her neck. It made her remember a picture she'd kept in her quarters, a picture that burned in the fire that claimed *Twenty-Five*. She'd loved the man in the picture, loved him so much she could have broken in two for it, but she no longer remembered who he was. She still saw his shadow, sometimes, darting through the trees, looking at her from across the clearing with black eyes burning, whispering into her dreams.

The Tribulation sun was high in the sky the day Ash and Kate opened their first box of moleculars. These were new: silver-red, eight-pointed stars that glistened in the sunlight and spoke of flame, whispering sibilant death. *Deletion.* They hummed at both women and shivered as Ash lifted one from its bed. *Glory,* it said. *Glory. We are together again.*

Kate's hair was loose, tossed by the breeze, winding around her throat in fluttering strands. She was the most beautiful thing Ash had ever seen.

"Will it hurt?" she asked.

"More than death itself."

"And we have to do this?"

Ash ran her finger down the moleculars' curves and valleys, thought of silver blood, of Joseph Solano, of the man she'd loved whose name she could not remember, of the people and places she'd never see again, of the Vai who would never go home.

It was her turn to say it, her turn to take Kate's hand and tell her *it was the only way,* that disarmament meant death, over and over again, that they would start here and work through every single box in the damned, broken place, and end with the Heart. That disarmament meant that they could start to make up for what had happened in the graveyard above, among the liars and the cheaters and the people who were just trying their best, that they could end the war before it began. Before others died.

Before they died themselves.

It was a story she told herself every day, a story she believed sometimes. A story she had to believe.

"It's going to be okay," Kate whispered. "I'm here. I'll always be here."

"I know," Ash said.

Forgiveness was a tricky thing.

"Then let's begin," Kate said.

Ash opened her hand and dropped the screamer on the ground.

The bright light blasted out the overhanging trees and the clearing grew boiling hot. Ash's skin charred. Kate's bones crumbled. Their breath boiled. Ash writhed. She threw herself to the ground, clawed at the sky, screamed at gods in which she no longer believed. Kate's esophagus twisted, and her stomach burned, and the sky fell and—

—and then it was over, and they were left gasping on the ground, whole and safe and thinking straight, the victims of a terrible clarity. Between them was the weapon, spent, a form without a void. Deleted. Nobody would ever be able to use it again.

"One down," Ash whispered, picking up the next one. Kate swallowed and nodded. *This one will be easier,* she thought. *The next one is always easier.* She could repeat this over and over again, but it could never drown out the memory of dying. It could certainly not drown out the memory of love. *Death,* she thought, holding her lover's hand, and her chin went back, and her mouth opened, and the blue light took her, and the screaming began.

*Eight hundred to go.*

# ACKNOWLEDGMENTS

Writing a novel is the only team sport I enjoy, and I am gob-smackingly fortunate to play with the best in the game. I am indebted to my agent, Dorian Maffei, and to my editor, Jen Gunnels, as well as to everyone at Tor who made sure this novel sang. Thank you for believing in the crew of *Twenty-Five*.

My deep gratitude to everyone who beta read or commented on the many drafts of this novel, including John Appel, Phil Margolies, Beth Tanner, Jo Miles, Christopher Spooner, Chelsea Counsell, Tim Shea, Jill Seidenstein, Jennie Goloboy, and Jennifer Mace. My thanks, as well, to the Viable Paradise work group that read the first chapters—some of the names above, as well as Susan Taitel, Valerie Valdes, Amanda Hackwith, and Teresa and Patrick Nielsen Hayden. Thanks to Kjell Lindgren for the chat at the '17 Nebulas about surgery in space; to the staff at the Orange County Library System and the Enoch Pratt Free Library, for research guidance; to UnitedHealthcare, Empire Blue Cross, and Cigna, for the, uh, um, *inspiration;* to the staff at Atwater's and the Red Canoe Cafe for serving me gallons of coffee; and to the doctors at Albany Med who saved me from the blood clot that eventually inspired Ash's story.

*Twenty-Five* and her crew have been around, in some form or another, since my time at Nazareth College. So, to the legion of writers and creatives who believed in me and challenged me to be better all these years, a very tight group hug: Viable Paradise 20, Clarion UCSD '17, the Maryland Space Opera Collective, the Orlando Writing League, #Broken_Dagger, 38th Argo, the Niskayuna Acting Troupe, the Isle of Write, the '02–'07 staff of *The Evangelist,* and my current fabulous local writing circle in Baltimore, including Sarah Pinsker, Kellan Szpara, Michelle Appel, and Christopher Rose.

Thank you to the many writing mentors who encouraged me along the way, including James Breig, Kate Blain, James Edgar, Mary Van Keuren, Sherwood Smith, Denise O'Toole Kelly, Mary-ellen Potts, Virginia Skinner-Linnenberg, and Sr. Monica Weis; to my amazing parents, Richard and Sandra Dietlein, who had no idea what they were getting into when they bought me that word processor in 1992; to my brother, Michael Dietlein, my original collaborator and partner in crime; and to my daughter, Claire, my North Star.

And, finally, to my husband, Glenn, who believed in me from Day One of this long journey: thank you for helping me finish my own version of the Dopey Challenge. Love you always.